ReignStorm

lp rothrock

Other books in this series
Reign Fall (Book 1)
Blood Reign (Book 2)

Jacket design by Rocko Bishop and Lea Rothrock
Element designs: lightning by vectorpouch/Freepik; leaves by rawpixel.com/Freepik;
Tunnel by ID 115421039/Dark Cave @Mulder photo/Dreamstime.com; filigree by
pikisuperstar/Freepik

ISBN: 979-8-9933184-4-8

For Deb Shaw
*Without you this story might
have never been told*

Reign Storm

Prologue

A long time ago, in an alternate timeline

From the side, the dimensional tear didn't look like much. Tenn finally found it quite by accident, after he'd gotten off his horse to relieve himself and followed his quail dinner out of the bushes, bow drawn.

In the late afternoon shade under the trees, the flashing pink, white, and blue light was barely noticeable, but the burning edges of the hole looked strange in midair. At first, he mistook it for a dangling tree worm, writhing in the golden sunshine coming through the leaves, but the charred black part didn't make sense, and when he got closer, he could make out the shifting, shining light coming through.

He'd ridden for days, combing every inch of the forest, and now that he could see what he'd been looking for, he doubted he'd have noticed it without stumbling on it somehow. It was tiny. About the size of an oak leaf, although size didn't matter, and he should know that by now. What mattered was that this was a hole into the second dimension, and something evil sat, or stood, or whatever they did, on the other side of it, wanting to get out.

Tenn gave it a wide berth. Thirty feet at least, Servant had said, right? Dinner forgotten, he laid his bow on the ground and walked slowly around a perimeter, his eyes fixed on the dancing light. Strange, how it hung in the air like that—flat, like a hole in a cloak you couldn't see. From the sides, the dangling worm, but front and back were all burning edges and sparkling middle.

Thirty feet were too far, he could barely see the confounded thing. Wary, he walked closer, watching for any changes or signs of threat. At twenty feet, he stopped. Eyes still on the tear, he dug the lightning weapons out of his pockets and hefted them in his hands. With some effort, he tore his eyes away from the light and looked down.

In his left hand, he held the pink stone cylinder with two metal prongs sticking out of one end. The prongs would carry a lightning bolt between them, generated by the holder's own energy. The pink rock conducted the energy from the hand to the metal. Very useful weapon in close quarters, especially since it gave a light shock if you weren't too upset, and a real hair-smoker if you were. Not a good choice for this situation, though.

His right hand held the other weapon. This pink cylinder had no prongs, or anything else sticking out of it, but it had a button on the side and a lens in one end. The lightning would be generated if he shined the little white light onto something that emitted a sufficient energy, like an animal, or a person. As the monks explained it, the second energy source would enable the completion of something, and the lightning would whatever whatever. Tenn had only used it once, just to see what it would do, and the result was that he understood by the bits of deer flesh dotting his face and the surrounding trees that the weapon was no good for hunting.

But it could work for this. Jase, who was probably the monk who invented the thing, practically told him that much. The rest of the brothers left through their dimensional escape hatch, and what did he say? Keep the light off the edges, or something like that. If it wasn't going to work, he would've said so.

How in saints' names was he supposed to keep the light off the edges, though? The white circle would be bigger than the tear at this distance. He'd have to get a lot closer to only hit the hole. So much for that thirty-foot safety zone. But if some monster stuck his head out, maybe he could shock it with his other hand, so he didn't put the first cylinder back in his pocket after all.

Tenn stretched his neck to either side and rolled the tension out of his shoulders. Sunlight streamed through the leaves behind him, dappling the forest floor and obscuring the strange pink and blue sparkles hanging in the air in front. Better that than looking toward the sun, though. Tenn stretched his neck again and stepped forward.

"I wouldn't do that if I were you."

The gravelly voice scared the fire out of him. He jumped fifteen fingertips off the ground and sideways, the pink cylinder in his left hand crackled like crazy, and his right arm thrust out, training the little white circle onto a pile of rocks about five strides to his right.

Tenn jerked the circle back and forth, certain the guy had to be hiding in the pile somewhere. "All right, you reeking chamber-pot, where are you?"

"Right in front of your eyes, Tenn," the voice said, and as it spoke, the big rock turned. Several smaller rocks floated up into the air beside it, making a hand that reached around behind the big rock and pulled up a head, which looked at him as it was set up top. "You're going to get too close, and the monks will be really annoyed with me if I don't try to stop you."

Tenn frowned. "Nod, what are you doing here?"

"I thought that was obvious. I'm here to save your mushy pink skin."

"I'm not pink!"

"Uh huh. The point is, if you get much closer, that hole will suck you in. See the ring around it?" Nod waved his hand in a big arc in front

3

of them. "No leaves, branches, or grass— nothing left but rocks and dirt. That's what it does."

"All right, all right," Tenn said, disgusted and backing away. "I can't let the lightning touch the edges, and I can't get close enough to keep that from happening. That was all the plan I had." He gazed at the offending hole. "Has anything come out of it?"

"Not that I've noticed."

"Have you seen anything that looks like it's possessed by an evil entity?"

"Not since my wife left me."

These guys, always the jokesters. "What do you suggest I do, then?"

"Me? I don't have a suggestion." Nod shook his rock head. "But Servant seems to think there's nothing you can do."

"Yes, that I know." Tenn sighed and scratched his head. It went against his grain to give up without trying. In fact, he couldn't do it. "I've got to try, Nod. I'll regret it forever if I don't."

"Your choice. I can't really stop you unless I avalanche your bony flesh, and if I did that, you might die, and the monks would still be mad at me, because the Royal Family is going to need you at the palace. So, do what you want." Nod shrugged his arm and tilted his head.

"Where's your other arm?"

"I didn't have enough good rocks here," Nod answered, looking around.

A flash of inspiration cheered Tenn up immeasurably. "Hey, can I hide behind you?"

Nod's expression looked about as skeptical as his rigid features would allow. "I don't know about that. I can't be sure it won't suck me out of the rock."

"You don't have to stay." Tenn walked up to Nod and put a friendly hand on his shoulder area. "Just move your boulder to about ten feet from the hole, and go back to your own dimension. I can put the circle inside the edges from that distance, I'm almost sure."

4

"Hm, well I suppose I could. Let me find some legs."

Tenn glanced at the shimmering light in the tear, then watched Nod search the surrounding rocks. Soon enough, he came up with some stumpy legs, which he laid out and scooted himself onto.

"You could have just scooted over there," Tenn said, "it's ten feet. What do you need legs for?"

"Because I have legs, all right? Just…let me do this my way."

"Fine, sure, absolutely." Tenn nodded and suppressed a smile. Whatever dimension these rock guys came from, people were the same all over, weren't they?

"Are you even ready?" Nod asked.

"Oh, yeah. Um, hang on a sec."

Nod made an exaggerated sighing noise while Tenn checked his weapons. The prongs were silent, but ready, and he positioned the button on the other cylinder under his right thumb.

"Let's go."

Nod moved forward, his round legs sliding over the moist, dead leaves with barely a sound. Tenn stepped behind him, keeping his eyes on the tear. As they got closer, the leaves disappeared from the ground, and Tenn could feel a strange pull in the air around him. It reminded him of the pull he felt in the ocean, many years ago when he was in training. Underneath the waves, the ocean dragged at him relentlessly, wanting him, making him fight to stay where he was. In the ocean, the fight strengthened him, but he didn't think this would be the same.

He huddled behind Nod, making himself as small as he could so no body parts would be exposed to the sucking hole. At about ten feet, Nod stopped and turned his head completely around to talk to him.

"I don't feel anything." He sounded disappointed. "Would you like me to stay and help?"

"You bet I would," Tenn said, hunched, sweat running down his neck. The pronged cylinder cackled in his hand and he inched his left hand down to the small rocks at the end of Nod's arm. "Here, can you take this? Use it if anything comes out of the hole. Just stick the prongs into it, and be as mad as you possibly can, but not panicked. Got that?"

5

"Sure."

"Other than that, I don't know what you can do, except block me."

Nod's little finger rocks took the cylinder. "I can do both of those things. Here, I'll hold up my hand." Nod positioned his rocks out to the left of his boulder, bent at the elbow area, hand holding the cylinder level with his head, effectively making his upper body wider. "Does that help?"

"Yeah." Tenn eased his head to the side of Nod's body, and brought the pink cylinder up to a tiny crevice between the upper arm and lower arm, which had just enough space for the circle to shine through. Supported by the rock, the cylinder felt stable in his hand. If he sighted in short glances, and didn't move his hand, he could keep the circle on the hole without giving the hole enough time to possess his face.

That was the theory, anyway.

He peeked and trained the white circle onto the flashing lights. Careful to hold his hand steady, he slid back behind Nod. "Is the circle still in the hole?"

"Yes. But there's something else in the hole, too."

"What?"

"Something kind of pinkish-purplish, moving around."

Oh, crap. What in all hells was that? "What's it doing?"

"I can't tell, it's miniscule."

Right. Well, One willing, it wouldn't be anything in a minute.

The circle still hung in the depths of the tear when he peeked again. Nod's vision must be astounding, because all Tenn could see was the sparkling pink and blue, same as before.

"Did you see it?" Nod asked.

"No, are you sure you're not imagining things?"

"I'm not imagining."

"Don't get testy, I'm just saying I didn't see it." Tenn's reply was cut up by the first sizzles of the lightning arc. He peeked; the air between the weapon and the hole had come alive with flickering white sparks. Lightning fragments appeared, joined, broke apart and faded in rapid succession. The pull started to bulge his eyes before he remembered to duck behind Nod again.

"It's doing something, Tenn…" Nod's voice sounded worried, and Tenn had to look again. The hole had become entirely pink, framed by the burning edges, and without flashes or sparkles or light. The white circle lay on the pink, and as they watched, a purple eye appeared and looked back at them.

Tenn startled, and jerked the cylinder only slightly, but it was enough to swipe the edge. A shower of sparks erupted, and the hole got bigger, revealing more pink and another eye. Through the sparks, a long pink streak thrust itself from the hole, to the side of the lightning. It came out flat as a shadow, bigger than both of them, the tip angled like it was cut. Two blazing purple eyes stared down at them from a hot pink hatchet of a head.

Fear hit Tenn like a hammer, and the lightning frazzled. The thing moved into the fear energy, its glow surging, eyes stretching upward, and ragged mouth falling open in ecstasy. Horrified, Tenn released the button, the lightning stopped, and the purple eyes came down and found him. He wanted to run, but couldn't. The creature lunged toward them, and Tenn and Nod both stumbled backward and fell. It hovered above them, pulsing with power, eyes watching them with triumphant glee. Tenn scrambled backward, but Nod couldn't, and he reached up with the pronged cylinder and stabbed it into the monster.

"NO!" Tenn shouted, but it was too late. Nod's terror fed into the thing, making it writhe, and grow, and burn until the brightness was blinding. Then its power blew back out and Nod exploded. Rocks flew through the air every which way, and the pronged cylinder hurtled out over the trees and disappeared.

Tenn had gotten far enough away that he wasn't terribly hurt. The entity stretched toward him with those gleeful, wicked eyes, and Tenn knew that he had to get out of there or the thing would possess him just like the monks had said. Several of Nod's rocks had landed close to him, and he picked them up one by one and threw them into the angular face. They went right through it. Still, he kept backing away, throwing everything he could reach, until a lucky rock hit the dimensional tear, and stuttered the burning shape of the monster, taking it by surprise.

The mouth opened again, and the rage that came out screeched unearthly. The rock itself disappeared into the other dimension, and the entity was sucked backwards with it, enough time for Tenn to turn himself over, claw to his feet and flee.

Thursday

The present

Chapter Th. 1

"State your business."

The bored voice traveled back to Hellen, eking past the four restless people standing in line in front of her. A dim reply could be heard, something about a trip to the fish market, and the two scowling sentries let the girl pass. The line moved up.

Three people to go. Hellen's stomach knot tightened a little bit more. Earlier, it had seemed like a great idea to disguise herself as a rotund chef and waltz the contraband right out the front door. No running, no shooting, no imminent death. Did she drop her brain somewhere in the forest? Because it was clearly not with her while she concocted this jewel of a plan.

The summer sun blazed in the sky, well on its way to noon. Hard, dry dirt reflected the heat and light so it felt like a desert. Sweat rolled down Hellen's padded body in streams. Of course, abject terror could have something to do with that. Back in the day, they'd all thought things couldn't get any worse. How wrong they'd been.

The line moved up. Both people in front of Hellen were delivery guys, returning from the palace to wherever they worked in town. Probably not the food store, because this checkpoint was for the peons on foot. Folks with wagons and carriages had to use the checkpoint at the gate, where the road passed through the wall. She almost missed the days when the wall went only around the town, instead of going right up to the palace like it did now. It was probably her fault Dagge changed it, he was so furious about what happened the night John Treslo died.

9

Three years now since Tomius Dagge had killed the King. A year and a half since he sacrificed John to one of those dimensional monsters of his. How time flies. The line moved up.

While the young man in front of her showed the soldiers his signed receipt, she scouted Adia's escape plan again, just in case the chef disguise went terribly wrong. The path was bleak. This part of town had become known as the bottleneck, a narrow passage created by the two walls Dagge had built from the existing wall to either side of the main palace entrance. Naturally, when the new sections of the wall were built, the handy climb-over spots John had put in for her were left out, and since running back to the palace would be stupid, the plan was to lose any pursuers in the town.

Fortunately, the merchant district lay ahead and slightly to the left. Without trees and plants, which Dagge had removed during his Pacification Program, there was little cover, but Beau and the others were making up for it in their own special ways.

"State your business."

Hellen snapped out of her mental chase scene and bent to the task at hand. "I have to go to the market to get some parsley. We can't serve the Overlord his plate tonight with the rotted mess I found in the refrigerator this morning."

"I don't recognize you."

Sigh. "Of course you don't, I'm new. Brought in all the way from Rofland, for my skills in the kitchen."

The second guard ceased his continual scanning of the bottleneck between the palace and the town, and came over. "There a problem, Speile?"

"This woman says she's a cook, and she looks like she's got the padding for it, but her neck ain't fat, and that don't look right to me."

Hells' bells. Figured she'd get an observant one. Hellen huffed herself up and cranked up her attitude. "I'll have you know, young man, that slender necks run in my family. In fact, we are known for our graceful carriage, and much admired for it where I come from. I don't appreciate your rudeness!"

"Suck me, lady. I don't care what you appreciate. Frisk her, Vyn."

If he touched her he'd know it wasn't flesh she was hiding under her clothes. Better to make a scene. When Vyn came for her, she let him have it. "Don't you touch me! Don't you DARE!" She slapped at him like an old lady. "I will NOT be manhandled!"

The people in line behind her bunched up and fanned out to the sides, worried looks on their faces. Hellen dodged the young soldier, backing away toward the town and yelling as he came at her, "Help! Help!"

"Hey, leave her alone, man," a strong-looking young man called from the crowd. "She's a cook, it's not like she's dangerous."

"Shut up, piece a shit, or you'll find yourself in the dungeon." Speile shoved him back with the butt of his rifle.

Her moment had come. Vyn had backed her away far enough, and she surprised him by grabbing his shirt front, pulling him to her and slamming her knee into his groin. He surprised her by wearing a cup. For a moment, she stood there stunned, watching the slow smile spread across his face, then she popped him in the larynx with her knuckles, threw him to the ground and ran.

Behind her, Speile set off the alarm—three shots from a bullet rifle into the air. In seconds, soldiers would be pouring into the bottleneck from the town and the palace. She had no time to spare. Her feet crunched over the dry dirt pell-mell, and she yanked off her white apron as she ran. The bulk under her clothes felt heavy and awkward, but she couldn't take it out just yet.

She made the curve where the new wall met the old at a full run. Behind the merchant shops, several small outbuildings would offer her some cover until she got to Luhe's fence. If she ran fast enough, the soldiers wouldn't make the back of his and Vartile's place in time to see.

Without the trees and big leafy plants, the back of the merchant district looked poor and desolate, bleached pale in the summer sun. It

11

still made her sad, even all these months later and in the middle of running for her life. That's how much she hated it.

Shouts rang out from the bottleneck. In about twenty more strides, she'd be at the outbuildings and they wouldn't be able to see her anymore. Thank One cooks wear sensible shoes, and she hadn't opted for a showgirl disguise or something equally dumb.

She ducked past the side of a low-roofed shed in back of the bakery next to Vartile's. Out of sight, she paused long enough to quick-look the best route to Luhe's fence. Between here and there were two more sheds and the low wall hiding the power meter. Hellen bent over, reached through her legs and grabbed the back hem of her skirt, which she pulled up and tucked into her waistband. Instant pants. She took the straw hat off the nail by the door, clapped it on her head, and darted to the next shed.

As soon as she appeared, some overzealous action-figure started shooting at her. A laser pulse zipped by her shoulder and exploded a small chunk out of Vartile's house. Soldiers were closing fast. Hellen crouched and ran past the last shed, where the wind took her hat, and over behind the low wall. Luhe's fence was just a few strides away, but the soldiers were almost to the outbuildings, and she couldn't let them get that close to her.

From behind a trash can at the back of the shop, a figure wearing a straw hat and a padded mockup of her clothes stood up and lobbed a small ball through the air. It arced to the second shed and hit the ground nearby. Firio grinned at her and took off around the other side of the shop. Shouts pierced the air as the soldiers saw him.

Hellen hunkered down and waited for the explosions. A fireball would spew copious amounts of nasty, burning smoke, and six to nine unpredictable fountains of fire. Without a gas mask, they were very difficult to get around, so once it went off, she could go.

At the first detonation, she looked up and behind her. No one was coming around by the big wall, so her forward motion would be out of the soldiers' line of sight. Shouts and the hiss of releasing smoke filled the air. Pushing herself off the ground, she lunged ahead and ran down the side of the building to Luhe's fence.

Made of plain wood planks, the fence looked like any other fence in town, but when Hellen threw herself at the top of the end section, it flipped on a center axis and deposited her on the other side, where she rolled and landed on her feet. Luhe stood at the end of the fence, stabilized it after the turn and rammed a bolt through the mechanism deep in the wall, so it couldn't be turned again.

Hellen stepped over to the wall, opened her shirt front and started heaving the King's cloak from around her body. Vartile hurried down from the front porch with a padded shirt in her hands. Together, they wrenched the hot velvet out into the air, and Luhe bunched it up and shoved it in his shirt front.

Hellen reached into her waistband and brought up two rolled parchments, crushed and folded, but safe. Two more came from the other side, all of which she handed to Luhe. He inserted them down his pants' legs, picked up his decoy paintbrush and climbed the steps to the porch. Vartile pulled the padded shirt over Hellen's head and gave up her own straw yard hat since Hellen had lost the one she'd been wearing.

"Be careful!" she whispered, and climbed the porch steps to follow Luhe into the shop.

By this time, voices could be heard coming around the other side of the porch. Hunched over, Hellen hurried to the corner and peeked around—no uniforms yet in sight. Firio waited halfway up a lattice across the street, and waved her down the road with quick movements of his hand. She set out at a dead run, past where the soldiers were filtering through the smoke between the buildings, rubbing their eyes and coughing. A quick glance showed about fifteen soldiers in pursuit, with many more stacked up behind the shed. Bursts of fire and billows of noxious smoke still erupted from the fireball.

Several of the soldiers saw her, and she could hear them follow once they hit the street, but she had a good head start. The padded shirt Vartile made was much lighter than the King's cloak, and it felt good to stretch her legs and really run. Shouts behind made her look back, and she saw Firio hustling up the trellis and onto the roof. A handful of soldiers had started to climb up behind him, and several more ran into the spaces between the shops.

The idea was to draw the soldiers away from the merchant district, then lose them. She'd learned a few things from Cary and Firio during the times she was home in the last eighteen months, but she wasn't nearly as good as they were. She couldn't climb and jump as well, although she was better at blending into crowds and disappearing. Today her plan was to do just that. Tuesday was market day on the Plaza, and if she could beat the soldiers there, she could shuck her overclothes and she'd be home free.

A few shops down, an alleyway opened up to the left, and Hellen darted down it. Shouts echoed behind her. In the near distance, other shouts drifted down to her from over the rooftops, followed by laser fire. Halfway down the alley, running feet turned in after her, and a laser pulse exploded the bricks by her head. At the next road, she turned right, and faltered. Two blocks down, a barricade of soldiers totally ruined her day.

Chapter Th.2

David put the walkntalk up to his mouth. "Papa Bear, activate the north side, she's coming home."

"Roger that, Charming," Beau's voice crackled back.

"Not Charming."

"Gotta have a name," Beau said, and clicked out. David chuckled, shaking his head.

Through the binoculars, he watched Hellen sprint across the road and into the row of shops that lined the street. From his vantage point in the University Tower, the town pretty much lay in front of him like a map. The taller buildings to the left circled downtown, and he couldn't see the streets there, but fortunately Hellen wasn't that far east. Her tiny body wove through the spaces between the buildings, headed northeast, as did the soldiers chasing her.

To the west, Firio led his pack of soldiers across the rooftops toward the warehouse district. He jumped and flipped from building to building, leaving several behind as he went. At the edge of the merchant district, he dropped down into a yard, went over a wall, across an alley, back up a scaffolding, caught an eave, swung around the corner and vaulted onto the next roof. The last David saw, Firio disappeared on the other side of that building, and the few soldiers who had more or less kept up were trying to figure out where he went.

Back in town, several of the soldiers following Hellen broke off the pack and veered east, apparently trying to flank her. "Tortoise, Hare, four of them are heading your way," he said, and shifted his field of vision to where Grovet waited with a pair of mules. He backed the mules into the narrow space between the shops, and when the soldiers came running around the corner, they met with two upset animals, four flying hooves, and a shouting shopkeeper who wasn't really trying to get them out of the way. David smiled; he could hear the mules braying from up here.

Back west, Hellen had steered herself around a cul-de-sac to avoid being in the open. Half the remaining soldiers followed her around the backs of the shops, and the other half ran through the circle to try and get ahead.

"Sparrow, Raven, Wizard, you're on. Grizzle, pick her up at the shoe repair place."

Cary's voice drawled over the speaker. "You sure about that, champ? You know how she hates to be helped."

"We'll tell her you didn't want to miss all the fun."

"All right, then," he drawled, and clicked off.

Back at Grovet's, his wife Purda had come out with a tray of candles and their two yappy little dogs. They ran around barking at everything, agitating the mules even more. The soldiers started backtracking—one of them limped, and another held his side and grimaced as they hurried away.

The six soldiers who cut through the cul-de-sac split up to go on either side of one shop. Behind that shop, Dessara's wagon blocked the pass, and she loaded several large cactus plants into it very slowly. On both sides of the shop catty-corner to Dessara's, Donas had industrial nets strung up to block the ditches he had dug around his water line. *(Couldn't have customers falling into those!)* Farther on, Merv had placed stacks of pallets and full barrels of wine in his alleyway, and stood there with a clipboard pretending to count. In other places, wood panels had been made into a fence, hot braziers boiled huge pots of steaming water, and just about every passage was blocked or hampered by something. Only one path to NHQ had been left open, hand-chosen by Cary for the best ways to use his particular gifts. Everywhere else, the merchants stood in side yards and alleyways, milling around, visiting with neighbors, and keeping their eyes open.

Of course, Dagge might decide to kill every merchant in town for this, but considering everything Hellen had been doing for the past year and a half, she was worth it.

16

Chapter Th.3

When Cary dropped in front of her, Hellen was glad. She'd had enough, and just wanted this to be over. It was hard to tell how many soldiers were behind her, but more often than she liked, one of them would take a shot, and some wall or window or porch post nearby would shatter. Following Cary meant a whole new level of action, but if it worked, she was all for it.

They wound through the buildings in a general northeasterly direction, never in a straight line for long so as to make shooting difficult. As Hellen followed Cary through the last merchant district shops—lungs heaving, arms pumping, legs pressing around corners for traction—it occurred to her that when this was all over, and Adia had the throne again, she really was going to take that vacation. She'd earned it.

As they wended north, a lot of the old, cheaper houses had been torn down, and the commercial buildings in their place were typically plain brick, long, and one story with a flat roof. The terrain rose slightly as it progressed to where the University was, so quite a few retaining walls bordered the landscaped lawns up ahead.

Cary glanced back over his shoulder and grinned at her. *Uh oh.* Without slowing down, he vaulted to the top of a chest-high wall and took off to the left. Hellen planted her right foot on the wall, held the top with both hands and sprang up after him. Momentum could sure do some crazy things.

On the foot-wide top, she followed Cary around the corner, up the incline and onto a decorative ledge that reached halfway up the building. At the corner of the building, which had Greyven Eye Clinic in big brown letters, Cary grasped the edge of the roofline and swung himself up. Hellen eyed the distance between the roof and the top of the wall as she approached—her center of gravity wasn't in her shoulders, like a man's, so she wasn't sure she could do it.

"Just get started, I'll pull you up," Cary said, arm reaching down over the low wall that lined the roof.

A laser pulse exploded the brick in front of him. Hellen hunched and Cary ducked down. To her left, the wall she was standing on dropped about fifteen feet to the loading dock. Across the paved driveway, two big metal trash bins had been shoved against the opposite wall, and the corner of the building on that side had an antenna mounted on the brick. Perfect.

She dropped down, landed with a roll and dashed for the trash bins. Cary's voice drifted down from the roof, but she couldn't hear what he said because soldiers had reached the eye clinic and were shouting behind her. Hands on the bin lid, she jumped up, put one foot beside her hands and hauled herself to the top. Only five feet of wall to go, but she had no momentum; she grasped the top, planted her right foot, then her left, but her feet kept slipping and she scrambled, getting nowhere.

A laser pulse ripped through her padding. To the side of her actual flesh, fortunately, but it was a real motivator. She was just making progress when Cary's hands reached down from the top of the wall and yanked her up by her shirt. Atop the wall, they lunged for the antenna, climbed to the roof and hurtled down the length of the building to the other end. The midday sun beat down, and the hot dusty roof bounced it right back up into their faces. What she wouldn't give for a drink of cold water. Or a beer.

Shouts and laser fire blew past her. One of the soldiers had climbed onto the roof and was running toward them, rifle at his waist. Cary ran ahead, put his foot on the low roofline wall and leapt to the roof of the next building. Hellen followed, landing with another roll. Across that roof they ran, trying to keep the stairwell door and water cistern between them and the soldier's line of sight. Another jump, and they lost him. Judging by the cry and the thud, he flubbed the leap and plunged to the ground. Another roof, and two more, and they were almost to NHQ.

A lot of the buildings in this area were abandoned. The one that hid the northern base of the Resistance was no different—it used to be a clothing accessories shop, but stylish accessories had pretty much gone the way of the dodo since Dagge took over. On the roof next door, Cary slowed a bit toward the end, bent down at the back corner, and with a quick look around, let himself over the edge. Hellen peered down as she reached the spot and saw Edren Taymer waiting for her beside the overgrown lattice that marked the location of the escape shaft. When he saw her see him, he bent over, grabbed the lattice, and jumped down the underground slide.

"Give me your clothes!" Cary called.

Hellen dropped her padded shirt and skirt down to him, leaving her with the tank top and light trousers she'd worn to the palace. She placed her hands on the edge of the roof and turned to face the wall as she lowered herself down. With one leg, she kicked the wall and pushed herself away to land in the grass. Cary had her clothes on by the time she reached the ground, and he grabbed the hat off her head and said, "See you back at HQ." With a wink and a grin, he jogged out into the road, tightened the hat string under his chin, and caught his breath while he waited for the soldiers to catch up.

Hellen ran to the lattice and looked back at Cary, who saluted and waved her down into the hole. She grabbed the lattice and obliged.

After the searing stress and bright heat of above ground, the cool damp darkness of the basement was a tremendous relief. Safe at last, she bent over in the middle of the room, hands on her knees to try and catch her breath. Edren climbed the several rungs set into the wall beside the metal ramp, and latched the spring doors at the top. Back down on the floor, he leaned the camouflage panel in front of the hole to block it from prying eyes.

The Resistance had had to start taking more precautions when the soldiers moved into the downtown buildings. It happened right after the Winter Festival—Diit had burned down all the barracks, and someone got the great idea that the army should kick out anyone who might be left, and use the three- and four-story structures for housing. Several tunnels had to be walled up again. John's stonemason, Rack, and a crew of six or more worked day and night to get the basements and the drainage tunnel sealed before the troops could catch them at it.

They'd had to move Adia back out to the monastery at that time, too. With the soldiers around 24/7, it was just too risky to have her that close. Not long after they moved her, the raids began, and everyone sweated until Beau and some of the others came up with ways to disguise the existing tunnel openings in basements—shelves that rolled away, wood panels, stuff that didn't look conspicuous. Unnecessary openings got walled up, and the Resistance tightened its belt some.

"Don't worry about Cary, he'll lose any stragglers." Edren watched her with a wrinkled brow. Her face must be frowning or something.

"Yeah, I know," she said. "Cary is the least of my worries." She half-smiled up at him.

In the dim light from the high windows, Edren didn't look at all like his father. Short and square, he gave the impression of being immovable—like if you were to run and try to tackle him, you'd hurt yourself and he wouldn't move one jot. His hair was black as pitch, and his eyes were a smokier blue than Chief's, but he had the same ready smile, and she was glad to see him.

"Well, Edren Taymer, when did you join this ragged bunch of reprobates?" Hellen stood straight and held out her hand. "I wasn't sure we'd ever see you in the trenches."

Edren took her hand with a shy grin. "It's been quite a few months now, probably since right after you were last here. Beau convinced me the Resistance could use an artist, and I guess he was telling the truth." He laughed a little and gestured her to a few chairs.

Hellen knew Edren hadn't wanted to follow in his father's footsteps—probably the first Taymer ever to refuse the mandate of the first-born son. His nature was not as much a fighter as being Captain of the Kingsguard or Chief of Police would need. Chief may have insisted if he hadn't had another son to take the responsibility, but Edren's brother Byron was happy to join the force. Chief kept him out of the Resistance for their mother's sake, but Byron joined immediately after their father was killed. Dagge had dismantled the town police anyway, and put Wharton in charge of keeping the proverbial peace.

The hard chair felt great to Hellen's tired legs. She leaned back and blew out a deep lungful of air; her breathing had eased and her heart rate had about returned to normal. Just a few more minutes and she'd be ready to make the trek to HQ.

"Papa Bear, this is Dwarf, over."

"Read you, Dwarf." Beau's voice sounded loud and strong in the speaker.

"The bird is in the nest, sir. Repeat, the bird is in the nest."

"Roger that, Dwarf. Hello, Tallulah, it's good to have you back." Edren held the walkntalk up toward her.

"Glad to be back, Papa Bear. I'll see you soon."

"Roger that, ma'am. Over and out."

Edren leaned back and tucked the walkntalk into his pants pocket. "Whenever you're ready, we can leave."

"Okay," Hellen said, "but I need to run a quick errand before we go." A frown squinched Edren's face. "It'll be quick, I promise, you don't even have to wait. I can find my way. I have made the trip before."

"No, I'll wait. I just have to let HQ know, but that's no problem."

Hellen studied him. He looked fidgety all of a sudden. "As long as we're stopped, why don't you give me a rundown on what's been happening in town? Beast couldn't tell me as much as I'd like, stuck as she is out in the woods."

"Wharton's got the place pretty sewn up these days. Patrols move in alternating patterns, and they switch up, but Beau's got it figured out. He knows where they'll be when. Search raids started right after you left. The sabotage at the mine really pissed Dagge off, and he ordered search and seizure on all the houses in town. The soldiers took everything valuable they could find and turned it all over to Dagge. He had them make a big pile of it in the bottleneck, and announced that all our treasure was now his, to pay for the carapaz we stole. It didn't matter that we only buried it in a cave-in, and he dug it up almost immediately. The next morning the pile was gone, and no one knows what happened to it."

Retribution. In Dagge's mind every move, every event was all about what they'd done to him; this country, these people, existed only for his own use. Since he'd been in power, the people's loss had become immeasurable: freedom had been lost to the wall, prosperity to carapaz, and lives to violence. Their rights to education, self-determination, and privacy had been summarily sacrificed to a madman's idea of control. But someday he would find out just how wrong he was about that.

"How are you spreading information? Last I heard, Dagge was installing cameras around town, to catch people who were putting up flyers."

"We've started publishing." Edren got a twinkle in his eye. "That's why Beau recruited me. I draw. Eilin, one of the woodcarvers, makes blocks out of them, and we have several writers. We crank stuff out with the letterpress, staple it, or sometimes bind it with glue and cardboard, and pass it around. In the last three weeks alone, we've recruited seven people from a short story about a blacksmith who's really a superhero." He laughed. "Beau really liked that one. David worked up a new symbol, too. Three thorns together, so they look like a fire. The sabotage folks use it, and I stick it in wherever I can. The soldiers never stop us to look at our books or comics, but if they did, it would just look like fiction."

"Brilliant." Hellen nodded appreciatively. The pen *was* mightier than the sword.

Chapter Th.4

Adia waited on the top floor of the pyramid, communing with the pigeons, and occasionally leaning against the edge of the broken wall to soak her face in the sun. Wolf waited with her, curled up on the cool stone between the cage and the part of the wall that wasn't broken. She could tell where he was because he snored and farted in his sleep.

Behind her, the messenger pigeons cooed soothingly in their cage, occasional wing flaps the only disturbance in the perfect summer day. Perfect aside from the monumental stress of having asked Hellen to fake her way into the palace yesterday so she could steal the royal cloak and the palace schematics. Of course, escape was never going to be easy—Dagge had increased the guards around the palace after Adia had ramped up the civil disobedience and sabotage. But night had at least seemed like a better plan than broad daylight. Nevertheless, despite all efforts to convince her otherwise, Hellen planned to walk out the front door this morning in some stupid chef's disguise.

Aside from that, the day was perfect.

A cool breeze coming down off the mountains caressed her face. She could hear the Apex Mountains towering behind her. The wind moaned through them, rocks slid and bounced down the sheer cliffs, and the snow dripped and shifted as it melted into the countless streams running down into the Rocky River. The peaks and shoulders of the range felt like a big, dangerous friend at her back, and she liked that.

In front of her, the forest—also a friend. Even safer than it was three years ago, because Dagge wasn't wasting his time on incursions into it, like he and Pulari used to do. For the last year and a half, Monk's Glen had been left to its own devices, and Adia wasn't sure Dagge would like it if he knew what really went on in there.

Hellen told her a long time ago that the rock giants had come back. They'd found new rocks, and stationed themselves over the dimensional tear, like before. The tear was bigger now, after the 2D monsters came out of it, but it wasn't as powerful, and without any enemy soldiers to feed on, it remained containable. Good news, all around.

She also said the monks were active in the woods, that she ran into them sometimes, when she was home, and they always said the same thing: "It's urgent that you complete your destiny." Thanks, guys. No pressure, right? She said it got to where she went the long way around every time she saw a glowy light in the trees.

Still, that warning was why Hellen had been gone so much of the last eighteen months, and why she'd struggled through until she got the job done. After that horrible night at the palace, when Dagge infected so many of his guests with those freaky magenta toys of his, Hellen's one-woman mission had been to follow them wherever they went until she killed them all. It had been easy to tell who initially got them, because they were pretty much the only ones who went home, but not so easy to find the bodies they moved into later.

By Hellen's account, the lucky ones were the people who got shot that night. Queen Eladora died at the party, but she was not one of the lucky ones. Hellen said the young Queen had been Dagge's first victim, and was the first one Hellen shot, but not until after the monster had already taken her.

Not to be thwarted, Dagge sent Eladora's lover, Rabinette, back home with one in her. The citizens of Rofland were devastated over the news that Eladora had had a stroke, which was what she told them. Most of them didn't buy it, and after a while they rose up in protest, demanding that Rabinette be held accountable. Rabinette was supposed to manipulate the mourning population and get herself declared Queen, but no one liked her to begin with, and some assassin did Hellen's work for her.

Hellen didn't have to go to Shindao, either. The whole world was shocked when their State Advisor revealed that Emperor Mapo had

24

killed Empress Ming and Dr. Wan on the train home from Great Hand. Mapo was subsequently declared insane, and no one believed his story about Ming and Dr. Wan being possessed by evil beings. Their daughter took the throne, and Hellen heard that she reinforced the borders on her father's warnings, but struggled with doubt until Dagge moved into the other neighboring lands. Rumor had it that after that, her father was quietly returned to the palace, and kept a low profile there. These days, Empress Dalang's army was said to be among the best-trained and equipped in the world, and Dagge had made no move in Shindao's direction.

Pulari took one of the evil dead with him, and so did his General. Queen Nylah was one of the lucky ones, and had died at the party—from a heart attack, Pulari told everyone. Well, getting your eyes blown out by a laser rifle would give anyone a heart attack, wouldn't it? The closed coffin should have clued people in, but Pulari himself died shortly after he returned home, and Nylah's death became secondary. According to Hellen, the entire country was in an uproar, first people demanding to see the Queen's remains, then trying to mount an inquiry into the Winter Festival events, and finally the autopsy of King Pulari himself, which proved inconclusive.

The monster moved from Pulari into his son, and when General Hatch's body died, his monster moved into the next General. These bodies lasted longer; the 2D beings evidently learned how to adapt their energy output. Together, the new King and the new General sold the country out to Dagge. Backed by the General, the King, and carapaz, Dagge co-opted the army, and no one could stop the takeover from happening.

Hellen was there at the time; she'd gone to Pulari right away, after the Winter Festival. As she described it, when the army took over, soldiers started shooting people in the street. If someone didn't do what they were told to do, fast, then *bam!*, that was it. Hellen couldn't leave, though, until she'd killed Dagge's monsters. Unfortunately, she couldn't get to the young Pulari, or the General, and it took many months before Dagge's creatures inhabited bodies she could reach.

25

When she came home, she'd been very dispirited, but went back out again, to Valdia, barely three weeks later.

A similar situation had unfolded in Valdia. President Arburash and Senator Bunch went home possessed, and pushed an arrangement through by Executive Order, establishing a weapons-for-carapaz trade that gave Dagge a consulting position in Valdia's government. The people went crazy, and mounted protests and demonstrations, but Arburash and Bunch pressed on until their bodies died. Hellen was in Pulari at the time, and there was no way to track who got possessed next, except to wait for news reports about the next crazy thing someone did. Meanwhile, back in Great Hand, Wharton was amassing a new army, sending recruiters out to all corners of the world, and mercenaries were arriving in droves on the promise of high pay and exciting work.

Months later, one of Dagge's monsters took the highest-ranking General in Valdia, and opened the border with Great Hand under heavy guard. Dagge's army flooded in, established martial law, and no one could stop the takeover of that country. Hellen was in Valdia by then, and when the General died, the monster moved from him to his wife. By then, they'd gotten very sly about whom they took, not always the most powerful people, but often the innocuous ones in the background. The General's wife had access to a lot of powerful people, and at the General's wake, her dead body was found alone in another room. Her autopsy was also inconclusive, which said everything. Hellen was in Valdia for a very long time, following the trails of sudden deaths, unable to get to her targets, until she finally completed her mission and returned home yesterday.

Yes, Hellen had been busy. Out of fifteen evil-dead henchmen, she'd killed five at the party, which left ten. Two of those went to Pulari, two went to Shindao, and two went to Valdia. Six, plus the one in Rofland, made seven more dead. That meant three left, given nothing had happened that Hellen didn't know about. Diit said that Dagge never let his gruesome toys all be in the same place at the same time. He'd learned his lesson, she supposed. And if they changed bodies, no one knew about it, because they were all just rank and file soldiers.

Smart, she had to give him that. It made her glad he didn't know she was alive.

A soft flutter of wings zipped by her head and landed on the cage behind her. Adia turned, walked to the cage, and felt around on the top of it for the messenger pigeon. It avoided her grasp, which frustrated her no end, and she had to locate the drape on the stone ledge, then toss it quickly over the cage and trap the bird underneath. With gentle hands, she fished the bird out from under the cloth, took the message from its leg and put the bird in the cage. Careful, she unfolded the scrap of paper and felt the raised letters.

S A F E.

"Thanks, Papa Bear." She pushed the paper into her pocket and said to the dog, "Come on, Wolf, let's go do some gardening. Hellen's all right, she'll be coming home later, and we should pick some cucumbers." Wolf's big paws scratched on the stone and his head nudged her hand. She rubbed his ears for a couple of seconds, losing her fingers in the long hair around his neck, then turned and led him into the cool of the monastery.

Chapter Th.5

Tomius Dagge leaned against the stone banister and stared out over the town from the big half-moon balcony above the front portico. He happened to hear the three-shot alarm while he was crossing the big foyer, and ran up the main staircase to watch as much of the drama unfold as he could. By the time he burst out onto the balcony, the fireball had belched a smokescreen, and whoever caused the trouble had apparently disappeared.

Hard to believe the stubborn stupidity of some people. How many things was he going to have to take away from them before they realized fighting would only make it worse? He hadn't wanted to cut down all their trees and plants, they'd made him do it by pulling shit like this. Likewise, he hadn't wanted to take their trinkets and valuables—none of it was worth much, anyway. What he wanted was simply for them to do what they were supposed to do. Work and obey. How was that too much to ask?

Ever since the banquet, the defiance had taken on a different flavor. The Thorn emblem had changed. It looked like a group of thorns now, or a small fire or something. How many others had crawled up out of the shitpile to join Hellen? Too many, clearly, annoying him like a never-fucking-ending cloud of gnats. Well, if those morons were brainless enough to keep it up, they'd find out he could play this game as long as it took to win.

Off toward the right, he could barely see the edge of the crowd in Victory Plaza. Traveling merchant stalls lined the open area, goods and food hanging from makeshift roofs, or displayed on tiered racks. Customers milled in the street, many of them facing west, toward the shouting and running. Too bad he didn't have his long-range rifle. He'd give them something to gawk at.

The chase in town had moved out of his range of sight, so he spun around and went back inside. He'd hear what happened soon enough.

In the palace, he stormed through the double doors on the east side, and turned right to go down the main hall to his sitting room. He'd finally given up trying to rename it the War Room; it had been a stupid idea anyway. The conference room downstairs made a much better War Room. It had a giant globe and everything—perfect for planning strategies on a global scale. He smiled to himself, suddenly feeling a little better.

Down the hall, he met a maid coming out of the servants' hallway between his bedroom and sitting room. She was older than most of them, but he'd discovered over the last three years that the tired cliché was true—it really was hard to find good help. In his experience, they either had to be disciplined and didn't survive it, or eventually they just left and didn't come back. He'd had to hunt down a few of those, and kill them, but it wasn't always worth the trouble.

The girls that had to be disciplined were usually the pretty ones he slept with, caught blabbing about one thing or another. Unfortunately for the servants, he had a harkener, and trouble sleeping. None of them knew how he learned what they were saying, and the rumors about him being a sorcerer or a demon pleased him. Never hurt to have that kind of reputation. Pillow talk was supposed to be private, anyway. Didn't their mothers teach them that?

At any rate, this old maid wasn't likely to make it onto his bedding list. She was here because so far, she had managed to do her job right.

"Hello, Rose," he said, "what were you doing in my room?" He put a slight edge on his question to see if he could rattle her.

"Overlord, sir." She curtsied and didn't meet his eyes, which he liked. "I was cleaning your bathroom again, sir, since I know you like it to be fresh and spotless."

Well, that was true, he did like it to be fresh and spotless. "How many times a day do you clean my bathroom?"

"Four, Overlord. First thing in the morning, again at lunch, once in the afternoon, and the last time in the evening."

Really? He hardly even used the bathroom that often. "Why do you do that?"

"Because you never know, sir. It might need it."

This whole time she never once raised her eyes.

"Look at me, Rose."

Slow and hesitant, her gaze came up in stages to meet his. At the last moment, she shook her head a tiny bit, and put a fraction of a smile on her face. "Thank you, Overlord."

"For what?"

"For being so kind as to speak with me."

He laughed. "I wish everyone was that easy to please. Tell you what, go find that idiot accountant, Robert Treslo, and tell him I said to give you a raise. Four percent." He smiled at her and patted her on the arm. "Dismissed," he said, and brushed past her on the way to his sitting room.

"Yes, Overlord. Thank you, sir."

He held his hand up in acknowledgment and turned through the sitting-room door.

****

Roberta stood where she was and watched him walk away. It had taken every ounce of self-possession she had to look Dagge in the eye and smile. He hadn't seemed to notice that her heart was pounding and she couldn't breathe, or maybe he assumed it was fear. Part of it was fear, of course—fear she'd be found out for who she really was, because death would almost certainly follow. For her children, too. She retrieved her cleaning bucket from the floor, crossed the main hall, and went through the door into the long servants' hall.

When she first came to work here, over a year ago, she'd stayed terrified 24/7. With John gone and the university shut down, she'd needed a job, and having another set of eyes and ears in the palace seemed like a no-brainer for the Resistance. Most of them actually tried to talk her out of it, though, and Elzbieta, who took over the nursery after Zola was killed, even offered her a job so she wouldn't have to see Dagge every day. But Roberta wasn't having any of that. She refused to cower after what Dagge did to John, and she promised herself she'd do whatever she could to bring the megalomaniac down.

So far, that hadn't been much of anything, but she'd managed to pull off the alter ego, and even Robert had settled into having her at the palace full-time, going by another name. Roberta was now Rose for most of her day, and a lot of people only knew her by that name. In her heart, it seemed a fitting tribute to Thorn.

Rose tucked her cleaning bucket into the cabinet and went to find her idiot son.

Chapter Th.6

David dragged his weary butt through the front door of the house, because that's where his mother had told him to go as soon as his watch on the University Tower was done. She still didn't want him "running around with the rebels," not after what happened to Dad. "David," she'd said, "forget it."

So here he was, at home again, with nothing to do. Yes, nothing was better than working in Dagge's carapaz mine. Thank One he hadn't gotten the slip of paper summoning him for that. His mother would say there's much to be thankful for. Robert would say he should get a job.

Easier said than done these days. Dagge had shut down so many of the local businesses —all the ones that weren't his idea of necessary—that the pickings were slim for everyone, and worse for young people without much experience. At the ripe old age of twenty, he felt a bit like his best years were behind him.

How the hells were they going to get this country out of this mess?

"Joey!" he yelled, dividing his vocal trajectory between the stairs and the doorway to the living room.

"Yeah!" Joey's voice drifted down the stairs.

"What's for lunch?" The kid may be eighteen, but it was still important to jab the little brother at every available opportunity. Some thumps and the sound of hurrying feet were deeply satisfying. David smiled on the inside, and put a scowl on his outside.

"What do you mean what's for lunch?" Joey appeared at the top of the stairs. "You didn't tell me to make lunch. I don't know what we have." He stood there, hesitant to come down for some reason.

David walked slowly around the banister and positioned himself at the bottom of the steps. Hands on hips, he let his head drop forward, and he shook it slowly. Then without warning, he launched himself up the stairs, eating them by twos and threes, and knocked his brother onto his face with a flying tackle as he tried to escape down the hall. On the ground, Joey flipped over onto his back and tried to fight his older, bigger brother off.

"Stop it! STOP!!" Joey hollered and laughed, half panicked, and oh-so red in the face.

"What are you gonna do, sissy? Huh?" David teased him from his new vantage point straddling Joey's stomach.

"Stop!" He laughed and whined at the same time. "David, really, you're going to make me pee!"

David, in the midst of little slaps on Joey's cheeks, took this as a sign of victory, and held his arms up in the air for his applause. Joey took advantage by reaching up and twisting the skin in the general area of David's nipples, which meant of course that David had to retaliate. Joey immediately resumed the posture of the vanquished.

"Okay, okay! You win! Seriously, I have got to go to the bathroom!"

"Say, 'You, David, are the victor for all time.'"

"Don't be a jerk!"

"Say it!" He snapped his hands up in the pinching position.

"YouDavidarethevictorforalltime!"

"All right then, you may pee." David stood and helped Joey up. Mom wouldn't be happy if he peed on the carpet, and she'd know. She always knew everything.

"Jerk." Joey punched him in the arm as he hurried by, squeezing his knees together.

David grinned. "Want some lunch?"

"Sure!" Joey said from the depths of the bathroom, all annoyance forgotten.

"I'll meet you in the kitchen," David called over his shoulder, feet already light on the steps.

Without Dad, life in the Treslo house had changed a lot. They'd all gotten used to having Mom home after the university was shut down, but her new work schedule meant she didn't get home until dinnertime, six days a week. Her seventh day was a half day, and she was usually so tired, David and Joey did all the cooking and cleaning on that day, too. It only seemed fair.

Most of the time, though, it was just the two of them here, fixing meals, cleaning, tending the garden, doing the schoolwork Mom whipped up when the public schools closed. Robert went m.i.a., staying at the palace for everything but sleep, and he mentioned one morning that he'd been trying to finagle a bed in recent months, too. Just as well, the vibe was better without him around, and David was glad he didn't have to look at his pompous face. With Joey, sometimes David felt like he was the Dad now, and he tried to be a good one, but it sucked not having a social life.

A lot of the kids he'd gone to school with were gone—killed by Dagge, or fled with their families before the wall was built. Some of them were working in the mine now, and not much chance he'd ever see them again. A few had joined the Resistance, but when he brought that little pearl up to his mother, she just glared at him.

The house looked pretty much the same. Minus the silver tray his parents got as a wedding present, and the painting by Monroe, which used to hang over the fireplace. David and his mother both had been surprised the soldiers knew it was valuable. Or maybe Robert tipped them off, he wouldn't put it past him. Brother or not, the guy was an asshole.

In the kitchen, David opened the fridge and peered inside. Raw vegetables crowded the shelves, wrapped in damp paper towels, ends and leaves poking out every which way. Looked like time to do some bartering with Brander's Dairy, and old Ms. Chokry the Chicken Lady. With this much haul, maybe he could even get a couple of pork chops from Mr. Maa, who occasionally butchered a pig and loved greens of all kinds.

Ah, he could almost taste the good food in his future.

None of that, however, solved the lunch puzzle for today. He shifted a few things around, and between the milk and the bundle of

34

young kale he'd picked this morning, a tub of leftover chicken pot pie beckoned. "Thar she blows," he whispered.

"What is it?"

Joey's voice in his ear startled him. With a lurch, David bumped against the open fridge door, rattling all the condiments in a flurry of tinkling glass. "Krikey, Joey! What'd you have to sneak up on me for?!"

"I didn't sneak! I walked up to the door," he made a smooth sweep with his hands, "and looked in the fridge with you."

"Walk louder," David groused, and had to shake his head at how much he sounded like his mother. "Grab an oven pan to heat this in. Did you wash your hands?" There he went again.

"Yes, I washed my hands, I'm not four," Joey grumbled, pulling a casserole dish out of the cabinet below the stove. "Do you know how much you sound like Mom?"

David took a deep breath, set the tub of leftovers on the counter, and closed the fridge. "Yes, I do. Sometimes I can't believe what I hear coming out of my mouth."

"Me neither." Joey gave him a sideways look, and David had to laugh.

A knock on the front door interrupted them. It could always be soldiers, so David liked to answer the door himself. "Preheat the oven to 400, put the pot pie in the casserole dish, I'll be right back."

Joey didn't say anything as David walked out of the kitchen.

In the foyer, he put his game face on. Without bothering to check the peephole, he grabbed the handle and yanked the heavy door inward. On the other side of the threshold, wearing light trousers and a tank top, blond hair short and wavy, stood Hellen.

"Can I come in?" she asked.

"Of course!" He stepped aside to let her pass, then closed the door after a quick visual check around the neighborhood. All clear. Hand on her arm, he guided Hellen to his mom's office, hoping Joey wouldn't come investigate.

Minus the brief glimpses he'd gotten today through the binoculars, he hadn't seen Hellen since the night his father died. It had been a hard night for both of them, and they didn't get a chance to speak at all once they got back to the warren. A lot had happened since then, but her showing up here brought all those grim memories rushing back.

He'd heard that she took his father's death hard, and he wondered if that was why she showed up here. If it was, maybe he could help. He understood that she had to kill his father, that she had no choice and Dad would have wanted her to.

"Is everything okay?" he asked in a low voice as he shut the office door.

"I need to talk to you about something, before I mention it to everyone else."

"Aren't you supposed to be at HQ? Isn't there a party or something because you're home?"

"What?" Her forehead squinched, and she sounded surprised. "Is there a party?"

David paused, mouth hanging open. "You're kidding. I just opened my big mouth, didn't I?" His eyes rolled, and his head fell back, and he was such a loser.

"Nooo, don't feel bad! I'm excited! Want to go with me?"

"Go where?" Joey strode into the room, through the back door from the kitchen.

"Nunya, buddy." David moved to head him off. "This is a private conversation, and you are not invited."

"Eat me, David," Joey said as he tried to dodge around him. "Who is that? And what HQ?"

With his bigger bulk, David forced the annoying little brother back out the door, giving him a final shove before he closed the door in his face. "You do not get to go to a party without me!" seemed a lot less irritating all muffled like that. David smiled as he walked back to Hellen.

"Nunya?" Hellen asked, grinning.

"Nunya business. Which it ain't, know what I'm saying?" He smacked his fist with the flat of his palm.

Hellen laughed. "I was never around boys much; I grew up in a girls' orphanage. You guys are hilarious."

"Oh, well, not all guys are hilarious, we're just special that way."

"Naturally." She nodded. "Both your parents are special, after all."

"Yeah, about that…" Might as well take the opportunity to bring up the subject.

"No worries, David. I feel sure you understand what happened in the palace that night. Why I had to do what I did. This isn't about that."

Okay, that answered that question. "So…all right then, we're square. What's up, Junika?"

She smiled again, and laughed a little. "I haven't heard that name in a while."

"It's how I first knew you. In fact, Hellen was a little hard to get used to, and when they call you Tallulah, I forget who they're talking about."

"Me too," she nodded. "In Valdia I was known as Dolores. For the first two weeks, I didn't know who people were speaking to half the time. Tallulah definitely sounds like somebody else."

"Just one of your many personalities. You might need to see a shrink about that."

"I tell you, if I'm not crazy already, I'm going to get there before it's all over."

David laughed. "You're not crazy, at least not any more than the rest of us."

"Thank you." Hellen shook her head. "I'm not sure that's really comforting."

"Right," he laughed. "Have a seat. Would you like a drink? Some lemonade? I think we have some lemonade. We have water."

"No," she said, and sat down on his mother's little divan. "I'm going to head over to the party in a minute, since it would be rude of me not to show. I just wanted to put an idea in your head."

"Okaaay." David leaned against the desk, facing her. What could she be up to?

"You know who's at the monastery, don't you?"

He nodded and put a finger to his lips, gesturing with his head in the direction of the back door.

She nodded and lowered her voice. "While I've been away, she's been there all by herself. Well, Diit goes out there sometimes at night—he's her valet—and he takes stuff like bread…things she can't do for herself. But during the day she spends a lot of time alone. Too much time, and I thought it might be a good idea for you to go out there. Keep her company, help her cook and stuff. Your mom says you're really good in the kitchen, and you have a garden, and chop wood, and frankly, Adia could use the help."

Truth was, she had him at "all by herself." He'd like nothing better than to get out of this house, and go spend some one-on-one time with an intelligent, interesting, beautiful young woman. Yet, something was missing from this picture. "But you're back now, aren't you?"

"Technically, yes. However, I want to get started again on finding the tunnels, and I thought your being there would—" She stopped mid-sentence. "Do you know about the tunnels?"

"You mean the storm drainage system under the town?"

"No, the tunnels the monks built, deeper than the pipeworks and storm drains in town. These tunnels run from the monastery to the palace and four other places we aren't sure about. Your Dad never said anything to you?"

"No."

"Crap. Well, don't feel left out. The King told your Dad and me about them before he was killed—back when he thought Camberton was the real danger, and he was trying to find an escape route out of the palace. The tunnels were a Royal Secret, but he was desperate, and swore us to secrecy, too. In fact, your mom got highly frustrated with your Dad for keeping so many secrets, but he was trying to protect you guys. He figured the less any of you knew, the better."

"Didn't turn out to be such a great idea, did it?"

"No, I suppose not. Anyway, I thought your presence at the monastery could ease some of my guilt for not being there."

"Fair enough, but if all the tunnels start at the monastery, why not look there?"

"Funny you would mention that, because your Dad and I both looked, and Adia has looked, or felt, over and over, and nothing. We could use a fresh pair of eyes."

Oh, to work with the Resistance, to escape this town and go off on an adventure, to rescue a princess (okay, not technically correct, but still) and help save the Kingdom. How badly he wanted it. How his very soul yearned for the chance.

But what would Mom say?

Hellen read his mind, apparently. "Let me ask your Mom. I think I can convince her."

"If you think so, you got it. What about Joey?"

"I'm glad you asked that!" Joey's shout muffled its way through the door.

"Well..." She looked surprised. "He's old enough to stay by himself, isn't he?"

"No, I am not!" Joey shouted.

"Yes, he is!" David shouted back. "But he really hates being alone, and he might get into trouble if left entirely to his own devices."

"I would definitely get into trouble!"

"Shut up, Joey!" Sometimes it was hard not to pummel the brat.

"Maybe he could go, too," Hellen barely whispered, "but I need to think about it. I'll let you know soon."

"Sounds like a plan." David stuck his hand out for a shake, and Hellen took it.

Chapter Th.7

Ten minutes after she left David, Hellen was back in the neighborhoods on the north side, where the residential area faded into the commercial area. Dagge had left the trees and plants alone up here, because all the activity of the Resistance had focused on downtown, and he must have figured the culprits were nearby. It irritated her that he was right.

Lately, though, Adia's strategies had branched out to other parts of the town. On Hellen's first trip home, she'd asked about the lightning weapon, because Vartile had mentioned that some of the local science nerds were studying carapaz. Hellen gave Adia the weapon, and she sent it to Merv, an ex-professor who apparently discovered that carapaz produced enough energy to make the weapon work.

The cave-in in the mine had been the latest in a string of carapaz-related explosions. The discharge was still slow, and therefore risky, but in one week a delivery worker was able to explode a few stones at the train-loading site, and he passed the weapon to a miner the next week, and the miner caused the cave-in. Later, the miner said the guards thought the carapaz was exploding on its own, and none of them wanted to work there anymore, or handle the carapaz at all. Given the danger of getting caught, exploding carapaz struck Hellen as more of a novelty than anything really useful, but the fact that the energy weapon worked on it might be good to know someday.

Grateful for the landscaping, she squeezed through the row of bushes beside Ruby's Sandwiches and Soup. Without the padding and the hat, she felt fairly sure the lunch crowd wouldn't suspect her as the woman who'd been running from guards just a couple of hours ago. Not that any of them would have seen her, it was just how her mind worked these days. Constant paranoia. It would have been better if David had walked to the party with her—two people instead of a single woman—but he argued that his Mom would kill him, and he was probably right.

Roberta had really clamped down on the boys after John died. Beau got to talk to David some, because Roberta immediately signed both boys up for self-defense classes. Beau had mentioned during one of her trips home that David really wanted to join the Resistance, but Roberta flatly refused. She'd told him she wasn't going to lose her children like she lost her husband, and NO ONE better argue with her about it. Beau said David dropped the subject out of kindness to her, but one day it would almost certainly come up again. If the son was anything like the mother, there could be no doubt. The Tower watch he pulled this morning would've been a soft tap on that door.

Click-clacks on the concrete beside her brought her up out of her reverie. Over her right shoulder, a hand was just about to make contact with her shoulder, and she slapped it and jerked away instinctively. The hand snatched back, startled, went to the woman's chest, and the mouth above it gasped.

"Oh!"

Hellen peered at the smooth, round face, the black hair hanging straight to the jawline, and after a second of piecing the parts together, recognized the woman. "Anji Oh! What are you doing here?" She reached out, wrapped her arms around the woman's body and gave her a delighted squeeze.

"Well, I'm looking for you, oddly enough!" Anji laughed and hugged her back. "I knew you'd be in Great Hand somewhere, and—"

"Let's step right over here, okay?" Hellen pulled her by the arm to stand under a big tree at the edge of the property. In transit, she glanced around to see if anyone watched, but no one made eye contact or glanced away.

"Okaay." Anji pitched forward precariously on her high heels as she tried to accommodate Hellen's pace. "Dolores! You're going to make me fall!"

"I'm sorry. Are you with someone?" Hellen didn't have a lot of spare life for small talk. They reached the tree, and she led Anji around to the more hidden side, which was, ironically, by the low-traffic crossroad.

"No, I crossed the border on my own, and that was no picnic, let me tell you."

Hellen gazed at the familiar face, so out of place here it bumfuzzled her. Anji had been a good friend during her time in Valdia—gave her a place to live, and vouched for her so she could get a job at the diner where she worked. Nicest person she ever met, and that was saying something. What on earth made her come to Great Hand?

"The border's terrible, isn't it?" she replied. "The guards treat everyone like criminals." She glanced around again, still no watchers. "Seriously, dear, what are you doing here? You do realize it's a lot harder to get out than in. Is something wrong? Do you need help?"

"Well…" Anji's eyes avoided her gaze, and filled with tears. "I lost my job right after you left. Bangko fired me because I recommended you and you disappeared without giving notice or anything. That's what he said, and I said he was a rat and a cheap boss, and didn't deserve such good people working for him anyway." Her laugh was light, but had a stress pitch, and Hellen could read anxiety in the lines around her mouth. "I know this is unexpected. I can go back if it's a problem, I kept the apartment…"

"I would love for you to stay." Hellen laid her hand on Anji's arm. "I'll see if I can find you a place to live, and maybe even a job, at least for a while. This isn't the easiest place to have a life, you know. Jobs are scarce, but I know some people." She grinned and sought her friend's downcast eyes. "Okay?" Pause. "Okay?"

"Okay," Anji said. "I knew I could count on you, Dolly. Thanks."

Such a weird nickname. Way perkier than Hellen felt. "No problem." She smiled, even though she, in fact, had a pretty big problem. The only people she knew who could take Anji in were people who called her Hellen, and sometimes Tallulah. How was she going to handle that?

"Can you get a room for a night or two while I make some arrangements? There's a boarding house not too far from here, and I'm sure they could use the business."

"Yes, of course." Anji nodded. "I shook the rat down for my paycheck before I left."

"Good girl." Hellen wrapped her arm around the smaller woman's shoulders and they set off up the street.

Chapter Th.8

Dagge lay on his cushy sofa and dropped a few peanuts into his mouth. The salty taste pleased him, and the crunch satisfied him when he chewed. He dropped a few more in. He wasn't hungry—just ate lunch, in fact—but his mouth wanted something, and peanuts did the trick. So what if he had put on a few pounds in the last couple of years? Not like anyone who mattered was seeing him naked these days.

Wharton should be knocking on the door any minute. In fact, he should have shown up an hour ago. The report about what happened in town this morning had gotten way past due. With all the money he was spending on the military, they should've had the criminal in custody yesterday, before she made fools of them all. No doubt the Thorns, or whatever they called themselves these days, were laughing in their beer, because he'd have heard by now if the soldiers had caught anyone.

Ten to one it was Hellen. At that checkpoint, she had to be either leaving the palace or going to the palace, and who else would have the grit to do that? Or enough knowledge of the palace to make a foray practical? No one but her. Sadly, as narrow as her previous escapes had been, she wasn't likely to push her luck and try to kill him a third time. He sure hoped she did. His body still reveled in the memory of that night in the dining room, pressing her hard against him, the rifle between them like a huge erection.

But the insurgents' m.o. these days was sabotage. If you can't kill the Big Dog, give him fleas, right? At first it was mostly just irritating—a power outage on the firing range, shut off water supply to the downtown barracks buildings, some kind of noxious odor in the swamp cooler there—all stuff that had to be dealt with, took time, and made his men cranky. Later, the sabotage got more creative, like exploding carapaz, and the cave-in at the mine. He may not know they did it, but they did it, and he would've just killed everyone on duty, but he'd been through quite a few laborers that way, and he was gonna run out if he didn't stop.

Hence, the retribution programs. They got creative, he got creative. What kind of punishment would he need to come up with now? Naturally, he wouldn't know until it could be determined what the sabotage was. But it felt good to have something to look forward to.

Knock knock knock.

About damn time.

"Come in!" The door swung open. Wharton came in and closed it behind him, then moved to stand at attention in front of the sofa. He looked tired, and not at all happy.

"Overlord, sir, we lost the suspect on the edge of the northern commercial zone. A subsequent search of the surrounding area was unsuccessful."

Dagge sat up without taking his eyes off his General. "Is that it? Three hours, and that's the extent of your report?"

"Sir, our efforts were continually impeded by..." He floundered for a second. "...a very well-organized series of environmental delays. She had help, too, from one of the fugitives who always eludes us. The suspect also had two or three doubles, and they appeared and disappeared, so they were impossible to follow. Sir."

"Environmental delays? Elusive fugitives? Wharton, that's pathetic."

"Yes, sir." His mouth turned down.

"I assume you spoke with the guards at the checkpoint. What's the description of this suspect?"

"A middle-aged woman, possibly overweight, wearing a white apron over dark clothing, claimed to be a recently-hired cook here at the palace."

Possibly overweight. That meant possibly not. Some kind of padding, maybe. "Hair color? Eye color?"

"One says light hair, one says dark hair, short or pulled back, but neither noticed eye color. Light skin."

Hellen, Hellen, Hellen. What were you up to? Unless she'd put on more weight than he had (which was doubtful, considering all the running around she'd been doing), she was hiding something under her clothes. So, it was thievery, not sabotage, unless she stole his bath towel or something. He chuckled at the thought.

"Half rations for the troops—three days. It might help their performance to remind them what it's like to be hungry. Dismissed."

"Yes, Overlord." Wharton snapped his heels together and bowed slightly, then about-faced sharply and left.

The men would grumble, and get surly, but there was no denying they had gotten soft. He knew how easily it could happen. In a few days, he may well have an idea of what his next move should be, and after going hungry, the soldiers would be ready to do anything he asked.

Chapter Th.9

Indeed, it was a party. Hellen walked into HQ with Edren, and found a whole roomful of people milling around with drinks and cake. A suppressed cheer went up when they realized she'd finally made it.

"What, you can't even wait for me?" She grinned and greeted the friends she knew well. Hugs for Grovet and Purda, Dessara and Donas, Byron, Elzbieta, Eilin...too many to list. Beau barreled his way through the crowd and wrapped her in his big arms.

"Ah, it's so great to see you again. My best student!" he said, lifting her up and spinning her around until she laughed. "We worried about you every day, you know." His head pulled away and he gazed up at her with twinkling eyes.

She hugged him to her again. Yeah, she knew what he meant.

On her feet again, she tugged her shirt down and searched the gathering for the other people she needed to hug. Vartile first, then Luhe and Cary, who handed her cake on a plate. She took the cake, but no fork came with it, so she dropped any pretense to manners and used her fingers. "I'm so glad to be home."

"We're so glad to have you back," Vartile said, leading Hellen to a semi-circle of chairs facing a dilapidated sofa. Hellen settled herself on the sofa, and Luhe set a glass of possibly lemonade on the floor beside her.

"It's lemon cake, so they kind of go together," he whispered.

"Thank you, Luhe, you're a darling," she mumbled around her mouthful, eating like a starving person.

He winked at her and stepped away to lean on the back of his wife's chair.

The circle of faces brought a smile to her heart. The few trips she'd made home from Valdia hadn't been long enough to see

47

everyone—just Adia, Vartile and Luhe, and a few lessons from Beau and Cary—and it felt really good to see them all. These people had come to mean so much to her, and she didn't realize how much she'd missed them. They were her family, every bit as real as blood, and just as precious.

"Did everything go all right after the drop this morning?" She directed her question to Vartile, and popped the last bite of lemony goodness between her teeth.

"Smooth as silk," Vartile said. "All of them under lock and key now, ready for tomorrow."

"Before we talk about the meeting tomorrow," Beau interjected, "I'd like to hear about what happened in Valdia." A chorus of agreement flew around the group, and heads were nodding. "If you're up to it," Beau added.

"Are you kidding? This is the most up I've been in months, I'm dying to tell you guys what happened." A swallow of lemonade washed the cake down, she licked her fingers and set her plate in her lap. Around the room, all eyes faced her direction. For someone who had lived the past year and a half undercover, it felt a little exposed. Sheesh.

"As you know, I was in Valdia when Dagge's army crossed the border. Early on, the news media told everyone it was nothing to worry about, just a readiness exercise for Valdia's military, but by the end of the day they stopped saying that, and were telling people to stay in their homes.

"General Dubin had given a press conference the day before, and said the towns along the border would see some military activity, but if people stayed far away, they wouldn't be in any danger. So people did, and no one died until the third day, when Dagge's soldiers opened fire on protesters in Downey. By then the people had gotten the idea that it wasn't an exercise, but any protest was too little, too late.

"I knew the General had to have one of those things in him, but I couldn't get to him—too many people around him, he kept traveling from place to place, and I just couldn't keep up. He lived for about a month more, and started looking pretty bad, but when he died I had no idea who the monster went into. Then his wife died, and I knew it had to be her, but there were so many people at the wake, there was no telling who it took there.

"In the meantime, I was also scanning the papers for sudden deaths in some social or work-oriented circle other than politics or the military. I found a series of unexplained corpses of people who had dropped dead in banks. They were all muckety-muck bankers and financial types who had recently been loaning money to other countries. It struck me as a move Dagge would make, so I traveled to Cacint City, where the biggest financial district is.

"I got lucky there. The president of a large bank had just died, while in a meeting with two other bankers. It had to be one of the two. Fortunately, bankers don't generally travel with an entourage of soldiers, so I was able to get close enough to see them by eating in the same restaurants, or just positioning myself so they had to maneuver their way around me on the sidewalk.

"See, if I looked into their eyes, and one of those things was in there, a tiny flash of purple would generally give it away. I discovered that in Pulari. The trick was always to get close enough. When I pinpointed the banker who carried the monster, I followed him on the sly until I could get a shot over his back fence."

The room was quiet. Most of them couldn't imagine having to do what she'd done, that was plain. Beau, however, was nodding.

"So you found my friend in Downey, I take it. Did he supply you with everything you needed? Contacts, weapons, papers?"

"He did, Beau, and I owe you both a debt of gratitude."

"You owe me nothing, Hellen. We all owe you."

Several murmurs of agreement peppered the crowd. It gratified her heart that they didn't judge her for killing people. Her own heart wasn't quite so kind.

"What happened with the second entity?" Cary stood behind Beau, his arms crossed over his chest.

"I went back to Stesin to see if I could pick up the trail. It was cold, of course, but I kept scanning the papers and listening to the news for anything that might be a clue. Dagge's takeover had changed the social order, but not all that much. Soldiers were in the streets, and checkpoints had been established on the roads, but life went on normally for the most part. I'd only been in Stesin for a day, went to a diner, and I ended up with a place to live and a job at the diner. The waitress there was a terrific person, and there's more to that part of the story, but I'll talk about that later.

"For months I hung out in the restaurants around the government buildings whenever I could. I loitered around the doorways of the capitol, snuck into the private wings more than once. I never saw anything there, but several times in restaurants, I thought I saw purple in someone's eyes. I'd follow them out, but I'd either lose the person in one of those electric surreys they have, or when I got close, it turned out I was wrong. The sudden deaths had become less frequent, so I was stymied for quite a while.

"In the end, I got lucky there, too. I sat in a city transit tunnel one night, alone, waiting for the magnetrain home. I'd spent hours that day scrutinizing all the political types in some stupid, trendy restaurant, and when I glanced at the woman who sat next to me on the bench, she was looking at me with these glowing purple eyes. She was a homeless woman, not anyone I would have looked at, and she was smiling like she knew who I was and what I was doing there."

Hellen had to stop talking for half a bit. She swallowed and cleared her throat, because the fear she experienced that night still leapt up in her when she thought about it.

"I haven't told Beast about this yet, but I'm going to tell you, and I'll tell her tonight so that if anyone mentions it at the meeting tomorrow, it'll be okay." She drew a deep breath. "The thing was there to take me, I'm pretty sure. I mean, it could've possessed me without me even knowing, from behind, but I think it wanted me to know. I think it wanted to gloat." A short, incredulous laugh escaped her. "It leaned toward me and said, 'Tomius says hello.'"

Her throat convulsed, and she couldn't coordinate her muscles enough to swallow. Tiny shakes of her head were all she could manage until she worked through the spasm and forced the swallow down.

"It terrified me." She nodded her head in agreement with herself. "How could he possibly know? My name was Dolores Kutchins, I'd traveled all over, in and out of disguises, and no questions ever asked. Not once did anyone look at me strangely, or search my bag, or treat me any differently than anyone else. As far as I could tell, I raised no suspicion whatsoever.

"But there it was, talking to me in the perfect disguise—a woman few people would even see, and almost no one would miss when it killed her." For a moment she had to pause, and look at the plate in her lap. "What it didn't know was that I wore my carapaz knife—the one Rack made for me—in a spring-loaded arm band." She held her right hand out, palm up, and looked at it. "I had it on every day, just in case I was attacked, or in case I got lucky. Well, I got better than lucky, because something told me to stab her in the eyes first, then the heart, and that's just what I did.

"It screamed. You should have heard it. When I stabbed it in the eyes, this deafening screech filled the station, like a thousand rusty hinges at different pitches. It was horrible. I stabbed it in the heart and ran. At the bottom of the staircase, about twenty strides away, I glanced back and the creature was jabbing out of her, all around, looking for me, its eyes torn and dripping purple globs that disappeared in midair. The homeless woman's body fell forward onto the floor, and the thing went with it, powerless to do anything but die with her."

Hellen let out a shaky sigh and hung her head again. It felt good to get that off her chest. Adia had done very well last night, listening to the bulk of her story, but all the detail about this bit struck Hellen as too much more for one sitting. Now she had to tell her, so the big meeting tomorrow night wouldn't risk getting awkward, and it would be better to go ahead and 'fess up, anyway. It was just that the whole "I'm okay with you risking your life" thing still seemed new, after all those months Adia wanted to strangle her for it.

51

"Now we know carapaz can hurt them, more than just in the heart," Cary said. "That could be really useful."

"Yes, it could!" Grovet nodded enthusiastically. "I'll tell Merv, and he can get the science folks on it right away."

"And I'll tell Rack," Cary offered. "He can see about getting some more large pieces, for weapons or whatever."

"And I'll tell Beast," Hellen chimed in, "so she can add that to the arsenal in her head. Who knows, the way she thinks, we may end up with a carapaz cannon before it's all over."

Quiet descended on the room. "Hey, this is a party, and I for one need more cake!" Beau's voice made her smile.

"Me too!" she said, and stood up to follow him to the desk where the cake sat waiting. A generous chunk landed on her plate, and she picked it up whole and stuffed the end into her mouth.

"Who needs forks?" Beau grinned and shoved an entire piece into his open maw. Hellen got tickled and started laughing around her mouthful. She had to put her plate down and focus on chewing before she choked.

Vartile pushed her glass of lemonade into her field of vision. "Good job, Beau," she teased. "Hellen survives every other damn thing, and you kill her with dumbassery." Beau's mouth was so full, cake came out of his nose when he laughed, and he couldn't answer.

Hellen took the drink, tilted it up to her mouth, and her cake dissolved into the tart wetness. "Ah!" She smacked her lips in satisfaction, and watched Beau as he fought the rest of his piece down his gullet. When it looked like he had slain the dragon, she handed him her glass and he finished it off.

"That was amazing," she said. "I never saw cake come out of someone's nose before."

"And I've never done it, so it was new for both of us," he said, and Hellen patted him on the back.

"What was the rest of the story about the waitress who helped you in Valdia?" Luhe had walked over to join the cake group, and stood with his arm resting on Vartile's shoulders.

"Oh, right!" Hellen said, putting her plate down. "I wanted to talk to you guys about that. Hey, everyone!" She stepped closer to the main group still sitting around the sofa. "The lady who helped me in Valdia showed up in Great Hand today." Surprised looks bounced around the group. "She spotted me outside Ruby's. She lost her job because of me, and spent her last paycheck to start over someplace new."

"And she came here?" Purda asked.

"Only because she knew I'd be here," Hellen explained. "She figured I would help, and I'd like to. But really, it'd be you guys helping her, and I wanted to ask if anyone could give her a place to live and a job."

"Wait! Before we all jump on the june bugs, let's talk about the risk factor." Byron Taymer had his hands up, trying to settle the crowd before it got excited. "I think it would be a mistake to allow any stranger, even one as commendable as Tallulah's friend, access to our operation. Anyone who helps her will have to be prepared to keep certain things from her. Are we agreed on this?"

Murmurs ran around the room. Hellen was glad Byron brought this up, but she had to admit, she felt a little defensive. "Byron's right, of course, we can't let just anyone in. I will say, though, that Anji has been a staunch ally, asked no questions, even when I was gone for hours, or days, with no explanation. I'm not saying we need to tell her anything, just that I don't think she'll pry."

"So it's a matter of who has the ability to keep her apart from the activity of the Resistance, and the warren, in addition to who has the space and the work," Vartile said.

"Yes." Hellen nodded. "Possibly for the entire run, or perhaps until she proves herself."

"That eliminates me," Vartile shook her head, "on both counts."

"I have space," Purda said. "She can have our son's old room."

"If she doesn't mind dogs and candles," Grovet finished.

"I'm sure she won't." Hellen smiled gratefully.

"I can hire her temporarily," Elzbieta said. "We've been busting our butts through the busy season, and the nursery's far enough away from the action that she shouldn't be exposed to anything that'll make her curious."

"Be aware," Byron said, "that you may have to lie—"

"Like she thinks my name is Dolores, so we'll have to tell her Hellen's my middle name or something."

"And you'll definitely have to keep secrets. Are you prepared to do that?"

"I can do that," Elzbieta nodded. "I kept my first pregnancy a secret for a whole year."

The room got stone quiet. Everyone stared at her.

"It's a joke, people, come on!" she grinned.

Chapter Th. 10

Streaks of sunset had the clouds on fire behind Hellen by the time she reached the monastery. The journey from the warren to home was as easy as could be expected these days. Still rocky, of course, but the trees and bushes had grown up some, and guard was light since the soldiers had moved into town. Dagge had evidently become complacent, protected on the south and west by the treacherous Apex range, controlling Pulari on the east, and having Great Hand locked up behind a wall. Or so he thought.

Over the last year and a half, the path around the back of the palace had become a bit worn by various members of Adia's council. Beau, or Vartile and Luhe, sometimes Cary, would leave HQ by the tunnel under the wall, come up in the rocky outcrop, and hike around the fringe of trees next to the mountains. Other than a couple of tricky spots, where the cover got thin, the path was pretty safe, and it looked like no one veered from it. In some places, even she could see the packed dirt and bare spots, and she wasn't a tracker. One forbid Dagge ever stumbled onto it.

Every full moon, three or four of them would make the trip to the monastery to see Adia. Hellen had shown them the way the first time she came home, after the initial few weeks she spent in Pulari. That much alone time had made Adia a little crazy, and Hellen knew she had to get some people out there once in a while to keep the future Queen from becoming a cautionary tale, or worse.

By the next trip home, Adia was doing much better. She had a garden started, and a big pile of firewood, and acted like her old self. Beau had taken care of repairs and things that needed to be done. Vartile and Luhe had stocked supplies and cleaned the corners, and Cary had mostly hung around Adia too much until she had to tell Beau to bring him sparingly. As Adia described it, lots of plans got made during those visits, via talks that lasted late into the night.

Tomorrow would be the full moon, but this time Hellen planned to take Adia to the warren for an all-council assembly.

When she stepped around the last jut of rock, the monastery appeared, dark and foreboding. Home sweet home. Hopefully she hadn't gotten too spoiled living in a place with solar power and a fridge.

In the increasing gloom, as she navigated the protrusion of boulders that used to be the west wing, she noticed that the cut stone of the front entrance looked older and moldier than ever. Or maybe it was just the light. Here, the trees grew closer to the building, and the sunset had little purchase. A few beams glinted on the moss and vines that had taken over, masking the entire front in heavy shades of green and black. Hellen kept moving. Past the entrance and around the corner, the fading sunlight still shone on the pyramid, turning everything there orange.

Standing at the corner, Hellen took a minute to appreciate how far Adia had come. Below the pyramid, a line of stakes and rope edged the path from the kitchen door and went around the bit of garden Beau and Luhe had made in the yard. Bushy plants reached and spread, looking very happy in their little home. A few glints of yellow and orange and red meant they were doing their job. Or at least Hellen assumed so—in truth she had no idea what kinds of plants they were.

She could go around that way to the kitchen door, but the foyer inside the front door had her disguise chest in it. Even though she wasn't really disguised, she'd left her pajamas there this morning, and was really feeling the need to put them back on. Hellen turned back and made her way across the viny, moldy front.

With one hand, she pushed the heavy rock slab that constituted the door. As massive as it was, it hung so perfectly it moved at the lightest touch. Those monks, they really knew what they were doing.

A low growl greeted her from the dark. Her heart skipped a beat. "Wolf, it's just me," she said. She hadn't been around enough for the dog to get used to her comings and goings, and the last couple of days had had a few tense moments like this. With a small shove, the door opened far enough for Wolf to come forward and give her a sniff. Hellen waited on the doorstep until he wagged his tail.

She'd found him in Pulari over a year ago—a skinny, disheveled pup skulking around his mother's body, which lay dead at the side of the road. Three red splotches stained her white coat, dried blood coated the cobblestones around her, and she was left there, forgotten. So sad. No doubt she'd tried to protect someone, or maybe her pups, and the rest of them ran or got taken by the soldiers who shot her. This one had managed to get away.

Hellen's conscience wouldn't let her leave the puppy there, but he was hard to catch. He kept a wary eye on her, and wouldn't let her get close to him until she bribed him with food. Even then, she had to be quick, and he struggled like crazy when she scooped him up and tucked him under her arm. More food, and petting, and ridiculous-sounding sweet talk eventually made it okay, and she was able to carry him home in the bag slung over her shoulder.

Adia had laughed when Hellen put him in her arms. His white fur was fuzzy and soft, he licked her all over her face, up her nose and in her ears, and she fell in love with him on the spot. They'd been inseparable since. He was probably the best present she could have given the lonely Queen.

These days, Wolf looked a lot like his namesake, but with a squarer nose. Bigger than his mother, he had a formidable bulk, and it was a good thing he hunted for food, because there'd be no way for Adia to feed him otherwise. In fact, she said he often brought food to her, and she did the best she could with the rabbit and squirrel carcasses—gutting, skinning, and cooking—because she didn't want to offend him. And sometimes she was just that hungry.

With his tail wagging and his tongue lolling out, he didn't look quite so scary. Hellen patted him on the head and walked into the foyer, pushing the big door closed behind her. Wolf backed away and watched everything she did. Perfect guard dog, she must say. Funny how sometimes you don't know what you truly need until it turns up. She sent One a little prayer of thanks.

"Well, Wolf, what's for dinner? Huh? Is it squirrel? Is it squirrel?" The big head cocked to the side, and obviously, he knew what she was saying. "I'm not having squirrel." She shook her head as she slipped off her walking shoes and reached for her pajamas on the hook by the chest. "Oh no, I'm not having squirrel, because I brought chicken—"

"You brought chicken?" Adia's voice surprised her from the archway to the great room. Hellen turned and looked at the young woman standing there. Aside from the scars, she looked much like she had when she came home from school three years ago. Her dark hair hung nearly to her waist, her brown eyes twinkled, and she hardly gave away the fact that she couldn't see. Wolf trotted over to his mother and nuzzled her hand.

Hellen smiled while she changed her clothes and listened to Adia's happy voice. "Oh my gosh," she said, "I can smell it. It smells heavenly. It's Vartile's oven roaster recipe, isn't it? Mmmm, I haven't had chicken in weeks. Can we eat now?"

"Yes, we can," Hellen replied from the depths of her pajama top.

"Come on, Wolf, let's go get plates!"

The two of them disappeared in the direction of the kitchen, and Hellen switched her trousers for the soft pj bottoms on the hook. Nighttime delivered a drastic drop in temperature here, so she snuggled her feet into the warm-ish rabbit booties Adia made last winter. Several big holes rather spoiled the insulation, and the fit was irregular to say the least, but Adia made them all by her lonesome, so Hellen loved them. Ready at last, she fished the chicken out of her bag and went to meet her family at the big stone table.

When Hellen entered the room, Adia had forks in hand, and was in the process of retrieving napkins off one of the shelves Beau had mounted for her. Plates already waited on the table, and Wolf lay beside the back door. A fire popped in the big fireplace, water steamed in the iron tea kettle, and two cups sat on the stone oven with tea strainers sticking up out of them.

With a tiny chuckle, Hellen marveled. Before she left for Pulari, Adia could not start a fire, or cook food, or even get around the monastery without having to concentrate. Now, here she was, accomplishing those things so easily, running the Resistance, and even the dog was trained. Once she set her mind to it, the transformation had been astonishing. All the way around.

"Would you like some tea?" Adia dropped the forks and napkins in their places and went to check on the water. After waving her fingers through the dissipating steam, she grabbed the hot-holder to remove the kettle from the swing rod that positioned it above the flames. "I've gotten to where I love tea," she said. "It's a comforting thing to do, and it helps me if I don't have any food."

"I would love some tea," Hellen said, even though it reminded her of sitting with Tomius in his quarters, and all the stuff that followed. She shook her head and drove the memory out. "What's in it?" she asked, watching Adia pour the water while she unwrapped the chicken. Wolf got very interested in what she was doing, raising his nose into the air, nostrils quivering.

"Blueberry leaves and lemongrass, mostly. Plus some dried blueberries and apple skins. Vartile brings me herbs and stuff, and I dry them in the oven. This batch is pretty good...I've made some that were a little rough, so you're lucky." She chuckled as she walked the cups over to the table. "Wolf, don't even think about it." She turned to him a little as she sat. "You'll get yours after we eat." He yawned and stretched out full length, head resting on the floor with eyes closed.

"That's remarkable, Adia, how do you have him trained so well?" Hellen pulled the bird apart and divided the portions between them. Tonight, they could eat as much as they wanted, no saving anything for later, and even if they ate every bite, there'd still be plenty of scraps for the dog. The tender bird gave up its pieces with hardly a fight, and the juice ran down Hellen's fingers until she had to lick them. Adia sat across the table, nose forward like her dog.

"We understand each other," she said, and Hellen wanted to laugh. That much seemed plain. "He knows I can't see, and he takes care of me. In return, I love him—I talk to him, and share my bread and cheese when the hunting doesn't go well, and I take him with me everywhere. We're buddies."

"So, I don't think I ever asked you, why 'Wolf'?" Hellen picked up her napkin, wiped her hands, and laid the napkin in her lap. The breast piece beckoned, and far be it from her to resist. "I mean, why not 'Fuzzy' or 'Whitey' or some other name?"

"Well now, 'Whitey' would be a dumb name for a blind person to give a pet, don't you think?" Adia's hand gingerly touched the pieces on her plate and settled on the leg/thigh combo. "And 'Fuzzy' wouldn't work for a grown dog, give us some respect…" The thigh went into her mouth, and she ripped a big chunk off, then had to poke at it with her fingers before she could get it all in to chew. "Oh, this is so fabulous!" She squeezed the words out around the food, grease shining on her chin in the firelight.

"I hope you have more manners in front of your council," Hellen teased.

"You're kidding, right? Beau's the one who's always telling me to stuff my face. He says he worries about me out here, and lately he's taken to bringing me canned goods like sardines, which are…such a mixed blessing. But Wolf likes them, don't you, baby?" Wolf sat up eagerly, saliva dripping off his hanging tongue. "And to answer your question," she said around the thigh clamped between her teeth, "Wolf gets to have a fairytale name just like the rest of us." She bit down and tore off another bite. "Except you, since you were first." After she chewed for a few seconds, she amended, "Well, John was first, but Thorn works with Rose and the whole fairytale thing, because that was part of the Beast story. Anyway, he wouldn't have counted because that was before we thought of it, like you."

Hellen swallowed her bite and took another. "I love that you chose 'Beast.' Did I tell you that already?"

"No."

"It's so mysterious, and powerful," she said as she chewed. "Perfect for the leader of a Resistance. People who don't know it's you will expect some big, scary guy." Amused, she watched Adia devour the leg and thought how perfect that name was in other ways, too. How on earth would the Queen ever be able to mix in polite company now? The two of them were going to have to plow through etiquette lessons all over again. For both their sakes. Hellen shoved the tender part of the breast into her mouth and said, "Are you ready for tomorrow?"

"I'm so ready," Adia said, her chicken leg combo landing on the plate, nothing but skin, bone, and cartilage. Her napkin made a brief appearance, swiping across her mouth and soaking up the excess grease on her hands, then it disappeared into her lap once more. With light fingers, she felt around the remaining food and picked up the wing. "I think having all the puzzle pieces laid out in front of us will help us figure out where and how to look for the tunnels." She pulled the tip off the wing, laid it on her plate, and chewed the meat out of the center section. "And having eight pairs of eyes on it will help us be sure we haven't missed anything. Is Roberta coming, do you know?"

"She should be. Vartile said her half day is tomorrow, so she'll have plenty of time. She could even go home first." Another bite, and the empty breastbone got laid to rest. Dark meat next, although she was getting close to full. Leg, then. She dismantled the combo and sank her teeth into the juicy muscle. Heck yeah, Vartile could cook. "Someone else might be coming, too. At my invitation."

Adia stopped eating and put her bones down slowly. The expression on her face had gone cautious. "Who?"

"John and Roberta's son, David," Hellen replied, as nonchalantly as she could. "He could be a great help, he's got his Dad's keen mind, and Roberta's too, so he's like them together. Plus, he's funny like them." She retired her bone to her plate and sat back, satisfied.

Adia's mouth pursed, and she frowned. Several silent seconds later, she said, "Remember how I told you a long time ago that it was awful not to be able to see other people's faces?"

"You bet I do."

"Well, I've learned that there's compensation for that." She leaned her forearms on the table, on each side of her plate, and faced Hellen with a small smile. "I can hear in your voice that you're hiding something. I can tell by what you said that your idea, most likely, is to have him around on a regular basis, to 'help.' And I can surmise from the fact that you mention his sense of humor that your intent is to get me to like him. What I'm not really sure about is why. Got any clarification on that? Hellen?"

An absurd giggle bubbled up and burst out of Hellen's mouth before she could stop it. She should know better than to try and pull a fast one on Adia these days, but the direct approach wasn't going to work, either. So, what did that leave her?

"You're right," she admitted. "I have a plan, and it's very logical, so you'll probably like it." Talk about a shot in the dark. "And as long as we're talking, there's something else I need to tell you, about my last night in Valdia."

Chapter Th.11

Dagge sat at the desk with his harkener in his lap and listened to Evening at the Palace. Too bad it wasn't more of a show. These days, even the new servants learned quickly not to say things out loud that they wouldn't want him to hear. What a mime performance it must be in the servants' quarters. He should surprise them by sneaking up on them sometime.

The thought was almost funny, but he felt cranky and it didn't quite make him smile. Problem was, he was bored out of his mind. When you have people who do everything for you, what was left? Trouble, usually. Bring it on. Please.

His eyes landed on the young valet standing patiently beside the doorway to the bedroom. The kid had worked for him for three years, and kept showing up every day, even after he threw the knife at him and put a big hole in his leg. It was kind of funny, really, the way his wig bobbled when he went down, and then he apologized for bleeding on the carpet, like it was his fault. Service. What a weird profession.

The knife incident came right after the Winter Festival party, when every inflamed cell of his overstressed brain momentarily topped out. He didn't actually mean to do it, not like it was a plan or anything, it just happened. At that point, most servants would have left, so the fact that the valet stayed, and showed up the next day with a bandage and a crutch said something about his loyalty.

Diit wasn't a bad kid, just annoying. He'd been a footman, he said, but hadn't worked at the palace for very long, and would be happy to keep working even with a regime change. Not all of them said that. So, he'd kept him around, even though the hovering and helping drove him crazy, and the constant presence and attention forced him to yell sometimes. How did the King stand it?

"Diit, I won't be needing you anymore this evening, you may retire."

"If you're quite certain, Overlord."

"I wouldn't say it if I wasn't certain. Leave me."

"Yes, sir. Have a good night." He bowed briefly and exited through the doorway to the servants' hall.

Dagge breathed a sigh of relief, glad to be alone again. He shoved the harkener into the desk drawer and got up to stretch his legs. Considering his mood, it could be time for a little knife-throwing practice. To the side of the desk, the giant portrait of Old King Som smiled benignly at him from its place leaning against the wall. It used to hang in the foyer, but the palace was under new management these days. For a long time, Dagge had the portrait stored in the museum with the rest of the family. After the Winter Festival snafu, though, using Ol' Kingy for target practice gave him a satisfying sense of power. He looked forward to shredding all the other Beldenets and their careful expressions one by one.

Nowadays, the six-foot-high painting was one of his favorite decorations, almost like having the old guy back. Only, instead of scowling at him every time he stood in front of the desk, now Ol' Kingy smiled like he was his best friend. And even when the big knife landed between the eyes, or sliced off the end of his nose, the face still smiled, and Dagge liked that. Eventually, of course, the whole King would just be a ragged mess, but as of now, he could still find plenty of places to bury the blade.

At the moment, his knife stuck out of the King's neck, right where the jugular would be. Not a bad throw, if he said so himself, one of many lethal strikes he'd made on the waist-up likeness. He walked up to the picture and yanked the knife out of the wall; it pulled through the neck, leaving an angled slit, and he imagined the blood, just like he did every time. Nice.

A quick glance over the body told him where the best targets would be, if he wanted to make the picture last. Still some places in the neck, and the head, and the stomach, but he wanted to leave most of the face, so Mr. High and Mighty could smile and smile as he repeatedly died. Plenty of non-lethal targets, too, for those days when practice was just a lark. However, that was not today.

Before he walked away, he fingered the big hole in the chest. It reminded him of the night he plunged the knife into the real Som Beldenet. The canvas hung in tatters around it, sagging loosely in the fancy white shirt and Royal Schmoyal cloak. How many times had he made that chest throw now? Twenty? Thirty? The wall behind the painting had become a splintered disaster of wood paneling, and he'd had to insist to the stupid valet that he didn't want it fixed.

The hole was a monument to Hellen, really, and her infuriating habit of killing off his best men. Well, not men exactly, but whatever. Single shots to the heart, usually, except a knife the last time, at an underground station in Valdia. Both eyes in that one, too, for some reason…pure hate, perhaps, or anger, both of which appealed to him. She became more worthy with every kill, didn't she? He had to give her props for managing to get so many, too. She did get around.

All his perfect work ruined by one woman. All besides Ming and Wan. He still couldn't believe little old Mapo had been able to kill his wife. He'd thought for sure the sweet guy wouldn't be able to do it. And who knew he'd have the skills to take out Wan, who was so smart and fit. Word never got out about how the murders were done, but Mapo saw how Hellen killed the others at the party, so he knew what it took. Had to give him props, too, although he was going to enjoy revenge on the man when it was time to take it.

Shindao had not fallen, and Rofland never made, either, but he'd done what he wanted to do with the others. He made the expansion into Pulari and Valdia, and now he had more weapons, more army, and more power. Between that and the carapaz, who was going to stop him? As soon as the chemical and biological weapons were ready in Valdia, he'd extend his reach into Bemont from there, into Heance from Pulari, and both of those countries had major port cities. Once he owned the ports, he could control a great deal of trade for the entire continent. If you want to control the world, you have to control the money.

The scientists had told him the death rate in Bemont and Heance would be about forty percent, and biological toxicity would last maybe five years. The rest of the world would be terrified, naturally, and some of them might come after him, but if the virus didn't get them, the army would. And if they started bombing, well, he'd have bigger bombs, and if they got bigger bombs, he'd make even bigger bombs. He could go on like that as long as it took to win. The one thing he wasn't worried about was dying. Fate had bigger plans for him than that.

Five paces away from the desk, he whirled around and faced the King. Between the slits in the nose, and the forehead, and the temple, the eyes watched him. No matter where he went, stood, sat, squatted, the eyes still watched him, unmoving, unblinking. They watched him execute his plans for expansion, watched him take the young pretty maids right there on the desk, watched him pace through all the sleepless nights and get fat. Yeah, well watch this, Your Asswipeness. He threw the knife, and blinded one of those eyes forever with a solid *thunk*.

Chapter Th.12

"You want him to stay here?" Adia said, aghast. "Hellen, I don't need some teenage boy complicating my life. Wolf is plenty."

"He's John's son, Adia. He's really smart, and Roberta has him trained up right, he can be a big help to you."

Adia didn't know what to say. On the one hand, the idea of having someone around appealed to her. Truth be told, talking to Wolf was largely unsatisfying, even with the whines and pants he gave her. It would be nice to carry on the occasional two-sided conversation while Hellen was off trying to save the world.

On the other hand, a boy? Just turned twenty, Hellen said, so technically not a teenager, but probably still as raunchy and self-centered as any of the guys she knew in college. The prospect sounded more taxing than anything. For One's sake, she was trying to run a Resistance here, the last thing she needed to deal with was a boy. He would be a distraction, and a source of aggravation. And even without all the Resistance stuff, never would she be the best candidate for patiently teaching a boy how to treat a woman.

"I'm not convinced," she said. "What do you think he can do that will be such a great help?"

"He can help with the garden, he can chop firewood, he can hunt for food…"

"I have people who do that."

Hellen paused, then said, "He can help you find the tunnels."

Aha. The news came as a relief, at least it wasn't a blind date, har har. "That's the crux of it? That's what you're hiding, you want him to try and find the entrance to the tunnels?" Adia took her napkin out of her lap and laid it on the table. "Why didn't you just say so?"

"Because I know you. If I told you that, I'd come home tomorrow and find you chipping away at the fireplace, with half the rocks piled around you on the floor. Then Rack would have to come back out here and fix the fireplace like he had to fix the wall behind the sink."

Adia chuckled. "I'm not going to take the fireplace apart. I still think the entrance is somewhere around the pump handle in the kitchen. But okay, I'll let David come here and help me." She pulled the skin and cartilage off her bones and laid them on her plate. Hellen piled her own scraps on, to which they added all the meat they couldn't eat. As a crowning touch, Adia scooped out all the goopy middle of the carcass, and with both hands, she lifted her plate off the table, twisted her body around and laid it on the floor behind her. "Here you go, sweetie." A rustle and scrape came from the corner, and Wolf's raspy tongue licked her face. His stomach growled impressively as he dug into the remaining chicken. She turned back to Hellen. "But if he's annoying, you will never hear the end of it."

As much as Adia tried to suppress her smile, she couldn't. It broke out with a breathy laugh, because how could she not be happy? Her stomach was full, her best friend was home, and they were going to see some people tomorrow. She'd get them to describe the schematics, and she could run her hands over the cloak, and something would tell her what she needed to know to get their kingdom back.

Her father's cloak would speak to her. It had to. Its deep blue velvet shimmered in her memory, the gold embroidery shone in its fantastic whorls and lines. How she couldn't wait to touch it again! The excitement of the coming day made her heart soar. Even the idea of babysitting didn't dampen it.

"What do you think, Hellen? Will we figure it out tomorrow? Will we find the thing that will make the difference?"

"I hope so." Hellen's voice came from table level, which meant she had laid her head down. She must be tired.

Adia reached her hand out, palm up, and felt Hellen's hand slide into her own. "I'm so glad you're home...did I say that yesterday?"

"Yes," Hellen chuckled, "once or twice." The strong fingers gave hers a firm squeeze. "I can't tell you how glad I am to be home. Oh, I forgot to mention that I ran into that friend from Valdia, in town here." Her voice moved up from the table to head height again, her hand pulled away, and Adia heard boney clinks on her plate. "Anji...the one who helped me so much? She lost her job, and decided to come here on a whim and find me."

"Really?" A dark cloud materialized on the horizon. "That seems peculiar, why would anyone want to emigrate to a country they might not get back out of?"

"I don't know, but she's here, and I have to help her. Don't worry, I've got her set up for now, working with Elzbieta, and Grovet and Purda will let her live with them until she has some income and we can find a place farther away from the warren."

"I'm sure everyone understands that they have to keep all information related to the Resistance from her. Right?"

"Of course, Adia, we all know that. We have lots of practice, keeping it from people who live here. I know it's awkward, but I couldn't say no. And she doesn't know about you, or this place, and she won't."

"All right." Adia nodded, even though misgivings weighed her down a bit. "But keep me posted, will you?"

"Yes, of course I will."

"Hellen, I think we should talk about what happened with the homeless woman in Valdia. I understand why you didn't want to tell me last night—I was tired, you were tired—but I think it's important that we discuss how Dagge knew where you were."

"I've got no answers for that, Adia. He obviously has spies. Someone was probably waiting in Stesin, knowing I'd show up there sooner or later."

A low growl from behind perked Adia's ears. Hellen stopped talking, got up almost silently and walked away toward the door. Wolf's feet padded after her. Several seconds passed, and a friendly voice called from the foyer.

"Wolf! Come!"

A distant scrape of nails on stone made her smile. Diit always talked to Wolf first, which was very smart. He also brought things for the big dog to chew on, keeping him busy for the rest of the evening while they either talked, or Diit taught her things like sewing (which she hated) and cooking. He'd been a great valet, and kept her sane for the last year and a half, she had to admit.

"Miss Hellen!" His voice echoed in the empty foyer. "It appears your efforts this morning were successful."

"Yes, Diit, they were." Hellen's voice was softer, and Adia had to strain to hear. "Thank you for warning Cookie I was coming. She had the clothes ready, and even had an alibi for getting through the checkpoint."

Wolf trotted into the kitchen, around the table, and settled into his spot on the floor behind her. Happy chewing sounds filled the space between the table and the wall, bouncing off the dumbwaiter and the bank of intercom pipes in the corner. Hellen's and Diit's voices came closer as they made their way through the great room and into the short hallway that led to the kitchen.

"Did you see your friends in town? You mentioned that you wanted to touch base with everyone. I'm sure they're happy you're back."

"Oh, I think they were. They threw me a party," she said brightly. "We had cake and everything. I forgot to tell you that, Adia!" Hellen's voice entered the room. "Vartile made a cake; we all saved you some. Beau and I had two pieces each, it was delicious. Beau is such a classy guy, he shoved his entire second piece into his mouth at once, and when I laughed, he laughed, and some came out his nose." Hellen cackled when she said it, and it made Adia grin.

"Good evening, Your Highness." Diit's voice greeted her from between the doorway and the table.

"Good evening, Diit," she answered. "How was your day?"

"It was fine, ma'am. Overlord Dagge sends his regards."

"Very funny, or it would be if that name didn't make me want to vomit. What an unfortunate waste of good chicken that would be, too. Did you bring anything?"

"I did at that, ma'am."

A bundle, or bag, or something else soft and not-too-heavy by the sound of it, landed on the table in front of her. Her nose did first duty, but all she could smell was the clean linen scent of palace laundry. "What is it?"

"Don't tell her," Hellen said quickly, "let her open it."

Adia put her hands on the bundle, which felt like a sheet knotted around something. Inside, more knots, and under that it wasn't soft, it was hard, so it couldn't be Monster Growlyface, or Hoaryhead, or any of the other toys she used to own. Her heart ached a little. Whatever happened to those?

Untying the knots turned out to be harder than she expected, but Hellen wouldn't let Diit help her. A few growls and grunts later, she'd dismantled the last knot, and by then she could tell what lay bundled in the blanket inside the sheet. Flipping the corners of the blanket aside, she unfolded the protective covering, and there lay her father's crown.

Images jumped to the front of her mind—her father at her mother's funeral, standing beside her in the Grand Ballroom, sitting across from her in the official carriage. How he looked down at her and smiled during one of those interminably long functions, then pulled a jellybean out of some secret pocket in his cloak. She'd never asked him about it, and now she wished she had.

The crown in front of her felt cool to the touch. The gold was smooth as glass, and she remembered how it shone in the light. Cut gemstones had been set into the front of it—a large ruby at the center, inverted teardrop-shaped and surrounded by raised filigree. The other stones fanned out to either side, decreasing in size, and round—diamonds, sapphires, then emeralds, and finally two small rubies on the outside. When she lifted the face of it toward her, it felt heavy.

"Diit…this is overwhelming. If you'd been caught with this, he would have killed you."

71

"Yes, ma'am, I know. But after Miss Hellen retrieved the cloak this morning, the crown became available. It seemed wrong to leave it in the vault."

Became available? Diit had the strangest way with words sometimes. She put both hands around the base of it, and raised it into the air. "Honestly, I wasn't sure I'd ever be this close to my father's crown again."

Hellen's voice was soft, but firm. "It's not your father's crown, Adia. It's yours."

Chapter Th.13

One of his favorite things was to prowl the palace in the dark. He slipped down the hall silently in his bare feet, passing the empty royal chambers, the potted plants, and the fancy little tables with flowers on them. He could smell the flowers as he passed—the thick, sweet air slowed him down and he waved his arm impatiently to clear it.

Past the royal bedrooms, and their ghosts, he stopped at the door to the governess's room. The wood squares of it teased him, blocked him, faintly glowing in the moonlight from the foyer, and he laid his hands on them. This was the last place he saw Hellen, really saw her face. He'd been far away, but he could still see the resoluteness on it, and the fury, and the desire to kill. It excited him.

He opened the door. Pale blue light flooded the room from the tall windows on the opposite wall. The curtains were sheer, and the shadows of leaves swayed and ruffled on them. In one window, a blur of the big moon hung like a watching eye. Funny, the King or Queen of Great Hand was supposed to be the Great Eye, once upon a time. Before he killed every last fucking Beldenet.

He stepped inside and closed the door. To the left, in the middle of the separating wall, was the set of double doors that led to the nursery. They'd been left open—all the connecting doors were to be left open now—and he stood in front of them, looking all the way down to the secret passage.

Well, not so secret anymore, was it? Now it was a big hole in the wall.

Hellen had made a fool of him twice. The banquet didn't count because he won that round. She got away in the end, but she didn't stop him. He planted his beautiful creatures in all the world leaders, just like he wanted. Snooty book types were saying, "Tomius Dagge changed the balance of world power in one historic night." How many people could say they did that?

But spreading his power would be so much easier if he still had all fifteen 2Ders. He could've owned the entire continent by now. *Hellen, Hellen...you shouldn't have killed them. You shouldn't have betrayed me that way.*

She could've been his Queen. She looked like royalty. She acted classy, and knew her shit. They would've been beautiful together. Beautifully deadly.

But she ruined it. They could've had everything, and Hellen chose treason instead.

Anger tilted his brain, ignited the slow burn in his chest, and he took off running toward the dark old stone.

Fury consumed him as he neared the wall. He slammed the meaty sides of his fists onto the undamaged half, and pounded the papered paneling. He kicked the little pictures of goats and rabbits, and pressed his body against the cool bleeding through his thin shirt. If he could push the wall down, he would, right into the bathroom behind it, all the way into the mausoleum of Adia Beldenet. From deep in the hot pit of his gut, a roar surged up and out of him, scraping and straining his throat, bursting out of his mouth like lava and spewing all over the wall.

"She deserves to die."

The whispery voice snaked out from the secret passage doorway and hovered in the air beside him. He stopped moving and went quiet, listening. He watched the doorway to see who'd come out.

But no one did. So he moved slowly to the doorway and peeked around the corner. The passage was empty and dim, the hole of the stairwell pitch black. A cool breeze lifted his hair and chilled the sweat on his face.

"She was never good enough for you." The voice sighed up from the blackness, echoing off the stone. "You made a ridiculous mistake. People laugh at you for wanting to marry a servant."

74

The voice wasn't real. It couldn't be. No one would dare speak that way to him.

"What is she but a stupid slut?"

"SHUT THE FUCK UP! SHUT THE FUCK UP!" Dagge spun away from the wall, fists at his sides, and bellowed into the empty space. He stomped, and swung, and filled the room with his madness.

No one would come running. He'd stopped that months ago, when the first servant who showed up got beat to death for his trouble. That had happened in the sitting room; the news had come earlier that day that the second 2Der in Pulari had been killed, and he guessed he didn't handle it well. After the man's screams woke everyone else up, the servants all understood not to interrupt the Overlord when he was upset.

So, he could howl as much as he wanted to. Once the sparks started in his head he couldn't stop them. They took over, and had to burn themselves out no matter what they took with them.

Like now. The fire in his brain blinded him—what he really wanted was to destroy something, and with long steps, he hurried through the secret passage and into the room on the other side.

The room had sat untouched for three years. He was saving it for Hellen, for when she came to live here in the palace with him, and he knew she'd like to have this room just the way it was. It would be important to her, and she'd see that he wasn't heartless at all. She'd been wrong about him after he killed the King. It wasn't personal, it was ambition, and ambition was good.

The scale model of the palace sat on its table near the far-left corner of the room. It had never occurred to him to see if the secret passages were marked on it somehow. Or even included—wouldn't that be lucky? He'd tried to find the others after Treslo was killed, because there had to be more than just the one, but no one he called in seemed to have the grey matter to figure it out. That was why Hellen had been able to get into the palace again, and run around doing whatever she did without getting caught.

He had to find those passages.

In the blue light from the windows, the model looked like some ghostly fairy lodge—its structure was too modern to be a castle. He lifted the roof off, and peered down into the exposed rooms. From the front entrance, the two-story foyer and Grand Ballroom took up the center of the layout. Tiny steps curved up to the balconies, and tiny tables and chairs overlooked the ballroom floor. To the right, a long theater took up half the length of the building. Tiny seats faced the stage, where miniature set pieces had been arranged into a living room. Behind the stage, several little backdrops hung from bars, and tiny lights came on when he flipped a switch.

Man, was she spoiled.

The lights were useful, though. He peered down the hallways and tried to see into the first-floor rooms at the back. Too many walls and halls and the stupid top floor made it impossible. As far as he could tell, all the little parts were there—the plants in the greenhouse, the kitchen stuff, little beds in the servants' quarters upstairs. In the opposite corner, the atrium, with its trees and plants, and even two miniscule birds glued to the catwalk. So far, no sign of any secret passages. But if there were any, there'd be some in the Royal Snooze-rooms.

Bedrooms and guest rooms took up nearly the entire left side of the palace. On the bottom floor, the fanciest guest rooms faced the floor-to-ceiling windows of the east wall. All the front walls of those rooms had been left off so people could see easily into the slavishly decorated spaces. As far as he could tell, all the side walls and floors were just basic structures, with nothing hidden, no secret stairwells, and no trap doors. How disappointing.

Just as he was finishing his examination, he raised his head to look at Adia's room, and surrounded by shards of plaster and painted paper littering the floor, a hole had been gouged through the wall adjoining the nursery.

Who the hells did that? No one was supposed to come in here. Three years ago, after the princess died, he'd ordered that the room remain undisturbed. Not even the maids came in here, according to the dust. Who then? Why risk punishment for a prank like this?

There was the time during the banquet that the 2Ders were in the nursery. The wall was open then, and maybe one of them got in here and did it. Hard to imagine, considering how dysfunctional they were at first, but who knows? They'd proved their smarts since, so it was possible. But why? He bent his head down and squinted through the hole, then he put his finger up to it and felt the edges. They were rough and ragged. He shoved his finger into it up to the first knuckle.

Fit like a charm.

Friday

Chapter F.1

Adia leaned over and stroked her mare's neck. She hadn't been riding much for a while—it was hard to manage a horse when you couldn't see, and there'd been few opportunities for anyone to take her. Consequently, Starseed had gotten a little bridle-shy, and fond of her makeshift stable in the base room of the pyramid. Adia could tell she spent most of her time in there, because of the poop that had to be shoveled out.

Hellen's horse had disappeared a while back, probably found her way home, but Hellen wasn't the least bit distressed over it. Not much of a rider, she pointed out, especially after the two days she'd spent on horseback in the forest. After that painful experience, she said she'd rather walk anywhere on her own two feet.

Hence the quiet footsteps scraping along the rock in front of the horse; the reins in Hellen's hand flapped lightly as she swung her arm, or rustled as they brushed her clothes. Starseed's breath whooshed out as she chewed on her bit and tossed her head. Her hooves clopped on the rocky places and thudded on the soft ground between. Underneath Adia, the squeak of the leather saddle sounded comfortingly familiar.

To their right, in the last half hour or so, the forest had come alive with sound: birds twittered and called; wind soughed in the branches high above; squirrels chattered and ran up trunks or through dead leaves on the forest floor. In the distance, a big cat screamed. Awesome, but a tad scary. Adia hoped she'd never meet her face to face.

At the base of the mountains where they traveled, the warm summer air and the cool air off the peaks were duking it out. First one, then the other swirled around her, buffeting her face and arms, keeping the flies away. Pure heaven. The hood of her cloak lay on her back, and strands of her hair tickled her cheeks as the wind played with it. Later she'd have to put the hood up, to help her look more like a shadow in the rock or something, but for now she could enjoy the morning without the sweat.

And better not to sweat too much, considering how many people she would be around today. The last time they made this journey, not counting the trip back to the monastery, was the first time everyone saw her after the murder, and the fire, and Dagge. No one had known she was even alive then, and it was funny to remember how she felt, not wanting people to see her scars. Now she hardly thought about them. Her hand went up to her face—her fingers felt warm on her cheek as she traced the uneven skin around her eye, over to her nose, and down her jaw. It would probably be different if she could see them. But she couldn't.

Her hand dropped back to the saddle horn. The sun must be up over the treetops now, she could feel the radiance on her arm. Ahead of her, Hellen stopped the horse and walked back to talk.

"We're at the palace. The stable's not too far ahead, and it's probably time to put the hood up." She dug around in the saddle bag while she talked. "Diit said he'd talk to Artour this morning, do you want to stop?"

Few people at the palace knew about Hellen, and even fewer knew about her, but the ones who did had been hand-picked for their trustworthiness. Diit kept a tight rein on them, and so far the word hadn't leaked. Artour was one of the few—he had taken care of Starseed, and all of her and her father's horses, as long as she could remember. He was a genius when it came to the care and training of anything equine, and it was because of him that she had Starseed now. And to be honest, Starseed could use a little dose of Artour for a while.

"If I leave her at the stable, how am I going manage the rest of the trip? The ground will be too uneven, I'll face plant every five feet."

"I'll piggyback you, you're not that heavy. Besides, with cloaks we'll be even less visible than four horse legs. If you think she needs some working, I say let's leave her."

"All right, yes. She does need it…don't you, baby?" A few pats on the neck, and Starseed tossed her head again. "Want to see Artour? He'll take care of you, won't he?"

"Hood up, then. I'm taking you over some rock, so hang on."

Adia grasped the saddle horn firmly and prepared herself for extreme tilts, which were still better than piggybacking. Beggars couldn't be choosers, she supposed. One of these days, she should just bite the bullet and learn this path. Or maybe they should kill Dagge and reclaim the kingdom so she wouldn't have to.

Chapter F.2

Hellen checked back over her shoulder as she pulled Adia's horse up over the mound of rock and down into the hollow on the other side. The path around would have been a lot easier, but the cover was better this way, and she didn't want to risk someone besides Artour seeing them. The sound of the mare's hooves was bad enough, but at least they could conceivably be written off as falling rock.

Adia's hood was up, and the grey of the cloak blended nicely with the mountain backdrop. Her own cloak was brown, not too bad a match for the occasional streaks between the rocks, and she was feeling pretty comfortable with their camouflage. Maybe when the time came, she should crawl up to the exercise paddock so she could really look like dirt.

Hm, apparently her internal sarcasm generator had been around Adia too long. Which was funny, because she hadn't even been around Adia much lately. Maybe she was just happy about going back to the palace, risking being seen again, and the likelihood of a joyful reunion with the festering sore in charge. Sounded like a real party.

Krikey, time to put a lid on that thought train. Not helpful. Hellen refocused her attention on the fences behind the stable and the upcoming maneuvers.

Artour stood in the nearest enclosure, with a horse on a lead, running around the paddock. It looked like the white mare John rode into the forest when they went together to find the monastery. Hellen's heart twinged the tiniest bit. He was so funny to watch—Dimebox was a good-sized horse, but John's feet looked like they could just about touch the ground when they were out of the stirrups. How he hated riding her, but she was gentle and patient, and evidently strong as an ox.

"Stay here while I get his attention," she whispered, handing Adia the reins. "If you hear trouble coming, duck and cover."

"Duck and cover?"

"Get down and squat like a rock or something."

"Oh, that's better," Adia snarked. "So appropriate for a Queen."

"What do you want me to say? Your Majesty, please debase yourself by lowering your Royal Posterior to the ground and covering your Royal Visage with thine appropriate-colored apparel, should some peon maketh noise in the immediate vicinity."

"Hey, I like that!" Adia sighed in fake wonderment, a big smile showing all those perfectly-straightened teeth.

"Smarty-pants. Here are the reins, keep a good ear out. And wait for me, the ground is too uneven and there are too many trees for you to come, no matter what you hear."

"Bossy, aren't you?"

"When you're responsible for keeping a blind woman safe in a madman's back yard, you can be bossy, too," Hellen answered, patted her on the leg and turned to navigate her way through the strip of trees and bushes.

From here, the distance to the back paddock was only a dozen strides or so, but there were a number of young cedar trees and other bushes that provided good cover and helped make the path safe. As she got closer to the fence, she instinctively crouched lower, and became seriously tempted to crawl, even though it wasn't necessary, because Artour remained alone.

At the last clump of cedar, after one more careful look around, she stepped out to flag Artour, and the back door of the stable opened. She dropped face first into the scrub, and got up close and personal with several dead twigs and a couple hundred insects.

"Artour!" Wharton's voice bellowed over the sound of hooves on the soft dirt.

"Yes, General!" The hooves stopped trotting and slowed to a walk. Hellen could hear the mare's heavy breathing and the quiet sound of the bridle as she shook her head.

"We'll be leaving for the mine earlier than usual, so the horses will need to be ready at 0730 hours."

"Yes, sir. Will you be taking Chief or Gumshoe?"

So, they still used the names Adia and the King had given them. Seemed out of character for someone like Dagge, but maybe it was too much trouble to change them all, and why kill a stableful of good horses?

"Chief, I think. Has his cut healed?"

"Yes, sir."

A moment of quiet prompted Hellen to raise her head ever so slightly and peer out from under the side of her hood. Wharton stood looking at Artour, his hands on his hips. "I thought Gumshoe had been sent to the smithy with the camera on his bridle."

"He goes today, sir." Artour nodded once, and Hellen could hear the tension in his voice, but he didn't waver his posture. "His shoe has to be loosened, and he wouldn't cooperate. Several of the groomsmen got either bruised or bitten. But they'll get it done, and he'll be taken in later."

"It's a priority, Artour. Are you the stablemaster or what? Overlord has no patience for excuses, the horse should have been there yesterday, and unless you want to be strung up in the plaza, you'll get him there immediately. Is that understood?"

Yes, sir, of course. I'll go right now." He pulled Dimebox toward him, grabbed her bridle, and took her in straightaway. Wharton followed.

Hellen ran over her options. She could take Starseed in herself, leave her in a stall and try to get out without being spotted. Or, she could leave the horse in the paddock, in which case she'd be found later, but no telling by whom. Or, they could take the horse with them, and have Cary bring her back. Or….

The back door of the stable opened again and a young man in a wide-brimmed hat came out with several saddle blankets. A clear, tuneful whistle came out with him, slicing through the air as he laid the blankets over the side fence, counted them, and lifted the top one off.

Hellen watched him, frustrated—if only he would go in for five seconds, she could get out of sight, get Adia, and they could leave. But no, he stayed out there, shaking blankets, laying them neatly side by side, and generally moving as slow as molasses. Behind her, Starseed whinnied, and the young man's head came up like a shot. It was Cary.

"Cary!" she hissed.

He tossed the blanket in his hands onto the fence and hurried over. "How long have you been here? Where's Adia?"

Hellen glanced around reflexively. "Don't call her that, are you mental? Beast is behind me, waiting with the horse."

"I'm sorry." He shook his head in small back-and-forth jerks. "I keep forgetting. I just got used to…never mind." He leapt over the fence. "I'll get the horse and take her in. You guys can go on and I'll catch up with you."

They walked together into the trees, Hellen looking over their shoulders to see what the catch was relative to this good fortune. "What are you doing here?" she asked when it seemed evident that there was none.

"Diit woke me up way before dawn and told me you needed my help."

"He came to your house?"

"No, I was asleep on the couch in the warren. I knew you two planned to be there early, and I wanted to greet you."

"Really?" She grinned and looked sideways at him. "Greet me, or her?"

Adia sat motionless, head turned slightly toward them as they approached. Underneath her, Starseed watched, head bobbing, and Adia reached a hand out and stroked her neck. "Cary Roades, you turn up in the most surprising places, don't you?" she said.

"I do try," he said, hurrying forward. "Hello, Your Highness." He stopped very close to her, and skipped the head bow, which Hellen didn't like. "Let me take her," he said, and his hand reached for the bridle. "I'll get her into a stall and catch up with you. Do you need a hand down?"

"No, that won't be necessary," Adia said, and swung herself down from the saddle. Between the two of them, they pulled the reins over Starseed's head, and Cary took them.

"Are you going to walk? Do you have a cane or something?"

"No…"

"I'm going to carry her, it'll be faster." Hellen stepped in to head off the interrogation. They didn't have time to explain the finer points of navigating for the blind.

"I'll do it! Let me go put the horse away, and I'll come right back. I'll be half a minute, I promise."

"I don't know, Cary." Several sticky points popped up in Hellen's mind—most of all, how would Adia feel about it? She glanced over at her.

"I don't see why not," Adia answered, a small smile flirting around her mouth. "If you're sure it won't be too much trouble."

"Psh! Are you kidding?" Cary's face split into a wide grin. "It would be the highlight of my day. My week! My year!" His voice faded as he hurried off toward the stable, Starseed breaking into a trot behind him.

"I'm stunned." Hellen turned to Adia with a wasted smirk on her face.

"Are you now?" Adia's own smirk said they were on the same page.

"I thought you had reservations about him."

"I do, but that doesn't mean he can't overcome them. Everyone needs a chance to learn, and some humble servitude might be helpful for our cocksure rabbit, don't you think?"

"I'm not sure humble servitude is what he has in mind."

"Perhaps not, but that's what he's going to get."

"You're sounding pretty cocksure yourself." Hellen chuckled.

"Well, if a queen can't beat him, she sure can't join him." Adia smiled in return.

85

Chapter F.3

Dagge pushed his chair away from the table and threw his napkin on his plate. The early mine inspection had been Wharton's idea. He had the quaint notion they stood a better chance of catching someone red-handed that way—like the rebels might have something planned for the regular official visit. Dagge didn't think the rebels were that stupid, or that industrious. Not since Hellen had come home. More likely, they were holding meetings and planning what to do with whatever she stole.

Legs stretched out in front of him, he listened to his stomach gripe and moan about the bacon and eggs, or maybe it was the biscuits. Whatever it was, he wished he hadn't eaten. Riding wouldn't be any fun with a brick in his gut. In fact, the whole trip to the mine had taken on a sour taste, and the best part of his week had been ruined.

No, he wasn't crabby, he had every reason to be pissed. Before bed, he'd convinced himself that Hellen would come back to the palace last night, to try and kill him again. He waited up all night for her, and she never showed. It made him feel stupid, because he knew deep down she probably wouldn't try again, but a good operative never underestimates the value of surprise, right? No doubt she figured he'd think she'd stop, and then it would be logical to do the opposite. But a person could go crazy outthinking themselves that way, and he shook it off.

Instead, he turned his chair and faced the shredded painting of the fat king. Ever since the night of the banquet, he'd taken all his meals in the Officious Dining Room, surrounded by scorched holes in the walls and vomit-stained carpet. The vomit itself had to be cleaned up, of course, and the blood, but the evidence of his triumph was still there, and he gloried in it every time he ate. It made him feel good.

These days, he didn't have to worry about people coming to visit the palace, anyway. Even his allies weren't inclined to come. He'd sent a few charming invitations to army officers in Pulari and Valdia, and they were always declined just as charmingly. Everyone was busy, and couldn't get away. The nature of the world these days, he supposed.

The fat king smiled down at him as if he approved. The canvas hung in tatters below his chest and under the table, but the food on the table still looked as sumptuous and intact as ever. The effect was a bit like royal torture; he could see the food, but he could never eat it, because his stomach hung in wide strips all the way to the floor. Now, there's a creative approach.

Through the tatters he could see the stairwell up to the music room. The shelves up there had been torn out, just like the wall in the nursery. Exposing Ol' Kingy's secrets. The other end of the narrow space behind the fat king painting had been knocked out, too. The exit there was just a door into the servants' hall, but they hadn't been able to figure out how to open it, so pickaxes and sledgehammers were called in, and they did the trick.

Otherwise, he'd been too busy to knock out many palace walls. Just like today, it was always something. The trips to Pulari and Valdia had slowed down, once the military got entrenched and he made a few rich assholes richer. Money talked louder than just about anything. At least until the time came to put those assholes in the crosshairs.

He pushed himself out of his chair and took the shortest way to the south door, which happened to be through the not-so-secret passage. The canvas brushed him as he passed through, into the dark of the old stone walls. All the peepholes had been slashed in the process of tearing up the painting, but as he walked down the length of the narrow room, he could see the table through the gaps the way Hellen must have seen it that night—still in its U shape, the same chairs, same decorations. If ghosts were real, there'd be plenty of them in there, too. He turned and went through the hole into the servants' hall.

To the left was a door to the Grand Ballroom, to the right, the passage to the back hall that ran the width of the castle. He hadn't been in the ballroom for months, maybe even years. Had he ever been in there? Once, at least, but there didn't seem to be much point anymore. Not like anyone was going to be dancing.

He turned right, then left at the back hall, and at the far end, by the hallway that led to the south door, stood the valet, holding his riding boots.

"I noticed that you didn't have your riding boots, Overlord, sir, so I took the liberty of bringing them to you in case you might want them."

"Yes, of course I want them, Diit. You always bring them to me, don't be stupid."

"Right, sir. Please forgive me."

Dagge waved his hand impatiently and sat on the bench by the south entrance. The valet set his boots in front of him, knelt and slipped off his loafers. Dagge grabbed one boot, then the other, and shoved his feet into them, pulling on the leather until his heels set. Booted and ready, he stood and went out the door.

The path to the stable had a slight downward slope, so it always ended up being a hard, fast walk. Normally he liked it, but even the reminiscing this morning didn't erase the tired from his brain, and all he felt was the jarring in his knees and hips, and the uncomfortable tightness of his belly. Eyes on the ground in front of him, he didn't see Wharton until he reached the big, open doors of the stable.

"Good morning, Overlord. It's a fine day for a ride."

Dagge glanced up. Wharton stood beside his chestnut gelding, in front of three other soldiers who stood beside their horses, adjusting saddles and affixing weapons. He stopped and eyed them carefully. One by one, they realized he was looking at them, and stood at attention. Their eyes remained fixed ahead as he walked closer and examined them. The first, a short, muscled guy, had clear green eyes. The second, taller, and equally muscled, had brown eyes. The third, tall but lean, had blue eyes, with a touch of purple. Dagge smiled.

"Sephone is inside," Wharton said, "she has a scrape on her flank from a broken board. Artour said she must have kicked her stall

88

sometime in the night, possibly a rat or raccoon or something got in there."

Damn. Plainly, he wasn't meant to have any fun today. He scowled and went in.

Artour stood at his mare's rump, putting some kind of ointment on with his fingers. She waited patiently, tied to the bar in her big, nice stall, facing away from him. Her head stretched around when he got to the door, and he walked over and put his hands on her, stroking her neck and nose.

"Overlord, sir," Artour said, stopping long enough to bow.

With a pat, Dagge moved down Sephone's body to her rump and inspected the bloody patch. Several straight lines ran horizontally through her hide, right on the curve of her muscle. He peered around the stall until he located the splintered boards, which used to be the feed trough.

Several steps across the empty space, and he was looking down at the damage. Rats, raccoons, no the hells telling. Bits of apple, carrots and peanuts littered the straw on the floor, but no dead bodies. Too bad.

"Overlord, sir—"

Dagge held up his hand and Artour stopped talking. In the row of stalls behind this one, a strange horse with a strange saddle stood in a stall with another horse, yanking its head against the reins, which were evidently tied to something. "Whose horse is that, Artour?"

"It's my niece's, sir." He walked up and stopped by Dagge's side. "She asked me if I would gentle her a little, and I told her if I had time, I would try."

"Your niece has a very fine saddle." He turned to look the stable master full in the face.

"Yes, sir," Artour nodded. "Her husband gave it to her, he comes from…a family that used to have money."

His eyes had dropped to his hands, which fidgeted with the towel he was holding. Classic lie posture. It could have been discomfort over the topic, since people tended to do that whenever the public torture subject came up, but he knew it wasn't that.

He knew, because that saddle, and that horse, belonged to Adia Beldenet.

Chapter F.4

Adia felt the sweat run down Cary's neck and onto her arm. He may be in excellent shape, but that didn't mean he wasn't feeling the strain, carrying her over mounds of rock and under low-hanging branches. Not to mention the cloak she'd insisted upon to blend them in with the cliffs behind. His breath had started puffing right around the turn north, when the sun began to hit her in the face between the trees, positioned as she was in his arms across his chest. His arm and chest muscles were hard and well-defined, not exactly comfortable, but appealing in a primal way.

"Cary," she said conversationally, "how do you manage to stay in such good shape? I mean, you're obviously very fit, but you can't be running around jumping off buildings all the time, so how do you keep your muscles so strong?"

"Well…" He huffed and grunted as he stepped down, wobbled a bit, and stepped back up. "I do pushups…" Adia lurched backward, her hands clasping around his neck as he bent to the side, presumably to avoid a branch. "I dig." A few breaths passed. "Wherever Beau tells me to." He bent forward, and Adia's arm tightened around his neck. "And I chop wood for you," he said with a small laugh, "even though you don't let me do it very often."

"You guys be quiet," Hellen said from several paces ahead.

Cary slowed, stopped, and set Adia down. Voices could be heard from beyond the trees, in the field west of the palace, probably where the barracks used to be. She turned her ear toward the sound, but Cary's breathing drowned it out. Frustrated, she stepped around behind him, and tripped on a rock. Her body stumbled forward, but Cary's strong arms caught her, and she didn't fall.

"What are you doing?" he hissed.

"I'm trying to hear around your breathing," she shot back. "You're as loud as Starseed!"

"I was…! You try lugging a hundred extra pounds!"

"Shh! Shush, you two!" Hellen's hand smacked at them, catching Adia on the arm.

Adia lowered her voice. "It was your idea, Big Man."

Cary stepped away, which was fine with her. She felt around carefully until she located the tree trunk Hellen had hidden behind. Hellen squeezed her hand briefly and let it go. Adia stood still and listened.

"Overlord says we don't clean this up 'til the cows come home."

"What does that mean?"

"I don't know, but Cap says Overlord likes this mess just the way it is, so we don't touch it."

"There's nothing else to do out here. Are we s'pose to just walk back and forth all day?"

"Yes. We're on guard duty, that's what we do."

"It's stupid." Several boards got dropped. "There's nothing to guard out here but these burned-out shacks, and who wants anything to do with them? We should be closer to the palace."

"He's got more guards at the…look, we do what we do. If you don't like it, tough."

"Yeah yeah." Pause. "Can we smoke?"

"Sure. Cap says as long as we keep it behind the buildings and don't catch nothing on fire." He snorted. "That Cap's sure a real smartass sometimes."

A long pause then. Adia leaned over and whispered in Hellen's ear. "What are they doing?"

"Lighting cigarettes."

Oh, right. Of course.

"How long is Overlord usually gone on mine inspection?"

"Few hours."

"Then we can smoke anywhere, can't we? I mean, as long as he's gone."

"He didn't go on mine inspection today. Weren't you at the stable when he strung up that stable guy? He was pissed about something and didn't go. He sent the General to the mine, then Overlord went out the back."

Adia's stomach dropped into her shoes, and her heart leapt into her throat. She must have made a noise, because Hellen's hand pressed over her mouth, and she had to move it to breathe. Hellen's fingers wrapped around hers, and they stood there, hands clasped, listening.

"He's gone, though, right? So we don't have to ditch the smokes, we can keep walking."

"Are you a moron? Cap says keep it behind the buildings, so we keep it behind the buildings. For all you know, Overlord could be watching from those trees right there, and he'd kill you as soon as look at you if you broke the rules. Gimme that, asshole."

"Hey! I wasn't finished!"

"You're finished now. Let's go."

The voices faded as the two soldiers moved away. "You don't have to be a jerk."

"And you don't have to be an idiot. I hope."

Hellen turned to face her. "I have to go back; if Dagge finds the trail, he can find the monastery."

"I know," Adia said. "I'm afraid he'll kill Wolf! Wolf won't have the sense to stay away, and Dagge'll kill him, I know he will!" Tears threatened behind her eyes, and her voice came out hoarse with them.

"I'll go," Cary said beside her. "Wolf knows me, and Dagge doesn't, so maybe I can bluff my way through if he sees me."

"Not happening, cupcake," Hellen said. "It won't matter if he knows you, he'll kill you on principle. But he won't kill me. Not right away, at least, so I'll have a chance to escape if he captures me."

"Hellen, you can't risk it. I can't let you, even for Wolf. You're far more important. To all of us."

"Adia, Dagge can't find the monastery. If he does, he could easily realize you're alive, and if that happens, he will launch total annihilation against us. No one will be spared. I have to see if I can lure him away before he finds it."

"Hellen…" Adia wanted to find words that would stop all of this. She wanted a plan, an alternative, a reason why Hellen was wrong. But there was nothing. No argument, no idea, no help she could offer, and she left it at that. Fear gripped her, and stole her power to speak.

"Cary, you have to get Adia to the warren. Tell the others what's happened, and what I'm doing. NO ONE is to come into the forest, is that clear? I'll do better on my own." Adia heard the saddle bag drop to the ground, and Hellen's voice drop as she rummaged through it. "Beau will be especially hard to stop, but you have to make it clear to him that he needs to protect the Queen. Do you understand?"

"Of course I understand. But I can protect Adia, are you sure you can't use Beau's help?" Cary's hand latched onto Adia's wrist, and she wondered if he was aware of it.

"Cary." Hellen's voice took on that no-nonsense edge that Adia was all too familiar with. "Do not argue with me. I know what I'm doing." Something plunked back into the saddle bag, and Hellen stood up. "Adia." Hellen's hand took her left arm above the elbow. "Go ahead with the meeting. Important things need to be discussed, and done. I'll get there when I can." The hand patted her as it released, and Adia heard the click of Hellen's spring sheath.

"I know I don't have to tell you to be careful." Adia's voice barely breathed out around the constriction in her throat. "Are you going to kill him?"

Hellen's air came out in a small rush. "I don't have a gun, so I doubt I can. I don't think I want to get close enough to try with my knife, but if I get lucky, you bet I will."

"We don't know if he's alone. He may have taken any number of soldiers with him," Cary said.

"No, if I know Dagge, he's alone. He'd want it that way." Hellen moved to go between her and Cary, and Cary's hand released her wrist. "Get to HQ as quickly as you can, hide the path behind you—we can't afford for him to find the warren, either. And you look out for her."

94

"I will," he said.

"Hellen…"

"Yeah?" Hellen turned to her.

Adia paused, not knowing what to say, then she put her arms around Hellen's shoulders and squeezed herself to her chest. "I love you."

Hellen's arms came up around her, and she laid her chin on the top of her head, like she'd done since Adia was tall enough to reach. "I love you, too, my darling girl."

Golly, that about killed her. She swallowed the tears down and let Hellen go.

Chapter F.5

The trail wasn't yet cold by the time he found it. Too much bare rock interfered with the prints, and he'd had to scour a sizeable area before he could put all the pieces together. From what he could see, a woman with a horse came from the east, the woman walked to the paddock, a man came and got the horse, then the man left with the woman to the west. The man's prints also came from the west, sometime earlier, so Artour had an accomplice.

He walked beside the trail with his eyes on the ground. Leafy shadows spotted the dirt and rock, moving in the breeze and annoying him. The trail wasn't hard to read, though, except for a couple of rock pads. It was easy enough to pick the trail up on the other side, but he had to examine all the edges to make sure no prints went off in another direction. So far, they stuck close to the mountain.

Considering who the horse belonged to, the footprints were probably Hellen's—right size, right stride. She was sure getting around these days. Why didn't she ride the horse? Not much of a rider, he remembered her saying, but at least that would have hidden her footprints.

And why did she bring the horse to the stable? Did they really think he wouldn't notice? Granted, there were a lot of stalls, and a lot of horses, but Starseed had been standing practically under his nose. No chance he wouldn't recognize her if he saw her.

Artour should have been smarter than that. He'd been a decent stable master, and too bad he had to hang him. How awful for your last decision to be a stupid one.

In a low spot, where the rock receded back to the jagged edge of the mountain, he bent down to examine the dirt. There'd been a lot of activity on this path. The dirt was packed, all the forest debris and plants trampled. A tiny carcass of a dandelion lay flattened…but older than this morning, more like last night. Yep, prints going east, same size, same stride as the fresh prints going west. He continued on.

Behind the stable, when he first found the trail, he could have gone either way. If he'd gone west, he may have caught Hellen himself, but it was the path east that intrigued him. Where did it come from? A hideout in the woods would explain a lot—like how Hellen could disappear, and suddenly reappear doing some crazy thing. Like how Adia Beldenet's horse could show up after all these months, looking well-fed and wearing a saddle. And once he thought about it, if Hellen didn't ride the horse because someone else was on it, a hideout in the forest could explain why the princess's body was never found.

Yes, he could have gone west, and possibly caught Hellen red-handed, but the far more subtle and exciting approach would be to find the heart of the rebellion. With Hellen busy elsewhere, he could locate the rebel base and surprise them later, when they were home. The thought of descending on the hideout, unexpected and fully in control, thrilled him.

And as far as the path west was concerned, the 2Der he sent had enough skills to find whatever waited at the end. He had strict instructions not to kill anyone yet, and not to capture, but only to watch and see and report. Later, the fun would be in surprising whoever Hellen's buddies were, doing whatever rat-ass thing they were doing.

Let them think they were safe, for now. Let them laugh at him, and believe they had the upper hand, because before long, he'd be the one laughing.

Chapter F.6

Hellen's focus was so absorbed in making good time back through the fringe of trees that she almost ran into the soldier sneaking along the trail. He was still a good thirty strides away, and she happened to glimpse him around the curve without being seen herself, so she ducked into an alcove of rock to gather her wits and ready herself for the ambush. How she wished she had brought a gun, but it hadn't seemed necessary this morning when they left. Stupid, stupid.

At least she had her carapaz knife. She never went without it these days—too much danger in her world. Its heft and girth fit her hand perfectly, its leather holder protected her whenever she released the spring. *Thank you, Rack.* Hellen tapped the tough layer on her palm nervously while she listened for footsteps. Knowing Dagge, and his twisted obsessions, the soldier was almost certainly one of his freaks. But even if it wasn't, the lackey had to die.

After more than a minute and no soldier, she peered around the edge of the rock to get a visual. No sign of him. Quite a few trees blocked her sight line, and she took a couple of hesitant steps out to scrutinize the shady spaces between. Still nothing. Damn! He must have seen her after all, and either he hid in the scrub, or he climbed up into the jagged outcrop beside them. He'd have a gun, too, and she didn't want to make herself a target, so she stepped back into the alcove.

Her cloak came off, hit the dirt, and she shoved the bottom of her shirt into her pants. Better to keep lean in a fight, no hanging, drapey pieces catching on anything. It had been a while since she actually had to throw down with someone, aside from Beau, who always had to show her some maneuvers when she was home. Thank One he did that, and hopefully she could remember a few, but her heart still pounded and her breath came short.

She closed her mouth and tried to calm the rapid breathing. Zen, or whatever. Reaching out with her ears, she attuned to all the sounds around her: the breeze in the treetops, birds, a distant hammering sound from the stable. In the mountains, a slight tinkle of snowmelt, a tumble of falling rock.

And there it was. A boot, or a belt, or some other firm thing scraping against rock. The sound skipped down from above her, a bit to the right, and maybe he knew where she was, maybe he didn't. Her best bet would be to get behind him, so she hunkered down and slipped around the right-hand wall of the alcove, flattened herself around the protrusion of rock just beyond, and glanced up the uneven cliff face to see if she could spot him. No.

Two laser pulses exploded the rock above her head. If he didn't know where she was before, he sure did now. She bent at the waist and hurried along the base to a narrow crack in the cliff, past the area the blasts seemed to come from. The sharp edges of the rock looked navigable at least as high as she thought the soldier had climbed. The crack wasn't deep all the way up, but if she hurried, she could get to a ledge at about the halfway point, and hide behind the outthrust of rock that shielded it at the other end. She sheathed her knife and prayed her brown clothes would somehow blend in with the grey.

One hand after the other, foothold by foothold she scaled the cliff. For a few awkward seconds it felt unfamiliar, but her body shook the strangeness off and muscle memory took over. It wasn't the same wall, of course, but not that different, either—still the reaching, the feeling, the grasping, the push/pull up. Luckily, there were lots of holds to choose from, the back of the cut to press against when she needed to, and it felt like she made good time. The last eighteen months of urban living hadn't spoiled her completely, after all.

As she got higher, the cut got shallower, and its protection disappeared. She clung to the cliff face and for a moment she really empathized with all the flies she'd killed in her life, just hanging on the wall, minding their own business, getting whacked. At least if they got lucky they could fly away, and that was a luxury she only wished she had.

Jaw clenched, dreading the likelihood of searing pain from a laser wound, she toughed out the last few feet with the sun on her back. But there was no laser fire, no grinning face below, no rocks dropped from over her head. All good. When she reached the ledge, and the relative safety of the formation at the other end, she sent up gratitude and took a knee to rest while she looked around.

Where was he? Her eyes scoured the side of the outcrop, along the steep angles and jagged formations that made the Apex range lethal for so many. Vertical daggers of shale thrust upward from the sides of the mountain, tethered to it by tall, flat tendons often with razor-sharp edges. They made passage tricky, but were great to hide behind, so he could be anywhere.

Getting behind him may have been a bad plan. He could just as easily keep following the path, and conceivably catch up with Adia and Cary. Or he could spy on them while they used the hidden entrance to the tunnel. What if he did that? She may not know until it was too late, spending all this time playing cat and mouse with no one.

"Hey!" she shouted, standing up and revealing her location if he didn't already know.

Nothing.

"I'll make you a deal! I'll turn myself in, and you can take me back to Dagge, but don't kill me." Lame deal, she knew, but she didn't have much to work with. Dagge wouldn't want her dead anyway, but she couldn't say "as long as you don't follow the not-dead Queen down the secret tunnel into the headquarters of the Resistance" now could she?

Below, and to her left, a soldier stepped away from the alcove she'd been in and turned to look up at her. "What do you know, if it isn't Hellen Parker." He leaned against the rock protruding to his right, set the butt of his rifle on the ground and crossed his arms on the tip. A toothpick or a stick or something stuck out of his mouth, and he moved it around with his tongue before he set it between his teeth. "Overlord was right about you all along. I didn't believe him—that it was you doing all these things—but he nailed it. You must have some skills."

She couldn't tell if it was one of Dagge's pets or not. From what he said, it seemed likely, but his eyes were too far away to be sure, and everything else about him was normal.

"Better be careful with that gun," she said, "you wouldn't want to shoot your eye out."

He smiled, looked away for a brief second. At least he had a sense of humor.

"It's a terrible deal," he said. "Maybe you can think of something better."

Her mind tripped; where was he going with this? Surely not sex.

"Tell you what," she said, "I'll come down there, and you can tie my hands, throw me over your shoulder, whatever, and I won't fight you." So she lied, sue her. "Or we can do this the hard way."

"Really?" He laughed and reached up to take the stick out of his mouth. "I always like the hard way."

Game on.

Chapter F.7

Dagge stopped. The trail dead-ended into a wall of rocks sticking out from the bottom of the mountain. No prints went around, and Hellen might have been able to climb it, but the horse couldn't have gone over unless it flew. Weird. And not possible, so he proceeded around, watching the dirt and needles and little plants carefully until he could pick up the trail again.

Halfway, he found thick scrapes in the dirt, ripped weeds like someone had dragged a couple of big rocks to this spot. But that didn't make any sense—the rocks blocking the trail were much bigger than the scrapes.

On the other side, the footprints and hoof prints resumed, next to the steep rock where they should be. They bumped right up to the boulders and looked like they went through. He stepped back and examined the formation. These rocks were a different color than the rest, they had more moss, and rounder edges. They didn't fit in, almost like somebody had put them there.

But how was that possible? The biggest boulder must weigh two hundred tons or more, no one could have put that there in the last couple of hours. There had to be a better explanation.

He turned and gazed at the forest. Supposedly there were legends about moving rocks in Monks' Glen. He'd always dismissed them as tavern tales, but since he'd seen the dimensional tear, his mind had become a lot more open. The warm green under the canopy looked idyllic, but he wasn't fooled. Creepy stuff went on in there, no doubt about it.

For the last eighteen months, the forest had been left to its own devices. After the day he caught John Treslo at the tear, he hadn't been back, and never sent troops in. Maybe that was a bad choice, but now that Pulari belonged to him, he didn't have to worry about incursions from some greedy asswipe anymore. And he had plenty of other places for his troops to go. Wharton went back in once, and said the tear had disappeared, or at least he couldn't find it, and after that any other trips seemed pointless.

Today, though, the forest beckoned. The mystery of the pile of rocks begged to be solved. Especially because they were helping Hellen, and her ridiculous rebellion, and how he'd love to just torch the whole place to teach them a lesson.

But not today. Today he had more important things to do. He turned away from the forest and continued following the path.

Chapter F.8

The hard way. Hellen dropped into a squat, as much behind the rock dagger as she could manage. She'd put herself at a real disadvantage, stuck as she was on the side of a cliff. But one thing she could do was jump; Cary had taught her that, and if she could lure the soldier to the crack in the wall, she could come down on him like a week's worth of bad news.

"Then come up and get me!" she yelled.

Zero response. Daring a peek over the edge, she found the path below empty. Fabulous. A quick survey up the rock revealed nothing, but the sound of a breaking branch pulled her eyes into the trees. In the low branches of a pine opposite her, he stood with his feet on either side of the trunk, his elbow resting on another branch, gun aimed right at her.

She felt like a target at a carnival shooting gallery. For the first time it occurred to her that maybe Dagge didn't care anymore if she lived or died. The idea was a game-changer, and she suddenly felt very protective of her hide.

With both hands, she reached up and grasped the dagger formation, then climbed to the top of the connecting tendon that ran between it and the vertical rock of the side. The thin top of the tendon was precarious, but she was able to keep the dagger between her and the soldier in the tree. If he wanted to shoot her, he was going to have to work harder.

Below and ahead of her were several ledges and gaps in the rock where big chunks of the mountain had apparently fallen to the side. The nearest ledge was small, but it was lower down, and in a pocket. Since getting off the exposed side seemed like the best idea, she made a precision drop onto it.

Her new position was very much like being inside a well. A gap let out on the front, but a maniac with a gun waited out there, and she sure wanted to find another way. A smaller gap opened on the side, but farther in it looked way too narrow, and the only thing worse than getting shot would be getting stuck.

If she looked down in the crack, though, she could see light. The bottom edge of the rock on the front side framed an opening that looked large enough for her to crawl through. Not the best exit point, but on the ground at least, she'd have a fighting chance. Conversely, she could go up, but if she climbed to the top of the rock, she'd be in the same boat she was in before, with a big, fat target on her ass.

She eased into the gap, supporting herself with one foot in the front and the opposite foot behind. Sweat rolled down her hairline, but she was glad she'd worn long pants and long sleeves; she shifted her weight from back to front as she lowered herself, using her arms, hands, and knees to increase the pressure.

Just as her shoulders reached the level of the ledge, the soldier jumped onto it and lunged at her, jabbing his left arm into the crack, and grabbing a handful of her hair. She released her knife and it sprang into her hand. With her other hand she grabbed his wrist, and with her knife slashed at his arm, cutting the flesh and scoring the bone. He let go of her hair, and the release of pressure and shifting of her body made her slip, and she began to plummet downward.

His wrist was still in her hand, and she held it tightly, slamming his body into the rock on either side of the gap, pulling him down until he crouched on one knee, his head dangling over her. In the relative dark inside the rock, the purple in his eyes glowed and grew larger, radiating with hate and fire until the hot color took up the whole pupil and she couldn't look anymore. He grinned and tried to pull back, but she had a good grip, and snarled up at him, "Tell Tomius I said hello."

Using her knife as a pick, she jabbed it into his upper arm, planted her feet on either side of the gap and heaved herself up. Above her, the soldier wrestled one-handed with his gun, trying to get it into the crack to shoot her. With every ounce of her strength, she pushed and pulled upward, plunging her knife into him, ripping downward as she pulled herself nearer his level. The blood running down his arm threatened her grip on his wrist, so she released it and seized the front of his shirt. His bloody hand tried to grab her throat, but she'd ruined the nerves and muscles in his arm, and his grip was weak. The gun came forward, his body hung half in the gap, and he pressed the tip of the laser rifle under his chin, and fired.

The magenta creature inside of him jumped out in several directions. Its flat-topped head sliced through the soldier's forehead, almost in Hellen's face. She recoiled, let go of his shirt, lost her footing, and slid back. Only her knife in the guy's shoulder kept her up.

The surge only lasted a couple of seconds, then the creature shrank back into the human form. It fired again, and the raging monster leapt out, stretching farther this time. Purple eyes glared down at her, and the half-visible edge of its mouth framed a hideous metallic scream. Harsh and long, it ricocheted between the rocks, vibrating her eardrums, her sinuses, and even her teeth. Terror engulfed her, and she wanted to flee, because surely the thing was going to take her, but it shrank again, and disappeared into the agonized face of the soldier. She could see then the charred hole in the top of his head, and brains spattering his hair.

A resolute courage swept up and hardened her. When it fired again, she grabbed the rifle, shoved it up through the guy's head, grabbed the tip, and used the front of his skull to pull herself up. The monster's face came entirely out this time, and she yanked her carapaz knife out of the man's shoulder and swiped it through the flat, angular head. The blade left a jagged trail through its face, and it screamed in rage as the top half of its head folded down like paper and disappeared into the air.

After that, the magenta began to flicker in all the places it stuck out from the body. The good arm released the rifle, and the barrel slipped out of the dying head. She caught it and turned it, jamming it into the gap at an angle. For a minute she dangled there, one hand on the action, her opposite elbow hooked in the strap, and watched the magenta face roar its last, an unearthly screech of pain and fury that shook her to her core, piercing her ears with frequencies she'd never heard. Long seconds later, the sound and the hot magenta faded, shrinking into flesh and silence, until the violent purple pinpoints in the soldier's eyes were no more.

Hellen looked at him for a long moment, then stabbed him in the heart to be sure.

Chapter F.9

A white wolf stared at him from fifty strides or so into the forest. It stood with its head down, ears up, tail drooping behind it. Dagge looked away, and kept walking. His knife hung on his belt, and a rifle hung over his shoulder, but he'd rather not kill the animal if he didn't have to. Not enough wild predators left in the world.

Dagge trudged along the base of a cliff, seeking out the trail as it disappeared and reappeared. There'd been too many strange piles of rock blocking his way. Strange tracks, too, of things that were dragged, or dropped at regular intervals, and they always led into the forest. But no footprints or hoofprints went with them, so what was he supposed to make of that? The wise thing was to check the entire area at the irregular spots, even though it made slow going. But he didn't follow through very far, because it was the footprints he was interested in. The other tracks made him nervous, even with his knife and gun.

Dagge considered the possibility that all of it was a ruse. That would be the smart thing, and Hellen was certainly smart. But he had a feeling the trail was real, and the rest of it was someone trying to confuse him. If he was right, and he surely was, the payoff for all this work would be huge.

Above him, the mountain loomed nearly vertical and stuck all over with spikes, which he really liked. New mountains, they said, but they couldn't be all that new, could they? At least over a thousand years.

The wind was his constant companion. It swirled around him in clashing gusts of warm and cool, buffeting his face, and bringing the scents of earth and snow. He peered up the steep rock beside him, into the stream of air coming off the frozen peak, and a piece of grit hit him in the eye. *Fuckin-z.*

108

He turned his back on the mountain and faced the forest, finger on his eye. The wolf had followed him, and stood under the trees watching, head raised and alert. Dagge gazed at him with one eye while he tried to rub the rock out of the other.

After a long few seconds, prodded by curiosity, Dagge took a step in the direction he'd been going. The wolf stayed still. He took another step, then another, and at three steps the wolf moved one step forward. Dagge stopped; the wolf stopped. Dagge let his gaze drop to the ground.

What was it doing? Lone wolves were generally either old or young males, and this one looked young, but large and well-fed. It didn't act like it wanted to eat him. If it did want to eat him, it would have attacked already, wouldn't it?

A small rock sailed out of the shadows and landed at his feet. Now, a real, normal wolf couldn't throw a rock, and the thing hadn't moved anyway, so where did the rock come from? The space under the trees was fairly open. A lot of pines grew here, bushes were scarce, and no ferns to speak of. Around the wolf, the forest floor consisted of patches of rock, pine needles and miscellaneous broken branches. Anything person-sized would have a hard time hiding, except behind the trunks, and even then they'd have to be pretty small and standing ridiculously straight.

But the rock didn't come from behind a tree, anyway. It seemed to come from the open area beside the wolf. Dagge blinked and squinted until his eye felt better, then he unsnapped his sheath and pulled his big knife out into the hot sun. A blinding reflection swept across his vision when he looked down at it. With a slight adjustment, he could see himself in the wide, polished blade. He needed a haircut.

The sun shone white behind his head, which meant he'd been out here longer than he realized. His reflection frowned and looked up at the forest, hand dropping to his side. The wolf sat farther back in the trees now, watching him with his mouth open and tongue hanging out, almost like he was taunting him, daring him to come into the woods.

But why would he want to do that, when the trail clearly followed the base of the mountain?

Someone must be trying to stop him from following the trail…someone who had trained the wolf, and knew how to hide. Or hells, this was Monks' Glen he was talking about, it had a portal to another world or something, and who knew what else. Maybe his soldiers weren't the only things to come out of it. Maybe he had enemies wherever they came from, and some of them were here too.

Screw 'em. Right now, he had more important things to do. He turned away from the forest and kept walking.

Chapter F.10

When Hellen found him, he was almost to the monastery. The monks once told her they had a veil around the place, but she didn't know how well that worked if someone walked right up to it. Would your hand disappear if you touched it? Not likely. At any rate, Dagge was smart enough not to take "trail disappeared" as an answer.

She'd moved deeper into the forest after she got past the palace, for better cover and less noise. But she'd been in such a hurry, she nearly passed him, squatted down like he was, peering at the ground beside the cliff. In front of him there was a pile of boulders that looked suspiciously like one of the rock giants. Apparently, they'd been called into active duty, which meant the monks were probably around, too.

Still behind him, she slowed, gazing through the trees from a good distance away, where the pine mixed with oak and the forest floor became irregular with roots. Careful to avoid fallen branches, her footfalls stayed silent on the carpet of needles and dead leaves. Trunk to trunk she went, her soft brown clothes making no noise, and her bulky cloak lying somewhere behind her on the forest floor.

Wolf knew she was there, but stayed ahead of her, all his attention focused on Dagge. Thank One he was there, because anytime Dagge stopped or turned, his gaze went immediately to the dog, and Hellen had time to secure her position if she needed to. She discovered that if she watched Wolf, his head tended to dip a little and his mouth would close just before Dagge turned and looked. He would continue walking when Dagge did. Very handy, since she didn't want to repeat the stupidity of getting spotted because she leaned too far out.

Lots of stops, detours, and backtracks stretched the stakeout interminably, but at least it gave her time to try and think of a plan. She hadn't been able to get the gun out of the gap. It had wedged in too tight, and she didn't have time to go back and try to retrieve it from above. Of course, if she'd known she was going to waste all this time watching him bend and squat, she'd have done it.

Hindsight was seldom helpful, though. In the here and now, she needed some way to draw him away from the monastery. A direct attack would most likely kill her. Out of shape as Dagge looked, he still had years of training and strength she couldn't match hand-to-hand. She could try to sneak up on him, and jump him from behind, but who was she kidding. However, if she could draw him into the woods, she could ambush him from behind a tree, and have a good chance of getting her dagger into his throat.

A weak plan, perhaps, but a plan nonetheless.

When she looked up at Wolf again, he'd moved farther back into the woods and sat looking at Dagge rather amiably, mouth open and smiling. Daring a peek around the trunk, she could see Dagge standing at the base of the mountain, facing the forest. He looked like he was trying to make a decision, but whatever his dilemma was, he tossed it aside and continued following the trail.

If only she'd taken the time to compromise the trail last night. She knew it was bad, and a risk, and if Dagge ever found it, blah blah blah. No point in wringing her guts dry over it now.

With a quick glance at Dagge, whose eyes were on the ground ahead of him, she sprinted forward, aiming leftish through the tree trunks on a path that would take her a little bit farther into the woods. The idea was to be close enough that he'd recognize her, but far enough away that it would take some effort to chase her down. Over tree roots and rain gullys, around rocks and trunks, she ran until she drew level with him, and then ran a bit ahead so he could see her. Wolf watched her, ears up, tail wagging slightly as she passed him. When she was sure Dagge could see her, she whistled.

It took him a second to find her. His eyes went immediately to Wolf, and Wolf looked straight at her, so Dagge was able to follow. He froze in his tracks. No question that he recognized her. His hand jerked to his big knife, and she wondered if he might throw it at her. Too far even for him. She smiled.

If he went for his gun, that would be different.

Chapter F.11

Sunlight gleamed on her head and shoulders, turning her short blond hair to fire and tracing the thin line of her nose. Even with most of her face in shadow, Dagge could still tell it was her—the wide stance, hands on her hips, tall and lean and strong. He suddenly became aware of his loins, and the divining rod in his pants drawing toward her.

The wolf's tail wagged, too, ever so slightly. She must be his trainer, or at least familiar, because she didn't act like she was scared of him. He sat there between them, head glancing back and forth, tongue lolling. Hellen didn't even look at the wolf, just kept her gaze trained ahead, and Dagge knew that if he could see her eyes, they'd be boring into his. He might have felt uncomfortable if he hadn't been flattered.

How did she get here? Possibly she turned around and came back, in which case the soldier he sent to follow must have gone on after the man. Good call, because their destination was far more important than following Hellen back this way. On the other hand, she could have spotted the tail and killed him.

Lust and admiration aside, all the damage she'd inflicted lately would definitely need retribution when he finally got her snagged and bagged.

"Hello!" he called.

No answer. What did he expect, polite conversation?

"Tell you what, I'll put my knife away, and we can meet in the middle and talk."

Nothing. Nada. Zip. In a show of good faith, he made a big, exaggerated move to put his knife in its sheath, and snapped it closed. Holding his empty hands up, he smiled and started walking into the trees. Hellen didn't move. The wolf, however, watched him warily.

After the bright sunshine and pale rock, the trees were a relief. Even the tall pines made decent shade, and it felt ten degrees cooler as he walked over the dappled ground underneath. Hands still in the air, he kept his eyes on Hellen, who stood about forty strides away. Less than half that distance, the wolf began to growl, and Dagge stopped.

"You might need to call off your dog," he said.

Still no response, but she did move. Her hands came up off her hips, she crossed her arms over her chest and walked out of the sun to lean on a tree. He could see her eyes now, and yes, she drilled him.

It appeared they were at an impasse. About ten strides in front of him, hackles raised and ears laid back, the wolf rumbled a long, low warning. With slow hands, Dagge reached for his rifle.

"I'm not going to shoot you. Or the dog." Slowly, with dramatic pauses, he lifted the rifle off his shoulder and bent to lay it on the ground. "I just want to talk."

Hellen watched him, unmoving. So did the dog.

Hands up, Dagge tried another step forward, but the growling turned into a snarl, the whole front of the dog's body lowered, and he gave it up.

His hands sank to his sides. "You'll have to come to me, I'm afraid. There's no way your friend here is going to let me pass."

After a moment, Hellen put two fingers up to her mouth and whistled. The dog snapped its head around and trotted off toward her. To Dagge's surprise, she turned her back and walked away, deeper into the old trees and juts of rock. The dog trailed behind, glancing back over its shoulder, still wary.

Dagge weighed his options. He could go back to the trail, or he could follow her. No contest, really.

"It's been a long time, Hellen. You look well," he said, passing in and out of the sun, navigating tree roots as he moved off the pine needles and under the canopy of the old oaks.

No answer.

"I was hoping I'd see you today."

She did stop and turn around at that. "Were you now?"

115

He laughed lightly and kept walking closer.

"I really was. I guess I've been thinking about you."

"I bet you have."

He laughed again, and smiled, twinkling his eyes at her. She was always a sucker for that.

"What's that scary grey patch on your face?"

Holy fuck...did she really say that?

"Did you hear me? Dagge?" Her fingers were snapping in his direction.

"Yeah, I heard you." All the sunshine had disappeared. "Why would you ask me that?"

"Because there's a—" and she glitched— "are you doing here?"

He had to think for second, and stare at her.

"You hate the forest. It's not like you're on a pleasure stroll."

She asked what he was doing here. Not about the grey patch.

This forest was fucking him up.

"I'm looking for you," he said, taking few steps closer.

"No you're not. And stay back."

The dog growled and lowered its head.

He held up his hands again and took a step back. Things were going off track, and he couldn't seem— "Why else would I be out here?"

Hellen crossed her arms again. "You're asking me? I have no idea."

"Oh, I think you do."

She didn't say anything, just tilted her head, and her hand came up and cupped her chin. Did she have some kind of binding on her wrist?

"I saw a horse in the stable today that reminded me of a horse that used to be around, but disappeared. And it had a saddle on it that I hadn't seen in a long time."

No response, just that steady stare.

He took a few more steps forward. "Still, I do remember who they belonged to." He watched her. "How is the Princess? Because I saw the explosion, and…let's just say I have my doubts about her ability to lead." Resting his hand on his sheathed knife, Dagge gazed at her, feeling every bit of the upper hand again.

After a few moments, she said, "Just so you know, I'll kill you if you come for her."

"Big words from someone who won't get within five feet of me."

"I'm not afraid of you, Tomius."

"Tomius again!" Delight lit him up. "I didn't expect to hear that. You've been so angry." Smiling, he fake-shivered. "But I know you're lying. Here, if this makes you feel better…" He unsnapped his sheath, pulled out his knife, and tossed it aside. "Now we're more or less even. But why you're running around without a knife or gun escapes me. Something up your sleeve?" He grinned and winked.

Hellen's arms lowered to her sides, and she readied her stance. "The Resistance will never stop, you know."

"The Resistance? That's uppity. Let's be honest, you are the Resistance. The rest of it's big talk for a load of bullshit."

Hellen's right hand started twitching, fingers tapping the palm…yeah, he had a feeling.

"Bullshit is killing the King, Dagge. *Bullshit* is stealing the throne. Bullshit is murdering all those people, and turning this country into nothing but a carapaz mine. You're the one who's bullshit."

Dagge was quiet for a moment, processing. "You clearly don't understand business."

Hellen snapped. She ran at him, a small pink knife in her hand. Tickled, he bent at the last second, planning to shoulder her in the gut and flip her over his back. But she rolled over him, landed in a squat and jabbed her knife into his side.

It surprised him how much it hurt. One hand on the wound, he staggered back, and for a moment, looked at her in shock. Then he got angry. He turned to find his own knife, and instead found the dog. The dog jumped, glancing off his chest and knocking him to the ground. It doubled back and was on him, pinning him, muzzle in his face. The blue eyes glared down at him, its ears lay flat and it snapped and snarled, lips quivering over its teeth.

Dagge turned his head, pulling his face far away from the dog while he flailed for the knife. Hellen lunged, but he reached it first, grasped the handle and plunged it into the dog's side. The animal yiped and recoiled enough for Dagge to shove him off and scramble backward. He held the knife ready in front of him while he got to his feet.

Hellen threw her knife and it stuck in his neck. It felt chokey and thick, and he reached up and pulled it out. "You can't kill me that easy." His voice sounded gravelly and harsh. He looked down. In his left hand he held a small fortune in carapaz. Fuckin thieves.

The dog jumped at him again, and Dagge hit it in the belly with his big knife, yanking the blade upward. The dog yiped dreadfully, in long, guttural wails, staggering to the side. Bright red poured into the white fur as it stumbled over to the nearest tree. Dagge turned to Hellen, a bloody knife in each hand. Sparks popped in his brain, and he suddenly felt like his body was too small to hold all of him.

****

The neck shot should have dropped him.

Why didn't it?

Where was Wolf? She couldn't see him, and she couldn't go looking because right now her world was all about Dagge coming at her with two knives. Blood ran down his chest, his arms were spread wide, his walk was wide, and his shit-eating grin was wide. She backed slowly. Emergency strategies zoomed through her head—she could certainly outrun him, but that would mean leaving Wolf, and he would die. Hand to hand would be impossible now that he had her knife, but she needed to do something before Wolf bled out.

"Hellen." Dagge kept advancing, gesturing with the knives like they were having a normal conversation. "Remember how good it was?

You don't have to be a loser. You could surrender to me right now, and one day I could make you my Queen."

What an absolute low-life fucking scum mold crazy-ass dick tick of the universe.

And a light went on.

"It could still be good, you know."

She kept backing away. "You'd make me your Queen."

"Well, there'd have to be some punishment first. Just enough so people would know that treason has consequences. Like Camberton. Only not so permanent." He grinned. "Then we could travel…see the world. Do every country." He rubbed the flat of his big knife across the bulge in his pants.

"If you mean sex, no thanks. You were lousy."

His smile faded into a grimace and his face went dark.

"It's probably the tiny penis. Not your fault. But that belly, whew! Cookie needs to put you on a diet."

As she talked, his face got redder.

"And do you know you have a bald spot now? Age will do that, of course. What are you now? 50? 60?"

He looked like he might explode. His hands white-knuckled the knives, arms stiff.

"Again, not your fault. I'm sure some women still find you attractive."

Dagge's hand came up with lightning speed, and the pink knife fired toward her. But it was his left hand, and his aim was off just enough to miss her eye and slice her cheek. As the carapaz disappeared over her shoulder, he came for her.

Hellen turned at a run and frantically searched the ground for her knife. It lay a few strides back, and she scooped it up, starkly aware of Dagge's heavy footfalls behind her. She knew this part of the forest well, though. She veered to the right, where rocks and tree roots made treacherous ground. With practiced feet, she navigated the gullies and roots, to duck out between a tall jut of rock and a tree.

Dagge was slower, but he wasn't stupid. He stopped not far into the tree roots and said, "Why don't you stay right here while I get my gun? But first I should check on the dog and make sure it's dead."

Fuck. Him.

She couldn't let him find Wolf. Fighting him might be a fool's game, but outsmarting him wasn't. She stepped back in the gap where he could see her, crossed her arms over her chest and leaned on the rock. "You're so hilarious. You think we put Adia's horse in the stable by accident? You think I'm here because I want to visit with you? You've been gone a long time. Following our trail. And you have no idea what's been happening in the palace. Because I am not the Resistance. And there are lots of ways in."

Fury and fear battled on his face for a few seconds, and he turned and ran.

Hellen found Wolf where he'd crawled behind the nearest oak. A broken branch lay on the ground beside him, and he'd tried to hide himself under the splayed limbs. "Oh, Wolf." Dropping to one knee, she examined the gashes as best she could without touching them. A light touch to his nose told her he was still breathing, though weakly. How could she get him to the monastery? The belly wound would make fireman's carry painful, but she didn't know if she had the strength to carry him in her arms. Not to mention, without knowing how bad Wolf might be messed up inside, she didn't want to risk his liver or something falling out. She was about to try and get her shoulder under him when Diit's white-stockinged legs stepped into her field of vision.

"Let me help you, Miss Hellen," he said in his soft voice. "I think we can do it together."

Her eyes traveled up his impeccable uniform and rested on the concerned expression under the big white wig. "Diit, what are you doing here? Dagge just left, are you certain he didn't see you?"

"Oh, yes, Miss. I'm certain. Why don't you let me carry Wolf…I think he's unconscious, so if you can help me lift him onto my shoulders, he shouldn't struggle or try to get away."

Diit pulled the branch to the side, and she got her arms under Wolf's front half and raised it. Diit half squatted and half knelt, leaning his shoulders down to take him. Careful not to traumatize the wounds, Hellen hefted and adjusted the big dog onto Diit's shoulders. Satisfied they had the weight even enough not to cause problems, she helped Diit stand, but when he started walking, Wolf's head bobbed and dangled behind his back. She couldn't abide that, so she held it up for him until they reached the monastery. Good thing for all of them it wasn't far.

Inside the foyer, they laid the dog in his favorite cool spot under the stairs, and knelt beside him.

"We need some clean water now," Diit said.

"Should I boil it? I'll have to build a fire, we didn't leave one burning."

"Bring some cold for now in the tea kettle. Once we clean the fur, we'll have a better idea of what we're dealing with. Do you have scissors?"

"I think so, I'll look. But I'll bring the water first."

"Fine." He smiled up at her. "Don't worry, Miss. If I have to go get the doctor at the palace, and bring him here blindfolded, I will."

That made her smile, forlorn as it felt, because she knew he would do it, and with a pat on his shoulder, she stood up to go to the kitchen.

Halfway through the great room, a blinding white light appeared at the opposite end, like a threshold, and swept toward her, across her, and she found herself standing in the other-dimensional monastery just like she and John had three years ago. A fire burned in the fireplace, the furniture was all gone, and a handful of glowy monks stood around her.

"Hellen Parker, it is good to see you again."

One of the monks approached her, and she guessed he seemed familiar, but honestly it was hard to tell. The facial features were nearly nonexistent, and more than anything they looked like cartoon aliens. But no need to say that, right? She could fake her way through.

"Yeah, it's good to see you too. Been a long time." She nodded, looking around. The foyer was also light and new-looking, like everything else. What must Diit be thinking?

"You would probably like to know that we brought you here so we could help the guardian."

"Help me what? I could have used help back there with Dagge, but that opportunity is past." She almost kept the irritation out of her voice.

"Not you, the guardian. You call him Wolf."

Well, bust her boots. She dismounted her high horse in a hurry.

"His spirit volunteered to guard the Queen; he has understanding about the forest, and the evil entity."

Then Wolf apparently wasn't just a lucky find, like she thought. Yet another door opened in her mind, and she should be used to that by now. Yet it still came as a surprise. So much more in heaven and earth.

"You're going to help him? He's in the foyer, do I need to get the water?"

"We have everything we need. Servant is in there now with him, and the repair shouldn't take long given his high vibration."

Well, that was good to hear.

"You received help with Tomius Dagge."

"I did, didn't I? And Diit helped with Wolf. Sorry. I guess I'm...just...tired."

"Understandably. Yours has been one of the more difficult Protectorships. You're managing adequately."

Was that a compliment or an insult?

"And here he is!"

Hellen turned and saw Wolf standing in the archway. He walked slowly toward her, almost shuffling, like he was exhausted. She knelt in front of him and put her hands on either side of his head. Tears came to her eyes, and she laughed at herself. Who knew she cared this much about a smelly dog? His blue eyes blinked back at her and he smiled. She leaned over his head and gave the top of it a kiss, rubbing his ears affectionately.

"He should be healed now," the monk said, "but he will need rest."

"Thank you. From Adia, too, she's going to...I don't know what." Should she even tell her? Yeeaah.... "Since I have to tell her what happened."

"Naturally." The monk smiled.

"What about Diit?" His quizzical look prompted her to explain. "He's the valet, he stayed in there with Wolf while I went to get water. What am I supposed to tell him about...all this?" She waved her arm to indicate the spotless room and the handful of glowing beings loitering around them.

"You won't need to tell him anything," he said. "He won't ask. Go and get the water, I will take the guardian back to the foyer, and when you return, and the wound is cleaned, it will be found to be less severe than it appeared. Only a scratch, so to speak."

"And he won't say anything about how great everything looked for five minutes?"

The monk chuckled. "No, for him everything was quite normal."

"Ooohhh." Hellen nodded slowly. "Okay, cool. It's too bad you guys can't just wave that light thingy over the palace and get rid of that festering wound living there."

"No one can accomplish certain tasks except the people to whom the tasks belong. That is the way of things."

Damn, that sucked.

She watched him walk Wolf back to the foyer, and as she headed to the kitchen, the light swept over her and all the shiny clean was gone.

Chapter F.13

Adia held her hands up and tried to quiet the room. "People…hang on. We can't send a big rescue party out for Hellen. She said she didn't want anyone to come help, and she would not want us to compromise the Resistance by putting too many people outside the wall." Silence fell around her. "Believe me, I have lived this worry for three years, and so far she has always come back."

"I know she can take care of herself." Beau's voice sounded tense. "But Dagge has skills in the field, and he could kill her before she even knew he was there."

"But the most likely scenario is that he wouldn't do that. Not with their history. Of course it's possible, anything is possible, but my instincts say no."

Across the room, toward the right, Vartile's voice spoke firmly, "Hellen had the element of surprise on her side, Beau, and I'm sure she saw Dagge before he saw her."

"Absolutely," Adia nodded once. "He would have been watching the trail."

"I'm just worried for her," Beau said, stress marking every syllable.

She understood completely. Hellen's absences had always been exercises in faith for her, and while it had gotten a lot better, the waiting still stretched her heart to the snapping point. "Tell you what, Beau, if Hellen's not back by nightfall, you and Cary can go look for her."

"Yes, ma'am," he answered, even before she stopped talking.

"I'd love to go," Cary's voice chimed in beside her. "What would you like me to do with Dagge's sorry ass when I find it?"

Several things ran through her mind, and not one of them was Dagge's sorry ass. First, Hellen had been very adamant lately about everyone calling her "Your Majesty" or "ma'am" or whatever. She said it was important that they think of her that way, because one of these days she was going to be on the throne, and they couldn't be calling her Adia. Second, the quip was funny, and she wanted to laugh, but third, should she let that level of inappropriateness go by unchallenged?

What would Dad do?

She smiled and said, "Bring him back alive. I want to see him in court." Time enough later to talk about respect in private.

"Your Majesty," Roberta said, "we don't know where they are, or if Dagge found the monastery. Has anyone thought to check the pigeon cage today?"

"That's right, how stupid. Beau, would you check your cage, please?"

"Right away, ma'am." A desk or table squeaked and scraped the floor, Beau "excuse-me'd" across HQ, and long strides disappeared up the steps.

"While we wait, I'd like to thank you all for coming. It's been quite a while since I've seen most of you—" (why did she keep using that word?) "and I suppose it'll be a really long time before I see you again." A shake of her head and a half-hearted laugh made the joke, sparking a good-natured chuckle in the crowd in front of her.

Probably most of the Resistance had squeezed into Beau's room. It had taken several hours after she and Cary arrived to contact everyone and assemble them here. The original plan had been to just meet with the council, but something in her felt like she should see everyone, or rather let them see her. It had been too long, and leading from that kind of distance didn't feel right anymore.

The council meeting would begin after everyone else went home. Beau, Vartile and Luhe, Cary, Byron, Merv, and Roberta all would stay, and if Beau and Cary needed to leave to go find Hellen, they could do it with their night glasses.

"Your Majesty," Purda's voice spoke up from the back of the center, near the town tunnel opening. "What if the Overlord finds the trail here?"

126

Well, that was a very good question. After they parted with Hellen, Cary had set her down a few times to go back and try to mask the trail, but she didn't think it would fool Dagge. Their hope was that he wouldn't find the opening, camouflaged in the rock. Still, that would only delay the inevitable. He'd order the army to dig until the tunnel was exposed, and every person at the end of every tunnel in the warren would pay in the worst possible way.

"If Dagge comes after us, we'll fight. Beau and a few others have amassed weapons, gas and gas masks, a few night glasses, and some other things, and we'll do what we have to do. Does anyone have a different idea?"

"I'm ready to fight," said Vartile, One bless her.

A number of "Me, too's" sprinkled the room, but Purda spoke again, her voice a little thin and high. "I'm not sure I'd be good at that. Killing isn't something I can picture myself doing."

"That's understandable. We're not all cut out for battle, but at the same time, if push comes to shove, I'm betting that we all have a survivor in us."

"There are other things that can be helpful in the push phase, too." Cary's voice vibrated the air beside her, she could feel it on her face. "Tunnels may need to be closed off, supplies moved, any number of things that don't involve fighting."

"That's right, Cary, thank you," she said. "And the end game will be to get as many of us to safety as possible. Obviously, we wouldn't be able to stop Dagge's entire army, but we can hold them off until the majority of us get away." Did she sound more confident than she felt? She sure hoped so.

"What's the exit strategy, ma'am?" sounded like Firio.

"Probably NHQ," Cary answered. Adia laid her hand on his arm, and he jumped like he was surprised to be interrupted. "What do you think?" he asked, loud in her right ear. The guy was really getting under her skin today.

"NHQ will be a good interim hub. As long as it stays off Dagge's radar, we can filter from there into the surrounding neighborhoods and at least hide for a while. We'll need to find ways out of the town, and we'll make those plans when we do. Cary, can you locate Beau's map of the tunnels for me?"

"Right now?"

His question came out more sincere than petulant, but it still lit her fuse. "Yes, now," she said, trying to disguise her very intense desire to throttle him.

He must have gotten the message, because he said, "Yes, ma'am," moved across the space in front of her and faded away toward the shelves.

"Even if Dagge does follow the trail to the wall, it'll take time to dig as far down as he'll have to to find the tunnel. In the meantime, we can prepare. Beau will have the best idea of what needs to be done, and we'll come up with a plan this evening."

"Are you sure we have time to wait?" That was Cary.

A scant second before the top of her head blew off, Roberta interrupted. "Your Majesty, I think I can answer this."

"Please do, Roberta."

"Cary, don't disrespect the Queen. Shut up."

A laugh jumped up into her mouth, and she had to suck air in and gulp it down to keep from guffawing. Even then, it took a few seconds and some lip pressing before she could speak.

"As I was saying, we'll have ample warning of invasion—" A scuff of feet on the stairs meant Beau had returned, and she stopped to address him. "Is there a message?"

"Yes, ma'am, Hellen is safe at the monastery!" A muffled cheer erupted across the room. Relief swept through her, and the world in general became a brighter place.

"Thank One," she said, amid the happy noises, all muted for safety. "That's encouraging!" Her voice rose to carry through the room, and she pushed herself off the desk to stand in front of it. "But we must remain vigilant. Dagge will almost certainly come looking for us, and unless we find out better, we should all plan for it. Prepare emergency measures, pack supplies you can carry in case of evacuation, move stockpiles to locations north as soon as you are able. And never forget he has a harkener. Does anyone have any questions?" No one said anything, and she added, "Council members, we will adjourn immediately to Vartile and Luhe's basement. Everyone else, thank you for coming."

Hand on the desk beside her, she felt her way around it and to the wall, where she found Luhe waiting for her. He stepped around to her other side, between her and the crowd, and buffered her from any chatters or well-wishers who might want to take up too much time. Purely awesome guy.

"Your Majesty," he said in a low voice as she took his arm. "Vartile and I have a surprise for you in the basement. I wish you could see it." His voice stopped in an awkward silence.

She grinned. "I wish I could, too, Luhe, I'm sure it's fabulous-looking. You'll have to describe every inch of it to me, okay? I'm not kidding, I want it all!"

"Yes, ma'am," he said with a laugh, and the two of them led the way down the tunnel.

Chapter F.14

Roberta stood by while the crowd dispersed, filing past her to exit through the tunnel, or queuing to go up the stairs. Many of them nodded at her, two reached out to touch her arm, but no one spoke. She liked it better that way, not having to answer the questions in their eyes.

When the room had emptied enough to make getting to the other side easy, she wove through the few lingerers and started down the tunnel to Vartile's. The rest of the council was probably already there, so she'd have to bear some concerned looks, but maybe no one would say anything. Vartile and Beau and Elzbieta had already tried, and as much as she knew they meant well, everyone meant well, she just didn't want to talk about herself.

Nothing had gotten better since John died. Well, no, that wasn't true, the boys were better. David had pretty much taken over raising Joey, and he was doing a good job. He understood the hardship she was going through, and didn't complain or shirk the duties. Joey took his cue from David, his schoolwork always done by the time she got home, and dinner on the table.

Robert got home later, and rarely said anything. He'd retreated more into his shells after what happened at the banquet. Roberta had tried to coax him into talking, but he flatly refused, saying, "Mother, I don't need to express my feelings." If she didn't know exactly how he felt, she might have argued.

Still, what she really wanted was to ask him how he felt about Dagge now. His comments about his boss these days were very guarded, and the tint of admiration had faded some. But she wasn't going to deceive herself about Robert's feelings. She wanted to believe his eyes had been opened by John's torture, but she wouldn't dare bank on it.

So, aside from David and Joey, nothing had improved since John's death, especially not her, especially not her heart. Every night she went home, she climbed into that big, cold bed and missed him so intensely it hurt. After cleaning Dagge's tonker all day, it was almost more than she could bear.

Her hand reached up and grabbed the heavy fabric of the curtain that divided Vartile's basement from the rest of the warren. In the dim light, on the back of her hand she could see the age spots and blue veins of a much older woman, the bony fingers and big knuckles of a crone. Somebody needed to kick that bitch's ass out.

Warm light and excited voices washed over her when she pulled the curtain aside and went in. The council members stood in a loose cluster, facing the backside of the shelves where the old sofa had always been. Once she could see around Beau and Vartile and Byron, she could see the Queen sitting on a beautiful, elaborate chair, smiling a great big smile.

"It's perfect, Luhe," she said. "My feet reach the floor and everything!" They all laughed, and she continued, "Tell me what everything is made of…what are the arms?"

Roberta watched her run her small hands lightly over all the parts as Luhe talked about them. She touched the carved wood of the armrests, the beautifully wrought iron of the high back, the brocade fabric of the cushion. Nothing went unappreciated or unadmired. Luhe and Beau and Vartile all got hugs, and promised to relay the Queen's joy and gratitude to the woodcarvers, if she didn't see them. Finally, settled in her chair, she called the meeting to order. The sofa was brought round, likewise a few chairs, and everyone made themselves comfortable in a semi-circle facing her.

Cary kept himself a little apart, his chair pushed back from the circle. If his face was any indication, he appeared to be sulking, and sulking could mean trouble, in the form of mouthiness or random expressions of disgust. Roberta kept a keen eye on him—she didn't have three boys for nothing.

"Is everyone here? Roberta?"

"I'm here, Your Majesty. We're all here, except for Hellen, of course."

"And she is safe at the monastery, hallelujah!" Beau grinned infectiously. "But I should tell you, there's more to her message than what I said earlier."

"Wait." The Queen held up her hand. "If it's not an emergency, let's take care of old business before we move to new business. Chief Taymer, how are the sabotage programs moving along?"

"They're meeting with some success, Your Highness, but throwing any kind of kink in the transport of weapons from Valdia has proven almost impossible. They've started using zeppelins to fly the shipments to Pulari, and we don't have anyone on the inside at the company they've contracted."

"Can't we just shoot them down?"

Cary's question hit the floor like a brick. Roberta looked over at him; his legs were stretched out, feet crossed at the ankles, and he slouched in his chair with his arms crossed over his chest. Yep, wearing some serious hurt-pride attitude. Too bad she didn't have the forbearance to feel bad about it.

Before she could speak her scathing response, Beau took the reins. "It's better if Dagge doesn't know the extent of our capabilities. He'd spare nothing to hunt us down and wipe us out. But perhaps we could get someone through to my contact in Valdia, and he could do some recruiting. I'm sure he'd be willing. We'd just have to work out the communication."

"Yes, Beau, put your feelers out for someone to go, we'll see if we can get a ball rolling there. Oops, that's new business...any other old business we need to discuss?"

"The next story is about ready to print."

"That's new business, too, Vartile."

"Dang," she laughed.

"Okay, apparently no one can think of any old business, so let's move to new business. Beau, what did Hellen's message say?"

"Let me read it to you." He pulled the scrap of paper out of his shirt pocket and unrolled it. "Safe for now, danger may head your way. Meet me flower bed tonight. Bring beast."

"Flower bed?" Luhe's puzzled face mirrored everyone else's.

"I think that means my house," Roberta said. "Rose and Thorn, flower bed...David said she showed up there yesterday." Tension squeezed her chest, but she didn't want to say what she was thinking. If she actually said what was in her mind—that Hellen wanted David's help, for him to get involved, to risk his life—it might make it true. And she didn't want that.

"All right then," Beau nodded, "we'll open the wall to the drainage system, and take the Queen through there. It should be plenty safe. We haven't had any activity from the barracks in a while."

"Are we all going?" Cary had sat up, eagerness fighting with the petulance still on his face.

"I don't think that's necessary, Cary." The Queen's reply was measured. "It sounds like Hellen simply has an idea she wants to work out with Roberta. It's not going to be a council meeting."

"Can I escort you, Your Majesty?" Beau's plea didn't fool anyone, they all knew he had ulterior Hellen motives.

"I'm counting on it." The Queen smiled. "Roberta, will you come with us, or do you prefer to go overland?"

"Honestly, I'm not sure I'm up to climbing out of the drainage ditch, so I think I'll go overland. It's not past curfew, so I'll be fine. In fact, if you don't need me anymore, I'd like to go —I'm very tired."

"Certainly you may go." The Queen nodded, and as soon as she said it, Roberta stood. "Maybe you can catch some sleep before we have to descend on you later tonight."

"Thank you, Your Majesty."

Merv jumped in, which was a surprise. He didn't generally talk unless he was asked a question. "Roberta, I want to give you this before you go." Everyone waited while he dug around in his satchel. What was it with nerdy types? When he turned back around, he held a carapaz cylinder out to her. "The crackdown at the mine is getting worse. We can't risk anyone carrying this anymore. I would have given it to Hellen, but I don't know when I'll see her next."

Roberta took it from him. It was heavy.

"What is it, Merv?" the Queen asked.

"Oh, I'm sorry, Your Majesty. It's the lightning weapon."

Ah. The legendary lightning weapon. Not good for anything but trouble. Still, John would be glad she had it so she could keep it safe. Somewhere in all his junk downstairs.

"Thank you, Merv. I'll hang onto it until someone needs it. Your Majesty." Roberta bowed her head and closed her eyes for a brief moment. "Vartile, can I go out your front door?"

"Sure you can," she answered. "I'll go up with you and let you out."

With a small wave to the other council members, she followed Vartile up the stairs.

Chapter F.15

Of course when he got back to the palace nothing was happening. Nothing had happened. And nothing was going to happen because he was going to kill every last one of those fucking traitors. Forget whatever Hellen was hiding in the woods. It was too remote, anyway. The real action had to come from the other end of the trail. In town.

On the other side of the desk, Wharton's mouth moved through the report on the mine inspection, but Dagge didn't hear a single word the man said.

Was the Princess alive or not? Was she a vegetable? Were they hiding her in the forest because she was too messed up to be seen? Fucking evil, sneaky bitch-ass forest, out to get him from the beginning. He should torch the place. That would solve a lot of problems.

"Overlord, sir, I need your permission to expand the work force."

"What? Why?"

Wharton looked at him with a blank expression. "Why do I need to expand the work force? As I said, we need cleanup crews for the areas where the explosions have taken place."

"Have there been more explosions?"

"Yes, sir. Are you all right, sir? Do I need to go over the mine report again?"

"No, Wharton, you do not need to go over the mine report again." Irritation flamed up in his brain. "You have my permission to increase the work force, and I want these explosions stopped."

Wharton stood silent for a second. "What strategy would you suggest, sir?"

"You've been doing pat-downs, right? Ramp up to strip-searches—surprise them with it. Humiliate them. Post a guard every three feet." He stood, pushing the rolling desk chair back so hard with his knees, it hit the wall behind him. "I'm sick to death of your incompetence, Wharton. You should have gotten a handle on this months ago. Now get out there and do your job. Dismissed."

Wharton bowed and exited without another word, his back stiff all the way out the door. Good, a little pissed-offness might get some shit done.

He took three steps away from the desk, and turned to look at the painting of the King. The dagger stuck out of the old man's ear, buried deep and straight, and the asshole was still smiling. No matter what he did, he just couldn't seem to wipe that smirk off. Maybe he could use some oil-coated canvas to start the fire in the fucking forest.

What he needed now was a good dose of revenge. Hellen had tricked him, plus his man hadn't come back so she must have killed him. Not much chance he'd still be out there looking.

But the important thing was that the trail went somewhere, and Dagge was going to find out where.

In two quick strides, he reached the dagger in the painting and yanked it out. Even with as many times as he'd speared the wall behind the canvas, the tip of the thick blade had a nice, smooth edge and a good point. His thumb checked the sharpness out of habit, but he already knew it was sharp. He loved that knife. Shoving it into his belt, he walked back over to the desk to get his laser pistol, and tucked it into the holster on his thigh.

Didn't want to forget the harkener. He slammed the top drawer shut and jerked open the bottom drawer. The shiny dish lay facing up, and he could see himself reflected in it. Fat bunched up around his jaw, his skin splotched red and grey, and the bags under his eyes had bags. What had happened to him?

Too much stress. No one had ever said anything to him about his grey patch. It had grown to cover his entire lower right jaw, down his neck a little, and after a few more months, spots started appearing on his cheek. He never caught anyone staring at it, either, so he still wasn't sure it was real. He'd asked one of the maids about it once—he had her in bed, and it seemed like a good time to ask someone—but she said she couldn't see it, and at first he pressed her, but when she still denied it, he let it go. That was when he began to wonder about his sanity.

They say if you question your own sanity, then you're not insane, right?

Both pieces of the harkener went inside his shirt. They were cold, and he pressed them to his skin to take the edge off.

He had a good feeling about seeing what was at the other end of the trail. Most likely it was a way over or under the wall. Chances were there'd be some kind of trail in town, too, and from that he could probably tell who Hellen's friends were. He could sneak around a little, see if he could locate the headquarters, and come back later with enough men to make a raid easy. If Hellen wasn't there at the time, a few hostages might bring her out of hiding.

Ready, he stepped back to salute the King.

"Don't worry, Your High-ass... I'll find them."

Chapter F.16

When the door at the top of the basement stairs closed, Adia turned her attention back to the council members in front of her. "Somebody fill me in on Roberta," she said.

Luhe answered across Vartile's empty chair. "I don't think working in the palace is good for her. She looks tired all the time and hardly ever talks. Of course it wouldn't be good for her, who'd want to see Dagge every day? Clean his tonker, for Pete's sake."

"It's worse than that," Beau spoke up from about 11 o'clock on the circle. "We all know what he did to John; yet she has to be polite when she sees him, and not let on how she'd really like to make him peel his own skin."

"I think she might feel like she's not part of this group anymore." Byron had sat beside Beau, 12 o'clock. "She doesn't make eye contact much, with any of us...with anyone, for that matter."

"You've noticed that, Byron?"

"Yes, ma'am. It's my job to be aware, and with Roberta, I'm seeing some danger signs. Not that I think she'd injure any of us, but she could do something like try to kill Dagge on her own. Before she gets herself in trouble, we need to bring her back into the fold."

"All right, if anyone has any ideas, get with me after the meeting."

Upstairs, the door opened and closed, and Vartile's feet hurried down the steps. "What did I miss?" she asked, breezing by Adia in a gust of lavender and sandalwood.

"Just some concern about Roberta," Adia replied. "I'd like to get your thoughts on that later, okay?"

"Absolutely, ma'am."

"The first business I'd like to discuss is the matter of the tunnels. Is everyone here aware that the monks built tunnels from the monastery to the town and the palace? They are supposed to be deeper than the drainage and plumbing tunnels, but so far, we have not been able to figure out how to access them."

"How many tunnels are there?" Byron asked.

"Shall I bring the cloak and the schematics, Your Majesty?"

"Yes, Luhe, please." Luhe's feet scuffed away to the other side of the shelves.

"To answer your question, Byron, we're not even sure of that. My father told John that the embroidery on the cloak was a map of the tunnels, so that's why Hellen snuck into the palace yesterday and stole it."

Luhe came back and laid a soft, heavy bundle in her lap. "Thank you, Luhe." She'd held the cloak earlier, let the soft aroma of her father's cologne wash over her when she opened it. How that scent tore her chest open. She'd buried her face in it and cried, smothering as best she could the weird bellowing wails she just couldn't seem to stop. Thank One she'd asked to be left alone.

"Let's all hold an edge of this, and spread it out over our laps." Vartile helped her unroll the soft velvet, turning it so the neck was in her lap, and she could run her fingers over the concentration of embroidery.

Scooting sounds made the circle smaller, and she could feel the energy of six people fill the small space. Breathing and noises surrounded her, murmurs and quiet laughs, scuffling and rustles of clothing as they reached for the edges of the cloak and sat back down. Adia felt the tugs on the neckline in her hands, and tightened her grip. The cloak was heavy, and wanted to sink in the middle.

"Let me get something to hold that up," Luhe said, and got up, coming back in a few seconds with something he slid into the space below.

It helped, and Adia could let go with one hand and feel the embroidery. "Somebody describe what they see," she said.

"It looks like…" Vartile whispered a few numbers. "Ten fingers pointing down from the neck. And that's funny, because they really look like fingers – shorter thumbs on the outside and everything."

"But the pinkies aren't shorter," Beau said from his vantage point. "In fact, they're longer."

"Yeah," said Byron, "they go from short on the side, to longer in the middle, then back up to short on the other side."

"And look," Merv said, "the bottom of this one is cut off, but also keeps going. Into the trim at the bottom. Is the other side like that?"

Luhe said, "Yes, it is. I wonder what that means."

"Do you think there are ten tunnels, Your Majesty?"

Okay, so Cary had finally caught on to the problem, before she had to speak to him about it. Maybe she wouldn't have to have that little talk, after all.

"That's a very good question, Cary." She smiled at him. "I don't know if John said anything to Hellen about that, but I'll find out tonight. Beau will be there, so if I don't see you, you can find out from him."

She turned away and addressed everyone. "If I'm the monastery, then what would be some likely destinations for some of these tunnels? The palace would probably be on my far left, for example, since I can't imagine there'd be a tunnel to the stable, or the mountains behind it."

"All right," Byron said. "If we start on your far left, then the shortest tunnel would go to the palace, and the other tunnels would be so long they'd end out of town."

"That'd be pointless," Beau said. "As someone who's dug a lot of tunnels, I can tell you, you don't want to dig more than you need. I'm going to vote that the palace tunnel is the longest, so it's the pinky, and the others over on your right are the only real tunnels."

"Five tunnels is more believable than ten," Adia nodded. "Let's go with that then, until we find out different. Let's fold this to get a better idea of the layout." They folded and scooted in. "If the palace is the pinky, then where might the others lead? What are the oldest structures still in existence?"

Luhe answered, "The stable in town has one of the oldest buildings."

"The well is from the earliest times, too," Vartile added.

"I think Mad Monk Tavern has some of its original building." Cary's voice sounded like he was getting over his wounded pride, which was good. "They say it was the first tavern in Great Hand, so it might be old enough."

"I think it is," Beau said. "They got some historical landmark designation some years back. The owner was telling me about it, and said the monks blessed the tavern when it was built." He laughed. "I gotta admit, I was skeptical, but maybe they blessed it for a different reason than just thinking a tavern was a great idea."

"Sounds like investigation number one. Cary, can you find out more about the building? Maybe take a look around?"

"Yes, ma'am. I'll do that tomorrow."

"Great. Mad Monk is on the plaza, isn't it? So the well wouldn't be a separate one, but the stable might. Byron, can you check on that?"

"Yes, ma'am."

"Thank you. We have places to start, anyway. Now we should talk about the possibility of Dagge finding the warren, and what we're going to do if he does."

Chapter F.17

Sunset had begun to streak the clouds when Hellen peeked out the front door of the monastery to make sure the coast was clear. Half of her expected to see Dagge's army waiting outside—row after row of men with guns pointed at her, and Dagge standing in front of them, evil smile plastered on his face. Thankfully, he wasn't there. Just the rustling of the breeze, a few frogs, and the sunset.

Hellen secured her knife in its holder under her sleeve, checked the spring release and pulled the sleeve down to cover it. Tonight she would also take a gun, and she might not ever leave home without one anymore, what with all the crazy folk around. Didn't pay to be unprepared.

Wolf whined behind her. He wanted to go, but was still too injured. She couldn't take him inside the wall anyway, so what would he do? Hang around and risk getting shot? "No, Wolf, you have to stay and rest." She bent down and petted his head, then led him to the space under the stairs. "Come on, I want you to stay right here and wait for us. We should be back way before morning. Look, I've got water here for you, and there's this to chew on, see?" She picked up a gnawed end of a chew bone and showed it to him. The big dog looked at her quizzically, then walked over to his pad of old blankets and lay down. "Atta boy." She turned back toward the door. "You bizarrely intelligent cutie-pie, you." At the door, she smoothed the black kerchief on her head, made certain the ends were tucked in, then picked up the laser rifle leaning against the jamb and went out.

Cool night air breathed down from the mountain, chasing away the heat of the day. It whistled through the pyramid, picked up the smell of the birdcage and the horse stall, and brought it right out to her. Shew! Gonna have to do something about that tomorrow.

Her path to the east side of town had gone unused for a long time. Better that way, since at least Dagge wouldn't be likely to stumble on it if he decided to try and visit again. Luckily, she went by landmarks, but she had mixed confidence about remembering one tree from another. "One, please get me where I'm going," she whispered, shouldering the rifle and heading toward the trees.

In the softening light, the forest looked beautiful. The warm glow of the setting sun washed everything in gold, backed on the other side by violet shadows, and it was very much like walking through a fairy tale painting. Warm and inviting on the one hand, scary on the other. Considering everything, she supposed that was appropriate.

Too bad she had missed the council meeting. Now that she'd come back home, she felt in a hurry to catch up on all the months she'd missed so she could move forward. The Resistance needed to find the old tunnels, especially now that Dagge could follow the trail from the monastery to the warren. If they could access the tunnels, everyone could disappear if they had to—the merchants, the miners, everyone— and he might destroy the entire town, but they'd all have their lives, right? They'd have a chance to start over.

But she wouldn't leave Great Hand. She'd never leave, not for good, not until Dagge was dead, or she was. What she really wanted was to take Beau up through the dungeon and put an end to this. Just the two of them, simple and quick. Beau could be trusted to handle himself, and handle whatever came up, including whatever unlucky soldiers currently held Dagge's demons from wherever.

At least she'd killed another one today, which only left three. Most likely, Tomius had kept the last few of his monsters in Great Hand to protect himself. The man did understand the danger of assassination.

Gloom had settled into the spaces under the trees, and only an occasional shaft of gold pierced the forest now. The floor had succumbed to shadows, and Hellen had to pick her way a little more carefully around the roots and gullys. She should have picked up some night glasses from Beau or Cary, but she didn't think of it.

Too bad she'd had to leave so much equipment in Valdia; she'd had night glasses there, along with a laser pistol she really liked. But her carapaz knife was the only thing without metal, and the borders had cracked down on everything since Dagge took over. She'd taped the knife to the underside of her arm, with a thin pad that didn't quite keep her from getting cut. It was worth it.

What to do about her friend Anji? She didn't seem like the type to really function well in a war, unless she was cooking for the troops, or maybe washing sheets and bandages. Sounded sexist, but even that might be too much blood for her. Possibly better to leave her out of it entirely, maybe try to convince her to go back to Valdia. She did say she kept the apartment, so she could do that. At any rate, she was probably wondering why her friend Dolores had disappeared, so a visit was in order first thing tomorrow.

In the meantime, she had to convince Adia, Roberta, and David that the Resistance needed him at the monastery to help find the tunnels.

Good luck with that, Hellen.

Chapter F.18

Dagge stood, bent over, looking in the ice box for something to eat. He'd missed lunch and dinner while he was searching for the ends of the trail, and he wanted to stew in his bad mood by himself. With, say, some cold lamb. He pulled the dish out, grabbed a bottle of milk, and shut the door.

A low-watt bulb burned in the exhaust hood over the stove, and gave enough light for him to see by. Careful to make as little noise as possible—so no one would come try to help him, for fuck's sake—he walked to the long table and set his food down, then lifted the end of the bench to move it out so he could sit. When he sat, a long exhale pushed up out of him, and he sank some.

Why couldn't things be easier? He knew the trail went to the wall on the west side, it had to, but he'd lost it shortly beyond the place where Hellen's prints turned back, and never picked it up again. He'd found where the fight was, between Hellen and his soldier, but he didn't find the soldier—just Hellen's prints heading east from there, and no sign of his. After hunting the area for quite a while, he'd gone on to the wall, and found nothing but several crumpled cigarette packs and a bunch of unidentifiable trash. Not even the harkener turned up anything. A few minutes ago, he'd stood by the rock at the back of the stable again, looking east and hating Monk's Glen.

Grumpy now, stomach growling, he pulled the paper all the way off the dish and laid it aside. Five little lamb chops lay on the plate, next to some shriveled carrots and several sprigs of mint; a pile of roasted potatoes took up the rest. The potatoes were his favorite. Gonna need a fork.

Only, he didn't know where the forks were. Twisting his body, he examined the kitchen for a likely spot, but there were too many drawers, and none of them jumped out at him, screaming pick me. Fuck it.

He turned back to the plate. With both hands, he grabbed a chop and stuffed the tender meat into his mouth. Ginger and pineapple, soy sauce and vinegar and sugar all beat the whangy lamb into submission. With one hand, he popped a couple of potatoes in, letting the butter and garlic blend in as he chewed. Then a carrot, sweet and tender. Two bites to clean the bone, and he moved to the next chop.

As he ate, he felt better, and as he felt better, he decided what to do about Hellen's friends.

Chapter F.19

David got up again to look out the window by the side door. It was dark, and he probably wouldn't be able to see the people coming from the drainage ditch anyway, but he couldn't help himself.

"David, sit down, you're driving me crazy."

His mother's voice had an edge to it, and he knew she was upset about this meeting, so he sat down, determined to make light small talk, and see if he could get her to relax some.

"Joey did well in his lessons today. He's making really good progress in calculus. I'm proud of him."

"That's good," she said, "I'm glad." Slumped in the chair at the far end of the table, she draped one arm outside the armrest, and the other lay on the table, hand flipping a pencil, end over end over end. Talk about driving somebody crazy.

But he refused to bring that up. Some things you just know without trying, and he knew a comment like that would be ill-advised. Instead, he said, "I heard today from Ms. Chokry that Nigus Pomrey has a dying oak he's cutting for firewood this year."

His mother looked at him, and he realized his blunder. "Joey should be able to bargain with him, trade labor for logs, or something. He's really strong…" He let his voice trail off, because the subject was only going to remind his mother that he himself would not be here, and at this point, there wasn't an upside to that.

To be honest, he wasn't sure how well Joey was going to manage by himself. Eighteen years didn't really read on him. More like fifteen, or twelve…probably because he was the baby. He'd been spoiled in a lot of ways, with Dad home, then Mom, and now him. They all did too much for him, because it was easy when they had to do it for the whole family. Consequently, he never learned to cook much, or clean well, or raise the garden from start to finish. He had watched negotiations for trade, but never handled them. Well, it might not be fair, but the kid was about to get a crash course in adulting.

A thud on the side door broke him out of his head, and brought him out of his chair. Before he could move to open it, the knob turned, and the door swung in. On the top step, with one foot coming inside, stood Robert.

"What are you doing home?"

Robert gazed at him, face immobile as he stepped up into the kitchen and closed the door behind him. "It's nice to see you, too, David."

David wanted to punch that sneer right off. Robert had always affected him that way, though, and he'd learned to get past it. "What I mean is that you haven't been home before midnight in a while, so I'm surprised to see you. It's not even 9:30. Did your boss drop your leash?"

"So clever. Probably not worth the three hours you spent thinking it up, but it is your time to do with as you please. You'll have to forgive me if I don't have a snappy retort, but I had to work today."

"Robert…"

"Are you going to take his side again, Mother? Because that would not be a surprise. The surprise is that I'm still allowed to live here. Am I still allowed to live here? Maybe I should actually ask."

"You stop right there!" Their Mom rose out of her seat slowly, both hands on the table, supporting her, and the glower on her face was directed at Robert, thank One. She leaned forward and spoke in a husky, careful voice. "I am your mother, and you will treat me with respect. This is your home, as much as it is any of ours, and I have never, ever acted like you were not welcome here. Even while I have struggled…with the admiration you give the man who tortured and murdered your father."

"Overlord did not shoot Father, some crazy assassin did that."

"Dagge…" she overran the end of Robert's comment, "murdered your father when he had one of his…HORRORS take

148

control of him! DO NOT take me to task over technicalities, Robert, Dagge TORTURED your father and KILLED him!"

Silent, Robert laid a folder on the table, put one hand on the back of a chair, and didn't meet anyone's eyes. "I'm sorry I've disappointed you. It was never my intent. I came home tonight to let you know that a bed has been approved for me in the palace, so I won't be coming home anymore."

David shot a quick glance at their Mom. Her expression was stricken.

Robert started to walk past the table, saying, "I need to pick up some things from my room, then I'll be going."

In a sudden rush, she started pushing chairs aside, and fighting her way around the table to him. David could see the tears glinting in her eyes, and her mouth had contorted into a ghastly frown. Surprised, Robert stopped, and she wrapped her arms around him, pinning his down, and broke into sobs on his chest.

Robert's stunned face would have been funny if their mother hadn't sounded so heartbroken. David felt a little bad for him, because he didn't know it wasn't all his fault, and he looked so awkward trying to pat her with arms that only moved from his elbows down. The two brothers made eye contact, and it was almost cordial.

"What's wrong with Mom?" Joey asked, walking through the den from the foyer doorway. He wore a bathrobe, and combed his wet hair forward, flinging drops of water onto all of them.

"Joey, go comb your hair in the bathroom." David ushered him out toward the guest bath. "Robert's just finally got a room in the palace, so he's moving out."

Joey's head whipped around, a half smile on his face.

"Just go." He nudged Joey into the small space. "Give Mom a minute, you can say goodbye before Robert leaves."

"You know, one of these days, David, you're going have to stop shutting me out of everything. I'm starting to get a complex."

"Right." David nodded, and closed the bathroom door.

Robert walked through the foyer doorway just as David turned to go back. They looked at each other, but nothing was said, and Robert continued up the stairs. David hurried to the kitchen to check the window.

Back in the kitchen, his Mom had collected herself, and stood by the sink, wiping her eyes with a cup towel. David crossed to the window, peered out, and saw nothing.

"I think I should go outside and stop our friends from coming in or knocking when they get here," he whispered.

"Yes, do that. Take them into the back yard, I can't imagine Robert will want to go out there."

"Okay." But before he went out, he took the couple of steps over to his mom and searched her face. "I'm sorry for this, Mom. I really am."

"I know, David." Her red eyes looked up at him. "I'll be fine, don't worry. It'll just take a while."

Joey opened the bathroom door, and brought a drum riff with him back into the den. Mouth wide open, he sang a wild guitar chord, playing the note on his comb, and landed back in the drum riff, all without messing up his hair, David noted. "What are we going to do about Joey, Mom?"

"I haven't decided. Go on, now."

Chapter F.20

Tired, and sad beyond belief, Roberta took a seat at the table while she watched Joey cross the den, lost in some song that played in his head. Her hand stole into her pants' pocket, and fingered the tiny bug she'd slipped in there a couple of hours ago. This morning, and for the last year and a half, the bug had been in the pocket of John's old coat, which still hung in the foyer on a hook, because she'd never been able to get rid of it.

She hadn't thought of the bug since the day she'd used it on John, and had to listen to Dagge torment him and Robert about that bar of music the Resistance had plastered all over town. That had been another one of the worst days of her life; she hadn't been sure whether either one of them would be coming home.

So much happened after that, it was no wonder she'd forgotten the stupid thing. John had opted for the lighter, shorter coat the night he went with Hellen into the forest…the night Dagge caught him and put him in the dungeon. David told her how the thing had taken him, that it had stretched toward his Dad, looking for him, and sliced into his body like a knife. Did he scream? Did it hurt him? She'd been afraid to ask.

Anyway, all that was past now. This morning she'd had three sons, and after tonight, two of them would be gone. There'd been no time to prepare for this, no final year of school, or last summer home from college. Her life kept dwindling, out of her control, out of her ability to repair, and she felt lost in it. What did she have to make her days worthwhile? How did her life get to be all about Tomius Dagge's tonker?

NO. She still had a son. She still had three sons, two of them were just going to be farther away. They weren't dead, for One's sake. And she could put this bug on David and keep tabs on him once in a while. Just to make sure everything was okay. If Dagge found the monastery, she'd know, she could send help. David would forgive her then.

"Joey, come here for a minute, I need to talk to you."

"Sure, Mom." He tossed his magazine aside and got up off the couch to come sit at the table. "What's the brief?"

A quick sigh escaped her. In a quiet voice, so Robert wouldn't hear, she said, "David's leaving tonight." His face fell. "Some friends are coming…they need his help."

In the foyer, Robert's footsteps thudded lightly down the stairs and tapped onto the tile floor. "I think I'm ready," he said, coming through the doorway and crossing the den. He carried a large duffel, which he set on the floor in the kitchen while he fiddled with his keyring.

Roberta stood up, and gestured to Joey to do the same.

Robert held a key out to her and said, "Here's my house key, I thought you might want to have it."

"I don't want to have it, Robert, I want you to have it." She took his big hand in both of her own and folded the key into his fingers. "This is your home, it always will be, and you never know when you may need the key."

He looked down, uncomfortable, as he always had when emotion got too close to him. "If you're certain," he said.

"I'm certain." She patted his hand and released it, and he put the key in his pocket.

"I should say goodbye now." His arms came up in a rare move to embrace her, and she stepped into them. They closed around her, loosely, the squeeze missing. The emptiness of it disappointed her, but she knew what it cost him to allow it. She wrapped her own arms around his back, and grief dripped out of her heart like blood. Their strange child, the one she worried about, the one who never fit in anywhere, how would life be for him? Would he ever be loved?

"Come home sometime, okay? I'll fix something you like for dinner, and you can tell me about…whatever you like."

Robert pulled away from her, his face veiled with that sardonic expression he so loved to wear. "As long as you cook it, and not David," he said. "He oversalts. Joey…" He turned to his youngest brother. "Don't be an idiot, okay? I know it's hard for you, but try."

"You're such an asshat, Robert. I'm glad you're leaving." Joey's face looked miserable, though, and his comment had none of the rancor it usually had.

Robert nodded. "Where's David?"

"He stepped out back. I'll get him." She shoved between Robert and Joey to go to the back door.

"Mother, I can see him on my way out."

"It won't take a sec, Robert, stay right there." Did she manage to keep the shrill out of her voice? She wasn't sure.

The soft night seemed so peaceful after the tension of the kitchen. Stars filled the black sky, and a light breeze found its way between houses and over fences to lift and ruffle her hair. "David!" she hissed.

David's pale face appeared from behind the bushes to the left. "I'm right here," he said, "has Robert left yet?"

"No, he wants to see you."

"Really? Not sure that's actually true."

"David, you go in there right now. It won't take two minutes."

"And," Hellen's voice drawled from the dark, "it will be smarter to play this out well. Wrap it up nice, Davy, and it won't come back to bite you."

"All right, fine," he said, and Roberta could almost hear his teeth gritting. He passed by her, went up the steps and in the door. She followed.

"At least I got to finish school—you'll always be stupid."

"Shut up, Robert! I really am glad you're leaving, you're worse than an asshat! You're a bunghole!"

Robert's laughter bounced over the sound of scraping chairs and Joey's fist pounding on the table. So much for familial bonding, but at least they weren't punching each other in the face. Yet.

"Well, Robert, I see you're leaving with your usual aplomb." David walked directly to the end of the counter, where Robert leaned with his arms crossed over his chest.

"Yes, David, I wouldn't want you to miss me," he said, and turned to face the two of them coming in from the yard.

"We will all miss you." Roberta spoke up loudly, pre-empting any smart remarks from the others. "You're welcome to come home anytime, and if things don't work out at the palace, you will never be without a place to sleep or food to eat." She stopped in front of him, next to David, and watched the two eye each other. "At least shake hands," she urged, ever the teacher.

Relieved not to have to hug, they stuck their hands out and met in the middle. A single shake, and they let go.

"Come on, Joey, you too."

Joey walked up the side of the table and stuck his hand out to his eldest brother. Robert took it, and gazed at Joey's face for a long few seconds.

"Ow!" Joey jerked back and Robert laughed.

"Aw, it wasn't that hard, you baby."

"Are you kidding, Robert?" David put his hands on his hips and frowned. Roberta sensed a problem coming on.

"All right, you three, time for Robert to go. Joey, your room might be the best place for you right now."

"But I didn't do anything! Robert's the one—"

"Joey! Do as I tell you."

Disgusted, Joey stalked off to the stairs.

Robert had picked up his bag and walked the few steps to the side door. Roberta glanced at David, but he didn't seem to be worried, so all their guests must have made it to the back yard.

"Take care of yourself, Robert," she said.

"I will."

"And I meant everything I said."

"I know. Thank you." Robert nodded once and went out the door.

Chapter F.21

Roberta had no idea what they wanted her to say. No, strike that, she knew exactly what they wanted her to say. David, Hellen, and Adia all sat there waiting, but she had nothing but dread and sorrow to give them, and that was definitely not what they wanted. They'd spent the last hour discussing Dagge, and the monastery, and tunnels, and David being needed to help figure it all out, and the truth was, there was only one answer they would accept, and that would be "yes."

To be fair, the Queen hadn't seemed all that enamored of the idea herself. She'd mostly left the talking to Hellen, except when the conversation was about finding the tunnel entrance at the monastery. All the business about how helpful David would be around the house got the silent treatment from Her Majesty. Roberta respected that.

Beau stayed out of it, which was smart, and Roberta envied him the option. David had talked to him about the Resistance; she knew because Beau had mentioned it to her after she started sending the boys for classes. He'd assured her then that he would never encourage either one of them behind her back, and she'd trusted him for it. She still did.

So why couldn't she just say "yes"? Well, there was Joey, and dinner when she came home, and wood chopping, and gardening, and the fact that David saved her sanity every single day. Oh, and let's not forget how half of her family was ALREADY GONE. She fingered the little bug in her pocket again.

"Let me be candid."

Perhaps she should have asked, but she didn't.

"The way I see it, my agreement, or permission, or whatever you want to call it, is just for show. The two of you, and I don't include Adia in this, have already made up your minds. This is what you think is best, and it will happen with or without my consent. Isn't that right?"

David and Hellen, sitting across from her on the other side of the table, looked at each other. Adia, at the end beside Hellen, stayed silent, listening. Beau, next to her, was also silent. Everyone was silent.

"That's what I thought," she said. "I don't blame you, it's perfectly logical for David to go out to the monastery and help. He has the skill set for it. It makes sense that someone should be there for the Queen, since Hellen plans to spend her time looking for tunnel entrances in town. All of that is very well-reasoned, and I cannot argue, so I won't. Joey is eighteen, he's a smart kid, and he'll learn to do whatever he needs to do.

"I do feel, however, that I really don't have a choice, and that you're asking me to sacrifice another family member to this cause. While I believe in the cause—I desperately want to see Dagge defeated and Adia on the throne—you must know that I cannot absorb the loss of my child dying."

"Mom—"

"Then we'll just have to keep Dagge away from the monastery." Hellen rolled over David like a loaded wagon. "We can do that, Roberta, I promise."

"How can you promise that, Hellen?" Her voice started rising, but she couldn't stop it. "You can't promise that. There's no telling what Dagge will do, and he knows something's out there, do you think he's just going to ignore it?"

"No, of course not," Hellen said, "but I really believe that for now he will concentrate on trying to find the warren entrance by the wall. For him, he wins either way, and after today, his main focus will be destroying the fighting arm of the Resistance."

"You're betting my son's life, you realize that. You're betting Adia's life, too. If Adia dies, it's all for nothing, anyway."

"That's why she needs me out there, Mom."

Roberta rested her elbows on the table and laid her forehead in her hands. "Yes, I know it's logical, David. And for the record, I consent. But it hurts my heart to do it."

David got up from his chair and walked around the empty end of the table to give her a hug. Too tall, he got down on one knee and wrapped her up. Laying her head on his broad shoulder, she wanted to cry, but she packed it down her throat instead. Time enough to cry later, when no one was looking.

"Roberta," Beau said when David stood up again, "I should tell you that David has been doing really well in combat training." His voice carried a smile in it. "Only a handful of people have actually managed to throw me, and David is one of those people."

David's face split in a big grin. "Ohh, you let me throw you."

"No, I did not," Beau said with a big smile. "You won that one fair and square—but I credit all those wood-chopping muscles."

"Hey, it's not just muscle, it's skills I got from practicing on Joey for the last fifteen years."

"Now that is believable," Beau replied amidst the general laughter.

"What are you going to tell Joey, Roberta?" Adia's voice was quiet, but there launched the next big question on her must-answer list.

"The truth, if that's okay with everyone. I don't see much point in trying to hide it all from him anymore. Robert isn't coming home, so Joey won't have to remember not to say anything. Blurting was always the danger. Do you have any objections?"

"If you feel like he'll be able to keep the secret, even if he sees his brother, then I have no objection," Adia said. "Is that the case?"

Roberta wanted to say yes. In so many ways, Joey had learned to master his passion, but Robert could aggravate him until he completely lost his cool. And with his cool went all control of his mouth.

"Robert would be the only risk," she said.

"Mom, give me some credit."

Joey's voice spoke up from behind her—she turned to see him walking into the den from the foyer, still in his bathrobe. He stopped at the end of the kitchen counter and leaned against it, facing them all.

"Joey, this is the Queen, please go put on some decent clothes."

"No, Roberta, that's not necessary. I'll pretend I didn't see what he's wearing." Adia grinned at her own joke.

"But, Joey, you do have to bow your head and all that," David told him, pointing at his eyes and nodding.

"Why? She can't see me."

"Joey!" Roberta scolded.

Everyone else laughed nervously, but Adia jumped right in. "That's very true, Joey, but my handlers tell me I have to expect people to do it anyway. And they're quick to remind everyone that they need to, so the sooner you do it, the faster we can talk about what you really want to talk about."

Joey stood straight, bowed his head and closed his eyes without another word.

When he raised his head, Hellen said, "Joey, my name is Hellen—"

"You were here yesterday morning."

"Yes, I was. I came to talk to David about—" Hellen paused.

"About leaving home. Yeah, I heard yesterday. You want him to go out to the monastery, but you said maybe I could go. Can I?"

Glances flew around the table, but Roberta kept her eyes on Hellen, waiting until Hellen's eyes met hers. "Is this true, Hellen?"

"Mom—"

"Hush, David."

"Roberta, I said I would ask, but I didn't. I…had several things happen after I left here, and that question completely slipped my mind."

Never had Roberta felt so out of control of her life. It hurt that Joey wanted to leave, on top of David wanting to leave, on top of Robert wanting to leave, on top of never ever having John again. If Joey went to the monastery with David, she would have a life full of nothing. How would she be able to face Dagge's tonker every day?

"You're all welcome to stay the night," she said, standing and not meeting anyone's eyes. "Robert's bed has fresh sheets, and David, you can get Beau a blanket and pillow for the couch. Please forgive me,

Your Majesty…I'm exhausted, and really must…" Unable to finish her thought, she turned from the table and left the room.

Saturday

Chapter S.1

At first, Hellen's voice seemed to come from a great distance. *Adia*, it said, echoing in her dream, *Adia....*

Adia woke with a start. Hellen was shaking her shoulder, voice impatient in her ear. "What, are you deaf now, too?"

"Ugh, what time is it?"

"It's almost five. We have to get out of here well before daylight, and I let you sleep as late as I could, so now we're in a hurry. Come on."

"Why didn't you get me up earlier?" Adia grumbled as she threw the covers off. "Is anyone else awake?"

"Yeah, David is, and I don't know about Beau, but he probably is."

Adia could hear Hellen moving around the room, and several soft items hit the bed, presumably her clothes. She swung her legs out, sat on the edge and started to unbutton the shirt David had loaned her. Shortly, she realized she wasn't going to make getting dressed without peeing first. Too much lemon water last night.

"I have to pee, really bad. How far down the hall is the bathroom?" A bit disoriented, she stood and felt for the doorway with her arms out in front of her, never her favorite position.

"Watch out, there's a chair there." Hellen's hands held her back, then guided her to the left.

"My mental image isn't really clear."

"No reason it should be," Hellen said. "You're at the door now. The bathroom is three or four steps to the right – perpendicular to this wall."

Ah, good, that helped. Adia put her right hand on the wall and her left hand out in front of her. Hellen's energy faded back with the bedroom.

Carpet felt strange under her feet. She shuffled on it to feel it scrape and tickle her skin as she navigated the hall. The palace had carpet, but she never thought about it when she lived there, so she didn't remember noticing how it felt. The monastery, of course, was all freezing stone, so carpet seemed like the best thing ever right now.

Her left hand bumped the wood door of the bathroom, and it opened. A humid rush of scented air cascaded over her, just before a wall of warm, damp skin pushed into her hand.

"Oh, Your Majesty, I'm sorry, I wasn't looking…"

"It's okay, but could you steer me to the tonker? I'm about to pop."

David paused, and she so wished she could see his face.

"Oh…sure…of course. Here, let me turn the light back on. Um, I guess that doesn't really matter, but here you are." He placed his hand lightly on her back. "No, here." He took her hand and didn't know what to do with it. "Um…"

"Tell me where it is like I'm standing at the bottom of a clock."

"Oh, right! It's at ten o'clock."

"Great, thanks," she said and started walking to the tonker.

"The tonker paper is there to your right, if you're sitting, and magazines…of course you won't need magazines…" His voice trailed off, and by the time she reached her destination, he still hadn't left.

"David, could you close the door on your way out, please?" She turned and stood there facing him, a little exasperated.

"Oh, right!" he exclaimed, and she heard the door shut.

The warmth had mostly gone from the bathroom, but the scent of soap and whatever else it was still lingered. She breathed it in, luxuriating in it. Perfume was an indulgence they didn't have much of at the monastery, and it smelled heavenly.

A sharp knock on the door interrupted her fun.

"Hey," Hellen's voice came in, and Hellen with it. "I brought your clothes, you can take advantage of a hot shower, how does that sound?"

"Oh my gosh, it sounds great."

"I'm putting your clothes on the floor in front of you, and I'll put some good soap on the floor of the shower." Her voice got muffled, the water started, some rummaging, and the shower came on. "Towels..." She pulled back out and started opening cabinets. "Are right here. I'm setting one on the edge of the counter for you. Listen," Hellen bent down and spoke to her face, "I know this is going to feel amazing, but you have to be quick, okay? We have to get out of here, and get through the grate before dawn."

"Yes, alright, I promise I won't dally."

"Super. See you in a minute." Hellen's energy left her space, and the door opened. "Have fun!" Hellen whisper-called, and closed the door.

Adia stripped and stepped into the steaming shower. She hadn't had a hot shower since they left Vartile's a year and a half ago. Cold showers, yes, thanks to the rig Beau had set up for her, and the occasional hot bath when she got ambitious, but hot showers? She didn't know she could be so happy over something so simple.

She let the hot water flow over her head and face; it penetrated her hair and ran in rivulets down her neck and body. Ohhh, she could stand like this forever...wash away the years, the hardship, the grief. All the terrible things that had coated her could just slide off and disappear down the drain.

Her hands came up and worked through her hair, rubbing the scalp, feeling the liquid heaviness down her back. Bending over, she felt around for the soap, and her hand bumped against a bottle. She picked it up and squirted some into her hand—it smelled tropical. Ecstatic, she worked it into a lather and soaped every inch of skin, savoring the aroma. Slick and happy, she rinsed, turned off the faucet, squeezed the water from her hair, and got out.

Two minutes later, she stood in the bedroom doorway, dressed and ready, but with the towel still on her head. "Hellen? Do you think they have a comb I can borrow?"

David's voice surprised her from across the room. "Sure, I have a comb, let me get it for you." He radiated scent and warmth as he neared her, and she found it strangely difficult to move out of his way.

"Excuse me, Your Majesty," he said.

"Adia, you're blocking the doorway." Hellen spoke up from probably the end of the bed.

"Yes, of course," she said, and stepped to the side feeling a little silly. Still, as he passed, she followed him with her nose.

"He says he'll carry you whenever you need him to. If that's okay."

"Yeah, that's okay," she said, as nonchalantly as possible, though it was difficult. Whew, this was getting weird. Admittedly, he'd handled himself very well at the table last night, with his Mom, and the whole situation, but this morning it was like her body and her mind were electrified by him. What the hells did she dream about?

She couldn't remember, everything happened too fast when she woke up. But what she knew was that she felt very happy about the day.

****

David felt like a total clod, and escaped the room gladly so he could regroup. *Cooome oooon.* He never had trouble with girls—one of the upsides of having a sense of humor. Except not so funny today, David. Magazines? What the *hells are wrong with you?*

Seemed like a good idea to close the bathroom door behind him, so he did; he didn't want to feel…audible. Or visible, if Hellen happened to come out of the room, because he needed to

Straighten up! He jabbed his finger at the mirror, then slapped the air in front of it, pummeling his own face like he used to do Joey's. *Still think you're hot snot?* He let his arms fall to his waist, hands toward

163

the mirror, and mouthed at himself, "Oh, and could you close the door *on your way out*?!"

All his air sighed out of him. He was going have to be around her all day, so he needed to get some cool. All day? Try all year, maybe. Or more.

Holy cow.

His comb lay on the counter where he left it earlier. Her Majesty probably didn't want to feel around on a bunch of guys' bathroom counter, and he couldn't blame her for that. He checked himself in the mirror, which was completely pointless, he realized. With a short nod, he turned and opened the door, flipping off the light with the comb in his hand.

In the doorway of Robert's bedroom, the ladies were laughing, which could be bad or good.

Chapter S.2

Hellen buckled her regulation knife onto her regulation belt. Her carapaz knife was already strapped to her arm, but who knew, the army-issue version might come in handy. "I've got some things to do in town today," she whispered, "so I'm only going to take you partway."

The four of them stood in the dark of Roberta's kitchen, trying not to wake Roberta or Joey. David had set his pack on the table for her, next to her rifle, and they waited while Beau finished tying his shoes on the sofa. Adia and David stood together, backed up against the end of the counter, eerily illuminated by a tiny bulb torch David had trained on the floor.

"What? How am I supposed to find the monastery?"

"I have a really great compass; I'll let you borrow it."

"You can't be serious."

"Look, I'd take you all the way if I could, but I have a situation I have to deal with. It's urgent."

"What about my bag?"

"I'll strap it onto your back. It'll counterbalance the front weight."

"Can I help?" Beau joined them in the kitchen.

"Have you ever been to the monastery this way? Through the forest?"

"No," he said, "but I can read a compass."

"I can read a compass!" David retorted.

"Ssshhh!" the others said.

"The thing is, if I'm off by one degree, we could spend all day, all night, who knows how long, searching for the blasted monastery."

"No, you won't," Hellen shook her head. "At worst, I'll come along later and find you. Just stay by the mountain."

165

"I could carry the bag." Beau looked at her from under his eyebrows, like she was passing up a great opportunity, but she already knew that.

Hellen chuckled. "As great as it would be to have you with us all the time, we need you at the warren, to get people moving if Dagge shows up to dig under the wall. I'll come by HQ later to check in, before I go back out to the monastery."

"At least take my night glasses. It'll be easier for you to lead us to the ditch that way. I'll bring up the rear."

She took them with one hand and removed her cap with the other. "I'll give these back at the drainpipes."

"Or later. Whenever."

"Deal." She positioned the goggles over her eyes and replaced her cap. "Let's go then."

David handed Adia his light. "Turn this off by pushing the button on the end as soon as I get down the steps," he told her, and swept her up in his arms. Once he got her settled across his chest, he asked, "Are you ready? Is everything good?"

"Yes, I'm ready," she answered, rather sweetly, Hellen thought.

She turned away to put on David's bag and hide her smile. One arm went in the shoulder strap, then she turned to face them again, and put the other arm in, so the bag would hang on her back. Adia fiddled with the bulb torch, shooting the beam all over the kitchen. Hellen grabbed the rifle off the table, reminding her, "Don't forget to point the light down so David can see the steps."

"Right," Adia said, and the light pointed down. "Are you sure you won't need this when we get outside?"

"Nah," David said, "there's nothing difficult between here and the drainage ditch, I know the path well."

His light laugh made Hellen curious, but they didn't have time for stories. She opened the side door from the kitchen and peered outside. The sky was just beginning to lighten in the east, but the houses and trees in the neighborhood were swathed in black. Perfect.

Two wooden steps led down to the yard, and at the bottom she stopped to wait for David. He navigated the doorway, holding Adia off to the side a little so he could see the steps. Adia kept her light down, but the little round island shone on the grass, and Hellen turned Adia's hand so David could see. When he made the yard, Adia doused the light. Beau came last and closed the door behind him. Without speaking, they hurried toward the sunrise.

****

When they reached the drainage ditch, David set the Queen on the side and jumped down into the water. Crap, he didn't even think of that; spring and early summer brought more runoff from the mountains, and the creek bed would probably be full. Oh well, no help for it.

"Do you need the light?" the Queen asked.

Dawn loomed behind the wall, turning the low sky orange and giving enough light that David could make out faces, bodies, and the stones lining the drainage ditch.

"No, but turn around and let Beau lower you by your hands. I'm going to try to catch you so you don't have to get in the water."

"Is it deep?" She sounded perturbed.

"Sh!" Hellen, already in the ditch, shushed them. "Just let her down, Beau. Adia, it'll be safer this way, patrols won't expect anyone in the water."

"I'm not worried about safety," Adia retorted, holding Beau's hands as she backed down into David's waiting arms. "It's that wonderful shower that's going to waste."

With his Queen's rump first and foremost in his reach, David hesitated, not sure where to put his hands.

"Adia, David's going to have to grab you, okay?"

"Okay, okay, just don't let me fall," she hissed over her shoulder.

David cupped her hips on either side and steadied her while her feet slipped and scrambled down the paving stones. Up top, Beau knelt to keep hold of her hands until she got low enough that David could catch her against his chest.

"See, it's not that full, you're still going to smell great." Oh, sure, he just touched her butt, why not talk about how great she smells? He could add that to the epic list of idiotisms he kept making.

"Thank you," she said, not at all offended, if he could judge by her exposed white teeth. He smiled back before he remembered she couldn't see it.

"That's what I'm here for," he said, settling her more comfortably against his chest.

"Are you guys done now?" Hellen's wry amusement derailed all attempts at charm. No problem, though, he'd turned the corner, he could feel it.

Beau handed down the rifle, dropped into the water beside Hellen and said, "Let's go."

The water in the ditch was only knee deep, but they had to be careful not to make splashing noises as they walked. Patrols would become a problem when they got nearer the big drain pipes. There, silence would be doubly useful, since the soldiers usually talked. By Beau's calculations, the patrols in the area should be far enough away that they could make the grate without being seen. However, the soldiers weren't always strict about the schedule.

David had told them all about the grate after Joey had stormed off to bed, angry that David wouldn't let him go to the monastery. How could he let him go, when Mom had been so upset? But all Joey could see was that Mom was hardly ever home anyway, and he'd have to take care of everything. Why couldn't she move to the palace like Robert? "They always need maids," he'd said. The kid had no clue about some things.

After that, telling Hellen about Dad's grate opening had salvaged the night. Beau was happy, too, because it meant they could get more people outside the wall if Dagge found the warren. And good thing they were making this trip to the monastery, because it might be important for more people than just Hellen to know the way.

Ahead, Hellen's hand waved him to stop, and he crouched instinctively. The Queen's weight threw him a little off balance and she gasped. Hellen stepped back toward him and pressed her finger over the Queen's mouth. She nodded.

Not far up the ditch, two voices argued on the bank.

"I don't care what you think you heard, Tony, we're not gonna be working the mine."

"Oh yeah? And what makes you think you know? Did Overlord talk to you? Did he come down to your room and say, Vizo, I wanna talk to you about something."

Hellen's face had turned away from him, but he could tell by her posture that she was listening. Her head shook, and she waved them to follow her over to the side closest to the soldiers. She hunkered, so he did, too. The Queen's arms tightened around his neck.

Only about twenty strides separated them from the big storm drain outlets, and Hellen clearly wanted to get them there as fast as possible. Luckily, the rush of creek water across the ends of the pipes created enough splashing to cover their progress. Lucky, since the voices got closer.

"Don't be a dick," Vizo said, but that was all David heard because he was too focused on not getting his fool ass caught.

Three soldiers' heads came into view just before he made the cover of the first pipe end. Behind him, Beau stepped past his bulk and ducked in, too. David stood there, trying not to breathe audibly. The Queen tapped his arm and made to get down. Concerned, he released her and watched her carefully, but she just backed farther into the pipe, her hand on the far wall.

Above, the voices came right to the edge of the embankment, and he and Beau both backed up a little.

"I'm telling you," Tony kept talking, "the Captain's room is right by the lav. When ya gotta piss, ya gotta piss, and I heard what Wharton was saying."

"You heard him say every man in town? Starting today?"

"Now, I didn't say today. Probly the slips won't be going out til this afternoon, but whenever it is—today, tomorrow, next fucking week—these asshole townies got no idea what's coming." A girly chuckle floated out over the ditch, just before a thin stream arced through the air and into the water, producing a solid, ongoing gurgle. Shortly, a second stream joined it, and the discussion continued.

"That means more guard duty at the mine, don't it?" This question came from a third voice.

"Yeah, I reckon. I hear Overlord's fed up with that bullshit stuff exploding. He may be planning to just kill all the men in town. You know, get em all out there and mow em down, then there won't be nobody to blow up the damn mine. And then we'll have to do all the work."

"That's stupid," Vizo argued. "I'm telling you, we ain't gonna have to work the mine."

The first stream trickled off, spurted, then a zipper went up. The second stream dwindled, followed by a second zipper. A cigarette flew out over the ditch, bounced off the far side in a small shower of sparks, and landed in the water. The three voices faded away.

"You know, Tony, you don't know everything. Why do you always have to act like you got all the answers?"

"Because I do have all the answers, Guindo."

"No, Tony, you really don't."

A hand touched David's shoulder from behind, making him jump. He turned, and in the dim light, barely made out Hellen gesturing for them to come closer. Beau moved around to his right and stood next to Hellen, and David drew closer to the Queen, who still stood by the wall, her feet in the swirling water.

****

As much as she hated to give them up, Hellen took off Beau's night glasses and handed them to him. "Beau, will you watch until we get through the grate, just in case?"

170

"Of course I will. And keep those until later."

"You'll need them more than I will, it's dark down here." She pressed them into his hand.

"How far is the grate?" Adia asked.

All three of them turned to look, then Beau answered. "Forty strides, give or take."

"We need to hurry," Adia said. "Beau, as soon as we're through, head back to the warren and mobilize everyone. Block the tunnel under the wall, and as many secondary tunnels as you can, especially the ones to people's homes. Let's make him work for it. Move supplies to NHQ and points north. Hellen, if you're coming back to town, you'll need to get Cary and Firio to buckle down on searching for the other tunnel openings. We have to get as many people to safety as we can."

"I know those guys, Adia. They're the patrol I snuck away from that day! And coming from Tony, that information is not reliable."

"But we can't afford to risk it. Dagge could easily do a sweep of the entire town, round up all the men for mine labor. He knows that would cut the Resistance in half, demoralize us, and leave the rest of us to defend HQ once he starts digging. And he will start digging now, don't doubt it."

"Should we stay here? Help in town?" David asked.

"No, we need to find the tunnel access at the monastery—tunnels won't be very useful if no one can get out." She gave Hellen's wrist a squeeze. "Hellen, I don't know what to tell you about your friend. I know you want to help her, but I don't see how we're going to be able to do that, given the situation."

"I know. I'm going to tell her to go back to Valdia. It's not safe here."

"We'll bring her back when this is over, I promise. Now, we should go."

"Charming, you got this?" Beau asked.

"Not my name." David's arm went behind the Queen's legs, and she stopped him.

"Your name is Charming?" Her forehead was scrunched.

"Sadly, yes."

Adia smiled. "I bet we can find a better one."

"Ma'am, I am ready for a better name."

"Let's work on that then. Whoever you are, you're going to need your hands, and I can make it to the grate from here."

"Are you sure?"

"Yes, I'm sure."

It came across as a bit summary, and Hellen felt a little bad for David as he moved away.

David didn't say anything, just turned and led the way out of the drainpipe. Hellen knew that Adia had simply switched to command mode, but he probably felt a little blindsided, which was understandable. He had to get used to it sometime.

Hellen took Adia's hand and tucked it into the crook of her right arm. "Stay down," she said, and they followed David out.

The bag on her back made the trip awkward, and Hellen found herself wishing she'd moved it to her left shoulder while they were in the pipe. Too late now, though, they didn't have time to stop. She shifted it the best she could, but it still kept bumping and sliding between them. At least the bottom of the ditch was level, so Adia could navigate without that much help.

At the wall, David stopped, and they ducked low. Hellen took the opportunity to shrug the bag off her shoulders and take a look around. In the increasing light, she could see the beginnings of details, and the grass and weeds around the ditch were looking green instead of grey. Halfway around her slow circle of observation, she saw one of the patrol guards walking back to the ditch. Maybe it was Guindo—he looked bigger than the other two, but she couldn't be sure. Hellen moved Adia between her and David, and handed over David's bag.

"Here, take this." She wrapped Adia's arm around it. "David, what's the problem?"

"The latch won't work. There's probably dirt in it."

"Get it to work, we're about to have company." The dark sides of the ditch and the forest beyond the grate would help them blend in until the guard got close, but if he happened to look up, and in the right direction, they were sunk. Hellen looped her rifle strap over her right shoulder and flipped off the safety, just in case. Always mindful these days, she reached and laid her hand on the Queen's cheek. Adia pressed it to her with one hand and leaned into it. It was as much of a goodbye as they were going to get.

David swore under his breath, jiggled the grate, and it opened. With a glance back, he moved Adia under the wall, tangling for a second in the branches and leaves floating past their legs. David's bag in her arms, Adia fought the current, which was much deeper and faster through the narrow passageway. David stayed close behind, bracing her with his hands on her shoulders, steering her through the gate and to the side where she'd be blocked by the wall. Hellen could hear him whisper something before she pushed the gate closed behind him. She dug the compass out of her pocket, and stuck it through the grate. David leaned forward, his dark clothes nearly invisible against the backdrop, thank goodness, and reached across her to grab the latch and raise and lower it so she would know. As he leaned back again, he scooped the compass out of her hand, and she hissed "East southeast."

With a quick swipe of latch-dirt onto her face, Hellen turned, snatched a floating glob of sticks out of the water, and started walking toward Guindo. All 250lbs. of him walked on the grass toward the ditch, maybe thirty strides away. Unfortunately, she happened to be looking at him when he looked up and saw her. She prepped herself to talk her way out.

"Hey, what are you doing?" he hollered over at her.

"Cleaning the sticks out of the grate," Hellen said.

Guindo stopped and stood on the bank where the creek ditch met the drainage ditch. He stared at her, cradling his rifle in his arms.

"It's clogged," she said, "I'm going to go outside and clear the debris."

"I don't think so. You're gonna come identify yourself, or you're gonna be wearing a big ugly hole in your head."

That struck her as a convincing argument.

173

Those two better be hightailing it up the creek.

Chapter S.3

David turned to the Queen to pick her up. The water, no longer held back by the dam of sticks and leaves at the grate, had made a wave up to her shoulders in its hurry to get out. She shook and her lips were deep purple, and so much for that shower she'd been happy about. He really wanted to wrap her up in his arms, but should he?

"Your Majesty, let's get you out."

"Yes, that would be s-s-splendid," she said.

Her arm stretched up to go over his head, and he bent his chest into the water to put his arm behind her legs. She tried to help him by jumping, but she got caught in the current instead, and he had to catch her to keep her from slamming the grate. Her arm tightened around his neck until she was practically on his shoulder, leaning on his head so for a few seconds he had a hard time keeping his balance in the anxious flow of water.

Once he turned upriver, they got it sorted out (*can you say upriver even though it's a creek?*), and in his arms she relaxed some, in spite of still shivering. Too bad he wasn't warm and dry for her, but oh well. Better than the water.

A few steps up the creek bed, and he realized too many rocks and holes made it stupid to continue; he'd be going down and taking her with him. All forward motion faded to the right, and when he reached the bank, he stood with her feet facing it.

"We need to get out and walk, the creek bed is too dangerous. But it'll be better—we'll get dry, your lips will go back to their normal color, and I won't be dunking us in the water."

"Yes-s, okay." She nodded, and tensed. "Where do I go?"

"Forward, I'll lift you up, and…"

175

He checked the bank above her. Not likely he'd be able to talk her through that, so he said, "You hang on until I can climb up and help you from the top."

She leaned forward as he lifted her to the bank. "Handholds at two and eleven, feet at eight and…two? Can you do two?"

"Are you crackers? Come on."

"Okay, six then, or five-forty-five-ish."

They got her hands to the right spots, and he helped her with her feet, then he scoured the side for a climbing spot for himself.

"David!" her voice cried, and he turned to see her grappling for a hold with her left hand, fingers scoring the dirt, breaking clods off that went crashing into the water. "It broke, and I can't—"

Her arm swung wide as one foot slid down the bank into the water, pulling her other foot down as well. David rushed up to her and caught her before she fell all in. Both of her arms went around his neck, and she hung face to face with him. Her nose felt like an ice cube on his cheek; warm breath came short and quick underneath it; icy skin chilled him through their wet clothes, and he pressed her to him without thinking. Her cold cheek nuzzled into the warmth of his neck, and he willed his body heat into to her. In a few seconds she stopped shivering and leaned back again, her sightless eyes wide and dark in the lavender shade, wet tendrils of hair stuck to her cheeks and forehead. The scar on her face looked purple, and reminded him of one of those flowery paintings by Verneuse.

"Can you help me from the bottom?"

"Yes, I can certainly do that, Your Majesty."

"Thank you," she sighed. "All right, I'm ready."

Her hands went up again, and he got her situated, then hesitated before the actual pushing, because…

"David, will you just put your hands on my butt?" Her voice had an edge of impatience that reminded him of his mother.

"Yes, ma'am," he said, planted a palm on each cheek, and vaulted her up. He could hear her laughing as her legs disappeared over the rim.

By the time he managed to climb the bank, and land himself on the ground beside her, she looked pretty normal—color in her cheeks, lifelike lips …and some kind of a smile. When it came to women, it wasn't always easy to know what kind, but he decided to believe it was a good kind.

"Ma'am, what are you smiling about?"

****

To be honest, Adia didn't know why she felt so tickled. She should probably be worried about Hellen, but she'd spent so much worry in the last three years, and it never did any good for anyone. Thank One, Hellen had always proven her fears wrong, so for the moment she allowed a little happy.

"That whole 'launch up to the top of the bank' was fun. I felt like I was in a slingshot."

Her thoughts went a little errant as the mental image of him in a wet shirt flashed through her mind, his hair dark with wet and the thin fabric clinging to him, revealing everything.

Whew. No kidding.

He laughed a little and said, "I aim to please, Your Majesty. I'll let my mother know all that wood chopping has not been in vain."

"Please do, it's important for parents to know they're making a difference."

"Absolutely."

The smile in his voice made her picture even white teeth, and John's twinkling eyes. How she wished she knew what he really looked like.

"Are you ready to go?" he asked.

"Yes, I believe I am." She tried not to sound too enthusiastic. "Same old, same old?"

"Same old, same old," he said, raising her right arm and sweeping her up on the opposite side from the way it was earlier. "You know, you're really helping me out."

"How's that?" she snorted.

"Gotta balance my workout," he said, and started walking. "I make Joey do all the carrying when we chop firewood, so my carry muscles are all out of shape. Yeah, it's a shame to be unbalanced like that, so I might ought to carry you three times a week or something. With your permission, of course."

"Of course," she nodded quickly, "and as much as I would really like to help," (and she might just do it), "do you think my handlers would approve of me being used as a workout tool?"

"Hm, perhaps not. They're sticklers, aren't they?"

"Ye-es," she drawled.

"I guess I'll just have to find a different way then...but you never know when you might need to walk out in the woods. For something important, you know, like flowers."

"Exactly." In fact, she suddenly perceived quite a few flowers in her future.

Chapter 5.4

Hellen waded up the ditch, making as much noise as possible, trying to draw Guindo's attention with exaggeratedly moving her gun strap off her shoulder and holding it up in a surrender posture. "It's me, Brucella! Brucella TaSwinn, remember?"

"You ain't TaSwinn. She had dark hair, and wasn't so skinny as you."

"Aw, I know," she said. "I got sick, and lost a bunch. And I bleached my hair."

"You bleached your hair?"

"Yeah, just for grins. Blondes have more fun, right?"

Guindo squinted at her as she walked across the shallower water backflowing into the ditch toward town, and up to the bank opposite, where he stood.

"I don't know about that," he said, with zero humor. And after staring down at her for another couple of seconds, he said, "Brucella TaSwinn disappeared into the forest way over a year ago, and we ain't heard of her since."

"I didn't disappear," she said, like she'd heard this story a million times. "I told you I thought I saw something, and I did. I went to the palace and told the Overlord."

"You did not." He ridiculed the very idea.

"I did!"

"What could you possibly have seen that would get you even in the same room, even in the same building as the Overlord?"

She glanced around like she thought someone else might hear her, then she gestured for Guindo to lean closer. He squatted, skepticism all over his face.

"I saw where those freaky soldiers of his came from. No kidding, Guindo, I left you and Vizo and Tony right there at that gate, and something led me back into the woods. I kept going and kept going, and I found a hole in the ground. I saw one going back down into it."

Not true, but planting rumors could be very useful.

"A hole to where?" He grimaced, kind of a cross between confused and horrified, but at least he wasn't questioning her identity anymore.

"I don't know," she said, and hung her rifle on her back so she could climb out. "I didn't get close enough to look." Hands on the rocks, she started up. "But after I told Overlord, he sent me to Pulari. I only got back two days ago." A hand appeared in front of her face as she pulled herself past the top of the rock-paved side. She grabbed it, and Guindo hauled her to her feet.

"Thanks," she smiled and rubbed her nose on the other side with her other, newly disgusting hand.

"Bruce, you got dirt all over your face now."

"Do I?" Ha ha.

"Yeah, it's on your nose…"

She reached up with both hands and tried to brush it off. Uh huh.

"Aw, you're just making it worse," he said, shaking his head and hanging his rifle on his back.

Hellen had a brief crisis when he stepped up to the edge of the ditch and unzipped his pants. What do women soldiers do when a man soldier pulls his dick out? Depends on the people involved, no doubt. Probably not look. She swung her gaze over to Vizo and Tony, who stood some distance away, arguing.

"I'm going to walk over there to Vizo and Tony," she said, taking a few steps.

"Not yet, you're not." Guindo's stream hit the water behind her. "You never explained what the hells you're doing out here."

"Didn't I?" Well, crap. "I'm looking for you." She turned back toward him, sort of. "I've been assigned to your patrol again."

"Is that a fact?"

180

"Yeah! And I'm glad, I got tired of all that bullshit in Pulari. They're all dumb as stumps."

Guindo tucked it in and his zipper went up.

"Say, what's the story on the rebels here?" She changed the subject before he could grill her anymore about her nonexistent orders.

He turned toward her, his brows frowning and the left side of his mouth in a sneer. "There's no story, what are you talking about? They're just a bunch of lame-ass pretenders. They cause trouble once in a while, but it's pointless. Overlord's going to have the whole world before he's done, and there ain't nothing they can do to stop him."

Something in her gut shifted and she felt sick. All the progress she'd made, killing his evil undead, and Guindo was right, it could mean nothing in the end. Oh, they could always imagine how much worse it might have been, but if they couldn't stop Dagge from marching through country after country, killing people, hanging their bodies in public places, then what was the point?

Obey or die? Maybe, but also Obey and Die. When it came down to it, she'd rather die fighting than rot from the inside out.

"Who you got, Guindo?" Tony's voice called over to them as they neared.

"It's TaSwinn. She says she ain't been disappeared at all, just over to Pulari."

"Oh yeah?"

"She don't look like TaSwinn. TaSwinn had dark hair, and it was longer." Vizo's finger traced a line back and forth over his shoulder, like they might be confused about what he meant with the word "longer."

"I cut it, Vizo, and bleached it."

"You bleached your hair?" they said in unison.

"Shut up, alla you," Guindo barked. "We got to hurry back to the plaza now so we won't be late for shift change."

The other two waited for Guindo to pass them and take the lead. Vizo turned after him, and then Tony…after a good, solid look at her.

181

"Hey, Tony, how's it going?" With a short nod, Hellen fell in at the back of the group, insanely grateful that their shift was almost up.

Chapter 5.5

Harkener in hand, Dagge strode quickly across the west meadow toward the place where the rock outcropping nearly met the wall. Maybe he could catch a few early birds underground, and if one or more of them happened to use the exit, all the better. Because if word was out about the mine recruitment today, there should be plenty going on in the fucking insurgency.

He'd thought about asking Wharton to come with him this morning, but decided against it. So far, he still wanted to keep his plans close. Except for the obvious stuff, like putting out the call-to-work slips. Master stroke, if he did say so himself. Noncompliance meant death, and what was not to love about that?

To his left, a fair distance away, stood the remains of his last run-in with the rebels—a graveyard of partial walls, charred edges, and a single plank giving the finger to the sky. Somehow, that really spoke to him.

No one on the grounds actually saw the person who drove the fireworks wagon into the barracks, and how was that possible with so many people around? He'd interrogated soldiers and servants for hours, and got nothing.

Never would he host another big party. Too many people, too many opportunities for things to go wrong. The night had been going so well, too—five-star food, lots of good wine (or so he heard), the limerick poet—but it sucked in the end, thanks to Hellen. And her doomed friends. All her fucking, doomed friends.

Well, he'd teach them some respect. He'd just been too busy, taking over two countries and manufacturing weapons. But now that things were rolling, he could take care of this little "problem at home." (Someone in Valdia had actually said that, but they wouldn't be saying anything else, would they? People needed to learn to mind their own business.)

The fringe of evergreen trees straggled out toward the end of the outcrop. A few pines dotted the space between the rock and the wall, and that was where he headed. Damned bold of those fuckers to sneak right through his yard this way. Maybe he should get some dogs for patrol detail. Wouldn't that surprise them?

He veered toward the wall and turned on the harkener, holding the small dome up to his ear and the silver dish toward the ground in front of his feet. Facing the wall, he swung the dish back and forth in slow arcs as he walked among the trees. At first he heard nothing, then in a westward sweep, he picked up a hammering noise...or a chopping noise.

A pick, perhaps. Two. No, three. Were they digging a new tunnel?

Back toward the outcrop it faded, and there were other sounds...scraping, mostly. Bumping. Toward the town it faded.

A slight adjustment to the right gave him voices. He tightened the focus on his harkener and turned up a quiet conversation between a man and a woman.

"What if we don't find the tunnels? "I'm terrified," the woman said in a wailing whisper, "that we won't get away, none of us. That Dagge will catch us." She paused, and when she started talking again, he could hear panic edging her voice. "We'll be hanging on poles, all around the plaza, like he did with the Newhili family, and all those others. Dying slowly, some of them. Eaten by crows. One help me, Luhe, I can't see myself managing torture. I just can't!"

Wails burst out of her then, and the man shushed and comforted.

"Hey...hey...I promise you, Vartile, I will borrow a gun and shoot us both if it looks like that's going to happen. I promise, okay?" A pause while the only sound was muffled crying. "Besides, we're going to find the tunnels. David's gone out there, and they won't rest until they find them, you know that. If it looks like Dagge's getting too close before then, we can take our chances in the woods."

Dagge turned quickly and started back toward the palace. No doubt the wife would agree, but it didn't matter either way, because sometime soon they would both die. This morning he'd send a patrol to this part of town. Ask some questions, take some names.

If they were so confident they could get to the woods, there must be another way to get outside the wall. Probably near the forest, plus no telling where else. He knew he was right about Treslo. It was a good thing he got rid of him. Though technically, Hellen got rid of him, and that little irony always made him smile.

The important thing, and it could be very important, was the knowledge that there were secret tunnels "out there," and the traitors were looking for them.

"Out there" could only be one place. That fucking forest. All the more reason to burn it down.

The upside was the fear he could already taste in the air, because they knew he was coming for them.

How he loved his harkener.

Chapter 5.6

Roberta hurried down the soft carpet in the silence of the big hall. On her left, the royal staterooms kept their secrets—a long line of closed doors surrounded by ghosts. She could feel them in the cool shadows, between the stained-glass skylights and their stretched color patterns on the wall.

Her wooden bucket swung against her left leg, filled with bottles of nicely deodorized spray, paper wipes, and her towel. A blue work dress hung plain and simple to her calves, her shoes were sensible, and her apron lay folded over her shoulder. If anyone saw her, she was just going to clean Dagge's bathroom.

Cookie told her as soon as she came in that he'd left early, carrying his "infernal listener." Roberta had grabbed her stuff and headed upstairs, not even bothering to don her apron. No time like the present to do what she needed to do, and she might not have much time to do it.

The dark rectangle of the small servants' hall came up quickly, and she turned into it and stopped. Bending her knees, she set the bucket on the floor so she could dig in her left pocket, and used her right hand to pull the apron off her shoulder. Her fingers ran along the bottom seam of her pocket until she located the bug, and she took it out and held it between her index finger and thumb. The bit of sticky tack she'd put on adhered to her thumb and she left it while she put on her apron and picked up the bucket. After one last check down the main hall, which was empty, she half ran to the servants' doors, and instead of turning left into Dagge's room, she turned right into the sitting room.

None of the servants, except Diit, were supposed to go into the sitting room. Diit cleaned and fetched, and Wharton came up sometimes for meetings, but for the most part, Dagge guarded his lair with teeth and claws. "No servants" had been the rule since before she worked here, so if she got caught, there was always the possibility that Dagge might kill her. He'd killed people for less.

A high sunrise streamed through the balcony doors and suffused everything in orange-yellow. Two large, white columns dominated the middle of the room to her left, and a strange arrangement of furniture inhabited the space to the right. Between the two areas, and around the columns, were miscellaneous statues and urns and decorative things. The overall impression was a mess, but not because it was messy. More…haphazard, perhaps. An interesting illustration of Dagge's mind—cluttered and chaotic on the one hand, but with shelves along the walls that were neatly ordered, and nothing out of place on the carpets or floor.

Across the room, in a shadowy alcove, the dim outline of a large desk beckoned to her—just the sort of place she was looking for. If she had to, she could hide behind the chair or duck under the desk, and maybe he wouldn't see her at all before he went to the balcony, or the bathroom, or wherever. *Sigh.* Who was she kidding? But the intel would be worth it for the Resistance. Forewarned is forearmed, as they say. No telling how many lives this might save. In hurried strides, she navigated the statues and urns, crossed the aisle of light next to the opposite wall, and slipped gratefully into the twilight of the alcove.

Eyes on the desk, Roberta veered for the chair and brushed against a curled strip of fabric dangling from the wall. It caught on her arm, and she lifted it free with her hand, feeling the thick paint. Surprised, she stepped away from the wall and looked at the painting of the King. His likeness held together in strips and threads, the kind face mutilated like some horror show. One large eye gazed at her, the other was a blind, gaping hole. Grief stabbed through her and she flinched, rattling the contents of her bucket.

As if every other thing in this kingdom wasn't enough to satisfy this monster's appetite, he had to deface even the portrait of King Som Beldenet. The anger and pettiness of it appalled her. Dagge won, and it still came to this. Somewhere inside her, the well of resolve hardened even more, and she turned her attention back to the desk.

The tall chair was spun toward her and after a moment's pause, she sat. On the right, the bottom drawer was half open, and inside Roberta could see a pair of handcuffs, and a bunch of stuff she couldn't identify. Otherwise, the desk gave nothing away—the drawers were closed and top was clean as a whistle. Nothing like her own desk at home, which couldn't boast a bare inch, what with all the books, and papers, and calendar planners she never could bring herself to throw away after the university closed.

Not even a lamp she could attach the bug to. Or a pencil cup, or any other innocuous thing. It would have to be under the lip, or in the top drawer, perhaps. She pulled out the shallow one in the center, and found a haphazard assortment of pens, wrinkled scraps of paper, clips, a few envelopes addressed to OL Tomius Dagge, and a thick white piece of painted rubber.

On the top of the rubber, toward the edge, a blue balloon knot stuck up out of the paint. Roberta pulled it toward her to look at it. From the darker recesses of the drawer, more blue was dragged forward, and in the light Roberta could make out the Thorn emblem, drawn on the balloon with brown marker.

Seeing this evidence of John hit her in the heart. Internal bleeding filled her lungs, and every body cavity she had. Why would Dagge keep this? As a reminder of his failure? What kind of sick mind wants that?

Or maybe it's a reminder to hate. To seek revenge, even.

"Mother, what are you doing here?"

Robert's voice launched Roberta right out of her skin. Her hand shoved the balloon back into the drawer without her mind being involved. Jumping out of the chair, she faced her son, who had hurried into the room from the doorway.

"Robert! You scared me." She tried to laugh it off.

"I don't know what you're doing in here, but you need to get out right now. Overlord will be back any minute, and if you get caught in here, he'll kill you. I can't believe I caught you snooping in his desk."

"I wasn't snooping."

"When you're looking through someone's private space, it's called snooping." Roberta opened her mouth to speak, but Robert cut her short. "I don't want to hear it. Out, right now. I'm going to put these requisitions on the desk, and when I turn around, you need to be gone."

Roberta locked eyes with Robert, and saying nothing, scraped the bug off her thumb and onto the side of the drawer while she pushed it closed.

And that was when Tomius Dagge walked in.

Chapter S.7

Adia hung her arm lackadaisically around David's shoulders and let him do all the work. She wanted to see how long it would take him to say something, because he was panting and sweating. It was a test, she had to admit. Even sweaty, the feel of his hair on her arm was luxurious, and his muscles made an excellent chair.

"Um, Your Majesty, is something wrong with your arm?"

"No," she frowned, and glanced her non-functioning eyes up at it like she was checking to be sure it hadn't, you know, gotten hurt somehow. "It's just fine. Why?"

"Because it's just hanging back there, and I thought maybe your muscles gave out or something. Are you feeling weak? Do you need a drink of water or some rest?"

"Oh, no, I'm fine." She opened both hands into the air, and let them drop down.

David tripped and lurched forward, sending Adia's heart into her throat, and she seized his neck with both arms, tensed her body and hung on for dear life. So much so, that she'd wrapped herself around his head and under his chin, and didn't even notice when he dropped his hands away.

He stopped his forward motion, stood for a few moments, and said, "You all right?"

"Yeah." She relaxed a hair, onto her forearm on his shoulder, then down his chest some...

And he started walking, arms swinging at his sides.

"I kind of like it this way, it's a lot easier to keep my balance on these tree roots. Excellent idea, Your Majesty."

Part of that was muffled by her chest as she shifted her grip to accommodate not being able to hold her legs up. As they sagged, she turned her body to face him, until she hung from his neck, futilely trying not to drop. "David!" she half-cried out, half-scolded.

"What? Is it hard to do that by yourself?" His voice spoke down to the top of her head, and her face bumped repeatedly into his chest as he walked. "Yeah, I can see how that might not be comfortable. Here, let me help you!"

Pausing for a moment, he worked one arm between them, up under her legs, and shrugged her into place. Her own arms stayed around his neck snug and tight, and he landed her on his chest and started walking again.

A few strides later, she said, "I suppose I should thank you for helping me out back there."

"If you like."

"I do. Thank you."

"You're welcome. I'm more than happy to do it."

His voice sounded so sincere, it made any more comment unnecessary. For a second she wanted to lay her head on his chest, against his neck, and she almost did, but she stopped herself in the nick of time. Day two—let's not forget it's only day two—was way too soon for that kind of intimacy. What was she thinking?

She changed the subject. "Dad said we should always thank the people who help us." Pause. "He thought a whole lot of your Dad, you know."

"Yeah, I think he did." David grunted, stepping over something. "My Dad admired yours, too. He always wanted be the kind of man your father could depend on, and I'm glad for him that he was. For both of them, really."

"Yeah," she said. "I'm glad I got to know your Dad a little. I wish you'd been able to know mine."

"I do, too, Your Majesty."

"It's hard having lost them, isn't it?"

"In every way imaginable."

A deep sigh rose up out of her gut, gasping for air with every intent of it blowing back out, but in the big middle of it, her own spit sucked into her lungs and she had to cough, sounding like she was dying, with her face at her armpit so she wouldn't cough on him. "Sorry," she croaked when she could get enough air.

"I'd pat you on the back, but I figured if I tried to bounce you up and down on my hand, it might not be that great. Would you like me to stop? I'll stop."

He set her feet on the ground, and she bent over, hands on her knees, and cleared her throat. How attractive.

"There is nothing around you for eight feet or so. The closest potential ground hazard is a tree root in a gully, and that would be to your…seven o'clock, if you're the middle of the clock."

"Okay, great," she said, pleased that he knew the clock thing. "And otherwise I'm clear?"

"For eight feet. In any direction."

"So if I walk nine feet this way…"

"You'll go down a hill, and possibly roll into a tree. Or a bush."

She stopped, nodded, and sauntered back the other direction. "This way?"

"A tall set of rocks."

Tall rocks? Her interest threw in like a set of knives, and all thoughts of teasing evaporated. How many stories had she heard from Hellen that started "I went to go see the rock guys," or "the rock giants said…" whatever whatever. Almost every time the woman came home. Hellen got to talk to the rocks plenty, but cooped up in the monastery like she too often was, the Queen had never once had the chance. Not cool.

"How tall?"

"Fifteen feet, probably."

"Do me a favor," she said, putting her hands on her hips and pacing a little. "Walk around it and see if you notice any parts that look like human body parts. Like a hand, or legs and feet."

"Really? All right."

His energy stepped away to the right, and she tracked his progress through the old leaves. Around the back the footsteps faded, then she could just hear them coming from the left, and they stopped.

"I don't see anything."

Damn.

****

"Maybe you should look harder."

David jumped and yelled out involuntarily.

"What is it?" the Queen asked. "Are you okay? Is it a rock giant?"

Dressed in a pair of rumpled pants and a plain white shirt, his Dad looked pretty much like he did most of David's life.

"I'm okay," he called around the rock.

"Hello, David." His Dad came toward him with his arms out, and if he was honest, David wasn't sure he wanted to get that close. But what was he going to do? His heart pounded as he stepped into his father's arms and let himself be hugged.

The energy was incredible.

David pulled back and examined his Dad closely. He could A) engage his inner problem-solver and approach this scientifically, in which case he'd have to deny the possibility that his father was really here and dismiss it as some sort of trick or hallucination, or B) He could accept the evidence of his eyes and let his world view expand.

"Amazing, right? Someday this will all be yours." He moved his hands in a display gesture in front of his shoulders, grinning. Still the same old Dad. David found that intensely reassuring, and chose option B.

"You look the same, but you feel different. Not quite as solid. Like if I squeeze too hard, I'll go right through you."

"Maybe we can test that later."

"Um…okay? If you don't think it would be messy?"

"I don't think so."

193

David called around the rock again. "It's not a rock giant, Your Majesty. It's Dad."

"It's your *Dad*?"

"It's me, Your Majesty!"

Dad led the way around the rock, and they found the Queen rooted to her spot, eyes wide.

"Your Majesty." Dad stopped and his head went down. "Did we ever tell you that the Treslo line is descended from the monks?"

"Yes you did, I'm happy to say. Otherwise, I'd probably be unconscious."

His Dad laughed, that same deep laugh he always had, and David felt a sudden stinging in his eyes. He'd never expected to hear that laugh again.

"Can I hug you?" she asked.

"You sure can," his Dad said, and stepped over to wrap his big arms around her tiny frame. They stood like that for a long moment, his Dad bent over, the Queen with her head on his shoulder, smiling.

"You feel positively glowing," she said, her face turned up to him as he stepped back again.

"Sometimes I do actually glow," he replied, his brows up. "I've had to practice manifesting on this plane, and glowing is one of the levels."

"This is so crazy." David laughed, put his hands on his hips, and shifted around, not knowing what to do with himself.

"Hellen sees monks in the forest all the time," the Queen said. "They glow, according to her. But as far as I know, she's never seen your father."

"No, this is my first time."

"Is something wrong?" David asked.

"Way to cut to the chase, my son. Good thing, because I can't stay long." He waved David in and lowered his voice. "I'm not exactly authorized to be here."

"Are you breaking monk rules?" the Queen asked, a smile in her voice.

"No!" His Dad held up a hand. "Not exactly. No one specifically told me I couldn't...talk to you." He glanced around, and leaned in again. "But there is a non-interference clause."

"Yeah, that's what Hellen said." The Queen reached her hand out to him. "Don't get yourself in trouble."

Dad shook his head. "Don't worry about me. You're the ones with the problems."

Chapter S.8

"What are you doing at my desk, Rose? In fact, what are you doing in this room at all?"

She bent to pick up her bucket and hurried around the end of the desk to stand in front of Dagge. "This young man was just telling me I shouldn't be in here," she said. "I didn't realize it's actually forbidden. I just thought..." She trailed off, because all the staff knew no one but Diit was allowed in here, and there wasn't anything she could say that would be believable.

"Roger, did you catch her in here?"

"I did, sir."

"What was she doing?"

"It looked like she had the drawer open, sir."

Roberta's heart sank. Robert didn't lie well, she knew that, and if he'd tried to do it, Dagge would've gotten him too. She sucked it up and faced the music.

"Is that true, Rose? Were you looking in my drawer?" Dagge walked around her and to the back of his desk.

"I did look in your drawer, yes sir."

"Did you find anything interesting?" The harkener clattered onto the desk, and he yanked the center drawer open.

"Not really, sir. Just some...pens, and...papers."

"And this? Did you find this?" Dagge held up the flap of John's balloon, the limp blue part dangling, the brown Thorn emblem swaying with every move he made.

"I did see that, sir, but I'm not sure what it is."

"Let me tell you what it is, Rose." He half-sat on the end of the desk, fingering the shard of balloon as he talked. "This is treason. This

196

is one man taking everybody else's lives into his own hands and RUINING THEM!"

He shouted so loud, his spittle hit her in the face, but she didn't dare raise her hand to wipe it away. Instead, she lowered her eyes, and tried to control her quaking fear. Dagge stood, and loomed over her, bringing the balloon up to her face clasped tight in his fist.

"And I'm going to say I think you know exactly what this is. I think you know this person, and maybe you came in here because you're a spy. Is that right? Are you a spy?"

Lying didn't come easy to her, either, but what else was she going to do? She put a shocked expression on her face. "Overlord, sir, I am not a spy. I was just checking to see if everything was clean enough! I know how you like things—"

"Then you know I like the servants to STAY OUT OF THIS ROOM! YOU! TAKE HER TO THE DUNGEON!"

Robert laid his papers on the desk, and didn't look at her as they exited.

Chapter 5.9

"Can you help us find the tunnels?" Adia asked. First things first.

"If I do that, they'll ground me. I can't tell you any secrets. David, have you made any progress with the book?"

"What book?"

"Didn't your Mom give you the carapaz book?"

"No. Is that like a monk thing?"

John sighed, and was quiet for a few seconds. "Yes, it's a monk thing. You're supposed to sleep on it. I never got much out of it, and I gave it to her just before I got captured. But don't be angry with her, there was a lot going on, and she probably forgot."

"Or she didn't want me to have it. You have no idea how she-bear she got after you died."

"Well, you can't blame her, considering. We'll find a way to get it to you, I promise. In the meantime, Your Majesty, what I *can* tell you is that you're right about Dagge digging to find the warren."

"Can you tell us if the town tunnel goes to Mad Monk Tavern?"

"He's looking down. Does that mean no? He's looking up. That might mean yes."

"Does it go to the well?"

"He's looking up again."

"Guys!" John said, "I can't do this! Looking down and looking up do not constitute replies."

"He's winking," David whispered in her ear.

"It's been wonderful to see you, John, but right now we have some urgency to find the tunnels. Will you be back?"

"As often as I can. But I might not manifest this fully."

"How do you manifest? Is it a push kind of thing?"

"David, interrogate your father later."

"Don't you want to know this stuff? It's like, the most world-changing truth there could ever be, and…don't you want to know it?"

"Of course I want to know it. But our people will need a way out of the town very soon, okay?"

"Yes, okay, you're absolutely right, I'm sorry."

"We can talk later, son. But both of you, before I go, there's one more thing. Roberta's been taken to the dungeon. She's safe for the moment, but that won't last long."

Chapter S.10

David jerked and jolted over the uneven forest floor, the Queen clinging to his back, bag resting on his hips below her. The new arrangement made it easier to see, not front-heavy, and he could use his hands if he needed them. Occasionally, he'd let go of her legs to grab branches or check the compass. She held on like a champ.

Conversation had fallen off, too, giving him time to think about what it would take to get Mom out of the dungeon. So far it was looking like he'd have to go in and get her. Maybe he could find the escape tunnel. Or knock a guard out and get the keys. And a gun.

But what about the Queen? He couldn't just leave her alone at the monastery. If they ever got to the monastery. At this point the chances of falling into a gully and breaking his fool neck seemed really high. Then the Queen would really be screwed. How did Hellen manage this stress all the time?

Granted, the way was beautiful—birds singing, early sunbeams shining through the trees. If the worry factor hadn't cranked up, he could appreciate it. As it was, he'd rather wave a magic wand and be there.

As far as he could tell, they were headed in the right direction. Given that one wrong degree at the outset would make a huge difference in the resulting destination, he just had to hope they wouldn't be wandering around out here for hours. For pity's sake.

A rain gully/tree root obstacle absorbed his attention for half a minute, then when he looked up, he saw a huge wolf standing in front of them, watching. Its ears were up, and its open mouth showed two rows of sharp, gleaming teeth.

He stopped. "There's a huge wolf about fifty strides ahead," he whispered.

"What color?"

"White."

Before he could even finish the thought, Adia wriggled her legs out of his hands and climbed down his back. "Wolf! Honey, come!"

To David's amazement, the wolf smiled and came loping over, going right to the Queen, who had taken a knee to meet him. Arms wide, she smiled with her whole face when he rushed up to her, and she wrapped him in a hug. "Wolf, this is David." She waved her arm in David's direction.

"Hello, Wolf." The dog looked up at him, still smiling, which David took as a good sign. "I didn't know you had a dog," he said.

"Well, Wolf is no ordinary dog," she said, standing. "Watch this. Take us home, Wolf. Home."

Cussed, if that dog didn't turn around and start trotting away.

"Let's go," the Queen said, her arms up, ready to climb onto David's back.

"Yes, ma'am. I'm bending my left leg, step on up."

Chapter S.11

Hellen couldn't get away from Guindo and the goons until the sun was well up and their shift ended. By that time, Anji was probably wondering what the hells had happened to her, especially since she was supposed to see her yesterday. Damn.

No time to run by Roberta's and borrow some clothes, either. Anji was just going to have to accept the soldier's uniform, like every dodgy thing Hellen did in Valdia. If it came down to it, a lie would be easier than the truth—and she felt pretty primed for that, having just lived a lie for the last several hours.

Anji's room at the boarding house had a separate, private entrance on the side. Hellen had stayed long enough when she brought her in to locate the door via the wraparound porch, and today she went up the smaller side steps to get to it. No need to panic the good people at the desk by making them think a soldier was coming.

Anji answered the door before Hellen even stopped knocking; her brows were knitted in a frown, until her mouth dropped open in recognition.

"Dolores! What are you doing in a soldier's uniform?"

"I joined the army."

She didn't know why she said it, but there it was. Now she'd have to back it up, or change the subject.

"Hey this is a nice room. I'm sorry I didn't make it by yesterday, things have been a little crazy."

"Well, I would guess so, if you joined the army." Anji turned and led Hellen into the quaint, rose-covered room, waved her to a chair, and sat on the bed facing her. "C'mon, Dolly, I know you didn't join the army. You couldn't say enough bad things about this regime when you were in Valdia."

"What do you mean? I hardly said anything!"

"True, but 100% of what you did say was bad. From a percentage perspective, that's a lot."

"Anji…" Hellen leaned forward and put her head in her hands, elbows on her knees. "There's too much going on here. It's not a good time for you to come, it's dangerous."

"What do you mean it's dangerous? There's nothing happening. I walked around town yesterday, and everything looks normal. I mean, apart from soldiers all around, but that is normal now. We have that in Valdia, too."

"Look, I can't explain, you're just going to have to trust me."

"Does this have to do with that uniform you're wearing? Because I know you did some things in Valdia that weren't…exactly aboveboard. But I never asked you about them. I respected your privacy, and I was happy to help you out." She paused, eyes on the ceiling, and when she looked back down, Hellen could see tears in them. "Now I need your help. You know I wouldn't ask, I wouldn't come here if I didn't need it."

"Please, Anji, for right now, go back to Valdia while you still can. You said you kept the apartment. I can give you some money to tide you over until you can get another job. Later, when things have settled, we'll bring you back, I promise."

Anji sat on the corner of the bed, her eyes full of hurt. "I guess I'm not as good a friend to you as I thought."

That felt like a lance to the chest. "You *were* a good friend. *Are* a good friend." Upset, Hellen rocked, rubbed her thigh, and glanced around agitatedly. "I just…"

"I'll find my own job. And place to live. Then I won't be putting you in a hard spot, and you won't have to feel responsible for me."

"It's hard to find a job."

"I can do it. Don't you worry about me. I've done a little bit of everything, and what I haven't done, I'll fake." She got up from the bed and walked to the door. "I know you probably want to get home and get out of that uniform, and I have work to find! I'll see you later, okay?"

Hellen got up and dragged her feet all the way to the door. "Please go back to Valdia."

Anji looked her steadily in the eye as she got near. "I lied. I didn't keep the apartment. I have nothing to go back to. Now, you can either be my friend or not, it's up to you."

With that, she waved Hellen out the door and shut it behind her.

Chapter S.12

The monastery wasn't as far as David was afraid it would be. Wolf turned out to be a very good guide—he went around the gullys, and took the smoothest path through the trees. No branches in the face or anything. Occasionally, he'd stop and wait for them to catch up, and when they did, he'd put his nose on the Queen's foot, and start off again.

For the entire last leg of the trip, the Queen kept up a running monologue that had been by turns funny, sad, and alarming.

"I miss my Dad terribly. So often I wish I could talk to him about the things we're doing, and get his advice. With so much of this—the Resistance, the people in danger, the tunnels and stuff the monks have said—I have no idea what he'd say. None of this was even approximated in my talks with him.

"Then there's Hellen. Dad would be so amazed by her now. She was my governess, you know. She was always really smart, and capable, but now she's like an agent or something. I never know when she's going to come home and say, 'Got another one today. It almost killed me. It was really close, but I stabbed it in the eye—or shot it in the heart, or cut off the top of its head—and now we only have x-number left.'" David could feel her shaking her head. "She's formidable. Speaking of formidable, how are we going to get your Mom out of the dungeon?"

"I don't know…I might need to get myself caught."

"Why?"

"Well, we know there's a way out, Dad just didn't have enough time to find it." David grunted, stepping up onto the stone entryway of the monastery. "*And*…now he knows where it is. Not that he would officially help, of course. That goes without saying." He released the Queen's leg, and bent his knee. "We're here."

"You make an excellent point," she said, holding his hand as she climbed down. "How would you get yourself caught?"

She was worried. Her voice had an ache at the edges that made his heart zing, no joke. "I could try to 'sneak' in."

"And what about when they shoot you?" Her eyes were blazing. Hard to believe she wasn't lasering a hole in him.

But he had a good reason. "What else are we going to do?"

"Let's send the pigeon to Beau and wait for a reply. He'll monitor and send right away, knowing we're out here."

Hand out, the Queen stepped forward until she touched the pitted, mossy surface of the rock slab door. "No offense, but going in without backup seems too risky for anyone, except *maybe* Helen."

"I'm not offended. Backup would be great. I'm a big fan of distractions, myself. And disguises. Whatever it is, after we're all caught, once we find the passage, we can get out."

"I can't tell if you're joking. But it doesn't matter. The better solution is to get your ass in here and find the tunnel," the Queen said with a crooked smile. Her hand moved to the side and found the seam, and with one hand she pushed. Voila, the behemoth swung inward.

"Would you look at that." David said.

"Where's Wolf?"

"He's to your nine."

With her forefinger, she tapped her nose and pointed into the dark. "Wolf, check home for me, okay? Check home."

David marveled to see the enormous dog trot into the dimness and disappear. In less than a minute, two short barks echoed from deep inside, and the Queen brushed her hands and started through the door. So much for her needing his protection, out here, all alone.

At least Wolf couldn't cook.

Inside, the old building was bare and gray. They'd entered into a large cloakroom, it looked like. To the left, a mirror leaned against the wall on top of a makeshift table. It reflected the light from the archway, and looked like an eye. A chest sat next to the table, and some kind of clothes hung along the wall on stone hooks. Hellen's, he imagined.

206

On the other side, stairs had been attached, like the ones in the palace dungeon. These had a railing, though, and went through a ceiling, like most stairs.

The Queen led the way, stopping to touch the side of the archway before walking confidently into the next room. Once there, she moved through the room like she could see—past the cushions, the low plank table, the end of the sofa, to the other side of the room. Impressive.

The dog met her at the end of a short hallway, whining softly. "Thank you, sweetie pie," she said. "You're a good boy." She rubbed Wolf's ears and neck. "Hey, David, let's go through the kitchen. The pigeon cage is on the top floor of the pyramid."

"Yeah, okay." David was lollygagging, his Dad would have said, but it was impossible not to look at everything: the perfect planing of the rock, the trapezoid stones of the archway, the intricate windows. He tried to keep moving, but there were carvings around the fireplace, and he took a hard right before the table. "Hang on…" he said. "Just…a quick…" His forward motion stalled as he examined the panels. All the daily life, he skimmed, but the monk being lifted on a net seemed strange. A game, maybe?

And there was one of the monks standing in line to go down a shaft. Hells yeah, that was the access to the tunnels. But not one identifying characteristic about where.

"Okay," he said, "one sec…" He shuffled around in the basket of kindling by the fireplace and found a twig to rub the carving with. So this was what it felt like to be an archaeologist.

"I've gone over these carvings until my fingers were raw."

Her voice was so close, he jumped. Which made her laugh. "Sorry," she said. "I need to learn to make noise."

"Where have you looked for the tunnel access?"

"Hellen and your father went over the entire monastery when they were here, and I've done a check of all the places I can reach. I feel pretty certain the entrance is through the kitchen, because the pump handle is the only place that has engravings on it, in a language none of

207

us can identify. At least, we assume it's a language, because what else would it be?"

"Why does it look like the shaft in this panel goes both ways, up *and* down? It must be inside the mountain."

"Up and down?"

"It looks like it. There's a tiny line above this guy's head, see?"

Oh, for pity's sake. He thought he was past this.

"I'm so sorry."

"You don't have to be sorry. It's not a big deal. Just put my hand on the line." The Queen held up her hand and he guided it to the carving.

"It's right under your first finger, above the guy who's going through the wall."

"Well, it's just the wall, right?" Her finger rubbed the tiny line.

"I don't think so. The other side of the passage is defined by the edge of the panel, and it goes all the way up."

"But that's the edge of the panel!"

"I'm just saying I think it means something. Can I see the pump handle?"

"Of course."

She led the way back through the hallway and into the kitchen, where Wolf was busy chewing the bones of a small mammal. David didn't need to know what it was, and hoped he wouldn't have to cook one anytime soon, because he sure didn't have a recipe for it.

The Queen stopped at the other end of the room, at a stone basin that had an old pump on the side of it. The metal must be extraordinarily hard, because it was smooth and rust-free. Symbols carved into the handle looked as clear as if they'd been done yesterday. Interesting.

The symbols themselves were spiky and stick-like. Lots of lines, and crosses, with some small geometric shapes embedded in them. He'd never seen any writing like it before. "Looks like writing to me. Or I guess it could be constellations. Not sure how that would be relevant, though." He bent over and peered under the handle, around the spout, and down the pipe. Nothing unusual. The basin looked solid, and attached to the floor. No seams to indicate an opening. "I don't know. I don't see anything."

On the left side, the basin was attached to the dumbwaiter, and beyond that, there was a bank of pipe ends attached to pipes that ran up the wall, across the ceiling, and through the various walls adjacent to the other rooms in the monastery.

"Is this an intercom system?"

"Yes." the Queen said. "It connects every room to the kitchen, and it's possible to hear the tiniest sounds—even Wolf's farts." She said this with such a twinkle, David laughed.

"Your Majesty, I'm stunned the word "fart" is even in your vocabulary," he teased.

"Oh, I know a lot more words than that, and we're going to have to put a halt to that 'Your Majesty' business if we're going to be working and living together. I can't be that all the time."

It felt like he had teleported into unfamiliar territory. He was so used to thinking of her as the Queen, he didn't know how not to. "What should I call you?"

"Adia, please," she said with a smile. "But Hellen would say you still need to call me Highness, or Majesty, or one of those things when we're with other people. That's just the nature of the job. Now, are you ready to send the pigeon?"

"Yes, ma'am, Adia." It felt light and frothy to say it. "After that, let's get to work."

Chapter S.13

It was taking way too long to get Wharton and a crew together to start digging at the wall. The man practically whined about all the other stuff he was in the middle of. Couldn't he see the importance of finding that escape tunnel? Of exposing it, and rooting out the traitors? All the rest of it was nothing next to that. The General's suggestion of stationing a patrol in the area until the trouble in the mine was solved nearly made the top of Dagge's head blow off. By that time, Hellen and her friends would have hidden everything, shut down everything, and he'd look terrible for killing them all for no reason.

Because make no mistake, he'd be killing them all.

Even Hellen. She'd passed her "use by" date with him, now that he knew just how evil she was. How can smart people be so fooled by love? If she came up to him right now, and offered herself, apologizing and penitent, he wouldn't forgive her. He'd blow her brains out.

But would he really? He liked to think so.

For the moment, though, he had other problems to solve. What was Rose doing in his desk? He'd gone through the middle drawer and checked everything in it. Nothing was missing. The balloon had been out of place, so he knew she'd looked at it, but why? Maybe she was Thorn. He puffed a derisive laugh—not likely.

Whatever it was didn't much matter anymore. She'd be dying soon, and whatever she found out would die with her. Maybe it was all the official "No" replies to the invitations he'd sent his so-called allies. He'd saved them so he could always remember who the assholes were. Of course, they were all assholes, and many of them had died for it. Still, he kept their rejections so he could gloat once in a while. It felt good.

Sitting at the desk, he peered into the drawer and ran his hands around the inside perimeter. A rough bump caught his attention. Leaning over, he saw a tiny black disc stuck near the front right corner with a small lump of sticky tack.

A bug. That bitch—unbelievable. Did she leave one in his bathroom, too? Were they listening to him shit every morning?

He crushed the little disc with his thumbnail, making sure he broke it before he hurried to go check the tonker.

They'd pay. Oh yes, they'd pay.

Chapter S.14

Hellen was at the warren when the message came from Adia. It said *Roses cut, drying in basement.* (oh, shit!) *Come home soon.* "Come home soon" meant there was more she couldn't put in. The language of their messages had gotten a lot sketchier as the threat level had increased. They'd agreed on a few code words—like "basement" for the dungeon—because it seemed like they might need them.

What was Rose doing? She hadn't been tasked with anything, except keeping her ears open, and that was mostly to make her feel better about having to clean Dagge's tonker. Now, the fact that she had become a person of interest to Dagge was terribly dangerous for all of them. The woman was hanging by a thread as it was, what would an interrogation do to her?

Beau had brought her the message. Around them, the teeming crowd in the warren dragged desks and shelves and whatever they could sacrifice to stuff the tunnel. Others carted rocks and dirt dug from the north side of the room, and they filled and packed the gaps as best they could.

Above their heads, the pounding and scraping of the crew trying to dig down to them was taking its toll. So far, they couldn't hear voices, so that was good. But everyone down below still looked like they hadn't slept in ten years. More than a little crazy.

But not Beau. The man was a rock.

"Do you want me to come with you?" he asked quietly.

Of course she had to go. Just in case something game-changing had happened. Ugh, she wished they had the monk tunnels open.

"They need you here, Beau."

"One of these days, you're going to realize I can help you."

"I do realize that. But I can't be selfish. What's happening here is urgent, and I can make it to the monastery on my own. Can I borrow your pistol? I don't want to carry a rifle, it's too cumbersome."

He peered at her for a moment while he took off his holster and handed it to her. "Of course you can borrow my pistol. Anything you need. I'll be looking for your pigeon, too, so don't forget."

"I'll send as soon as I get there."

To her surprise, he put his arms around her and pressed her to him. This wasn't the usual I'm-so-happy-to-see-you hug. It felt deep, and full body. She was surprised to feel her own body respond, hips pushing forward, electricity sparking in her loins. She'd never felt this with him before. Pulling back, she looked in his clear green eyes, and noted his expression. Did he feel it?

The gaze that met her was knowing. Patient.

How long had she been this stupid?

Now was such a bad time, though. Whatever this was would have to go on the back burner. Not forever, but preferably until the threat of imminent death had passed.

Or maybe not. Either way, at the moment, she had to leave. She leaned in and kissed him on the mouth, patted his cheek, and headed for the drainage tunnels.

Chapter S.15

Dagge had loaded a bag, and was busy strapping it to Sephone when Wharton found him in the stable.

"Sir, we've started trying to dig, and the top layer is rock for twenty-five feet in every direction."

"Move inside the wall and use explosives, Wharton. Blow them to hells."

"Sir, if we use explosives, they could cave in whatever's under there. We wouldn't be able to go in."

"Are you fucking kidding me? Are you stupid? Blow it all the fuck up, Wharton! Blow the entire fucking *country*, just block that tunnel, and do not let them escape. Am I clear?"

"Yes, Overlord."

He was closer to Wharton than he realized, or intended. But to give the man credit, his expression was still pretty unflappable. What did that mean? Even Wharton used to at least avert his eyes. *Note to self: work on scary-tyrant face.*

He turned back to his horse, and pointlessly checked his bedroll again. If he was honest with himself...but he didn't have to be honest with himself, did he?

"I'm going to do some hunting in the forest. Set some traps, maybe. If you need something, send me an instanote."

"Sir, the instanote system is insecure."

"Don't you think I know that? I didn't say send me state secrets."

A brief-ish pause. "Yes, sir, of course not." Another pause. "Will you be going in a particular direction? In case we need to find you?"

"Don't even try. The first man that shows up will die."

"Yes, sir."

"I should be back in a couple of days. If I'm not back by Sunday, you can send someone to look for me. Does that make you feel better?"

Brief-ish pause again. "Yes, sir. Thank you, sir."

What a moron.

"Begone from me, Wharton."

"Of course. Have a safe trip, sir." The general bowed ever so slightly and left the stable.

Taking Sephone's reins, Dagge led her out of her stall and through the stable. There, in the back corner stall, stood Princess Adia's horse. Nose in the feed bucket, she lifted her head and watched him as he passed the end of the row of stalls on his way to the door. He wasn't sure why he kept her. She was a fine specimen and all, but it felt more like…by having her he had a part of the princess. He could see her, caged up there, every time he went to the stable. And it felt good.

Especially since he was finally going to find that bitch.

Chapter 5.16

Lunch time had come and gone, and as far as Adia was concerned, so had her hunch about the kitchen pump being the tunnel entrance. David had dismantled the entire mechanism, she was pretty sure—though she didn't dare ask him, what with all the cursing and mumbling he was doing.

Fortunately, the cheese and crackers in David's bag had taken the edge off, and Adia sat with Wolf while David wrenched, and clanged, and generally insulted the pump.

"There!" he said at last, and Adia could hear the familiar scrape and rattle of the handle, then the sound of running water. "I didn't think I was going to be able to get it back together."

"But you did! Good job," she said, clapping.

"Thank you, I would have left it, but running water is a plus."

"Yes, it is. I know that from having to bathe with a single bucket of water back when it had to be fetched." Adia stood, walked to the garden doorway, and pushed aside the heavy tapestry Diit had brought from the palace. "Wolf, come. It's a bad time of day, I know, but will you see if you can find us some food?" She put her fingers to her mouth like she was eating. "Food?" The wet nose tapped her other hand, and the bushy fur tickled as Wolf went out. She let the tapestry down and walked over to lean on the dumbwaiter and talk to David while he fiddled around at the sink. "I'm sorry I was so certain about the tunnel access being in here. Now I don't know where to look. Nothing else seems likely."

"It still could be in here. I'll get my bulb torch and check out the closet."

"And I will...feel around the dumbwaiter again." Ugg. She huffed a small sigh as David's feet hit the staircase up to the bedrooms.

How many times had she done this? The dumbwaiter had zip to offer but smooth river rock, perfect, mortarless fitting, and a beautifully functional counterweight system (this last fact had been based on the experiments she'd done involving pots of steaming water, and dreams of a truly hot bath).

To her surprise, mumblings began to drift out the end of one of the pipes in the intercom system.

"Next time you feel like showing off, David, do something useful. She said it wasn't the handle, but did you listen? Nooo. You thought…what did you think, anyway? That monks could magically get sucked down a teeny-tiny pipe? Now you just look like an idiot."

Wow, he was berating himself. So unnecessary, though she did tell him he probably didn't need to dismantle the pump handle. Once he got the idea to do it in his head, there was no dissuading him. Now, what would her father do? Probably give David an opportunity to succeed at something.

"David…" she spoke into the pipe end, rather loudly. The mumbling stopped. There was a pause.

"Yeah?"

"I'm really hungry. Can we take a very short break to eat something? There's a vegetable garden out back, and I'm sure we can find one or two edible plants."

"Yeah, of course. Yes. Yes. I'll be right down." He sounded perkier already, giving her a little smile.

By the time his feet landed back in the kitchen, Adia had a bowl, a skillet, and several utensils out on the table. "I didn't know what you might want to make, so I grabbed what I thought was universally useful."

"Excellent! Let's visit the garden!"

A big smile on her face now, Adia grabbed the basket by the door, and opened the tapestry. David swept it aside for the both of them, and Adia led the way, her right hand occasionally tapping the guide rope that lined one side of the path. More of a habit now than anything, but she didn't mind it—it felt homey.

The path was wide enough that David could walk beside her. His energy had a ringing feel to it, that was the best description she could come up with. Everyone's was different: Hellen's was very steady and low-key, until she had a mission, then it sped up like a propeller; Beau's energy undulated like the ocean—a lot going on underneath; Cary had a blinking light in him, and it mostly blinked fast.

If somebody had told her four years ago that she'd be describing people in terms of how their energy felt to her, she'd have told them to have another beer.

The garden had been built by the monks, apparently, because the sides were very well defined by the rim of rock that extended down into the ground much farther than Adia ever planned to dig. She'd wondered many times if it could serve as a swimming pool, if they took all the dirt out, of course. Not likely she'd ever know.

One corner of the plot being all she could manage, gardening-wise, they didn't have to hunt too hard for what they wanted.

"Look at those tomatoes! Do you have any potatoes and onions?" David asked, clearly making his way to the tomatoes.

"We do, in the pantry. What are you thinking of?" she asked, far from faking an interest. In fact, her stomach growled, sounding like it was glad she asked.

"It's a dish I learned from my mom's cookbook, very delicious, and not dependent on meat, though we can add some if we want."

"Sounds perfect."

"Here, take these tomatoes, and I'll check this little garlic patch."

Since they were in a hurry, Adia didn't take her usual time tending the plants. She did find a giant cucumber, and three squash that she'd missed last time, but they weren't too big yet so she left them. David kept dropping things into the basket—she felt green beans, garlic, and a few big leaves of kale.

"That should do it," he said. "Can I carry that for you?"

"Sure."

He lifted the basket off her arm. "I hope you have some sort of oil to cook with."

"Fortunately, Vartile brought us some, because otherwise Hellen wanted us to try rendering rabbit fat."

They started back up the path "Do rabbits have very much fat?"

"No, they do not. I'm so thankful for Vartile." They laughed, and were quiet for a minute. She could hear the birds, and bugs, and the distant cracking of ice on the mountain. It felt so peaceful. Funny how much she'd changed.

After they passed back through the tapestry, David set the basket down on the table, and unbuckled his belt. She could hear it, and it caused a little flare of anxiety, she had to admit. "What are you doing?"

"I'm going to strap this tapestry back, if that's okay. It would be good to have the light. I guess I could have asked for rope. Do you have rope?"

"If we have some, it would be in Hellen's trunk in the foyer, but don't worry about it. I'll imagine you with a belt."

Adia listened to David wrestle the tapestry up, grunting, then bumps, buckle noises, and a scraping clang. Immediately, a mechanical sound emanated from the dumbwaiter, accompanied by scraping rock, gears, and a heavy thud.

"David, is that what I think it is?"

"Yes, ma'am. Lunch is going to have to wait."

Chapter S.17

At least being in the forest with a horse was better than going it alone. Two horses was all right if you didn't count one of them being spoiled rotten. He'd tried letting Adia's horse go, thinking she might lead him to the rebel hideout, but all the blasted mare wanted to do was head back to her comfy stable. Still, if they got close enough to the hideout, he was betting she'd give it away, so he kept her with him.

They walked under the pines. Cooler there. Freer, flatter. Plus the muffling effect, and easier to see into the shadows.

He hadn't been in the forest real long before he saw the white wolf again, somehow alive in spite of the gut wounds he gave him. Damn. That dog might have to be his when all this was done.

A little starvation could tame a lot of things.

Maybe Hellen would be turning up soon. What would he do? He wouldn't have to kill her right away, of course. They could talk, and who knew? Anything could happen. He might not have to kill her at all.

The wolf stayed parallel with him, just like before. Dagge kept glancing farther back into the trees, looking for a glint of blond hair, or a sexy shadow. So far, none of the above.

Then something did move. In the shadows, under a massive oak, a person stepped toward the trunk and disappeared. It looked male, though, large.

"You, under the tree! Stop and show yourself!"

He urged his horse into the forest, nudging her into a trot. As he got closer to the wolf, it edged away, but not far away. Sephone got a little skittish.

"Easy, girl." He slowed her back to a walk and stroked her neck. She still tossed her head and sidestepped, so he turned her away from the wolf, which made her calm a bit, and they resumed a roundabout path toward the mysterious shadow man.

He kept his eye on the tree. The asshat must be circling that trunk to avoid being seen, because Dagge got all the way past it, and there was nothing. No one had tried to escape to another tree, either.

Then he saw it. Several more trees in, a man stepped into the shadows from a patch of sun. Dangling down his back was a long grey ponytail.

Impossible.

Forgetting the wolf, and Hellen, Dagge looped the other horse's reins around a downed branch and kicked his horse forward, into the oaks.

It couldn't be who he thought. He'd gone behind another tree, but when Dagge got there, he was gone. Furious, he twisted in his saddle, the horse spinning and rearing under him. Frantically he looked, until he saw it. Farther still, by a different tree trunk, the shape stood facing his direction, hands on his hips.

The man walked slowly and deliberately to the edge of shadow, and Dagge could see John Treslo.

Chapter S.18

"What did you do?"

David dropped the tapestry, making it a lot darker in the kitchen. He'd have to fix that, in a minute. Right now, he needed to look down that shaft. "I tried to attach the belt to the first pipe end. When I did, it folded down, and the bottom front of the dumbwaiter lowered into the shaft. Come look."

Really? He said that? "I mean…"

"I know what you mean, no worries. Just make sure I don't fall down the shaft."

The Queen stepped over to the dumbwaiter, hand out. David cupped her wrist and guided her hand to the left side. "The wall is here. I'm going to raise the wooden dumbwaiter door, but before I lower the…platform, I guess…I'm going to pull out the bulb torch and see what I can see down there."

"We call it the cart. Let's raise it a bit so it's easier. I'll listen." She grabbed the cable and raised the cart over her head. Hanging her left ear out into space, she stood rapt. Hyper aware of the Queen's proximity to danger, David knelt as close to her as he thought he could get away with. At least he could block her fall.

The bulb torch revealed very little—a rock shaft dropped into the ground, probably forty feet or so. At the bottom, it looked like there was an opening. Definitely an opening, considering the cool air wafting up from the abyss. "Do you hear anything?" he whispered.

"Air. A faint sound of water."

"You can hear air?"

"Like wind, only much softer. Ssshhh."

While he waited, he explored the cable and pulley system. He didn't know the monks made cable, still in fine shape, even after all these years. How he wished he could apprentice to them, what amazing things he'd be able to learn.

"David, I want to go down."

"What?"

She was already lowering the cart. "You heard me."

"Your Majesty, I don't think that's a good idea."

"I'm not surprised."

"Anything could be down there!"

"Like what? Rats? Monks?"

"Snakes?"

"I'm not worried."

By then she had lowered the cart nearly to the floor, and stepped in. Not knowing what else to do, David stepped in beside her.

Chapter S.19

John fucking Treslo.

He stepped out of the dense shadow looking exactly like he did the night he died. Stringy gray hair swaying in front of his face, blood running down his arms, flap of skin hanging off his chest. Dagge sat on his horse, stone frozen.

How was this possible? Hellen blew the asshole's chest open. No sign of that on this guy. They burned the body, right there in the field beside the palace with all the rest of them. No sign of that either. What the fuck was this thing, because no way Treslo could still be alive. *Could he?*

Dagge's heart jumped into his throat.

What should he do? Could it hurt him? Could it fly over here and get him? His heart thudded. It choked him, made it impossible to breathe. He unsnapped his knife, whipped it out and threw it into John Treslo's head.

It went right through. Bounced off the tree trunk behind.

The whole scene glitched with lightning from the sides. It jabbed quick and with a crackle, then it was like a channel had changed. Treslo was there, but he looked like he always did. Ponytail, glasses, frumpy. This John Treslo glanced behind him and laughed. "That was good, Dagge. I mean that. Nice shot."

It sounded normal.

But it wasn't normal, nothing that dead could be standing here.

"What are you doing here, Treslo?"

"I came to see you."

A lump with the texture of wadded-up paper rose in his throat. He cleared it, covering with a raspy laugh. "Aren't you supposed to be dead? Oh wait, you are dead. I know because I took your heart out and fucking ate it."

"Was it good?"

Hysteria bubbled out of him; he couldn't stop it. His head lit up. More than just sparks this time, it was a whole fireworks show. Under him, Sephone side-stepped and turned, which pissed him off even more. He wrestled her back around as he talked.

"Don't lecture me, you sanctimonious piece a shit." Sephone reared a little. He closed his eyes a second and threw sand on the fire in his head. "Maybe I should learn to be a loser like you. Always bowing and scraping to better men. Even Ol' Kingy, weak as he was, was a better man than you." Sephone settled. "And now it's his little girl, isn't it? She the one ordering you around these days? John?" He smiled. "Because I know she's alive, and I'm on my way to get her right now."

Treslo stood there, quiet. *That shut him up.* Dagge started to turn the horse around.

"Did it though?" Treslo asked.

"Did what what?"

"Did it shut me up?"

Dagge stared at him. *What the fuck?*

"The fuck is this, you malefic ooze: you will not win," Not-Treslo said. "It doesn't matter what you do. You can grab everything for yourself. You can crush the people you hate. You can prop yourself up and tell the mirror you're a great man—all that wealth, all that power…a seat at the top of the world! But you don't have the hearts of the people, Dagge."

A bray of pure glee burst out of his mouth. *What kind of corny bullshit was that?*

"It's the kind of corny bullshit that makes the foundation of life, you dim-witted absolute parasite. In truth I feel sorry for you. Don't you know you can't get around without feet? Feet are amazing, important things—all these tiny bones and muscles carrying this enormous weight. They work together. Jumping, running, climbing, even standing all damn day, they achieve." His hands had come up in front of him, grasping the air. "People are the feet of a kingdom. They bear the weight. They support the structure. They do a phenomenal amount of work, and if they're with you, then you can accomplish greatness."

"What the fuck are you talking about? Greatness *is* being at the top of the world, Treslo. Greatness is everyone knowing who you are, and your name being carried into the future. Greatness is changing the world to suit you. I'm already great, and I've only just started."

Music surged around him. Movie music, for when the hero is doing his thing.

"All right then." Treslo's arms dropped to his sides. "Get ready to meet your own stupidity." The music stopped.

How long had his head been throbbing? Dagge reached four fingers up to his temple. His head felt hot. Every pulse whitened the world.

He wanted to beat John Treslo to a quivering pulp. But it wasn't Treslo, was it?

He didn't know.

"You know, Dagge..." The thing just couldn't stop talking... "I want to thank you for that night you made me peel off my own skin. That was an experience I would never have had otherwise."

"I'm glad you enjoyed it." He dumped more sand on the brain fire. The thing was trying to trigger him. What was it saying? Thanks for making me peel my skin? Maybe it was a demon.

"Oh, I didn't say I enjoyed it. I was still in there. I felt everything."

So this was about revenge, not rebellion. More sand on the brain fire. *The banquet.* That's what he was talking about. He remembered the banquet.

"How did it feel for Hellen to shoot you?"

"Honestly, that was the best part."

"Then you lack vision. We could have owned the world. So easily."

"Who wants the world? It's a mess, and a huge responsibility.'

"How can you be so stupid? It's luxury, and privilege. And power. It's living a good life because you're chosen. You're not like all the dirty, poor people."

That really did shut Treslo up. Whatever it was just stood there looking at him.

Dagge needed his knife. A pair of hooves in Treslo's face would get rid of him. Dagge nudged Sephone with his heels, but she shied and wouldn't go close. She reared back, and Dagge couldn't make her.

Treslo smirked. "Guess you don't want to get off that horse."

"For all I know you're a fucking demon."

He let Sephone back up and she calmed some.

"I appreciate that you're afraid of me."

YOU ASSHOLE! screamed in Dagge's head.

"I heard that."

"FUCK YOU!" That was all Dagge could think of to say. His mind had gone blank— something in his brain burst. He could feel it spreading; it was warm. His head fell back, but he barely noticed. His mouth hung open. Sephone tossed her head and did the foxtrot, and then suddenly everything was clear.

Dagge pulled his rifle from its holder on the saddle and aimed it at that smirking face. "You can talk your superior elitist bullshit, you dead fuck, but I'm holding all the cards. If you could stop me, you would've done it by now." Dagge fired a whole bunch of laser pulses, all the way up and down the body, and all it did was chew up the bark on the tree.

But Treslo wasn't smiling at all when he disappeared.

And when he did, there was Hellen.

Chapter S.20

The ride down the dumbwaiter shaft was a little tight, but Adia didn't mind at all. David's presence was becoming quite familiar to her, and though she couldn't put a finger on why, the effect was different from the one with Cary. Easier, like she didn't have to be on guard all the time. Like she knew David already.

They'd gone down pretty far, judging by how long it took, before the cart bumped on the bottom of the shaft. The wall had disappeared behind her. Fresh air cooled the back of her neck, smelling like rock and dirt. She turned around and took a big breath.

Adia stepped out, left hand grasping the wall as she made room for David to follow. "It's got to be dark, right? I hope you brought the bulb torch," she said.

"Right here," he answered, and she could hear the click of it coming on. "It's crazy dark. Okay, if the shaft is six o'clock, the left tunnel, to the palace, is at…nope, the room is too oblong. Four tunnel openings are side by side in the wall in front of us. It's a shallow curve. I'd say each opening is probably twelve feet in diameter. Want me to walk you to them?"

"Yes, please." David took her hand and hooked it onto his arm. Before starting, she backed into the dumbwaiter opening, and said, "Walk me to the closest end."

"Okay," he said, leading her toward the right. "The floor is mostly flat, and clear of debris. If we were to go farther to the right, there's another tunnel opening kind of back in the corner."

David took her hand off his arm and placed it on rock. "This is the inside wall of the index finger tunnel. Just six or so feet to the left is the middle finger tunnel."

"The fuck off tunnel." She grinned.

"I hear the monks originated that phrase," he said. "This tunnel probably goes to the site of an old inn called The Bunghole."

Adia laughed, so glad to be with a funny person.

But they had more serious work to do, and she needed to focus. Getting her bearings, she turned and walked to the other side of the index tunnel, hands out. When she reached it, she turned around and placed her back to it. "Would you lead me on a path directly in front of the openings?"

"Of course." He was there in a few quick strides, hand on her hand, tucking it into the crook of his arm. How did he know what to do? Someday she'd ask him.

"Stop and let me touch the walls, okay?"

"We're at the other side of this tunnel now. Want to touch?"

She stuck her hand way out and brushed the edge. "Good."

"Yes, ma'am."

"You know, also don't call me ma'am when it's just the two of us. It makes me feel…untouchable." *Did she really just say that?* "Distant."

"Oh, good, I was afraid you were going to say old."

She tilted her head up at him. Funny, it was her scar side, and she hadn't even thought about it.

"Um, I don't mean feeling distant is good."

"Just treat me like you know me, okay? Is this a monk thing? Because your Dad can be a goober too. Did he ever tell you the story about the time I surprised him in the dungeon? He thought he was seeing the ghost of my mother, walking down the hall. He fell over in his chair, on his back like a turtle—a cup of coffee in one hand, which he managed not to spill. Then he jumped to his feet, all in one motion. I don't know how he did it. Still not spilling the coffee. We laughed so hard once he realized who I was."

"He never told me about that! That's a great story," David said delightedly. "So Dad." She could hear the smile in his voice. "I've missed him this last year and a half. Losing him was hard on all of us. Especially Mom."

"I know what you mean," she said. "It's like part of your foundation crumbles."

"Yeah, it is."

By that time they were at the last tunnel, and Adia had done her counting and mental mapping. She stopped at the last tunnel and listened. For what, she wasn't sure. Some sound of the woman who sat at the other end, she supposed. But there was nothing. "Now take me around the wall, back to the dumbwaiter."

As they walked, she told him, "We're going to save your Mom, David, don't worry. Now that we've found the tunnel hub, this Resistance can really step up. We should go down the palace tunnel. You and me, right now. See if we can get to her."

"And what if it's a waste of time?"

"What if getting inside is a waste of time? Do you want to die? If we can't get in from the tunnel, we can try from the inside. But in case you don't know, your Dad couldn't figure it out. He sat in front of the sleeping platform, and he was convinced the mechanism had to do with a tiny hole in the side. Like a keyhole, but not shaped like a key. He never made it work."

"A keyhole," David repeated.

"There was an engraving above it that formed the shape of an arrow, too. It said "Hope is never really lost," pointing at the cell door. Not sure how useful that is."

"Unbelievable. Dad, you crazy genius, you." David laughed softly. "He figured it out. He gave me a box just before he died. He said it was a puzzle box, and it had a tiny keyhole, with that phrase written in marker above it. The key was the hinge pin. The hinge was fake."

They'd stopped, and David put his hands on both her arms. "If I can get into the dungeon, I'm 99.99 percent sure I can get us out."

Talk about mixed feelings. For once it wasn't Hellen who was going to do the dangerous thing. Hellen didn't have to risk her life in the hornet's nest, guns blazing or whatever. But David had no experience. Okay, he had a little—a year and a half ago when he helped Hellen get into the dungeon. That time he got caught, though, and

Hellen had to free him. But later he saved Hellen by whacking Dagge in the head with a gun. So, yeah, mixed feelings.

"David…"

"Adia, it makes the most sense. Dagge doesn't know me, doesn't know I'm with the Resistance, so he won't feel like he needs to kill me right away. I'll get caught doing something innocuous. I'll steal something, like food. Okay?"

She could feel her boat tipping. The brand new, strong, dependable lifeline she had just discovered was slipping through her hands. And she let it go.

Chapter S.21

Hellen had been surprised to see John in the forest, although overjoyed might be the better term. Tears welled up, and her heart hurt, and she wished she had time to sit a minute. It took a lot of the guilt off her to know that he survived, because the image that had stuck with her was the big bloody hole in his chest. That, and the horrible expression on his face just beforehand.

Clearly, his monk blood had qualified him for admission into their appear-and-disappear club. Which was brilliant, because him standing there meant she could avoid being seen until she was ready. Did he know that? She'd have to remember to ask him.

Then when John disappeared, she watched Dagge see her: the shift of focus, the slow smile.

"Well I should have known you'd be close by when Treslo showed up. You two were such buddies. I bet the fact you killed him still keeps you up at night."

"What keeps me up at night is the fact I didn't kill you. But I plan to remedy that at some point."

"Like today?" He eased his mare forward. "I seem to remember you wanting to make a deal one of the last times we met. Is that off the table?"

"Have you completely forgotten our last conversation? The one where we tried to kill each other?"

His horse stopped, and he looked at her blankly for a second, but snapped out of it. "I haven't forgotten. I see you're carrying a gun this time."

"I see you are too." She rested her eyes on the rifle across his lap, then let them shift left suddenly, and Dagge, always afraid of the

232

forest, took the bait. When his head turned, Hellen slipped behind the tree, because all in all, it seemed better not to be an easy target.

"Really, Hellen? That old ruse? I thought you had more skills than that."

"It worked, didn't it? Who's the loser?"

Silence. She had to wonder whether it was truly a good idea to piss him off. Ah well, too late now.

"What if I said I might be willing to make a deal?" she called out, readying her own gun.

"I'd say you're lying." Hoof steps started coming toward her again. A little faster.

"What if we call a truce right now, and you can take me to the palace and put me in the dungeon for the rest of my natural life." Eventually, someone would find the tunnel and get her out, she was sure.

"Why would I do that, when I know the Princess is alive, and somewhere out in these woods? You've been hiding her, but she's really the key to all this, isn't she? Don't bother answering, by the way."

Staccato thuds alerted her he was turning.

"See if you can catch me."

Chapter S.22

It felt good leaving Hellen behind, knowing he was threatening the most important thing in her world. Once the little Princess was gone, maybe she really would stop the nonsense. There wouldn't be any point in it.

The hideout had to be at the bottom of the mountain, given the trail, and the fact that once he'd moved away, the wolf stopped following him. He didn't find it last time because he didn't get far enough. Well, no more pissing in the wind. He was the only one that could end this.

If a Resistance showed up, he'd blow that thing to kingdom come.

Chapter S.23

Lunch had gone a lot faster than usual, as in down her gullet with lightning speed. Somewhere in the back of her mind, she hoped she hadn't embarrassed herself by doing one of those barbarian things—not chewing, for example. By way of comforting herself, she adopted the position that cooks were always glad to see their food enjoyed.

And krikey, it was good. David was going to be the best new thing since Wolf. After he got himself out of the dungeon, anyway. Because it sure sounded like he was leaving for the hoosegow today.

"I'm going to leave all my stuff here with you," he was saying. "I won't need it, and that way it can be here when I get back." He'd gotten up to take his plate to the basin, and Adia could hear him pumping the handle and rinsing it. "Oh, I do want to take a piece of wire. I'll need some to get the hinge pin out. Do you know if there's any around here?"

"Beau has some on the shutter knobs in the great room. We use it to latch them in the winter. It hangs on one knob in the summer."

"Perfect." The water stopped, the plate was set to the side, and David's footsteps came toward her. "Can I get your plate for you?"

"No, I can do it. It's better for me if I don't let you do everything." Oh, the irony. Considering she'd let him do everything since they got there.

"I understand, and I applaud you." He mimicked a cheering crowd, and she could hear a faint clapping of his hands. She had to laugh a little. In spite of her aching heart.

"Are you heading out right away?"

"I am. If you think you'll be okay."

"Oh yeah, I've spent lifetimes here alone."

"That's not reassuring."

"I'm sorry." She laughed lightly. "I just thought I'd have a respite for a while. But don't worry, Hellen will be here soon, and I can call Wolf back. In fact, let's do that right now." She got up, walked to the tapestry, and jabbed her finger back in his direction. "Don't touch my plate."

He chuckled, and she could hear her fork sliding as he set it back down. Once she lifted the tapestry aside, the sound of faraway, frantic barking froze her gut. Her arm flew toward David of its own accord, and she stuck her head out so she could hear better: definitely Wolf, clearly something bad out there. David joined her, and pulled the rug higher so he could see.

"He's less than a hundred strides away, hunkered down, and his hackles are up. He's facing to the side, so whoever it is, is close."

David yanked her back from the doorway and dropped the tapestry. Adia could hear the scrape of the pipe as David folded it down to open the shaft. "Dagge may be here, Adia. Let's get you down into the tunnels."

He couldn't even wait for the wall to get all the way down—he scooped her up and over, deposited her in rush, and started pulling on the cables. As the cart began dropping under her, she nearly wailed up at him. "He'll know you're with the Resistance, David! You won't be able to fool him, he'll know you're with me! Come with me. Hide!"

"If I refuse to tell him where you are, he can't kill me." The cart kept dropping. "I'm the only one who knows. Don't worry, I'll get out tonight, and I'll bring Mom. When you get to the bottom, step off so I can raise the cart again. We can't risk him seeing all the way down."

The cart kept lowering until it hit bottom, and she stepped off. When she did, it started immediately up again. David was the only other person who knew how to open the shaft, and there were no guarantees he'd be back.

Chapter S.24

After David got the Queen into the tunnel, and the wall back in place, and the wire off the window knob shoved under the insole of his shoe, he half-concealed himself in the great room, at the kitchen end of the panorama windows. Should he wait, or should he go out? A bridled horse trotted past the windows and disappeared into the pyramid.

Go out.

Through the back, where there were at least a few garden tools he could use to defend himself. Not really from a gun, though. That made him remember Hellen lived here, so he reversed direction and ran to the foyer.

In the foyer, he spotted a laser rifle, leaning against the wall next to Hellen's trunk. He needed to have a talk with her about gun safety. But for now, he snatched it up and made sure the safety was off before he hustled for the front door.

A gentle push pivoted the door just enough for David to peer out. Wolf's barking was much louder than before, and there, sitting on his horse in front of the monastery, was Tomius Dagge. Leader of the enslaved world. Overlord of Hells.

Fury leapt up in David like an animal. Suddenly he wanted nothing more than to kill that man, whatever it took. He wedged his hand in the crack of the door, and swung it open.

Chapter S.25

Hellen knew Dagge had found the monastery when Wolf started barking that nonstop bark. *Danger! Danger! Danger! Danger!* It felt like her heart beat had grown four legs and a tail. She wasn't far behind. She'd made good time, but had no plan. Dagge had a lot of weapons. Adia was hopefully crouched in some closet, and who knew what David would do.

If she could get inside before she had to confront Dagge, she could dig the pistol out of the bottom of her trunk for David. Barring that, even with Wolf and David there, it was looking like a one-sided fight. How she wished that laser rifle worked.

Chapter S.26

"Yes, sir, can I help you?"

David didn't know why that came out of his mouth, he was pointing the gun right at Dagge, and "help" was obviously not his intent. Still, no need to be rude. Yet.

Dagge just looked at him. Gauging his preparedness to shoot, no doubt. From his far side, his left arm folded up over the saddle horn, and he laid a rifle just like David's across the saddle in front of him.

"You'll need to drop that, mister." Wolf stopped barking.

Dagge smiled, slow and open-mouthed, like he couldn't believe what he was hearing, and wasn't it the best thing in the world? "Do you know who I am?"

"Looks to me like you're a trespasser at the moment, and I'd appreciate you getting off my land."

"THIS LAND IS MINE!" He practically convulsed when he said it, his face all red, and spit flying. David had heard Dagge was losing it, but seeing him snap made it too real. Maybe he should just shoot him right now. End this whole mess. Everyone would be so happy.

He tightened his trigger finger, so slightly. Could he? Could he take another person's life?

Dagge watched him, a half-smile on his face. Laughing at him. Not thinking David had it in him to do it. So he pulled the trigger.

Nothing happened. He pulled again, and again. Nothing.

Dagge laughed. "Forget the safety? I knew you didn't know your way around a gun." He started to climb off his horse, and Wolf darted forward, snarling. The horse goose-stepped, giving Dagge problems mid-dismount, having to grab the saddle horn and losing his gun. David darted forward, hit Dagge in the mouth with the butt of his

239

rifle, threw it to the side and swept Dagge's rifle up off the ground. Then he backed away, pointing it at him.

Dagge settled back into the saddle, mouth bleeding. "No question whether you'll shoot, now is there?"

"No, I don't suppose there is."

"Did you check to see if my safety's off?"

He hadn't. It was, and it killed David to be so obviously new to this, but he was still the one holding the rifle.

"I know who you are, you know. And there are so many things I want to say to you…but I think I'm just going to say this." With that, David squeezed the trigger.

And nothing happened.

He squeezed, and squeezed, and checked the safety, which was off, and squeezed again, and Dagge laughed a great big belly laugh, pissing him off even more.

"Hand print technology. It's the latest thing. You must be feeling very stupid."

Maybe, but he felt a lot better when he saw Hellen in the woods, heading their way.

Chapter S.27

Hellen pointed at herself, then to her left, letting David know what she was going to do. Not that she had a real plan. Whatever it would take to stop Dagge was basically it.

Wolf had backed off and gotten closer to the kitchen door. Getting past him would take some doing, unless Dagge got his gun back, and David wasn't looking like he would give it up easily.

David drew Dagge's attention by moving toward him, gun held like a bat. Dagge answered by facing the horse toward David. David moved back and forth, manipulating Dagge's angle to try and give Hellen time. She ran, pine needles cushioning her footfalls, hoping like crazy she managed to stay outside Dagge's field of vision. Once she squared with the horse's rump, she moved in carefully. Wolf didn't look at her. Good dog.

Dagge started easing the horse toward the back door. Wolf hunkered down and growled, then snarled as he got closer. The horse started tossing her head, and Dagge shoved his hand into his saddle bag.

What did he have in there?

Wolf lunged, making the horse rear. Dagge pulled something out of the bag and dropped it beside the dog. It started spewing fire and smoke within seconds. Wolf yiped, probably burned, and backed away.

David swung at Dagge's back while he was focused on the dog. The horse moved, though, backing away from the toxic smoke, and David missed, grazing Dagge on the elbow. Still rearing, and avoiding the smoke and fire, the horse turned to flee, and that was when Dagge saw her.

He dropped off his horse, and a sharp smack on the rump sent her running. Giving Hellen a smirk, he went for David, wrestling him for the gun. Hellen ran at them, but Dagge had gotten his hands onto his gun, and began to fire. He elbowed David in the face repeatedly, trying to take the gun from him. Laser pulses shot past her, and she ducked to the outside. Wolf had come around the fireball, and David tried to force the laser pulses up and away from both of them.

But he could only do so much. Dagge outweighed him and had more fighting experience, and Hellen couldn't get to them fast enough. She scrambled, crouching low, but Dagge yanked David around, using every trick in the book, firing wildly until he shoved David to the ground and got the rifle. Before she could get to him, he shot Wolf, and Wolf went down.

David, nose bloody and left eye swelling, jumped to his feet and kicked Dagge in the kidney. Dagge lurched, and turned, but toward her instead of David, and with a tight little smile, he fired.

****

A black hole opened in David's gut when Hellen fell, and he wanted to run to her, but he couldn't. Dagge turned toward him, rifle up, and David had to survive, or in five seconds there wasn't going to be anyone who knew how to get to the Queen.

"I'm the only one who knows where she is," he said.

"That's not that impressive when I can just go in there and find her."

"She's not in there. Go ahead and look."

Dagge stopped, and lowered his rifle to his chest. Almost nonchalantly, he walked toward David, and when he got close, he said, "I think I will. And by the way, I'm pretty sure I owe you this." Then he smashed David in the head with the butt of his gun.

Chapter S.28

As hard as she tried, Adia couldn't hear anything up top. She leaned, and paced, and stepped in and out of the shaft, and all the while silence sat around her, ancient and immovable. After a time, she wondered if she might be able to lower the cart and take herself back up. But the ropes wouldn't move—David must have set the brake.

The smoke smell drifting down the shaft a little while later was how she knew someone had set fire to the monastery. The rock wouldn't burn, of course, but the rugs, Diit's couch, Beau's kitchen shelves, Hellen's trunk, her mattress, their clothes and blankets…all flammable. Thank One Diit had taken the crown back with him that night, and her father's cloak was with Vartile.

And it also meant that whoever it was had won. David was either dead (she refused to believe he was dead), or on his way to the dungeon. Hellen hadn't gotten there in time. When she did get there, she'd probably find the place in ruins, and since she didn't know how to access the tunnels, she'd go right back to the warren.

Adia had two real choices, both just a few strides away from her. One: go down the dungeon tunnel. David told her he could get himself and Roberta out, and she could be there when they did. Potentially after a very long wait. Or, two: she could take the chance there'd be a usable exit in town, and figure out how to get to the warren from there. Given the well tunnel exit would be too exposed, and the index tunnel pointed straight into the forest…

Fuck off tunnel it was.

Chapter S.29

Dagge was feeling pretty good about himself when he got back to his sitting room just before dinner. It had been a long, but very productive day, and the only down side was that he'd had to kill Hellen. But was that really a down side? Because considering all the trouble she caused, it was best to be rid of her.

Wasn't it?

Standing by his comfy chair, he untucked and unbuttoned his shirt before he sat to remove his shoes. He was sweaty after all the exertions, and wanted to shower before he ate. Smoke smell still clung to him, and the young guy's blood was smeared all over his neck and shoulders. Boy, was he glad he'd taken the Princess's horse—it would have been a lot harder to get the guy back to the palace without her.

And what a shame he had to leave Hellen for the carrion eaters, she was still a beautiful woman.

Her death made him realize all the plans he still had for her. When he fantasized about parades in his honor, and celebrations of his greatness in gold-tinged palaces, it was always Hellen on his arm, admiring him. If he was honest with himself, he knew it was a pipe dream. The Hellen part, not the parades.

Someday he'd have parades.

After peeling off his socks, he stood and walked to the desk. Where was that valet? All these years of him hovering and being annoying, and the time he actually wants him around to take his clothes, he's nowhere to be seen. He yanked the fancy embroidered bell pull at the corner beside the King.

"Got anything you want to say, Kingy? I am going to find your baby girl, and I'm going to kill her. And there ain't nothing you can do about it." For good measure, he slid his big knife out of the sheath on

244

his belt, and stabbed it violently into the canvas head. There he left it, stepping back a bit to admire his handiwork.

He had everything that once belonged to Som Beldenet. He had more, two whole countries more. And before long, he'd have the daughter, too. Pretty much everything he'd ever wanted.

Except he wouldn't have Hellen. He'd shot her in the heart, just like she did Eladora, and John, and so many others. Teach her to steal from him, because those creatures were his. She stole their lives, stole their service, stole his future. It woulda been so much easier to take the continent if he had all of them.

So he was glad he killed her. She deserved it.

The Princess was his next challenge. He'd checked every room in the old building, every closet and potential hidey hole, and she was nowhere. If she was in the town, why was the guy in the forest? Unless he was Hellen's lover, but there wasn't any evidence he was living there. The evidence said two women had been living there, and at least one of them had a trunk full of disguises.

Hellen had a trunk full of disguises. Of course she did, because Thorn needed disguises.

Well, not anymore.

Dagge sat in his desk chair and pulled out the shallow center drawer. The trophy he'd picked up was stuck to his pocket and he had to peel the fabric down around it until he could get it out. Bringing it up, he laid his hand on the desk in front of him and looked at it.

It was a bar of Hellen's soap.

"Yes, Overlord, can I help you with something?"

"Where the hells have you been, valet? I rang five minutes ago."

"I'm sorry I was not here faster, sir, I was in the kitchen, going over the menu wi—"

"Fine, whatever. Help me out of these clothes."

It felt good to get the filthy shirts off. They had to be peeled away, stiff as they were with blood. Still, the valet folded them, and he took so long, Dagge started jerking his other clothes off himself. "Don't fold them, you dolt, burn them," he said, yanking his pants and underwear down, and pushing his socks from his feet.

Naked at last, he rubbed his package, scooped up the soap, and headed for his bathroom, calling, "Don't anybody bother me while I'm in the shower!"

Chapter S.30

By the time Adia reached the end of the tunnel, she'd tripped four times, scraped up both palms, and was bleeding from one knee. Smooth floors were clearly not considered worth the effort in ancient tunnel-building. Granted, a lot of that time she'd been distracted by what might have happened at the monastery. Did Dagge kill David? Would he know he was John's son? Would he put one of those things in him if he did?

The more agitated she got, the more she stumbled. Thus, she learned to focus on the here and now.

The tunnel trend had been uphill for a while, so the finish line would probably be a basement, or perhaps a sub-basement, or even a stairwell or dumbwaiter. Something not too terribly far below the surface, at any rate, and she clung to that idea like it was an inflatable boat.

Not too far back, she'd passed through a breath of air that tickled her face. Stopping briefly to investigate, she discovered a fissure in the wall, about as high as she could reach, and the air drifting in was warm, so most likely from the surface. That was encouraging.

When she finally felt the wall turn and become the end, she reached out with both hands and felt along it for any kind of panel, or secret lever, or hidden latch, or anything crazy monkish-like. There were lots of examples in the palace of what sort of things the exit activator could be, and she felt confident she could identify it if she came across one.

Turned out it was a pull handle in a hole beside the door. Gears were set in motion, locks disengaged, and the door released. Adia ran her hands over it. Like so many monk doors, it was a slab. She pushed on the far side to bring the near side toward her. A rush of cool air swept out; in it she could smell oiled metal and pencil shavings. No sound, though. She stepped into the space beyond, and pushed the door closed softly behind her.

Getting through the basement was tricky. There was so much stuff, she couldn't follow a wall, and just walked around with her hands out in front of her, taking little sliding steps so she wouldn't stub her toes or whack her shins.

Floorboards creaked over her head. Maybe it really was the Bunghole Inn. A nervous laugh coughed out of her, and she clapped her hand over her mouth.

The creaking moved quickly away into light thuds. In a few seconds, she could hear a door open higher up and not too far away. A voice whispered, "Hello?"

"Hello?"

"Identify yourself!" the voice said. A young voice, male.

"I'm a friend of Thorn's." If this was a soldier, that was a mistake. Too bad she didn't think of it in time.

A light clicked on. Footsteps hurried down the stairs. "Your Majesty! What are you doing in our basement? How did you get here?"

"Joey Treslo, is that you?"

"Yes, ma'am!"

"I'm so glad it's you! No kidding."

"What's going on?" He was in front of her now, pulling her by the hand through the random stuff.

"I've come from the monastery, and I want you to take me to the blacksmith's."

"How did you get in our basement?"

"There's a tunnel. And a long story, and I'll tell you on the way."

248

Chapter S.31

Dagge's dinner seemed especially good today. Pork chops, mashed potatoes and peas—the perfect victory dinner, as far as he was concerned. He threw the bone down onto his plate and wiped the grease off his chin with the fancy white napkin. A rumbling belch burbled up out of his belly, followed by a smaller one. Ahh, perfect.

He waved his hand for the servant to come get his plate and bring dessert. He hadn't asked for any particular sweet, so he didn't know what it would be. Whoever cooked down there had learned his tastes, and always pleased him. He liked to think it was because she cared, and not because, you know, death. With any luck, it would be something chocolate. No better way to end a good day.

His instanote buzzed, and he picked it up to look at it. Only two people had this number, and they both knew it better be important. Most people didn't even use instanotes anymore, since the signals weren't secure, but he liked the challenge of making messages complete batshit to anyone but his chosen few.

"Travel plans in flux. Will call tomorrow a.m."

That meant she'd secured a place to stay. And she'd be at their meeting tonight—usually late, never early. He messaged back.

"Not good enough." Which, of course, meant "Fine."

Simple, yes, and easily breakable perhaps, but it made little difference. When you're the guy with all the bombs, people don't generally mess with you.

A waiter bearing a tray hustled into the dining room, up the outside of the big table, and swept the tray down to his level before depositing the chocolate mousse in front of him. Delectable. With a bow of his head, the servant turned on his toes and hurried back out.

You know what would make the day perfect? He dug a big spoonful out of the little bowl, careful to get as much whipped cream as mousse. *To make a visit downstairs. Ask a few questions. Get a few answers.*

A warm feeling swept through him.

Chapter S.32

When Hellen's eyes opened, Diit and John were leaning over her, their faces frowning and concerned. Behind them, the sky was growing dark—long shadows lay across the mountain, and only a few areas still caught the sun. She'd never really noticed before how beautiful the monastery was, carved in graceful lines. Or how the rest of the mountain was such a contrast, with its sharp peaks and jagged rocks.

"We're overjoyed to see you, Miss Hellen."

That was Diit, of course. He was the only one who ever called her "Miss."

"I'm glad to see you, too, Diit. And John!" Her throat had closed on itself, and she had to swallow. "I've been hoping for a year and a half you'd show up. I…can believe you're here, because monk, but I can't believe you're here." Her hand had reached for him, and he took it. Tears came to her eyes and streamed down her temples, her heart hurting with feelings.

"Where's David?"

"Dagge took him to the dungeon, which is perfect. Let's just worry about you right now."

Wait a minute. Dagge shot her, didn't he?

Her head snapped up, and she looked down at her chest, which had a burnt, shredded hole in it. What. The. Hells.

"You're fine, Miss Hellen," Diit said. "The monks fixed you up, you just need rest now."

The monks were clearly out of the bag.

"They did?" She tried to sit up.

"Noo," John said, and took her shoulders in his hands, easing her back down. "You need to lie right here for a minute. Then I'll take you in, and put you in your bed, and you will sleep. Do you hear me? I am speaking from a position of all-knowingness."

Tears flooded her eyes again, and her chin pushed her mouth into a frown. "I'm so sorry I had to shoot you...I had to." The last came out in a bit of a wail, and the tears spilled down her cheeks. Her body shook with grief.

"I know that. I'm *glad* you did. I wanted you to, it was horrible. That thing in me, and Dagge... Listen to what I'm saying. Dagge already had plans to use my knowledge, and you saved a lot of people by stopping me. Do you hear? Do you?"

She couldn't speak for a minute. Literally a whole minute. All she could do was lie there and sob until finally she pulled a breath and said, "Okay. I hear." Then she shook her head, cried some more, and squeezed his hand. Hard.

He waited patiently.

When she was better, Diit said, "Miss Hellen, we should get you in."

They got her up to standing, and she realized Wolf was nowhere to be seen. "Where's Wolf? He was hurt, Dagge shot him." Tears threatened again. "And has anybody checked on Adia?"

"Adia went down a tunnel," John said. "She's fine, and discovered all by her lonesome that the middle finger tunnel goes to our house."

"You're kidding me. Of course it does. Is anyone home?" she asked as they got up under her arms.

"Joey's home."

"Good. And Wolf?"

"Wolf's inside, Miss Hellen. The monks helped him, too."

"Thank One." Her anxiety quotient went down eighty percent. "Why does it smell like smoke?"

"Dagge set fire to everything."

"What?! In the monastery?"

"I'm afraid so," John said.

So much for that anxiety quotient. She limped to the monastery door, each arm draped over a pair of shoulders. Head hanging, watching her step, all she could really see was the torn and blackened fabric sticking up from her chest. It was tempting to touch—she wanted to know whether there was still an open wound there. For the moment, though, better to concentrate on one foot in front of the other.

Chapter S.33

The trip across town with Joey was a mixed bag. Much of the time he remembered she was blind, and gave her warnings of things. Other times she tripped over curbs. She got to where she could tell something was coming by his gait. Thank goodness.

She'd asked if he knew the drainage system route to Beau's, but he didn't. Luckily, he did know about the secret room downstairs. Self-defense lessons, he'd said, and maybe some eavesdropping. She could relate to that.

In Beau's office, the door slid away, reminding her of the time she'd come for her one self-defense lesson. Funny that she'd been here so many times after that, and even lived just a short tunnel's length from here for quite a while, but she hadn't used this door at all since that first time. Vartile's was closer, and made more sense for a young woman with no horse.

The warren was a frenzy of activity. Creaks, scuffs, thuds, squeaks, and harsh whispers bounced up to her once she stepped through the door onto the stairs. Her hand lay on Joey's shoulder so she didn't run into him, but she found herself pushing almost immediately. The energy was piercing.

"Do you see Beau?" she asked Joey as they got to the bottom.

"No," he answered, "I don't see anybody I know."

"Ask the nearest person."

His shoulder moved away, and nearby whispers drew her in their direction. It was Elzbieta. "Your Majesty." Pause. "Beau's in the north corner. There's a lot of excitement over there. I don't know what it is."

"Is Hellen there?"

"I haven't seen her."

Hellen must have gone to the monastery, probably thinking she and David were in danger. What if Dagge caught her there?

"Take me please, Joey." Her hand found Joey's arm. "Thank you, El."

"Yes, ma'am." A warm hand patted her arm, and El moved away.

The trip across the room was nerve-wracking, but thankfully without incident. Joey moved quickly, which was good, but erratically, which was exhausting.

"What do you see?" she whispered.

"Lots of people. The printing press is gone. Shelves are almost empty, and some of the units are missing. Wheelbarrows are waiting in line to dump dirt. The left tunnel is full."

"What about the back corner?"

"It's crowded. The wall is dug out some, and it looks like the floor might be, too."

"Do you see Beau?"

"No, ma'am, not yet, and we're right up on it now. There are too many people."

"We need to get in there. Can you do it?"

"Heck yeah, I can do it." He pulled her forward. "Be ready, it's a slope, all right."

Joey started saying "Queen coming through. Make way for the Queen," and it was so stereotypical, Adia wanted to laugh. But it worked. People began to step back, crunching loose dirt under their shoes, accidentally brushing her with their arms. As they became aware, the crowd thinned around behind her, and whispered "Your Majestys" surrounded her like mist.

Way to go, Joey. "What do you see now?" she asked.

"Beau's sitting on the ground. His legs are gone."

What?!

"Oh, no. They're in a hole. There's a hole."

"How big?"

"Three feet across, maybe? Two feet tall?"

"Take me as close as we can get."

Beau's voice spoke to her from just a few feet ahead. "Your Majesty! I'm so glad you're here. We've found a…tunnel, I think."

Chapter S.34

The guards had done the lazy thing and put David in the second cell, right beside his Mom. He'd woken up to a raging headache and a voice hissing his name. Light trickled from the guard room, and he could just make out the bars of his cage, and then the hand waving to him from around the wall.

"David!" Fair to say she sounded a little anxious.

"Mom, I'm fine. I'm awake."

"Are you okay? I saw them carry you in. You have blood all over you."

"Dagge hit me in the head. I'll tell you about it later." David fished the wire out of his shoe, listening to the guards talk in waves—loud, soft, loud again. When he stood he felt woozy, but no time to waste whining. "Mom," he whispered, "I'm pretty sure I know how to get out." With one hand he located the hinges on the cell door. "Find the tiny hole on the front of your bed." He unwrapped his wire and worked the middle of it under the head of the knee-level hinge pin. How much time had passed since these had been used, or even looked at? Grime and corrosion might be a problem.

The key lifted right out. And hung onto the wire. It was magnetic. Fascinating.

"Here, take this." David reached the wire through the bars and as far around the end of the wall as he could. His mother took it. "Get it under the head of the third hinge pin, and pull the pin out."

While his Mom was bu— "Got it," she said.

"Okay, good. Now take the pin and push it into the hole." David did the same, only his wouldn't go. He could barely see it in the dim light, and it didn't even look like a hole, really. More like a divot. Ugh, what he wouldn't give for a bulb torch.

"Got it," his Mom said again. "There's something happening. The end of the bed is opening."

Sure enough, a light scraping sound was coming from her cell. Of course it was the end, just like the box. Dad was right about all of it! What a superhero.

Loud, raucous laughter pushed down the hall, reminding him.

So what was his hole's problem?

The problem was, it wasn't a hole. "Hand me that wire," he whispered.

"Should I put the hinge pin back?" The wire appeared around the wall.

"Yes. Then go ahead and get out," he told her, taking the wire. "I've got to clear out the keyhole over here."

"David, I can't leave you."

"I'm going to be right there. Start going down the tunnel, I'll catch up. If I don't show, you know who to tell. Please, it's better if we're not both stuck."

She sighed long and heavy, and there was a pause. "You better get a move on, then, because I'm going to be hauling ass."

He smiled. "Love you so much, Mom."

"Forever and ever."

He listened to her knees pop and her groans as she got down to the floor and scooted herself through the secret passage opening. The same light scraping, and it closed again.

Back to the stone bed. Lowering himself to one knee, he set the hinge pin on the top of the block, and straightened the tip of the wire. Going by feel, he found the divot and dug into it, scraping and twisting the wire until he could feel tiny crumbs fall out on the back of his other hand. He was just reaching for the hinge pin when he heard Dagge's voice coming down the hall.

In a blink, he grabbed the key and shoved it in the keyhole. The light scraping started, he pushed himself to standing, dropped the pin into the hinge and made the end of the bed in two steps. Just as he was sliding into darkness, the torch came around the corner, and he was gone.

Chapter S.35

The dungeon was just as cheery as Dagge remembered. Remarkable, really, as dungeons went—roomy cells, pleasant hallways. Of course, they didn't keep the torches lit, no sense in spoiling the prisoners. But even in the dark, it was much better than some.

The gatekeeper led him down the hallway, holding one of the fire torches Dagge insisted they use. Fire gave him the feeling of primitive times, and how the captors carried literal life in their hands. It was satisfying.

The light rounded the corner first, beating back the darkness, forcing the will of man into the depths. His will. He was the man. Everyone else followed.

The cells were empty. He stopped.

"Come here, you idiot!"

The guard stepped quickly over, shining the light into the first empty cell. Dagge shoved him aside and rushed to the second cell. Same nothing. He whipped around and examined the cells on the other side of the walkway. All four were empty. He grabbed the torch, and ran around the corner into the next set of eight cells—same story.

Either Wharton had lied to him, or they had escaped.

Chapter 5.36

David wished he had a bulb torch. First thing he was going to do when he had a chance was put one down here. Hells, a dozen of them, because the floor was mostly smooth, but not completely. The walls were mostly straight, but not completely. He had to focus and be on alert with every step. If this was what Adia felt like all the time, he had an entire new respect for how she managed.

His mom, on the other hand, wasn't managing so well. He'd given up talking when she told him not to talk on her account. Even the news about Dad only made her cry. They were happy tears, she said, but she didn't sound all that happy. Part of it was the dark, maybe. She'd never been a big fan, always preferring a small light burning somewhere at night so anyone who needed a drink of water, or the bathroom, or a snack, could see.

And the dark down here was absolute. No hand in front of the face, or dim outline of anything. Being completely surrounded by it felt like nothing existed. Everything you thought you knew was wrong. Or worse, irrelevant. All of life was an illusion, and now he and his mother were outside of it. Alone. Together.

At that point, he had to stop thinking about it. In an effort to help—not just the thinking, but the walking, and the oppressive silence—he listed every element, and every formula he could think of, in between warning his Mom of every rise in the floor, every lump in the wall, and every element he couldn't think of, and she never complained. Most of the time she said nothing, but she didn't fall, either.

The tunnel seemed to go on and on forever.

He wondered if Adia would still be at the hub. She could have gone down a tunnel. He'd set the brake on the dumbwaiter because he didn't want her to risk going up if things went south and Dagge was still there. She wouldn't have any way of knowing. So maybe she'd be mad at him, but at least she'd be alive.

"Mom?"

"Yeah?"

"You okay back there?"

"I'm fine. Actually, could we stop a minute? I need to rest for a little bit."

"Of course. Where are you?" He waved his hand slowly behind him, until it collided with hers. He grasped her wrist, and helped her down, then lowered himself near her.

"Tell me about your father," she said.

"He looks good. Healthy. He was wearing that old shirt you kept asking him to throw away." He laughed.

She chuckled with real delight. "He loved that shirt, and of course he would choose it for eternity." They both laughed, and it was sunshine in the darkness. "I'm surprised he didn't want a monk robe, though. Did he have that option?"

"That's one to add to the list of questions! I probably need to literally make a list, because there's no way I'll be able to keep them all in my head."

"So you can ask him questions—that's pretty cool."

"But he can't divulge any secrets. That was what he said."

"Well, shoot, that's what I mainly want to know."

He could hear the smile in her voice, and it made him so very glad. "But why he's not wearing monk robes is probably not a secret, so we're asking him."

"Dang straight."

They were quiet a few seconds. "I was in Dagge's office, planting a bug."

"You were planting a bug?"

"Yes, it's the same one you caught me listening to, that day your father and Robert were getting questioned by Dagge, in the palace."

"I remember that day. The voices coming out of the speaker were mostly hard to identify, but Dad was pretty clear." David was amazed by his Mom's courage. "You figured you'd eavesdrop on Dagge?"

"It seemed worth the risk. Chances are he suspected what I was up to, though, so it'll be a surprise if it works." She paused for a moment. "I felt like I was losing everything, David. And it seemed an unfair burden to put on Joey."

"No one wants to live through these times, Mom. You are not alone."

"I know." They sat in the quiet for a bit, listening to air. She slapped her thighs. "Are you ready to go? I'm ready."

"I'm not quite ready," his father's voice said beside them. His mom gasped, and he added, "I need to talk to my girl."

His mom burst into tears, and there was shuffling, and her sobbing got muffled. Pretty soon she started wailing and keening, and it was hard to hear, but she needed it, so they waited it out, until eventually the crying became hiccups, and she could talk again.

"I'm so glad to see you. Well, not 'see' you, I guess." She laughed once. "Touch you, for sure. You do feel different."

"I try to feel as solid as possible," he answered.

"You're just a little squishy," David said.

"I wouldn't call it squishy…more fluffy."

"Like I used to feel."

"No, more like poodle hair."

"Poodle hair!"

Roberta laughed. "Poodle hair is great. It doesn't shed."

"I shed."

"Still?" David asked.

"Probably not."

"How's Joey?" Always the Mom.

"He's good. He's with the Queen at the warren."

"How did Adia get to the warren? I left her at the hub."

"The middle finger tunnel goes to our house. It's not a secret now, so I can tell you."

David sat there with his mouth open. "All this time, if we'd only known."

"No kidding. Excellent work finding the tunnels, by the way."

"It was an accident."

"Half the stuff in the world seems like an accident."

"Sooo, you're on first names with the Queen now," his Mom teased.

"She's the one who insisted," David rushed to say. "She told me she couldn't stand all the 'Your Majesties' at home."

"Really? 'Cause I always wished you guys would call me that."

"You're a riot, Dad."

"Thank you, it's good to know I haven't lost my touch. Roberta? Are you still ready to walk? We have a way to go, and we probably should."

"Yes, I'm ready." More shuffling, and they all stood.

"Dad...do you know the way? Can you see in the dark or anything?"

"Oh, I am much cooler than that," Dad said, and in a couple of seconds, a soft glow started. As it brightened, it became the outline of his father, then more three-dimensional, while also remaining half invisible. Like he had a sheen on him.

"Dang! That is cool!" David said, and realized he could see his Mom smiling. "You're bright, Dad, we can see!"

That's what I'm saying!" his father answered, waving his arms and grinning. His mom put herself right under one of those arms, and they started walking.

"I can't really feel you now. Except I can feel...*you*. The John I know."

David couldn't help but watch his parents as they whispered to each other. His Mom's face was turned up to his Dad's face, who was looking back down at her. So much love there. He hoped he could have that someday.

"David," his Dad spoke up, "I hate to be a party-pooper, but Dagge has realized you guys are gone, and he's going nuts. He'll check every place he can think of. The monastery, our house, the smithy, none of those places will be safe anymore. He's looking for the tunnels already, and he'll guess that's how you escaped the dungeon. It'll take him a while to get through the rock, but he won't stop until he does."

"What do we do?"

"I can't tell you what to do. You guys have to figure it out. I'm sorry. I *can* tell you that Hellen's life has been saved."

"Hellen! I forgot Dagge shot her!"

"Yeah, you got a pretty stout wallop to the head."

David reached a hand up to his temple. It was tender, and he could feel a crust of blood in his hair. "How was her life saved?"

"The monastery has a convergence of energies, in frequencies that vibrate higher than the third dimension. The monks can use those energies for quantum healing. Hellen's asleep now, you'll find her when you get to the monastery."

"What about Wolf?"

"Wolf, too. They're both Protectors, and their jobs aren't over yet."

"Is Joey going to be okay?" his Mom asked.

David's heart tugged. She'd worked so hard to keep him and Joey out of danger, and here they were, right in the thick of it.

"Don't worry about Joey, Robie. Whatever happens, he'll be okay."

"That's a cryptic answer, John."

"I'm sorry I can't give you a better one."

Her mouth opened, like she wanted to say something, then closed again.

"Hey," his Dad said, looking down at her. "Don't be afraid, all right? Life here is a temporary condition anyway. The best thing we can do is make a difference for other people. Right now, Joey's making a big difference. You said yourself that you want to be the kind of Mom who makes a better future. That's what it's all about."

She took a sharp, deep intake of breath, and let it out. Her head nodded, and she tried to relax the misery on her face. David turned his attention back to the tunnel ahead. He felt bad for her, but was really glad his Dad had said that.

His Dad's glow didn't light the tunnel very far, so they walked up on the hub without expecting it. David went immediately to the shaft and pulled the rope to lower the cart. It didn't budge. "When I locked this, I wasn't thinking we'd need to get out."

"Locking it is exactly what you should have done," the all-knowing monk-father said as he walked over to the shaft. "You don't need no stinking cart, son." With a sly look, he pressed the back wall and voila, a door swung open. There, inside a tiny tower, a presumably spiral staircase wound up into the darkness.

"Well, I'll be doggoned."

His Mom, with a look of facetious wonderment, said, "Why, John Treslo, is this a secret?"

"They already found a way to get down here. This is simply a...technicality." While his mother suppressed a smile, his father said, "Allow me," and swept himself up the stairs like a hero. David grinned at his mother in the fading light, and gestured her forward ahead of him.

"John, wait, we can't see!" she called, a smile playing over her face as she hurried through the door.

Chapter S.37

Hellen heard her name called in her dream. It echoed from a distance, and as she turned away from the incredibly blue pool of water she was facing, her eyes opened to find glowy John leaning over her, flanked by David and Roberta. It had to be one of the happiest sights of her life.

"Guys!" She worked her way up to sitting. "I'm so glad you're okay. Where'd you go, John? You were a lot more solid earlier," she said, waving her hand through his shoulder. "Does that hurt?"

"No, it doesn't hurt, and didn't we have this discussion the first time we were here?"

"I believe we did, and it seems almost as weird now."

"How are you feeling?"

"Um, pretty good, I think. A little groggy."

"Well, you were dead, so I'm guessing it's an improvement."

"Thank you, David, for that reminder. Roberta, I'm profoundly glad to see you." Hellen slid off her sleeping platform and wrapped a hug around her friend. "We were so distressed when we heard you'd been taken prisoner. What did you do?"

"I got caught planting a bug in Dagge's desk."

"A bug?"

"I thought it might be useful. Wharton's in there a lot, and it never hurts to know things. No good now, probably. I'm sure Dagge went over everything with a fine-tooth comb, especially the drawer. Robert had caught me first, and the drawer was still open when Dagge came in."

"So, if Robert hadn't delayed you, we could be listening to Dagge right now."

"Don't blame Robert, David, he was just doing his job. I was the one out of place."

"Mom—"

"I don't want to hear it!"

Roberta had definitely reached her fill line for the day. Hellen took her arm and steered her toward the kitchen. "Let's see if we can find anything to make tea out of, what do you say? Dagge tried to set fire to everything, but it didn't all catch, so maybe there's something edible. Is anyone hungry? I'm hungry."

Thank One, as they navigated the hall and the steps from the second level to the kitchen, John took over the inane chatter duties, because Hellen wasn't quite up to snuff.

"This monastery can't burn down, anyway," John said. "Not only is it rock, but it exists outside the space-time dimension. Its structure can't be damaged. When the monks destroyed the west wing all those centuries ago, they were only camouflaging it. It still exists."

"Why did they camouflage it? What was in there?" David asked.

"At the time, it was where they did experiments, and invented things relevant to the 3D world. Like a science lab." He paused. "That's all I can tell you."

They reached the kitchen, and Hellen gestured for them to sit. John took Roberta's hand and pulled her to the table, but David began tossing remnants of shelves into the fireplace, lighting them, and drawing water for tea. Hellen headed for the pantry, looking for any usable remains of food.

"So, if you can't tell us any more about the lab," David said, "that means we can't go in, either."

"Not in this dimension. Someday you'll be able to go in there. Hey, that reminds me…Roberta, remember that little pink book I asked you to give to David?"

"I didn't give it to him."

Hellen got very quiet so she could hear this.

"I know. And it's okay. It's just time now."

Roberta nodded, but her head drooped, and she didn't say anything.

"What book? And why do I get it?"

"Because you're my son. Monk blood, and all that. It's more or less an instruction manual, I think. The monks made it out of carapaz, and carved the pages in a language we don't have here. The only way we can "read" it is to sleep on it, and hope it vibrates its way into your brain better than it did mine."

"Sounds sketchy."

"Tell me about it."

Crisis averted. Hellen walked out of the pantry with maybe enough food to get them by. David was checking the tins for tea.

"I'm game to try. Where is it?"

"It's at home, under my pillow." Roberta sighed and shook her head. "Seemed worth a try."

Hellen tossed sardines and crackers onto the table, along with a rogue can of peaches, some peanut butter, and a jar of Vartile's home-canned beets. Stomach growling, she sat across from John, grabbed an opener from the caddy, and proceeded to open the food. "Dagge will be back soon, now that you guys have gotten away. He'll be sending soldiers to all our usual places. If we're going to get the book, we need to go soon, and then make sure he doesn't find us. We can hide in the tunnels for now. I'll send a pigeon...oh crap, I was supposed to send Beau a pigeon!" She shoved her cracker into her mouth, jumped up from the table, and ran to the kitchen door. It was dark outside.

"Here, I got my bulb torch, you can use it."

Hellen caught David's torch and hurried out the door.

****

Roberta reached inside her bra, pulled her little listening dome out, and set it on the table. Old ladies seldom got frisked. "He has your balloon, John. The one the paint was in? I found it in the drawer."

"Really? Why would anyone keep such a thing?"

"Because every time he sees it, he gets angry all over again. It motivates him. He has an addictive personality, only his addiction isn't alcohol or drugs, it's power."

David had started a small fire in the fireplace, and put the teakettle on to boil. Once that was done, he joined them. "That explains a lot," he said as he sat. "He kills an entire family for the land, and then the land goes neglected. He didn't want the land for anything, he just wanted to be a god."

"I'm worried about Robert being in the palace," Roberta said. "There's no telling when Dagge might lose his temper and just…"

"He's a smart young man. He knows better than to piss Dagge off."

"He won't have to piss him off, John. He just has to be there. Dagge doesn't need a reason, he's crazy. All he needs is a victim."

"Robert made his choice, Mom. We can't save him from himself."

Roberta burst into tears, covering her face with her hands. John put his arms around her, and in the middle of her grief, she felt his arms become the hard, strong shield she used to know. It felt so real, it made her cry more.

"Robie, Robie…it's going to be okay." He rocked and soothed her for a little. "If something happens to Robert, he'll be with me! And I'll take care of him, I promise."

It mended her a little. The crying slowed, and she raised her face to John's shoulder. "Well, at least there's that." And John started laughing, then David laughed, and then Roberta laughed. They all laughed. It was the weirdest thing. But so good.

Chapter S.38

Adia leaned against the wall opposite the hole, Joey beside her. In her hand, she held the message from Hellen. Cary had brought it from up top, where Beau had him on watch and/or taking a break. He read it to her: *Bouquet is beautiful. Will pick more flowers. T.*

Her chest relaxed, and she felt like she could breathe. Hellen was safe. *Bouquet is beautiful* probably meant Rose and David were, too. If Rose was free, David must have gone to the dungeon, which meant he was right about how to get out. All excellent news.

But Dagge would also know they were gone. If not yet, then soon. Which meant nowhere would be safe—not the monastery, not the warren, not the flower garden. *Will pick more flowers* had to mean she planned to get Joey, who was supposed to be home. Did Hellen know about the fuck off tunnel? John would tell her; it wasn't a secret anymore.

She and Joey might be able to catch Hellen if they left soon. Save her the trip here, and get back to the monastery asap.

"Cary."

He was bending over in front of her, talking down into the hole. "Yeah, we just got it." Beau said something. Cary replied, "I gave it to the Queen. Where does the tunnel go?" He stood and backed toward her.

Joey's arm shot out and blocked. "Watch out!"

Cary pulled back as he turned. His breath smelled like coffee. "Oh! I'm sorry, I didn't mean—"

Beau's voice moved up out of the hole. "Your Majesty," he said. "The tunnel goes to the well."

"That's fantastic," Adia said.

"But it's blocked there, by the well. We'll have to dig around it," he said, pushing up into the warren.

"We can do that, right? A hole just big enough for our largest person to get through. How long do you think that'll take?"

"Two hours?"

"Beau, you're my hero. Let's get everyone to go home and pack like they're going camping. Spread the word. We want the whole Resistance. Ask them to be back here in a couple of hours at the latest."

Beside her, Cary's energy was agitated. He kept moving his arms, shifting on his feet. "It goes to the monastery, right? I wish we'd known about this for the last three years," Cary said.

"Believe me, Cary, we tried."

"Who tried? Nobody asked me, I would've helped."

"Ma'am," Joey said.

"Ma'am," Cary said. Only there was a tiny edge to his voice instead of sincerity.

Beau started to say something, and she held her hand up to him. "John Treslo tried. Is that good enough for you?"

"I'm not saying I'm smarter than John, but you never know who might get lucky."

"Ma'am."

"I don't have to say it every time." Getting a little testy.

Cary needed a job.

"Please go find a team of diggers, Cary," Beau said.

A pause. "Now?"

"Yes, now!" Beau barked. Cary's energy scuffed away. Beau called after him, "Pickaxes and shovels!" as he moved to stand in front of her. "I'm sorry, ma'am."

"Do not be sorry. You were perfect."

He huffed a light laugh. "We're trying to teach him manners, it's a tough go. He's so full of himself, there ain't room in there." They both laughed. "So, the biggest problem I see with this hole is how are we going to disguise it if they break through that rock."

272

Adia's mind spun, and she rubbed her fingers across her forehead. After ten seconds, it turned out disguising a hole didn't include a lot of options. You put something over it, because a tunnel sure wasn't going to fill in.

Beau stepped away, and Joey said, "He's looking around the room, but there isn't anything left but wheelbarrows."

"How many?"

"Five."

She took a step toward Beau, her hand reaching for him in the small space. "We'll have to use the wheelbarrows. Take the bucket off one and lay it in the hole, cover the whole end with dirt, and jumble the rest in a pile. It's a poor solution, but anything else will take too much time. We need to find someone who'll hang back and do that."

"I will," Joey said. "I can cover the hole, go home, and use that tunnel to go to the monastery."

"I can stay with you," Beau said. "And maybe we should ask for a few volunteers. The more the faster."

"Yes, ask for volunteers," Adia said, "but I'd rather you lead the group through the tunnel. If the soldiers find the hole, we'll have to fight. Once the way is open, let's start moving everyone out, okay? It's a big job, but I'd like to leave this in your hands. Are you willing?"

"Yes, ma'am, I am."

The smile in his voice gratified her heart. "Great. I want to take Joey and go back to his house to catch Hellen."

"It'll be safer and quicker if you take the drainage system. Cary's used it, he can show you."

"I'm sure Joey and I can figure it out. Do you mind, Joey?"

"Not at all, ma'am. I've been in the other end. There's only one outlet, it's easy."

"Great. Beau, can I get a walkntalk?"

"Joey, get Cary's. Tell him I'll give him another one." Joey's feet scuffed the floor as he ran off.

"Thanks, Beau." Adia reached her hand out to him and he took it gently. "We can all meet at the hub and get some rest before we tackle the next thing. Sound good?"

"Sounds great," he said. "See you there."

Sunday

Chapter Su.1

The chair back dug into Dagge's ass, feeling like bruises on the bony parts. He liked it, liked the pain because it reminded him of his own suffering. The fucking rebels, all of them, were a pain in his ass, and until he caught and killed every last one of them, he wanted to suffer. To be reminded, so he wouldn't lose the fire.

The fire felt good. It made him alive; it satisfied his need for something to feel. Rage burned, lust burned, and vengeance was all that mattered.

He watched the soldiers try to dig out the giant rocks that lined the floor of the dungeon. He watched them hammer on the rock platforms in the cells, and poke things in the little holes on the fronts. He knew they'd never get in that way—those asshole monks probably put spells or something on this place. The only solution would be to tear it all down.

He liked that idea.

He stabbed his fork into the can of peaches in his hand and brought up another slice. It gleamed in the torchlight, dripping thick juice down his arm. He turned it, anticipating the texture and flavor in his mouth, and the saliva ran. He swallowed, holding the tantalizing peach back from himself. Sacrificing. Proving he hadn't lost his edge.

His life was too soft. Like his belly.

The bustle in front of him made him feel like he was accomplishing something. Four cells were open, and pickaxes hammered away at solid rock. In the hall between, metal rods had been jammed into the narrow space they'd made around one stone. Even if it had been hours, some small progress showed, and he didn't care how long it took. There was an escape tunnel here, and he aimed to find it.

He popped the peach into his mouth, his arm moving in a snake strike, like the peach might get away if he wasn't fast enough. It exploded on his tongue, flowing down his throat and into his groin, nudging his cock to life.

The fire felt good.

Chapter Su.2

Adia had refused Cary's offer to be a guide. He'd come back with Joey, really wanting to lead the expedition, but she was firm. The people needed him in the tunnel. Or so she said.

Joey was doing mostly fine. Adia did have to remind him periodically to tell her what was coming—trash, holes, rocks, whatever. He'd forget, but he'd also move stuff out of the way for her, so it balanced. The curve was a bit of a thing. She scraped the bricks sometimes, but only lightly, so she couldn't really complain. Plus, he reminded her of the other Treslos. He talked a lot, like John, had a practical side, like Roberta, and sounded like David. It was comforting to be with him.

Adia hoped upon hope the ditch wouldn't be as full of water as it was this morning. Yesterday morning. Whatever. The point being that she wasn't in favor of wet shoes for the long trip back to the monastery. Maybe Roberta wouldn't mind if she snagged a pair of dry ones.

When they reached the big pipe ends, where the drainage system met the ditch, the air became fresher and warmer. Humidity hung heavy in the still night. Frogs croaked at the river. Joey stopped, presumably at the edge of the ditch, and she stepped up beside him. "Is your light out?"

"Yes."

"Can you see anything?"

"No, it's pretty dark, but I'm not picking up any indications of people."

She had to bite her lips so she wouldn't laugh. That brain thing sure ran in the family, didn't it? So adorable.

"Me neither," she said. "Let's go."

He led her out into the gentle, knee-deep water. It was quiet—made it hard to be silent, but they picked their feet up and did the best they could. Before too terribly long, he slowed down and whispered, "We're here, at the climb out."

"Okay," she said. "Can you get out?"

"Oh yeah, I do it all the time."

"Can you help me out? Either pulling from up top, or pushing from down here?"

"Let's go together. You don't have to see to rock climb this, just feel."

"Seriously?"

"Yes, ma'am."

Adia ran her hand along the rock in front of her. Up above, at about the ten, she found a good handhold, then she realized she needed a foothold, and had to bend to search for that. After way too many seconds wasted, she said, "Joey, it'll be a lot faster if you pull me up."

"Okay, yeah," he said. A few grunts and scrapes later, his voice came down from above. "My hands are right above you."

Adia reached up and found Joey's hands. He immediately started to pull, and Adia stumbled her feet up the wall, digging in and helping the best she could. The young man was strong, though, and didn't need much help. The trip up the wall, in fact, was a teensy bit like hanging onto a rocket.

"Thanks," she whispered, bouncing up onto the grass.

"You're welcome." His hand pulled hers down suddenly, and they were crouching on the grass. "Soldiers," he said, and pulled her hand forward. They ran quickly, Adia forcing herself to have radical trust. Every nerve cell in her body was screaming at her to stop and be careful, but she just kept repeating to herself, *please, One...please, One...please, One.*

"We're at a street," Joey said, slowing down. "There's a curb here." They crossed the street, up another curb he warned her about, and then up a mound he didn't. She recovered, though, and soldiered on. Her feet whished through grass, slapped over concrete, scraped through bushes, and slapped over more concrete until Joey said, "We're here. Three steps up."

His arm disappeared as he mounted the steps, and Adia heard the door open. She followed Joey inside, and a man's voice said, "Joey, what the hells are you doing with the Princess?"

Chapter Su.5

The rock was freakily indestructible. Dagge paced the floor of the hallway, hands on his hips, scowling at the sweaty workers, who were looking a little sullen, he noted. Maybe he should put a little fear into them.

"Every man in this room will be executed if we don't find THE GODDAM ESCAPE HATCH!" With a sweep of his arm, he knocked the chair he'd been sitting on, sending it crashing into the bars of the nearest cell. It flipped and bounced away, landing on its back on the other side of the hall. The men averted their eyes, hopefully imagining they were the chair. The silence stretched.

Then his instanote buzzed, ruining the moment. Wharton better have some good news.

But when he pulled the device out of his pocket and looked at the feed, it wasn't Wharton. Dagge whipped around and stormed to the guard room, took the stairs two at a time, and made a right turn into the back hall. *What the hells?* He remembered issuing strict orders never to come to the palace. Secret identities were meant to be secret, not paraded around in front of every Joe in the kingdom.

I'm in the room with the big globe, it said. The assumption being that he'd come right up, and what if he didn't? What if he'd been asleep? What if he'd been out, or in the tub, or any damn thing he wanted besides rushing to the War Room?

Except he did want to rush to the War Room. He practically flew down the hall, then the next hall. When he reached the closed door, he wrenched the handle and pushed it open so violently, it banged against the wall beside him.

There, sitting on the desk, was a short, slight woman. Her black hair hung to her chin, color-matching the soft, nondescript clothes she wore. And her sensible shoes. When she looked up at him, she smiled a cold, heartless smile. Just his type.

But he couldn't let her know that.

"I distinctly remember telling you not to come here," he said, crossing the room to her.

"Aw, boss," she purred, slithering off the desk and walking right up to him. "I didn't let anyone see me." Her hand fiddled with his shirt, prompting him to grab the small, cold fingers. "I gotta say, though, your security is a little lax."

He squeezed the fingers until she winced (*Ow!*), then let them go and pushed her out of the way. "Maybe you should do your job, and SHUT THE FUCK UP about everything else." There was a pause while he went around the desk and yanked a drawer open.

"Boy, someone's cranky."

The bottle in the drawer was still half full, but it wouldn't be for long. He lifted it out and set it on the desk. Several shot glasses lined one side of the drawer—he pulled two, and set them beside the bottle.

"Well, after that greeting, I wasn't sure I'd be asked to stay."

"I haven't asked yet." Bottle in hand, he sloshed the fire water into the glasses, pouring an equal amount onto the desk. When they were full, he picked one up and slammed it.

"Ohhh, I know what happens when you get a few drinks in you." She walked slowly closer and leaned her thighs into the desk, pushing her hips toward him. Languidly, she reached for the other shot glass, and tossed the dark liquid down her throat.

"I thought I told you to shut up." He poured another round for both of them.

"You did, but I'm not listening."

He chuckled at that. She never did listen. He wasn't entirely sure why he put up with her, but handed her another shot anyway.

"In case you're wondering," she said, taking the glass, "you like me because I get results. And I've got results now. Want to hear them?"

Dagge took his time moving the desk chair and sitting himself in it. While he dawdled, leaning back, putting his feet on the desk, she

281

downed the second shot. He smiled; he could always count on her to be thirsty.

"Will I like it?"

"No, but that's not really the point, is it?" When he didn't answer, she got pissy and leaned toward him, both fists on the desk. "Hellen's little friends have finished filling in the mountain tunnel on the west side, and you won't be able to get in over there. Not soon enough."

He looked at her, still not saying anything, holding her gaze until she looked away, tapping the desk with her nail. With a little laugh, she picked up the bottle and poured herself another, drank it, then offered him one. He declined. "Where's the other way out?"

Her face went dark, and she slammed the bottle down on the desk. "I don't know. I've tried to make them trust me, and I can't. What I know is that the people were packing like they were going on a big camping trip."

Dagge took the bottle and filled his glass.

"Hellen's dead," he said. "Her little friends won't be anything without her. They're a bunch of shopkeepers and professors, running away. You think I'm worried about them?"

"They have more going on than you think."

"I've got guns." Dagge stood, leaning in over the desk until his face was a single inch from hers. "And more important things to worry about. Like where is the Princess? Can you tell me that? Huh? Because I know she's alive. And she shoulda been at that hideout, but she wasn't. Oh, her stuff was there...but not her."

He leaned back, tugging his tight shirt down so it covered his belly. With slow, deliberate steps he walked around the end of the desk and right up to her. She faced him, and his hand reached up to catch the swinging black hair. He looked at it for a moment before he balled it up in his fist and yanked her toward him. "Those are the results I want, Anji. Now get the fuck out until you have them."

282

Chapter Su.6

Never having had brothers, or sisters, or siblings of any kind (not even a dog), Adia found the heated arguing between Joey and Robert nearly unbearable. While she had managed to find the table and sit, it didn't offer any relief from the storm of sound they were building between them.

"Where's Mom, Joey?"

"Stop asking me that! I don't know where Mom is! Last I heard she was in the dungeon. Maybe you should check there, and shut the hells up!"

"I know you know. You were all so righteous about this little rebellion. I can't believe I didn't turn you in as soon as I figured it out. Now I'm implicated right along with you. Do you realize Dagge didn't know "Rose" is my mother? What do you think he'll do to me when he finds out?"

"Then come with us," she blurted.

"Come with you?" Robert's voice turned toward her, and she could feel the focus of his eyes. "I hate to tell you this, but you're going to die. All of you. Do you know what he's having built in those weapons factories in Valdia? Not just bombs, and guns, and missiles, but biological weapons. Chemical weapons. There's a virus that melts flesh. One chemical blisters every bit of skin it touches, including your eyeballs. They blister, and the blisters pop, and then you're all bleeding ooze. I saw the report. You're not playing this game with a minor character. He knows what he's doing. The only way for anyone to survive is to follow him."

Horrified, Adia said nothing. They were going to be very lucky if they got away from here.

"How can you be such an ass?" That was Joey.

"At least I'm not a traitor." That was Robert.

"Robert! You ARE the traitor. How can you not know that?!"

"Gentlemen!"

The nonstop argument stopped. For a second.

How was she going to defuse this?

She stood. "We might all be better served by taking a step back."

"Your Majesty…"

"You're calling her 'Your Majesty?'"

Oh crap.

"Miss Beldenet," Robert said, "out of respect for who you are, were, to all of us in Great Hand, I will not take you prisoner. This time. If I ever see you again, I will, and I will take you to the palace without delay."

Adia was glad Roberta couldn't hear that.

"I believe you," she said. "And I appreciate your gesture. I know there would be certain advantages to bringing me in, and I consider it an honorable thing for you to give me fair warning this way."

No answer. Until Joey couldn't help himself anymore. "He's not honorable—"

"Joey!" she said sharply, and shook her head, hoping he was looking at her. He must have been, because he stopped.

"Joey, however, is a different story." Robert's voice had gotten a silken sound. "Taking him to the palace would tease everyone out, wouldn't it? There'd be a dramatic rescue, and all the important rebels would show up somehow. They'd sneak into the dungeon to free John and Roberta's baby son."

"Get away from me, Robert. Fuck you, asshole, get back. Get back! You're never going to catch me." Joey's voice moved, first to the right, then away, then to the left, then more left until his feet disappeared down the hall to the stairs.

"Robert, stop!" she cried, feeling her way around the end of the table and toward the den.

Shouting voices echoed through the upstairs hallway, screeching down the stairs in a storm. "Don't touch me! DON'T

TOUCH ME!" A loud thud shook the house. Several smaller thuds followed.

Adia felt her way to the doorway of the foyer. Someone was moving around upstairs, but she had no way of knowing who. "Joey!" she called.

No one answered her. "JOEY!"

Footsteps creaked on the upper story, coming down the hall and starting down the stairs. But not the light, easy run those boys always took, these were slower, and heavier.

"Robert, please don't do this. You have no idea what Dagge will do."

"He'll put him in the dungeon, just like he has everyone else. You can tell all your co-conspirators right away, and he may not even have to spend the night."

"Please don't. He's your brother."

A short laugh huffed out of him as he reached floor level, where he stopped for a second before moving toward the door. "That might matter to David, and Mom, but I'm more logical than that. If I can show Dagge that I will sacrifice my own family to help him, what choice will he have but to believe in me?"

Chapter Su.7

Hellen had to take a rest. Apparently, dying took a lot out of a person. Here she was, on her rock slab, in her room, wishing very badly that that asshole hadn't burned their rugs, and cushions, and blankets, and every useful comfort they had.

Stretched out on her stomach, she closed her eyes and let her brain wander. Sometime soon, she'd tell Adia she saw her father in those minutes she was dead, and the King looked well and happy. It wasn't her time yet, he'd told her, she needed to go back. He said time was getting short, and certain things had to happen. Dagge had to be stopped, or the whole world would suffer.

Didn't she know that already?

Think about something else.

On the upside, she also met her own parents, which was poignant and happy at the same time. The pictures she'd seen didn't do them justice; they were so full of life, and love, including love for her, and it wrapped her up and filled her with a bright joy. They told her they were proud of her, and had always watched over her. She felt so much healing to her heart, mending the loss as well as the muscle.

What a day. She'd been surprised that Adia wasn't here. John said she was at the warren with Joey, which was amazing. It meant she'd gone herself, and doing that alone was leaps ahead of what she would have done six months ago. Hellen felt so proud of her.

David had left to go down the "fuck off" tunnel (as he and Adia had named it—good for them), and see how he could help. Hopefully that meant bring Adia back. They were all going to end up here anyway, and Hellen would feel a lot better with Adia in her personal protection zone. And David could bring Joey back too, while he was at it. She'd said in her message that she'd do it, but felt fine about letting David handle that job.

No better person in the world.

Chapter Su.8

It had taken Adia a while to get out of John's basement—she hadn't anticipated needing to navigate it in reverse all by her lonesome. But she did okay, only running into things twelve times before finding the stridemeasure she dragged against the wall now.

The tunnel was longer on the way back, she swore. That could be something the monks would do, right? Some kind of crazy time/space manipulation?

Okay, maybe not, but it sure felt like it.

"I could hear you coming a mile away."

David's voice echoed in the tunnel, cutting right through the annoying scraping noise she'd gotten used to. Relieved, she dropped the offending end of the ruler, and let the rest of it fall between her feet and the wall.

"David, Robert took Joey to the palace."

"What?" His footsteps moved toward her, and she waited to feel his energy. When he was close, she felt the familiar ringing of him, which restored and comforted her.

"They fought," she said. "They were so angry with each other. Robert kept asking where your mother was. He thought Joey knew. Is your Mom okay?"

"She's at the monastery, and she's seen Dad, so she's much better. Was Robert going to turn Joey over to Dagge?"

"He thinks Dagge will just put him in the dungeon, like he did with you and Roberta." David's energy stepped away again, and she could hear his feet pacing on the rock.

He stopped. "And what do you think?"

"I think Joey's in real trouble."

"Damn!" His hands grasped her upper arms, and his face bent over hers. "I have to go to the palace, Adia."

"I know. Don't worry about me, I can make it to the monastery on my own."

"Actually, I need you to go back to my house and get the carapaz book. Can you do that?"

"Of course I can. I'm an old hand at your house now. Where is it?"

"Under Mom's pillow. Their bedroom is at the front, on the right."

His hands vanished from her, and his voice went down. Under it, the familiar sound of tying shoelaces. "When you get back to the monastery, there's a stairwell on the back of the dumbwaiter shaft. You just push the rock to open it. Hellen is sleeping."

"Is she okay?"

"Dagge shot her, but the monks healed her and she's going to be fine."

Too much to sort through right now. "The Resistance will be there soon. They found the well tunnel."

"That's fantastic!" David said, "But I have to go." His voice drifted back to her as he jogged away. "I need to sleep on that book!"

"Bye!" she called.

"I'll be back as soon as I can!" he answered.

And he was gone.

Adia picked up her measuring stick, and scraped along the wall the way she came. She was going to know this tunnel like the back of her hand.

Chapter Su.9

By breakfast time, he was starving. He'd been sitting in the dungeon most of the night, watching the nonexistent progress through the floor. Near morning, he'd had the dumbwaiter door opened, and when the smell of bacon and biscuits reached his nose, he was out like a shot. Up the hall, up the stairs, up the hallway to the kitchen, barking orders. Now he sat in the main dining room, his back to the Fat King, enjoying his three eggs, two biscuits, and five pieces of bacon. The potatoes were also good, and the coffee was perfect.

If the cook was trying to comfort him with good food, it was going well.

Shoving the last bite of biscuit and jelly into his mouth, he tossed his napkin on the table and pushed back his chair. He was beginning to regret sending Anji away. At least he could've gotten a good fuck—she was a spectacular lay, and after all the bullshit of the last few days, he could've used it. But oh well, then there would've been the awkwardness of getting rid of her, and he had more important things to do.

Just as he was about to exit through the tattered king's belly, the butler came in through the main door, calling his name. "Overlord!"

Dagge stopped and turned. The butler started the long journey up the side of the table. His expression wasn't happy. The man hardly ever looked happy, but this was a sour look, even worse than usual.

"Overlord, sir, the young Mr. Robert is here, and he has a…guest."

"And why am I being interrupted for that?"

"He claims you will be interested to meet one of the rebels."

Everything went still for a second. The hairs on Dagge's arms stood up, and the whole room came into sharp focus. This moment

290

mattered. Whoever waited outside in that hall was destiny. Excited, he stood.

"Have the guard in the hall escort them to my sitting room." He waved the butler back to the door and left through the secret passage.

In his sitting room he paced a bit and shook his arms out, trying to get rid of the sudden energy. His fingers ran through his hair. His shirt was tugged back down. He pulled his knife out of his belt and threw it into Ol' Kingy's chest. It stuck just fine.

By the time the knock came and the door opened, he was seated and ready.

It was a little hard to tell the two apart. Except for the fact that one was dogged by a guard. Other than that, pretty interchangeable. What did that mean, exactly? Was Treslo turning in his own family?

The guy was a suck up for sure. Wharton had brought him up, after he was found sitting in a dungeon cell with the door open, that night Hellen killed his old man. It was his father's fault he was down there, of course, since Treslo was a traitor, and most apples don't fall far from the tree.

This apple, though, was more like a pine cone or something, because he didn't have a save-the-people bone in his body. He'd said some cleaning woman had tried to get him to run, but he didn't want to do that. He wanted the Overlord to know that he was loyal, and believed in him. Ever since that night, he'd lived up to it, too—kept his head down and nose to the grindstone. The financial reports showed up on his desk every morning, always neatly precise, and if they ever ran into each other in the halls, he was always servilely deferential. What wasn't to like about that? Even when he was caught with Rose, he repeatedly said he was confronting her, and she confirmed it was so. Wharton had his doubts about keeping the guy around, but Dagge liked the idea of having that little piece of Treslo at his any potential whim. Even better that he was a pine cone.

Dagge leaned back in his chair and watched the procession walk over to the desk and stop. The prisoner was younger than Robert, but not by too much. He was skinny, and his hands were tied, which was good.

"Yes, Mr. Treslo?"

"Overlord, sir, I've brought you one of the rebels."

Dagge took his time running his eyes over them. "This young man looks remarkably like you. Is this your brother?"

"Yes, sir, it is."

Dagge laughed. "That's cold, Treslo."

The older one blanched, and got this stricken look on his face that made Dagge want to laugh even more. So he did. "You look like I pissed your birthday cake! What did you think, I was gonna give you a medal for turning in your own family?"

"See, I told you, Robert! You keep thinking—"

Then the guard tapped him on the side of his face with the end of his gun, and he stopped yakking. Probably some history there. Dagge could easily imagine this kid running his mouth until the guard got sick of it. Hells, he was sick of it, and it had barely started.

"What's your name, son?"

"His name is Joey."

"Did I ask you?"

"No, sir."

"Then shut up."

The mouth closed, and he gave the slightest nod. Good answer.

"Your name is Joey?" No answer. The guard nudged the back of his head with the gun tip.

"Yes, sir."

"What do you think about your brother bringing you to me?"

Joey looked over at his brother's face, still stricken-looking, and refusing to meet his eyes. "I think he's a traitor."

The brother's eyes got hard and angry, and he turned to face him. "*You* are the traitor. Just like Father."

"I wish I was like Dad! He was brave, and everything he did was to protect this country!"

"Everything he did was against the government of this country. That's the definition of treason."

With a quick, furious look at the government in question, Joey shut up.

"You have to admit, Joey, he's got a point," Dagge said. "If I were you, I might not use your father as an example."

Joey didn't speak, and kept his eyes on the floor. Too bad.

"Roger, what do you expect me to do with this prisoner?"

Joey huffed a small laugh and stood there shaking his head.

"Sir, they'll come to rescue him. He's John Treslo's son. My other brother, David, will try to free him as soon as possible. Maybe even this morning."

"Is David the one that was in the dungeon earlier?"

"Yes, sir."

"And is the cleaning woman your mother? Rose?"

After a short pause, he admitted it. "Yes, sir."

Joey had an anguished look on his face. "Can't you just shut up?"

"I see."

He couldn't believe he'd let it get past him. Rose was John Treslo's wife, all this time. Cleaning his bathroom four times a day. She could have tried to poison his mouthwash or something, and he never would have known the difference.

He wrestled the urge to launch out of his chair and attack. He wanted to roar and pound his chest like a big silverback. He wanted to swing out with enormous arms and knock them all across the room. He realized he was breathing through his mouth, and closed it.

"When David comes, we can...you can catch them, sir. You can see how they get out of the dungeon."

"Shut up, Rodney."

"I can't believe you'd get your own family killed, *Rodney*," Joey said. "You're a fungus. I mean, I always knew something was wrong with you, but I thought you at least loved Mom and Dad."

"Joey, now is not the time to show how stupid you are."

293

Dagge gave up, and stood. "Oh, I don't know, Roderick. I think maybe you're the stupid one." He took one step, two steps toward Joey. "But you're right about one thing, this is John Treslo's son. And they're going to come for him." Another step brought him face to face with the boy, and he found his eyes on the sparse hairs of his chin. He let his gaze travel up over the face, and the ghost of his father was there, in the clear blue eyes.

Trouble.

The guard from the dining room door stood next to and a little behind the boy. His eyes never left Dagge. Deep inside the pupil, a purple glow flashed like a sheen. The smirk looked permanent.

Dagge gave the soldier a short nod. The face went slack, mouth dropping open and eyes drooping. The knees began to buckle. Dagge backed away to the space in front of the desk, alerting both Treslos. Joey followed his gaze and spun around. The purple in the soldier's eyes got brighter, pulsing and glowing.

Joey thrashed to get his hands free. Robert grabbed Joey's arms and pulled him back, so Dagge had to hit him in the kidney. Robert went down, landing on his back. Dagge punched his face but the giraffe pushed him away, holding his arms. Dagge broke free, grabbed Robert's arms, and pounded his knee into Robert's belly.

A sharp stab pierced Dagge's back. He dove away and scrambled to his feet. Joey had his knife. He held it out in front of him and stood over his brother like a mama bear. "Robert, get up! Get up!"

Behind him, long blades of magenta had begun to shoot out of the guard's body. Stretching in every direction. Searching. Joey was more focused on getting Robert up. When the monster hit him, he was surprised.

The monster sliced through Joey's head and bent toward him, dumping the soldier's body on the floor. Joey's eyes blanked. "Run!" he told his brother. Terror all over him, Robert backed away, scurried to his feet and out the door.

Then Joey buried Dagge's knife in his own heart.

Chapter Su.10

David jogged as much as he could down the palace tunnel, but he had to stop sometimes and catch his breath, and let his muscles recover a little. Running for fun had never been his thing, and he felt like all the upper body muscle was maybe a detriment. Why hadn't he done some squats or lunges or something?

He'd toyed with the idea of stopping at the monastery to tell everyone what Adia had said, but he figured his Dad would know about Joey, and time might be short. What he really wished was that Dad would tell him how to get into the dungeon from the tunnel, but of course it was a secret, and blah blah blah.

It didn't seem possible to climb up the chute that he'd dropped down earlier—pure carapaz, he was pretty sure. Slick. He'd had to slow himself down with his feet, since he didn't know how it ended. Maybe the monks made it literally impossible to go up because they didn't want access into the dungeon, only out. That way, if the monastery was found, and by some chance the tunnels were found, the palace would still be protected.

Hopefully that wouldn't be the case.

"It is the case," his Dad said.

He was jogging beside him—David turned his head and they looked at each other.

"What are you doing, Dad?"

"Can we stop for a second? I have something to tell you."

"Stop?" He glanced ahead at the endless stream of tunnel in the light of his bulb torch, disappearing into darkness beyond. "Okay." They stopped, David's breath echoing off the rock around them. He bent over to try and catch it a little faster. "What is it?"

"I'll wait."

David stood up again, suddenly wary. "What is it, Dad? Is it Joey?"

"It is Joey, David. Dagge tried to put a monster in him, and he sacrificed himself to keep from being one of them."

David's heart, and stomach, and lungs felt like they disappeared, leaving empty space and blood draining through the hole. For an eternity he couldn't talk, he couldn't think. When he finally spoke, his voice came out husky and soft.

"I left him, Dad."

Then he shook his head, and had to move, pace, because Robert was there, Robert turned Joey in, and what did he think was going to happen?

His mind couldn't help imagining it. And he wanted to know what happened, but he didn't. It tore him up either way.

"Let me just tell you two things," his Dad said. "One, he killed the monster by not giving it a place to go. And two, he'll be with me soon. Please don't worry about him. This death was part of his soul contract, and he's a hero."

David couldn't help it, he sobbed. And why should he help it? Joey was a part of him—an annoying, funny, wise, integral part he would miss terribly. Miss being with him, and watching him become a man.

A profound grief shook David, and he put the heels of his hands over his eyes, pressing his brow while the pain leaked out of him. His Dad put his arms around him, and after a long and short while, it stilled.

"Why isn't he here, then?" David asked, when he had finally leveled out, and stood wiping his face and neck.

"Well, there's process. It's different for everyone." The conversation paused for a moment. "There's something else I have to tell you, too, are you ready?"

Ugh. "Yeah."

"Robert's been put in the dungeon."

"That's good news."

His Dad took a deep breath (*he breathes?*) and said, "I know you're mad at him, but try to be careful with your thoughts and words, especially around your mother. He's still our son, and your brother."

"He killed Joey."

"Joey killed Joey. Robert didn't believe Joey would die. Otherwise, he never would have done it."

"You have a lot more confidence in him than I do."

"Yeah, but I know everything now." The ridiculous expression on his face made David chuckle. Dad was always so good at that, it was kind of infuriating. "There you go, that's what I'm saying. Are you ready to go back to the monastery? Because I'm going to need you to be there when I tell your Mom."

"Yeah, I'm ready." They turned back up the tunnel and started jogging. "Thanks for not asking me to go rescue Robert."

"You're welcome," Dad said. "He actually needs to stay there, but don't ask me why."

Chapter Su.11

Tired hit Adia like a bag of bricks when she got back to the monastery. Her right hand was aching from working the stridemeasure, and her left hand clutched the carapaz book. At the dumbwaiter, she leaned the stick against the wall and pushed on rocks until the door opened. Nifty.

The Resistance wasn't there yet. Given that Beau was in charge, she shouldn't worry. He could manage anything. Most likely it was just hard to get out of town, especially with that many people. All the minor emergencies you had to deal with before you could get on the road.

Yep, pulling hard for minor.

Wolf was the one who greeted her in the kitchen, after she groped her way up the steps, stressed over whether the dumbwaiter brake was set properly, and climbed out the hole instead of lowering the wall. Honestly, it was a bit disappointing not to receive applause, but no one else was downstairs, not even in the great room.

There was food on the table, though, she could smell it. It made her stomach growl, and she realized it had been a while since she'd eaten. The scent drew her forward. She laid the book on the table and hovered over it, breathing. It smelled warm and savory. Saliva flooded her mouth.

But all that was driven right out of her head when a tinny voice spoke just behind her.

"Your Majesty?"

She whirled around. "Diit! You scared the crap out of me," she said to the bank of pipe ends. "Where are you?"

"I'm in your chamber, ma'am. I've been cleaning it up a bit, I thought you might need a rest before this evening."

"Thank you, Diit. I am bone tired, no kidding. Hungry, too, can I have something from the table?"

"Of course, ma'am! I'll be right down to tell you what we've got."

"That'd be great." She turned back to the table. Wolf joined her, and she stroked his neck as they leaned in, noses almost touching the food. There was roast chicken, and some kind of grilled meat. Bread, smelling so buttery. Cookie must have done this; that woman was getting a raise as soon as the kingdom was theirs again.

"I laid some blankets on your sleeping platform," Diit said as he came down the last few stairs to the kitchen. "It won't be as soft as your mattress, but perhaps it will be better than the plain stone."

"You're the best, Diit, I'm so lucky to have you."

"We are all lucky to have you, ma'am. Truly."

He put some oomph on the last word, and Adia didn't know what to say. She smiled, and her forehead squinched—she hoped she could live up to it.

The pump handle clattered, and Adia could hear the water run at the sink. "Hey, that's a great idea." She joined Diit to wash hands. "Is all this food for everyone?" Wolf made the familiar sounds as he lay down in his usual spot in front of the back door.

"Cookie and I thought everyone would be hungry," he said. "There's been a lot of work done, and not much time for stopping."

Interesting how he would know that. He'd been at the palace, hadn't he? Rinsing, she took a shot in the dark. "How close are they?"

"I can't say for certain, ma'am, but I believe it won't be long." The water stopped, and a towel rose into her hand.

"Let's wait, then. They're going to be hungry, too," she said as she dried. "What about David? He must have made it to the dungeon a while ago. Are they on their way back?"

"Master David is with his father. They're on their way back here."

"What about Joey? Did they get Joey?"

"Ma'am, there's something I need to tell you." A dish of some sort was set gently on the table. "Joey has died."

Stunned, Adia said nothing. Her brain had stopped.

"The usurper attempted to put a dimensional entity into Master Joey. The attempt was unsuccessful. Master Joey did not survive. The entity was also unable to survive, and Mr. Robert has been put in the dungeon."

Adia's knees felt weak, and she had to sit down. Finding the bench beside the table, she sank onto it. "Dear One, this is so terrible," she whispered. "I can't believe it. We just spent hours together; he's in my heart." Her whole body slumped. "I shouldn't have taken him with me. I should have let Cary do it."

"Ma'am..." Diit squatted in front of her. "Master Joey is a hero. He tried to save his brother, and sacrificed himself rather than become a pawn of dark forces."

"He sacrificed himself?"

"Yes, ma'am, he did."

Adia's head hung while she sorted through it, heart aching. "What about Roberta? Does she know?"

"Not yet, ma'am. Brother John thought it might be better if David was with them."

"Yes, of course." How would Roberta survive this? "Is she sleeping?"

"Yes, ma'am."

"Hellen, too?"

"Yes, ma'am."

"Good, they're going to need it. We'll hold vigil until John and David get back."

Chapter Su.12

Wharton stood rigid in front of the desk, pissed off to be called to the carpet for not a damn thing but doing his job. Dagge stood behind the desk, with his hands on his hips and that look on his face. Wharton wanted to punch it right off.

"Believe it or not, Wharton, I don't care how hard it is to get through the layer of such-and-such rock where you were *trying*...to find the tunnel that some *shopkeepers* had dug. Do you know how embarrassing it is to have an *army* that can't even dig a tunnel like some *shopkeepers* did? The important thing here is that you FAILED, and why are you a general? I clearly thought it was a good idea at one point, but now I think I have Changed. My. Mind."

Things hadn't been going well, it was true. But it wasn't his fault, and he was pretty sure he was in the big middle of being blamed for every shitshow thing that went wrong. Fuck him, then. Wharton kept his face stone and his eyes glued to a spot on the wall over Dagge's head.

"I'm tired of being outmaneuvered by a bunch of weak civilians, Wharton. I'm tired, and it's your fault."

"Sir, we can move inside the wall and raze the businesses. The smithy's over there, and it's an essential business we'll have to work around, but the tunnel has to lead somewhere, and we will keep tearing buildings down until we find it."

"Except you're too late. As usual. My spy says they've filled all that in, and they're going somewhere else. But you didn't know that, did you?"

Given all the shit on his plate, the report that the rebels were going somewhere else felt like good news. "About half the mine workers didn't show up for the last shift, sir. And there's been an issue with desertion in the troops. Did your spy mention that?"

Dagge was quiet for a few moments. Wharton didn't look at him.

"That's not her job," he said (so his spy was female). "It's your job." Dagge picked his knife up from the end of the desk. It still had blood on it. The carpet in front of the shredded painting was soaked. Two bodies had been carried away, but no one was saying what happened. Looked like it was so bad the boss needed a new bodyguard. The guy stood just inside the door.

"In fact," Dagge said with a smack of his lips, "your whole attitude seems to need adjustment. Who do you work for?"

Was he just pissed, or had Dagge finally dropped into the crazy pen? He'd been on the edge for a while, but there'd been a lot of pressure, and Wharton was inclined to overlook it. Lately, though—for about a year—he'd get this look in his eye, like his brain was spinning inside his head and he couldn't stop it. Sometimes he laughed, sometimes he killed people.

"You, sir."

"Yes, you do. And I say you have Disappointed Me. What do you have to say about that?"

"I would say that I was there for the last ten mine inspections. Sir."

"What did you say?"

"Permission to speak frankly, sir."

Dagge stepped in front of him, as much in Wharton's line of vision as he could get, since he was shorter. For his part, Wharton stared through Dagge's forehead. Then Dagge raised up on his toes, slowly, until he could meet eyes.

"Please, Wharton, speak frankly." Dagge sank back to his heels, keeping eye contact.

"When you start ignoring people, sir, that's when they get out of hand. You've been dealing with the rebels, I know, but the mine needs your attention, too."

"And the army? Does it need my attention?"

"Some of the soldiers have lost confidence in our mission. Reports from Valdia say that some of the old factions of their military have joined forces with the people, establishing pockets of resistance. Some of our soldiers have joined them, and more are leaving every day."

Dagge turned slowly, hands behind his back, gaze lingering until he stepped away. Behind him, the knife twitched in his hand. "First, I don't care about the soldiers, Wharton. They're expendable, and if they join the other side, we'll kill them. As long as we pay, we'll never run out of soldiers."

In a sudden burst, Dagge spun around and swung his arm toward the wall. The knife lodged in the king's head with a solid thunk, and Dagge had a smirk on his face when he looked back. "And second, dumbass, the reason I have to focus on the rebellion here is *because* of what's happening in Valdia. If we can't subdue our own people, everyone's going to try treason. But we crush the rebels here, they see it happen, and it weakens them. At the same time, it strengthens us— our ranks, and our reputation." He walked over to the knife and yanked it out of the wall. "This is what I'm trying to accomplish, and what have you gotten me?"

"Sir, I'm at the mine, which is constantly on alert for low-level insurrection. I'm in the dungeon, where even the officers don't see any point in trying. I'm at the completely useless digging outside the wall. I'm dealing with the soldiers every morning, and all day every day. They are the backbone of your operation, and rot has set in. They're freaked out by your...whatever-they-ares. Half the time, they're eyeballing each other, trying to figure out if one of them's one of those things. And as soon as the carrier is identified, it changes, and everyone's afraid it's going to get them next. The troops are destabilized."

"Are you a King, Wharton?"

"I am not, sir." Was he even listening?

"And you're not an Overlord."

"No, sir, I am not."

"That's funny, because I thought I heard Royal Asshole coming out of your mouth." Dagge stepped toward the desk, where he hiked a cheek and sat, tapping the tip of his knife on the carved edge. The tapping slowed, and got louder. "I'm waiting for an apology."

Never a good sign. He'd said that to some of the Lords at the beginning, and it didn't matter whether they apologized or not, it was still a gruesome death.

"I'm s-sorry, sir."

Dagge stood, and walked toward him slowly. "S-sorry?"

"I'm sorry, sir."

In front of him, Dagge crossed his arms, knife at his left elbow, head tilted, looking up. "Private Finch!" he called.

The young soldier stepped forward. His uniform hung loosely on him, and he had a lanky way of walking. Visually, he was an ordinary guy—short hair, pale, not real tall. Except as he walked toward them, his eyes flashed purple.

Wharton flinched, his hands came up, and his knees bent, ready to run. His head snapped back and forth between the other two and his weight had just shifted toward the door when Dagge lunged forward and tackled him. But Wharton flipped over as soon as he hit the floor, climbed over Dagge, gained his feet and ran for the door.

Dagge grabbed his right ankle, and stabbed into his calf. Wharton fell forward, flipped onto his ass and kicked at Dagge's head with his free foot. Dagge ducked in tight, taking it in his shoulders. Then Finch got to them, and grabbed Wharton's kicking leg, pulling it sideways very fast. Wharton twisted his hips, lying on his side, and bent toward Dagge, trying to wrench Dagge's hands away to get his leg free.

Dagge crawled like a damn spider up onto him. Wharton slapped at him and pushed him off to the right, half turning onto his back. Dagge grabbed his wrists and pulled them above his head while Finch came up the other side, still holding his foot. With his free leg, Wharton kicked at Finch, but Dagge wrenched his arms to the opposite side and rolled him onto his back. Wharton raised his hips and tried to roll away from Finch to get his leg free, but Finch held on. Bending his knee, Wharton pulled back to launch the guy, but in a surprise move, Finch pushed Wharton's knee all the way down, grabbing Wharton's belt on each side and crushing. Wharton tried to kick Finch away with his other knee, but Finch only leered above him, and rammed his knee into Wharton's balls. Pain exploded, driving all other thoughts away.

With a groan, Wharton pushed through the pain and kicked at Finch again, trying to knock him backward. Finch grabbed the free leg and held it under his arm, jerking with Wharton's frantic fighting, but not letting him go.

"Do it!" Dagge said.

Wharton bucked, trying to push Finch off his leg, and managing to raise him into the air. Almost dumped, Finch caught himself, pushed the bent leg out from under him, and sat on it, inside knee on Wharton's crotch. Finch leaned in, and the purple started to shoot out of him.

Wharton fought, but couldn't get away. Dagge had pinned his arms under his knees, and he couldn't get either asshole off no matter what he did. Terror possessed him. His heart tried to fight its way out of his chest. He screamed "FUCK YOU!" over and over as the thing came for him.

Chapter Su. 13

Adia had fallen asleep, sitting at the end of the big table, back against the wall and her head leaning on her hand. She'd dozed off to the sounds of Diit's hands fiddling with something, in his unhurried way, a short distance down and across. She couldn't help knocking out; it had been a long, exhausting day and night, and for the past hour, she had wanted sleep more than anything.

She woke when Wolf growled a speck. A confused second later, Adia shook off her fog and sat up. The dumbwaiter door slid open, the half-wall started down, and someone stepped over it into the kitchen.

"Hey, it's us," David said.

Adia stood, reaching her hands toward them. "Are you okay?"

David grasped her hands gently. "I don't know if I'd say that. But I'm surviving. It helps to have Dad here."

"Yes, of course," she said, and moved one hand toward the second set of footsteps. "John?"

"I'm here, Your Majesty." His warm hand took hers.

"Really, John? Your Majesty? You guys are family for us. All of you." She squeezed their hands as she spoke, then reached to hug David first. "I'm so sorry about Joey."

"Me too," he said over her shoulder. "Thank you."

They hugged for a bit, until John said, "Man, you're really a hug hog."

Adia laughed out loud. David turned toward his father, but kept her close. "You didn't raise no fool."

John laughed and Adia moved over to hug him.

"I'm glad you're still you, John Treslo."

"Me, too," he said. "I wish you could see how good I look."

"So do I!" She grinned.

306

"Master David…" Diit's voice came from standing height, but still the other side of the table. "I'm so very sorry your brother was taken from you. It's the people we invest the most love and time in that are the hardest to lose."

"Thank you, Diit," David said. "I have to say, I'll be really glad when he shows up."

"Me, too," John said.

For a split second, Adia was jealous. Not that she would ever wish such a thing away from them, but she wished her father could be one of them. What wouldn't she give to be able to talk to him every day? To know he was among friends and brothers.

Adia heard a slight scraping sound—Diit must have picked something up off the table. "Here, ma'am, I believe you have something for Master David."

"Yes! Thank you, Diit." She put her hands out and the heavy little book was laid in them. "We need to get you to bed as soon as possible." As soon as it was out of her mouth, she realized how it sounded. Her forehead squinched, her face got hot, and her mouth hung open. "I mean for sleeping. Of course." She laughed nervously, entirely too close to his muscled chest. Oh, dear One. She pushed the book toward him, and he took it.

"I brought some blankets for putting under your head, to pad the book," Diit said. Because he was the best.

"I'm hearing you loud and clear, my man. I need to "read" the book. My mind, however, is a little restless at the moment, and I'm not sure how I'm going to get to sleep."

"The book will help you with that, sir."

"Hey, I might love this thing."

Is Roberta sleeping?" John asked.

"Not anymore," her voice said from the stairs. "Your Majesty. John, I'm glad you're here." Soft hugging sounds. "Hi, honey."

"Hi, Mom," David said, his energy moving away toward his mother.

While David and John greeted Roberta, Adia spoke quietly to Diit. "I think now would be a good time to move this food downstairs. You and I can do it so they have time and space to talk."

"Excellent idea, ma'am. I've been packing the food back into the box, and there's a bag as well on the table behind you."

"Brilliant." Adia found the bag and hoisted the strap onto her shoulder. Arms wrapped around the bag resting on her belly, she said loudly enough for the whisperers to hear, "Diit and I are taking the food downstairs. You guys come when you're ready."

"We can help," Roberta said.

"No, it's not necessary. There's probably some tea, David. Maybe your Mom would like a cup."

"I would love a cup," Roberta said, moving toward the table.

"I'll take care of that," John said, just before the ring of the metal teakettle scraping on the fireplace stone.

Diit joined her beside the dumbwaiter. "Shall I go first, ma'am?"

"Please, Diit. Let's go, Wolf," Adia said, and waved her hand for him to go in front of her. As she stepped into the dumbwaiter, she listened to the sounds of the Treslo family settling around the table. There would be time to talk to Roberta later, to share her grief, after John and David broke the terrible news.

Chapter Su.14

Roberta sat at the stone table, her tea untouched in front of her. The loss of Joey was too big to absorb. Her heart felt frozen.

John kept trying to talk her through it. "He'll be with me," he said. "As soon as he adjusts to reality."

What did that even mean?

But she didn't ask. She didn't say anything. David put his arms around her, sitting next to her on the bench. He laid his head against hers. When John started talking again, she held her hand up to silence him.

She'd left Joey alone. Too much. Over and over. She thought the house would be safe. Their haven. Their home. Turned out it was the least safe place of all.

Robert, Robert... How could he do it? How could he turn *Joey* in? Joey never even did anything for the Resistance.

She'd left him alone.

"Please don't worry it, Robie."

John just couldn't help himself.

"This was part of his life plan. It was an agreed-upon series of events; you couldn't have stopped it."

Some tiny explosive in her brain went off, and she was suddenly furious. "What kind of bullshit is that?! Don't tell me that! What good could it possibly do for an eighteen-year-old kid to die? He hadn't even lived, John! He hadn't done anything yet!"

John opened his mouth and she glared at him. She just didn't want to hear it. In the quiet, her mind began to imagine Joey's last moments. The monster coming for him. How it felt when it…

"John, how did it feel? When the monster went into you." She didn't want to say the next, didn't want to know, but she had to. "Did it hurt?"

"It didn't hurt, Robie. It felt like it does when you touch something that's vibrating. Only…your insides are touching it. It doesn't hurt. Really."

"But the knife would hurt," she said.

And that did it. Her frozen heart broke and she cried, long aches of it. Tears for Joey, and all the things he would miss. For everything she had lost, and everything they had all lost. She cried for the broken world, and their broken lives, and her broken heart. Her face melted, awash in tears. Her mouth opened for the big, gasping breaths.

John came around the table and sat on the bench next to her. His shoulder felt firm, and she leaned into it. David released her and held her hand. No one spoke.

Eventually the earthquake subsided. Her sobs became sniffs and wiping her face on her sleeve. Nose included. "I'm sorry. This is probably disgusting."

"You're always beautiful," John told her. "And you can use my sleeve if you run out of your own."

"Thanks."

"Here, let me look." His hand lifted her chin, and she raised her eyes to meet his.

John brought his shirttail up and wiped her top lip. He rubbed around her nostrils, and even inside a little. His shirt was remarkably soft. No wonder he loved it, and she suddenly felt bad about telling him to get rid of it all those years.

She watched him as he worked on her with his eyebrows knitted and mouth slightly open. Her husband was all there—the man she knew and loved: the joy, the kindness, the humor of him; the brilliant mind and enormous heart; the courage, and commitment. How fortunate she was that she had married him…fortunate that he had fathered her children.

And Joey would still be Joey. Wherever he was, he was all there, and she could be happy about that.

John smiled down at her. "There. You're all dry and snot-free." It made her laugh a little.

On her other side, David sat watching them. "Want some fresh tea?"

"I'd love some."

He got up, whisked her cup away, and went to the fireplace.

"Can I talk now?" John asked.

"Only if you talk about something else."

"Okay, deal. Remember the time when Joey was five, and he did that fancy dismount off the couch and broke his arm?"

"That was gruesome, the way the bone lapped over," David said.

"Yes! And nurse couldn't find a vein in his hand, and the shot hurt him so bad? That was horrible. Are you guys trying to make me feel better or worse?"

"Better!" John said. "Of course I'm trying to make you feel better. That was a knuckleheaded choice, I'm sorry."

"It's okay." She laughed lightly. "Do you remember the time he brought that mouse home?

"Yes," John said. "He'd caught it somewhere, and he wanted to keep it."

"And we thought that was a bad idea."

"But we let him."

"And he surprised us. He took great care of that mouse."

"Remember the trick with the ball?" David sat across from them with Roberta's cup. "He could push it from one end of the table to the other."

"Except once I found mouse turds on the table, I had to move that operation to the floor."

"As I recall," John said, "they were fine with that. Joey played with him under the table. Didn't he even have an obstacle course for a while?"

311

"He did, that's right! He was going to start a mouse decathlon for a while." Roberta chuckled. "What was that mouse's name? Bippy Buppy? Doodle Doo?"

"Dippa Duppa Doo. But he called him Doopy," David said with a big grin.

"That's right." Roberta smiled and shook her head. "We were all so sad when he ran away."

"I don't think it occurred to any of us that he might run out the open door."

"Right? Didn't he love us? Joey was so heartbroken."

"Can't blame Doopy, though."

"I know. I'd've done the same thing."

"Me, too."

"Say, isn't there food downstairs?" Roberta asked. "I'm hungry. Can you eat?"

"No, but I can watch you."

Roberta reached up for a kiss, and before she could finish wondering whether that was okay, John had leaned down and given her one. "Oh good, I thought maybe kissing was not allowed, or something."

"No one has said I couldn't," John replied. "So unless that changes, I'm kissing." He kissed her again. "But real quick, before we go…what's this?" His finger pointed at the little silver dome she'd left on the table earlier.

She picked it up. "It's the receiver for the bug I had on you. You know, the day Dagge grilled you and Robert about that song? This morning I got the bug out of your pocket and put it in Dagge's desk. But I'm sure he found it; the drawer was still open when he caught me. It was such a big risk for nothing."

"Not entirely for nothing. We did get out of the dungeon," David said.

"True."

"Can I have that?" David asked. "I'd like to examine it."

312

"Sure," she said, handing it over. "I'm going to run upstairs real quick and use the water closet. I'll wake Hellen, too, and we can all go downstairs and...join the Resistance."

"See you in a minute." John watched her with such love all over his face, she kissed him again before she left.

Chapter Su.15

"Take Finch's body and put it in the burn pile."

"Yes, Overlord." Wharton bent over and hefted the skinny body onto his shoulder. Meat sack now, but the kid did turn out to be a badass for a few minutes. Dagge had to give him that.

"After that, forget the wall, send a squad into the west side of town. I want to know who's gone. Double the work in the dungeon, too. We're finding those assholes."

"Yes, Overlord," Wharton said.

He loved that.

"Well, get going."

"Yes, Overlord." Wharton turned sharply, Finch swinging on his back.

Dagge watched the body bobble all the way out the door.

Restless, he pulled his feet off the desk, stood, walked past the couch and over to the empty fireplace. Hands on his hips, he stared into the sooty hole. What was he going to do about Hellen's little friends? If the asshole traitors were packing to go camping, they had to be headed for the forest. Set up some commune or something. But finding them would mean going into the forest, which he still hated. If he went right now, it would be daylight, but hells, it would still take hours to comb those woods. He could send Fake Wharton. Maybe he should do that.

Only now that they found their tunnels, the bitch-ass whiner babies were bound to camp near the end of one. If he could just get down there, it'd be a lot easier to find them that way. Plus, he could find all the other places those tunnels went, and that was probably everywhere. But they probably all ended up at that old building. That was why the princess wasn't there; she got out through a tunnel.

She was probably back now.

He could make it to the hideout in about an hour. Except they'd probably have sentries hiding on the mountain or something. They'd be protecting the building now that they knew he knew about it. They'd be expecting him to come back. It would be more dangerous, too, since they'd have reinforcements, and maybe a few weapons. There'd be no sneaking up on them, either, backed into a cliff the way they were.

He needed a way in.

His stomach growled. Funny, he hadn't noticed he'd missed lunch. Why the hells didn't the valet come get him?

In the hall he made left for the stairs. Halfway down, he turned the corner, and met the valet coming up. "Where the hells have you been?"

"Overlord, sir, I was just coming to get you for lunch," he said.

"It's way past lunch time, idiot." He brushed past him, and continued down the stairs.

Dagge hurried briskly down the hall, fingering the instanote in his pocket and wondering what the cook had made for lunch today. He liked good surprises. And ice cream. He hoped he had ice cream.

The asshole rebels could wait. He knew what to do. As much as he wanted to smite the shitheads down himself, there was a better way to get it done.

Chapter Su.16

The sound of her people coming reached Adia long before they arrived. It was a bit of a hard wait, she must say. She paced the hub while she waited, and stood at the tunnel opening with Wolf when they neared. As they came in, voices were low, sounds of pack clinks and footsteps were like music. When they got close enough, she called, "I'm so glad you're here!" A cheer went up; joy hit her in a wave, and Wolf's tail whacked her leg. It made her laugh, and she opened her arms for them.

Beau came first. "Your Majesty. We're so glad we made it. It's the Queen, everybody!" A hush traveled over them, and she waited, smiling.

"We have food," she said, "thanks to Diit and Cookie. Please, come in and get settled. You've had a long night."

She stood there while they filed past her, Wolf leaning against her leg. Maybe they were in the way, but she wanted to feel the Resistance. These amazing people. All of them had just left their homes and everything they knew. Their future was uncertain. A fight was coming, and they might die, but they were here, ready to do what they could. Heroes. Every one of them.

As the last people passed, Adia turned to face the back wall. Hellen was back there, with Roberta, David, and all the food. Diit had lowered the dumbwaiter cart to put it on, then left to go back to the palace a bit ago. It still smelled great.

John had made himself scarce so he wouldn't give people heart attacks.

She said, "We can either camp here for a while, eat and rest, or we can eat and move on down the index tunnel." Packs were dropping to the ground all around her. Feet scuffling, grunts and groans. "Before you decide, you should know that Dagge was out at the monastery today. We're ninety-nine percent sure he doesn't know how to get into these tunnels. And as hard as it was for us to do it, he isn't likely to figure it out."

"I'm all for staying in the tunnel," Beau said. "I don't know about everybody else, but I'm wiped."

"Me, too," said Vartile. "But maybe we could just get a few hours, and then go unblock the forest tunnel. The sooner it's done the better, if you ask me."

"All right, how does everyone feel about that?"

A general murmur of agreement went around the group, and Dessara piped up from the back. "But shouldn't someone go up to the monastery and look out? Not to fight, necessarily, but just so we know if someone shows up."

"I'll do that," Hellen said. "I was planning to."

"We should post here, too," Beau said. "I have extra walkntalks."

"I'll take a shift," someone volunteered.

"Me too, Beau," came a voice from the back.

"Second shift," someone else said, echoed by a fourth.

"Thank you, everyone," Adia said. "Now, you must be starving, let's eat."

"Come get your chicken parts," David called out. "Or brisket. We have plates, here you go, here you go…raw vegetables, here you go, rolls. All finger food, folks. Napkins are to the left…"

David's voice reassured her, and she let it relax into the background as she puzzled out how she was going to get safely across the crowded hub.

"Can I give you a hand?" Cary said, approaching.

"I want to let it clear out a little first, but yeah, sure."

His energy stood beside her. A soft rustling sounded like he crossed his arms over his chest. "Good thing we found the tunnels, isn't it?"

"Very good thing."

317

"I wanted to see where it went in the other direction, but Beau wouldn't let me. He said we needed to keep the group tight and ready to go."

"Sounds like I put the right guy in charge." As soon as she said it, she realized how it would sound. Krikey, she didn't mean to imply Cary was the wrong guy. Even if it was true.

He was silent for a second, then he said, "It took us some time to get around the well. The dirt was solidified, like it had been fused or something. That's why we were late."

"Fused? That's weird. Good job getting through."

"Thanks," he said, pleased.

"Hey, kids," Hellen said, walking up to her, providing rescue because she was awesome. "I made a plate for you, Your Highness. If you'll come with me, we have a reserved area of dirt across the room."

"Oh my goodness, thank you, I'm ravenous. Cary, thanks for standing with me. You should get some food," she said, walking away, her hand in the crook of Hellen's arm. Facing forward, she said, "Your timing is almost perfect."

"Almost?"

"Well, half a minute earlier and I wouldn't have had to eat my own foot."

"Ah, well. If that's the worst thing that happens, you're doing all right."

"Good point."

"Your Majesty, can Luhe and I sit with you?" Vartile's energy moved in close to her left side.

"Please do," Adia said. "Beau, where are you?"

"Right here, ma'am!" His voice came from the food line.

"Come sit with us when you have your food, okay? We need to plan out some stuff."

"You bet!"

"Here, we're at our spot," Hellen said. "Let's put your back to the wall. Vartile, will you take her plate while she settles? I'm going to get a plate for myself, be back in a minute."

Adia put her hand on the wall and felt her way down. Sitting cross-legged, she took the plate Vartile offered, and listened to the people around her while she felt her food: chicken thigh, celery and carrots, and a roll. She picked the roll up immediately and held it to her nose, breathing it in. Then she shoved half of it into her mouth and bit it off.

Vartile laughed, but Adia didn't care. She was in heaven. "Ohh, this is so good," she said around the enormous wad. It was light, and buttery, and delicious, and she wanted to stuff the rest of it in, but decided to pace herself instead. As soon as she got that bite down, she went for the chicken.

Gradually, the sounds of people moving spread out, away from the dumbwaiter. Bit by bit, everyone sat. As they ate, talking and laughter filled the room—soft, then loud, then soft again. Byron Taymer was telling a story. Dessara's unique laugh made Adia smile.

A circle had formed around her. David sat to her left, Hellen to her right. Roberta, Vartile, and Luhe went around from David. Beau sat by Hellen. Cary sat by Beau.

Roberta said, "How are we going to prepare everyone for John?"

"What do you mean?" Vartile asked after a pause.

"I'll do it," Hellen said, and stood up. Adia put her hand on Hellen's leg, and Hellen patted it. "Hey, everyone, can I have your attention?" The room quieted. "A lot of people here know that I've been seeing monks in the forest for a long time." A murmur went up. "Don't get excited, they're not here to help. They can't 'interfere.' What you may not know is that John Treslo was descended from the monks." Another, louder, murmur. "Yesterday, he showed up again." Shocked silence.

"And here I am," John said from the dungeon tunnel.

A few cries went out, and there was some sort of ruckus at that end of the room. Adia stood. "Please don't be afraid! David and I met him in the forest yesterday. He's the same John we all knew, the same hero who started this Resistance. He's the one who made all this…" She circled her arms to include all of them. "…possible."

After a pause, someone started clapping. Adia joined, and David, who stood beside her, and Hellen, and more and more people until the hub was filled with applause.

"Welcome back, John," she said to herself, and smiled.

Chapter Su.17

Roberta watched John from her spot on the floor, still nonplussed by the fact that he was here. After a year and a half of bitter grieving, having him back shattered her sense of reality. A whole new construct had to be built, and she wasn't sure she was up to the task.

What she really wanted was for Joey to show up. She worried about the last hour of his life, and whether his spirit was damaged. His delightful, wackadoodle spirit. Tears stung her eyes.

"Aw, Thorn! We never thought we'd see you again. You are dead, right?" Beau walked down the center of the room, between the groups of people clustered along the walls.

"Dead as I'll ever be, Papa Bear." They met near the middle, laughed, hugged, and patted each other on the back. People watched them, mouths hanging open or clamped tight. Some stood, others sat, more and more began to smile. John, grinning like a kid, kept walking, waving his hand at people he knew.

He and Beau joined their group, and John stopped to greet the Queen. "Your Majesty."

"Do have a seat, John," she said. "Do you eat?"

"Sadly, I do not, because it smells so good, and who wouldn't want to eat everything they liked without gaining an ounce? Hello, honey." He leaned down, kissed her, and hugged David, who was still standing. When everyone sat, John sat between her and Vartile.

While they finished eating, he started entertaining the whole group with stories—about his and Hellen's trip into the forest, and the raccoon that ate their food. Everyone laughed, including herself. Then he talked a little about the monks, and more about the history of their kingdom.

"I know why the town tunnel was blocked off by the well."

Beau made a long *aha* noise, and said, "We thought it was blocked. What's down there?"

With a half-smile, John eyed the group.

"A long time ago, a member of the Royal Family was exiled for trying to usurp power from her sister. The two had been close all their lives. When their father died, Ephor became Queen, and Morla earned her place as the Queen's top advisor. Like all the Beldenets, they both had seeing gifts, but Morla's was more powerful—she could see the dead, and they would tell her things.

"As time went by, she didn't share everything she learned. She used the information to selfish ends, and didn't always warn the Queen when she'd misunderstood her own gift. The Queen's gift was visions, but they were symbolic and hard to understand, and she often made mistakes in their interpretation.

"Only a few years into Ephor's reign, Morla decided she should be Queen, instead of her sister. Rather than an outright attack, she started rumors among the servants, thinking they'd get out into the town, and destroy her sister's reputation. But it backfired. The servants were loyal, and one valet in particular took it upon himself to inform the Queen.

"Ephor was furious. She banished Morla to a hovel in the hills, guarded by two Queensguard. Supplies were delivered once a week, and she was to have no other contact with the palace.

"But the monks still saw her as a member of the Royal Family, and they wanted to help Morla. Ephor gave them permission to build this tunnel to Morla's house. That way they could get to her easily, and teach her about herbs and medicines, midwifery…things she could offer as services to the people. Morla, however, developed some side businesses of her own, and eventually she was accused of being a witch.

"By then, it didn't matter that she had royal blood, they hanged her and burned her, and that was the end of Morla Beldenet. The monks felt responsible; they blocked off the tunnel, and set the rules that we can't interfere, or reveal secrets."

"I can see why," Roberta said.

"How come we don't learn about this in school?" David asked.

"The monks have ways of protecting things. I can't tell you any more than that."

Groans and laughs surged around the room. "That's such a tease, John!" Vartile threw a towel at him.

"I might be the only other person here who knows about Morla and Ephor." Adia smiled and leaned forward. "When I was a little girl, I came across a very old book in the palace library called *Accounts of Dismaye*. I kid you not. It had the story of Morla and Ephor in it, only it said Ephor came to watch the burning, and 'didnae leave 'til it was doon.'" Laughs and groans went up. "I thought it was a fairy tale."

"It wasn't a fairy tale," John said, grinning. "Even the Beldenets have their black sheep."

The young Queen laughed, her smile beautiful, her body leaning toward David. There was something there, between them. Roberta was glad, though it made her heart ache for the danger they were in.

Still, love was the point, wasn't it? Someone she knew once said, "Grief is love with no place to go." It couldn't be more true.

But her love did have places it could go. How blessed she was to see John, and talk to him. That he could hold her, and still make her laugh. Others didn't get those opportunities.

She glanced over and found John looking at her. The rest of them were laughing, joking around, but he was quiet. Time stopped, and all the love, all the history they shared became the very air around them. It comforted her, and healed her heart the tiniest bit.

Chapter Su.18

There wasn't any way for Dagge to hide Wharton and Private Newsom from Anji. She was a good spy—she'd gotten into the palace in Pulari, and Dagge couldn't be certain she wouldn't sneak in here. But Newsom had to be close to introduce Anji to her new friend. Chances were she wouldn't take it well, and Wharton needed to be close so they could catch her.

Newsom didn't look as good as Finch had, but there was no help for that now. He stood by the fireplace, next to the door the valet always used. Dagge had sent the valet away. No point in extra witnesses.

While he waited, he played with his knife, pulling at the flaps of fabric that used to be the King, scraping the paint, running the sharp tip along the line of the neck and across the jaw.

It still satisfied him to have the old man at his mercy like this.

He moved the tip of the knife up, and lovingly traced the remaining eye. It would be his final blow someday. Blinding the Great Eye. He could hardly wait.

But it had to be a special occasion. In his fantasies, that occasion used to be the day he made Hellen his Queen. Sadly, not anymore. But sacrificing the Princess was a darn good substitute.

Public sacrifice would not only be spectacular entertainment, it would mean the end of any threat to his place on the throne. Or it might mean more threat, until more people died. Maybe even a lot more people, but at some point, they'd get the message.

Fun stuff. He was ready for that again.

Anji was late. Dagge looked at the clock, and it wasn't his imagination. Over half an hour late, and that was not like her. Did she know? Had she been spying? What were the chances she'd been in the palace all along?

Pretty good, he realized.

Fuck.

A tiny click drifted around the corner from the balcony. Newsom's head swiveled to his left, and Dagge peered around the corner, keeping his body behind the wall. Just in case.

Anji laughed at him, standing there with feet apart and guns in both hands. "Afraid I might shoot you, Tomius?"

Wharton started toward her, but Dagge waved him back. No need for him to be all shot up just yet. Besides, a little danger was the spice of life. "Will you?"

"Depends on you."

"What do you want?" He watched her slowly drift to the side, putting a column between them.

"Guaranteed safe passage. I'll go do as you asked, get the Princess, and you let me stay just the way I am."

"You could still get the Princess my way, so I don't see the advantage for me."

"I am the advantage, Tomius. You know we have a...special relationship."

Could he still pound her if she was one of them? He could try.

"I'm not sure that matters."

Silence. Then she fired, both guns. One bullet pulverized the wall over his head. Dagge jerked back and signaled to Wharton, who ran toward her. Dagge followed after, but when he rounded the corner Anji was already gone. Wharton ran out onto the balcony, Dagge right after him. Dagge could see Anji's small form racing through the meadow toward the trees. The rope tied to the railing was still swinging.

"Shall I go after her, Overlord?"

"No. She'll bring the Princess back, and then we'll see."

A husky voice barely made it out the balcony door. "I don't know if I can make it that long, Overlord."

Irritated, Dagge rushed back through the door and found Newsom on his ass, leaning against the wall. Anji had shot him in the side. Blood bubbled out with every breath.

Maybe they should find a temporary body. Or, it didn't have to be temporary—maybe the body should be someone else altogether. Anji had a point about the special relationship, and really, he wasn't all that jacked about one of the 2Ders watching him fuck her through her eyes.

Well then, if he didn't use Anji, who would be useful?

Why, Robert Treslo would.

Chapter Su.19

Hellen let her eyes travel over the people, scattered along the hub floor in clumps, talking. Lanterns and bulb torches glowed at intervals in the dark, a few of them lighting the bottoms of the walls in subtle sunbursts. Silhouettes leaned forward, heads down or turning, arms moving. Faces shone in lighted parts—laughing, smiling, speaking.

She was tired. Had lost a lot today. Her life for one, but maybe more than that was her immunity. No longer did she hold the "special place" in Dagge's heart. No more free pass. No more bargaining when shit really hit the fan.

What happened, she wondered. Did he just have enough, or did he snap?

All those times she saw monks in the forest, and they told her it was urgent that she "complete her destiny." Not that they ever explicitly said what her destiny was. But she could assume. They still had to save the kingdom. She had to kill Dagge, and his last however many monsters. If she didn't, Dagge would turn the whole world into ash.

Would him being crazy make her job easier or harder?

Ugh, she didn't want to think about that.

She steered her mind back to what happened when she died. So much love over there. Colors she had never seen. There was a being of light next to her the entire time—her angel, perhaps. Her parents...funny how she knew they were proud of her, because no one said anything.

And the King showed her the forest. It was on fire.

When she came back into her body, it felt terrible: all heavy, and tight, and in pain. But she was glad to be back, for Adia's sake. They had work to do.

Hellen hadn't told anyone about where she went, and she didn't know if she was going to. Adia, probably, and maybe Beau. Maybe Roberta. She'd have to see.

Beau was sitting beside her, being his strong, warm self. Making sure she had everything she needed. How could she have not seen his love for her before? The light he gave off when he looked at her said it all. Was this a good time or a bad time for love?

Screw that, all times were good times.

He was going to be unhappy with her soon, when she got up to go to the monastery. He'd want to come, and how was she going to say no? Again?

Maybe she shouldn't.

She didn't want to sit there alone in the dark, anyway.

"Your Majesty…" It was Merv.

"Yes, Merv, please join us," Adia said.

"Thank you, ma'am," he said, sitting in the space Luhe made for him. "I brought the crystal we've been working on for a power source. We've cut it into a four-sided equilateral pyramid. The carapaz is receptive, as you know, to the body's energy. We've found that if we connect physically with each other, and with the crystal, the output is multiple times the input. We can output an energy that would serve well as defense."

"Does it do the same thing Hellen's weapon does?"

"No ma'am. It beams straight out, like a giant laser."

"Wow. What happens to the person holding it?"

"That's been a problem. The crystal's like a capacitor—it gets hot and shocks."

"Do we have a way to mount it?"

We've been working on a rig, but it was too big to carry."

"We'll figure something out. Thank you for bringing it, Merv, now we can blow that boulder up if we need to."

"Yes, ma'am," Merv said, and pushed himself to standing. "I've been thinking about the dimensional tear, too. It's possible that a strong enough beam could seal it back up."

328

A red flag went up in Hellen's head. "How do we know it won't make it bigger? Or feed whatever infernal creature is on the other side again, waiting?"

"Theoretically," Merv said, "if the beam is large enough, and encompasses the full diameter of the hole, the energy should warp the time-space fabric…in a sense melt it so that it repairs and seals."

That all sounded really great. Theoretically.

But who was she to argue? Science was never her thing. If some giant monster came lumbering out a hole the size of the plaza, she guessed they'd deal with it then.

Hellen let the chatter fade into the background. It became a bell over her, made of glass, so she could watch the folks she loved: Vartile, grounded and easy as always; Luhe, strong and silent; Beau, who always took care of everyone; Roberta, looking as tired as Hellen felt; John, the bright spot in any room; David, taking his place beside Adia; and Adia, with her hand on his arm. They'd make an amazing team.

She felt blessed to be surrounded by such people.

Cary, however, wasn't handling Adia and David well. He mostly kept his eyes averted, but the thunderous scowl gave him away. No help for love. Hellen appreciated that he was choosing to keep his mouth shut tonight. There'd be plenty of time for courtship showdowns later. Hopefully.

Speaking of time, it was time to go. Hellen glanced up at Beau, and discovered he was watching her. She smiled at him.

"It's time for me to go to the monastery," she said.

"I'm going with you," Beau said, stowing his water bottle in his pack, and turning to face her, resolute.

"I'd like that."

His frowny face relaxed, and he smiled at her. "Good. Do you want to go now?"

"Let me tell Adia." Hellen turned to her other side, where Adia was engrossed in something John was saying.

Her hand went to Adia's arm, bringing Adia's face around. Conversation stopped, unfortunately.

"We're going to go," Hellen said. "Beau's coming with me."

Adia suppressed a smile. "Thank you for letting him go with you," she said, reaching her arms out to hug.

Hellen leaned in to her, wrapping her arms snugly around Adia's back. "Yeah, I didn't see any point in going it alone anymore."

Adia whispered in her ear. "Are you really okay? You seem…unsettled."

"I'm okay, I promise. We can talk soon." Hellen squeezed her, patted her, and pulled away. "Beau and I are heading to the monastery," she announced to the room at large, standing, making eye contact with Byron Taymer just in case they needed backup.

"Should I come with you?" Cary asked, half rising.

"No, it's better not to have too many people," Hellen answered. "Unless an army comes, so keep the walkntalk close."

Beau was unloading some things from his bag and piling them on the floor. "I've got travel tonkers!" he announced. "They're the ones with cat litter, but I don't have enough for everyone, so make of them what you will. Be kind." He grinned to a roomful of laughs and snarky comments, then hefted his heavy bag from the floor behind him. "We might not need you guys even if there is an army," he joked to Cary. "I got some stuff in here."

Chuckles and well-wishes breezed around, bypassing Hellen as she picked her way through their circle, hand landing on John's shoulder, squeezing Roberta's hand, hugging Vartile, who stood for exactly that, squeezing Luhe's hand. It made her wonder how much they didn't expect her to come back.

They weren't likely to run into an army, but you never knew. More likely, they'd run into a small, elite group of fighters, and that might be worse.

Hellen took the lead with her bulb torch, and they started up the stairs.

Chapter Su.20

David watched Hellen go. She'd been very different since she woke up, and he was worried about her. Beau would watch out for her, of course, but some things can't be healed by another person's love. They can just love you through it, if they have the stamina.

His Mom was suffering, too. It helped that Dad showed up, but they all knew she was worried about Robert, no matter how much she didn't say it. Never mind Joey. David hoped Joey would turn up soon, because it would help her to see him.

Thank One Dad could make her laugh in spite of everything. The sad look around her eyes would fade. Not completely gone, but better.

Aside from that, he had a hard time keeping his eyes off the Queen. *Adia*. Up close, she was so real—smart as a slap, and fun. Still strange to be in her orbit, though. He couldn't wait until it got normal. Given they survived this.

He knew what she was thinking. She was thinking he'd be able to unblock that forest tunnel.

It seemed a huge, impossible task. They didn't even know what it was blocked with. Dirt? Rock? Could they dig it out if they had to? David laid his hand on the book, tucked in the inside pocket of his shirt, it hung heavy. If he got nothing from sleeping on it, they might have to try blowing the blockage out with Merv's pyramid or something.

Adia's hand lay on his arm again. It felt cold, and he turned to look at her. Her chin was tucked, a posture he knew meant she was listening. He placed his warm hand over hers, and listened, too. Scrapes and jingles. Low voices.

"Tell me they're settling in to rest," she said.

David looked up. People were pulling out bedrolls and blankets. Some were carrying packs into the tunnel mouths. "Yep, that's what it looks like. Nice call."

"Thanks. I might be so tired I'm hopeful." She chuckled.

"Hellen and I brought you guys some blankets. They're under the dumbwaiter cart," his Mom said. "I'll get them for you."

"Thank you, Roberta. Would you pile some brisket on a plate for Wolf, too?"

"Of course I will."

Dad stood, offered his hands and pulled Mom up, then she stepped over to the dumbwaiter.

"Wolf," the Queen said, "Roberta will give you food." Wolf clearly knew what she said, because he got up and followed. David was amazed.

Dad said, "I'll be taking my girl over to the thumb tunnel, so we can talk without waking people."

"What's your plan?" the Queen asked, her face turned up to David.

"I haven't made one," David said. "Crash anywhere, I suppose."

"Can I lean on you? I'm freezing."

"I would be honored, but I have to lay my head on this flipping book."

"Oh, right. Of course." She shook her head.

David wanted to say she could snuggle up with him, lying there on the floor, but it just didn't seem right. She was the Queen. He'd barely known her for two days.

"You can lean on me, ma'am," Cary said, scooting over to her other side. He met David's eyes, a smirk playing around his mouth. David wanted to punch him.

"What's the matter, Dave? You look like you want to punch me."

"I'd love to punch you, Cary. Because, as usual, you don't know how to act. You don't push yourself on her."

"I'm offering, you moron."

332

"Guys!" The Queen stuck her hand up between them, eyes flashing. "I'm not the last donut. I won't tolerate you two arguing over MY decision." She let her hand drop. "I choose Wolf, you guys find your own places."

His Mom appeared with blankets, handed one to the Queen, and one to David. She also gave him a look that said *Don't be a dunderhead.*

"I hate to say this," Dad said to the room at large, "but sleep will have to be short. I'll wait until the last minute to get you guys up. But that tunnel has to be unblocked a.s.a.p."

Chapter Su.21

Dagge pushed away from the table with a happy sigh. After three years of hits and misses, the cook finally understood him. Every time. Carbs when he was upset. Protein when he wasn't. It was like she had a sixth sense about him now, which was good, especially for her.

Tonight, it was beef. Tender chunks in a dark gravy, with some kind of peppers, and onion. Served over rice, so a few carbs. But lots of beef. Because in spite of losing the rebels at the wall, and having to shoot Hellen, and all the things he should be upset about, he knew Anji would go to the monastery tonight.

And that made him happy.

Grabbing a toothpick from the cup on the table, he raised his gaze to the new sentry at the big hall doors. The guy looked a little ridiculous, posing there in his suit, but even without a uniform, he carried the attitude of a soldier. Gunstock to the floor, other arm behind his back, you almost didn't notice the pale skin and the sparse beard shadow. Especially if you happened to catch the purple glow in the eyes. No more bookkeeping for ol' Rodney. And no more kissing ass. Was that a good thing, or a bad thing?

He threw his toothpick on the table and stood, pulling his shirt down to cover his belly. He needed to get some longer shirts.

"Treslo!" he called, stepping swiftly to the left corner of the table, and starting down the long side. "What do you know about the rebels?"

"Virtually nothing, Overlord, sir."

"Not where the headquarters is?"

No, Overlord."

"Where the tunnel access is?"

"No, Overlord."

334

"Who's leading it now that Hellen is dead?"

"No, Overlord."

Dagge walked right up to him and got in his face. Except the guy was taller. What was it with these Treslos? "How 'bout this, Rupert? Is your brother one of the traitors? Well, not your dead brother. Your dead brother wouldn't be one of them. Not anymore."

Call it a test.

Dagge searched the eyes, but the purple didn't glow for him like it usually did, it stuttered. Newsom had died before they got the body to the right cell, and maybe that was why. If he didn't need Treslo intact, he'd just pump some laser fire into him, that seemed to perk them right up. But then the body didn't last as long, and this flatty probably wasn't worth it.

Anyway, once Anji got back with the princess, he needed Treslo to get into where the rebels were. They wouldn't turn John's son away. Or Rose's…that bitch. In fact, his new toy could probably hobnob with the top morons for hours, and they'd never know.

Won't they be surprised?

Chapter Su.22

David woke in a rush when he opened his eyes to his father leaning over him, a bulb torch lighting up his face from below like some scary movie. "Dad!" David jerked to the side and sat up.

"I wanted to jump start you."

"Well, it worked. I'm probably scarred for life."

"It's time to get up, son," Dad said. "How does your head feel?"

"I don't know. Tired, I guess." David wiped his face with both hands, ran his fingers through his hair, and wished he had a teethbrush. Around the hub, it looked like everyone else was still asleep. "Need me to help wake people?"

"Nah, Mom's got a bell. I just wanted to know if you feel any different."

"Hi, honey." Mom stepped over from the dumbwaiter.

"Where'd you get a bell?" David picked up the pink book, tucked it in his shirt, and got up.

"Diit brought it. He also brought teethbrushes and granola bars. They're on the dumbwaiter cart."

"Diit's here?"

"Hello, Master David. Would you like some water?"

"Aw, Diit, you're the best, thanks." David took the paper cup and drained it.

"Would you like more?"

"No, I'm good. But I'll keep this cup if you don't mind."

"Naturally, sir." Diit stepped over to the dumbwaiter and got another cup. "Miss Roberta, perhaps the people should be woken now."

Mom wasted no time, ringing the bell gently, picking her way between the bundles stretched out on the floor. Dad went along, saying good morning, and not using the flashlight effect, David noted.

Soft chimes filled the room. People began to stir. He was seeing lights come on when a warm, liquid sensation popped in his brain. It started in the middle, and as it spread, it faded. At first, he worried he was having a stroke, maybe, but nothing else happened. It passed. So, he walked over to get a teethbrush.

"Master David, how are you feeling?" Diit was heading toward the Queen with a cup of water.

"Funny you should ask," David whispered. "I just—"

"Diit," the Queen called, sitting up and rubbing her eyes. "You're here."

"Yes, Your Majesty." He kept walking, and took a knee beside her. "Would you like some water?"

"Please," she said, and held her hand out.

And it occurred to David that even an act as simple as handing someone a cup had to have symmetry to it. Grip and release in a fluid motion that people took for granted. Muscle memory, they called it. What if it was more accurately cell memory? Or even quantum field?

What if it was a matter of vibrational conditions having to be right for a given thing to happen? If a person is "off" they may drop the cup. If the other person is "on," they may catch it. But both elements have to be in accord for the transaction to be successful.

And what of vibrational frequencies? Cymatics shows that a single musical note can vibrate intricate patterns in sand on a flat tray. What could a single note do if projected from intricate patterns? It could make a net of waves, couldn't it? A net could be lifted.

A pattern came into his head. Fairly complex, at least a dozen major intersections. He tried to study it, but the image was slippery. The places he looked straight at would disappear, so he had to see by looking slightly away. That made it hard to—

"David!"

The Queen stood in front of him. "I waited as long as I could, but we've got to go."

David looked around. Most of the people were already gone, just his parents and Wolf had stayed with the Queen. "How long have I been standing here?"

"A really long time," his Dad said. "I made them leave you alone. Everyone can thank me later."

"You all right?" his Mom asked.

"Yeah." David nodded. "Is the water still here?"

"Diit left you some," the Queen said. "It's on the cart." She held a little tub out to him. "I saved a tonker for you if you need it. It's collapsible—you pull it open. Most people used theirs around the corner in the thumb tunnel."

"Thanks, let me brush my teeth, and run do that, and I'll be ready." As he turned to get the water, she stopped him with her hand on his arm.

"It's a rock," she said.

David grinned and pressed the hand still on his arm. "And I know what to do to move it."

Chapter Su.23

"Your brother did it. Or maybe it was your mother. Either way, if one of them could do it, you should be able to. I know you have access to this brain." He tapped his finger hard on The Thing That Was Robert Treslo's forehead. "Now get busy."

It blinked and stepped back, looking around at the floor, the walls, the bed…but not like it knew what it was doing.

"Just stop. Stop for a minute," Dagge said. Holding one hand up, he moved several steps closer, until he had to crane his neck to look in the giraffe's eyes. "What did your brother know, or do, or have, that you didn't?"

"Nothing."

He had to laugh. Guys and their pride.

"Obviously, that's not true." He walked away a couple of steps. "Roger, you're about to lose the Smartest Treslo award, unless you can find that secret passage. You do realize that you will die, at any time I decide your body isn't working out. If I were you, I'd get irreplaceable real quick."

Roger gazed down at him for a moment, then turned away, squatted in front of the bed and got his face really close to the little hole. "I need a light," it said.

"Wharton," Dagge barked, "get a light."

Wharton promptly left the hallway in front of the cell and disappeared down the hall to the guard room. Ahh, obedience was nice.

In the meantime, he was left alone with Roger. How tempted he was to plant a foot in his squatting ass. Just because he could. So, he did.

Roger fell face first into the slab, bending his nose to the side and landing the edge right on his eye. The expression on his face was hilarious. Dagge laughed, and it felt really good. How long had it been? Too fucking long.

Roger didn't say anything, but of course he wouldn't. Dagge watched him right himself, and stay squatting. Always submissive.

"I'll eventually kill you, you know."

It took a long time for the thing to reply, like in the beginning, when they didn't know how to use their voices.

"Yes, Overlord."

They were passably good for some things, but conversation wasn't one of them.

"Shut the fuck up," Dagge said. "Stand up and look at me, motherfucker."

It stood up and turned to face him very slowly. The suspense gave Dagge a chubby.

He searched the eyes again. The purple seemed stronger, maybe. Still stuttering, which was strange, since it should have gotten better by now. Where's a 2D doctor when you need one?

Wharton came barreling around the corner, holding a bulb torch out in front of him. Dagge reached his hand through the bars, and Wharton walked right by it and came through the door. What a moron.

It made him wonder if the flatties had different levels of smarts. The one in Wharton seemed really dumb, which was too bad, because Wharton didn't used to be dumb.

Dagge grabbed the torch out of Wharton's hand and went to give it to Roger. The guy moved in slow motion, and kept getting slower.

"What the hells is the matter with you? Get a fucking move on, Rodney." He shoved the torch into Robert's chest, but Robert wouldn't take it, and he had to fold his arm up over it to keep it from falling when he let go. "Are you useless?" He grabbed the front of Robert's shirt and jerked him closer. The bulb torch hit the floor. "I'm fucking going to kill you now if you don't pick that up and find that secret fucking passage! Wharton!"

"Yes, Overlord."

"Go get me someone, right—"

340

"Wait…" it said. "Overlord. I…am…" Then it made these choking noises, and jerked around. Creepy shit. Dagge wasn't sure if it was going to hock up some giant parasite or what. He stepped back just in case.

In a few seconds, it arched its head back, its body all tense, and then released again to normal. Dagge watched, hand on his knife, and when its eyes came down, they were purple.

"What's going on, Roger?"

"Nothing, Overlord. The body was resisting, but not anymore."

"Resisting, huh?" His hands jumped to his hips. "You sure you've got it under control?"

"Yes, Overlord. My strength was greater."

Dagge studied him for a long minute. The purple didn't blink or dim. "Do you have access to the brain?"

"Yes. There is no information about the secret passage."

"No shit." He nodded, then threw his hand out and jabbed the air with his finger. "That's why they call it a secret. Is there any information…that can help us figure out…where the fuck it opens!"

Somehow he had ended up on his tiptoes, shouting into the guy's chin. But the guy was unflappable, as Granny used to say. In fact, he had a smirk on his face, if you asked Dagge, and Dagge agreed.

"Wipe that fucking smirk off your face, asshole."

The face twitched and went through some contortions, until it settled in a frown. "I don't have any information about the secret passage."

Fucking moron. What was the point of having a smart body if the stupid flatty couldn't think? "Get out of my way," he said, pushing the giraffe aside. "You're staying in here, Ronaldo, until you find a way out. If you don't get out, your body will get thirsty, and hungry. At some point you will die, and no one will be here for you to jump into." Out in the hall he spun around. "What fun."

Wharton closed the bars behind him, and Dagge could hear him lock the body in as he hurried on around the corner. Treslo wasn't working out the way he'd hoped, but what could he do? Apparently,

Hellen had killed all the smart henchmen. He couldn't believe he let her get away with that.

Love was stupid.

Chapter Su.24

In her dream, she'd stood outside a small building, like a tavern or something, surrounded by trees. Several people were standing outside, all looking up over the building. Ming stood beside her, then turned to her and said, "Beware the dragon that comes as friend."

Turning her head, she looked up over the building, and Adia did the same. A dragon was there, black with tan cheeks and chest, and no wings. With great sweeps of its head, arms, and tail, it knocked down trees until limbs and branches filled the air. As it destroyed, it incinerated the forest with jets of fire. Beside her, Ming was gone, and Dagge stood in her place, also watching the dragon. The dragon stopped breathing fire, and looked at her. Then it leaned over the building, front legs crashing through the roof, open mouth coming down, down, and covering her with black.

Then her father stood beside her, under the night sky. They were in a clearing, standing in front of an enormous boulder. "The index finger points the way," he said, holding up his first finger. "David will know what to do."

"I miss you, Dad."

"I'm always here, Birdie Girl." But as he said it, he faded, and she'd woken on the hard ground, blind again.

Beware the dragon that comes as friend. The only friend that had come recently was Hellen's friend from Valdia. Hellen's description of her did not sound like a dragon type. Too bad Adia had to bring it up next time she saw her.

The forest tunnel dragged. They were all so tired, no one chatted or laughed. Occasional whispers broke the quiet, but other than that, the trip was a lot of shuffling steps, the rustle of clothing, and clinks from packs. Had they gotten slower? It seemed like they had. Adia remembered the first time she walked a tunnel it seemed like it would never end.

Most of the crowd had left her and David behind. Just his parents bringing up the rear, and they were back a handful of strides. Adia's hand rested comfortably in the scent of David's arm. The crook of his arm. She meant crook.

Good grief.

"Byron!" she called to the front, her voice carrying easily in the confined space. "Do you know any marching songs?"

"I know a few sea shanties!" Edren Taymer called back.

"That's perfect! Will you teach us?"

"You bet I will! All right, folks, I'll sing a line and everybody answer with 'That's the life at sea.' Ready?"

"READY!" the chorus shouted, eager to stay awake, probably.

"I saw a mermaid who swam with a fish."

"That's the life at sea!"

"She told me I answered her every wish."

"That's the life at sea!"

"She begged and she begged for me to come down."

"That's the life at sea!"

"Then when I did, I started to drown."

"That's the life at sea!"

"The wench had my ankle and pulled with her might."

"That's the life at sea!"

"She didn't expect I'd put up a fight."

"That's the life at sea!"

"I kicked toward her head with my trusty old boot."

"That's the life at sea!"

"And connected the toe with her sizable snoot!"

"That's the life at sea!"

"She let go my ankle and tooted a fart."

"That's the life at sea!"

"With a flick of her tail, swam down to the dark."

"That's the life at sea!"

"This lesson was sent from the angels above."

"That's the life at sea!"

"Don't ever drown for a mermaid's love!"

"That's the life at seeeeea!"

Laughter floated around the group, along with one or two suggestions for the next song, which they picked up immediately.

Wolf bumped her hand with his nose and trotted ahead.

Behind, John and Roberta caught up, and John started talking, his nose poking over David's shoulder.

"David, you know about carapaz, right?"

"I know it was easy to blow up with Hellen's weapon."

Adia said, "Merv and the science people have been experimenting with it for a while, but in a focused energy beam way."

"Well, it's all around us in these tunnels. They have a crystalline carapaz structure that the Resistance tunnels in town don't have," John said.

"We haven't been able to study the carapaz in its natural setting," Adia said. "These tunnels are a deeper layer of rock. And no one has theorized about how such a distribution of crystals could effect a generalized energy."

"You're a bit of a geek, aren't you?" David teased.

"Maybe. What's your point?"

John and Roberta faded back.

"I like it. It means I can release my inner geek."

"I'm thinking that passenger is already off the ship."

"Really?"

"Oh yeah."

His free hand touched hers again, like it kept doing. Landing briefly, and pulling away. At some point she was going to catch it, and make him hold her hand outright.

Very soon, maybe.

****

David found it almost impossible not to lay his hand on the Queen's and leave it there. Her hand needed warming anyway, so he could say that was why. But that wouldn't really be why. The why was that it felt like a bird, light and soft and delicate, and he wanted to protect it. Protect her. Not that Adia was delicate…on the outside, maybe, but inside she was pure carapaz. Like her kingdom.

She was a Queen, and capturing her hand might not be appropriate.

But didn't she open the door by telling him to call her Adia?

Yeah, not the same thing. Maybe he should ask. Sure, she was a Queen, but she was also a person, and they had a lot in common. Three years of Dagge had taught them that life didn't care how smart, or funny, or royal you were. If it wanted to blow up your world, it would. Death and oppression leveled the field.

But three years of being home with Joey had taught him that life is also built and rebuilt with other people. Mostly the people we care about, but also everyone. We weave our strands together, and it makes us stronger. Joey's thread had ended, and it made a hole, but the weaving went on because it had to. If you didn't keep weaving, the whole tapestry would fall apart.

The weaving with Adia was beginning, and David felt very good about that. Good enough to protect it.

Given the events of the last forever with Cary, he didn't kid himself about where the tension could end up. Cary was in full competitor mode, and at some point there was likely to be a meeting of the fists. David had been in a few fights, and could only wish the guy wasn't in such prime shape.

"I don't think Cary likes me."

"Why do you say that?"

"He gets a mean face when he looks at me."

"Really?"

"Yeah. It's not as scary as Mom's, though."

"How do you feel about that?"

He paused for a bit, then said, "I think he should work on it. If he could make his eyeballs really pop, that would help."

She laughed. Score.

"We'll be at the boulder soon," he said, "and I want to ask you something before we get there." She didn't say anything, just waited. "I suspect Cary is going to be…increasingly out of sorts with me, and I'm wondering how you'd like me to handle it."

Her head went down for a few moments, then she turned her face up to him. "I trust you to handle it the best way for you. I don't see you as a temper-ridden person, but Cary might be. I could see him pushing it to blows. Are you trained? Because he's quite strong, and agile, they tell me."

"I've been training with Beau, so I could probably get in a few licks. Woodchopping, too, but there's no way that would match what he does. I'm taller, but he's more cut. I don't know, I hope it doesn't come to that, but if it does, so be it. If you like, I'll describe every inch of my messed-up face to you."

She laughed. "That might be necessary. I wouldn't survive the curiosity."

"Who would?" He touched her hand on his arm, then pulled it away. Except this time she caught it, jolting his heart. She was smiling, her face tilted up to him. So much for needing to ask. David switched hands, wrapped his warm fingers around hers, and squeezed gently. "I want you to know that—"

He stopped, not knowing how to say what he wanted to tell her. In his whole life, he never realized how much communication happens through the eyes. He'd taken for granted that he could show humor, or anger, or love. Sometimes just a glance was enough. He shook his head. "I want you to know that I never expected…" Nope. "I want you to know that I have more fun with you than with anyone else I know. It's not just fun, either. With everything that's happened, we've gone through so much just in a couple of days, and…I feel lucky I got to do it with you, that's all. Better than anybody else."

Her eyes sparkled in the dim light. "I feel the same way, David Treslo."

Her hand squeezed his, and he smiled down at her. Even though she couldn't see it.

Monday

Chapter M.1

Wolf's barks echoed back down the tunnel, through the crowd and the soft conversations, all the way to Adia's ears. "He must be at the end," she said. "Cary!" she called. "How far ahead is he?"

"I can't really see him with my bulb torch," Cary called back. "But it doesn't sound too far."

"We'll need some room at the end," David told her. "To make the formation. I don't know how much, but maybe a lot."

"We should catch up with the others."

"Clear path, let's go." David gripped her hand and they sped up into a brief run. "Ten strides…five strides…and just ahead we have…Vartile and Luhe." They slowed to a fast walk.

"Vartile." Adia reached her hand out.

"Your Majesty." Vartile's voice came from the one o'clock, and her hand met Adia's.

"Walk with me," Adia said. Vartile's hand let go, there was some shuffling, and Vartile's warm energy moved to Adia's left side. They hooked arms. "David, will you run ahead and stop everyone at the distance you think is right?"

"Yes, ma'am," he said, and hurried off.

"Loud enough that I can hear you!"

"Yes, ma'am!"

"I guess the book worked," Vartile said.

"It seems so. Thank One."

"Excellent. That puts us one step closer."

"Yes." Adia liked the way that sounded. "I was wondering if you might take on a job for me."

"Absolutely I will."

"The group is going to need…a combination drill sergeant and den mother. Someone who can keep them moving in the right direction." Adia grinned. "I believe you are extraordinarily qualified. Plus, everybody loves you."

"And I love them, too. I'd be happy to be the den sergeant, ma'am, I can do it. Can I get Luhe to help me?"

"Of course you can. You can get anyone you want. And I must say, Luhe is an excellent first choice."

"Thank you, I thought it was quite good." Vartile squeezed her arm. "Hey, here comes Wolf." Vartile's pitch went up like everyone else's when they talked to the dog. "Hi, sugar!" Wolf approached, panting really loud. Adia was sure he was smiling, too. His nose bumped her hand, and she scratched his head. He fell into step beside her.

David's voice rang down the tunnel. "All right, everybody, we're going to stop here. The end is about thirty strides more, but we need room. Let's take five while the Queen catches up."

Vartile released Adia's arm and yelled forward, "Folks! Let's put the packs back here along the walls. That way we won't trip and break something."

"What are we doing?" someone yelled.

"No idea," Vartile said. "David is the man with the plan."

Talking and footsteps were coming back her direction, and Adia reached for the wall to get out of the way.

John stopped her. "Your Majesty, we should move to the front."

"Yes, all right," she said, admittedly sorry to give up the luxury of not being looked at. But, nature of the job and all. Hand on his arm, she followed John through the crowd.

"Coming through, coming through," he said.

Adia ended up behind John, out of the flow of people, holding John's ponytail, walking in his footsteps. She felt like a comedy act, and thoroughly enjoyed it.

A light stream of "Your Majestys" flowed to the sides as they walked past, along with some laughs, and people rejoining behind in a hum of conversation.

Vartile's voice rose over them. "Let's start back here. You guys bring your packs back this far! Against the wall past me."

The crowd thinned as they got closer to the end of the tunnel. John dropped back so Adia could take his arm again. Several males were talking ahead, voices echoing off the rock—Cary, David, and…Byron.

"Hello, gentlemen," she said, walking up.

"Your Majesty," they said.

Adia waited just a moment before she got on with it. "David, will you escort me to the rock?"

"Yes, ma'am, I will." A warm hand touched her arm. She ran her hand up to the elbow, and David pulled it in close. They walked to the rock. "It's about two feet in front of you."

"How tall is it?" she asked, releasing David's arm and touching the boulder's surface.

David answered. "About fifteen feet, we estimate, ma'am. Twelve around the belly."

She smiled at the thought of it having a belly, and rubbed it. It felt fuzzy and irregular. She ran her hands up and down, side to side, moving to her left until she reached the wall, then curving back around to the right to do the same. Bigger on the outside, too, for it to block the opening.

Their plan suddenly struck her as crazy.

"David says we need to make a formation?" That was Cary. Sounding…carefully neutral.

Dread burbled up in her. "Yes, Cary, but we have plenty of people, you don't have to do it if you don't want to."

"I want to help. Direct me, I'll get people in place."

"Sure," David said, sounding as surprised as she felt. "That'd be great."

Note to self: Stop thinking the worst. "John, is there anything you can tell us?"

"Well, the crystalline carapaz structure makes them durable and *conductive*." John whispered the last word. Like it was a secret.

"Ah, the walls are our friends." David said.

"Your best friends, *because of the confined space*." He whispered that last part, which couldn't have been a secret…obviously it was a confined space.

"Can we compress the formation?"

"Keep it to the scale of a given clock. Although, clock sizes vary. Consider the feet of the rock as the fulcrum. The center. Feet together. Also, multiples of a given formation operate the same, just with degrees of separation." The volume knob had gone from normal to nothing in the space of what he said. Just his lips moving at the end.

"You know you're not fooling them," David said.

"Repeats, then. Gotcha. *Are we ready?*" Adia whispered, enjoying play time.

"*Yes, ma'am,*" David whispered.

Byron said, "Cary, let me take your pack."

"Thanks." There were some rustles and grunts, and one set of jogging feet faded away.

"I'll get out of your way, too, gentlemen," Adia said. "John, are you…" She flicked her pointer down the hall.

"Yes, ma'am. I am at your disposal."

"Sweet. If you guys need anything, let me know." As she and John walked away, David started yelling. "I need volunteers!"

Adia immediately stopped and turned around with her hand up. Because why not?

Chapter M.2

Hellen and Beau sat among the rubble of what used to be the west wing of the monastery. The jumble of rocks and ivy made quite a few good places to hide, as long as you didn't mind spiders and the occasional snake. As long as they weren't poisonous, Hellen was okay, but it was hard to tell.

Like she wasn't jumpy enough. She half expected to see both Dagge and Wharton tonight. Dagge, because he would almost certainly want to make the kill himself, and Wharton just in case he couldn't do it alone. But who would they be expecting? Not her, being officially dead the way she was. Probably David, then, and whatever nameless others Dagge imagined were helping the Queen. He wouldn't imagine them to be too threatening, so he'd likely leave his pet monsters at home. Or maybe he'd have one. Knowing Dagge, it'd be a small contingent. Stealth and skill, steal and kill.

Beau had settled a few feet away from her, loaded for bear. He had a rifle with a night scope, a machete and a crossbow on his back, a knife on his leg, and a pistol on his belt. Another knife was tucked in his boot, and who knew what else was in the multitude of pockets all over him. Hellen got the feeling he'd been planning this moment for a long time. Thank One.

They both had night glasses, and kept their eyes on the trees. No talking, no fidgeting, just endless silent waiting. Hellen's legs were starting to ache, kinked up under her, and she was just starting to shift off her feet when Beau's hand reached over and lay on her arm. She stopped.

"Dolly!" A faint voice called out from the trees. "Dolly, can you hear me?"

"What the hells?" Hellen whispered.

"Do you know her?" Beau asked.

"She's my friend from Valdia. The one I told you about. What is she doing here?"

"Dolly, I'm lost…" Anji's voice faded and cracked, sounding like it was on the verge of tears. It jerked Hellen's heart, and she started to stand, but Beau's hand lay on her arm again.

"Hellen, you have to ask yourself, what is she doing here? What are the chances she'd show up by accident?"

"About zero. I know." She took a knee.

If Anji was working for Dagge, it would explain a lot. Like why she offered her a place to stay when she didn't even know her. Why she never asked questions when Hellen would be gone for days at a time. And why that last monster knew who she was, and *Tomius says hello*.

But if Anji worked for Dagge, it raised an even bigger question. Why didn't she stop her? All those pets of his she killed, and if Anji was watching her, and reporting back, why did Hellen get away with it?

Only one way to find out. "I'm going," she said.

"I'll have your back," he answered.

Hellen stood, and wound her way out of the rubble. She could hear Beau's feet scraping the ground, and when she looked back, his rifle was positioned on the rock in front of him, his eye to the scope. It was honestly so comforting.

With her night glasses on, Hellen could see pretty far through the trees. Anji was coming in from the left, following the line of the mountains, but keeping to the shelter of the pines. She didn't have night glasses, or a bulb torch, and she touched every tree she passed like it was a lifeboat.

Hellen felt her pain.

"Dolly!" she called again. Stopping, she cupped her mouth and moved her head in a long arc. "DOOOLLYYYY!" For a few seconds, she stood and listened, and Hellen stopped with her. What would be the best approach? If she was a friend, it wouldn't matter, but if she was a spy… Hellen opted for the keep-your-distance strategy.

"Anji, what are you doing here?"

"Dolly!" She burst into tears, shaking her head, and spreading her hands over her face.

Well, krikey. If it was a ruse, it was very convincing.

"Anji, Anji…" she said, taking a few steps closer, and making sure to stay out of Beau's line of shot.

"I thought I was going to die out here. I didn't bring any water, or a blanket or anything. I don't even have good shoes!" Hellen glanced at the little slippers she was wearing, and had to agree.

"What are you doing in the woods? You shouldn't be here."

"I wish I wasn't here! These woods are spooky. I heard some people say they were going to a monastery in the forest, and you would be there."

"First of all…bullshit. You didn't hear that unless it was Dagge talking. And second, you expect me to believe you happened to end up here by wandering around the forest? I know better."

After a drawn out moment, Anji"s demeanor changed. Gone was the goofy, sweet daisy of a woman, and she got replaced by:

"You're right." Her voice lost that squeaky quality it always had, both grating and endearing at the same time. Totally fake, apparently. "You were always so astute, I had to constantly provide alibis. It was irritating."

Hellen raised her rifle to her waist. "I'm not sorry to hear that."

Anji laughed. "Of course you're not."

"Is there something you want?"

Anji smiled. "There are lots of things I want."

"I'm afraid I can't help you with taking over the world."

"No? Then how about something simple? You come back with me to the palace, and we can work this out like adults."

"By 'adult' you mean my torture and eventual death."

"Oh now, I think you're jumping to conclusions. You were important to him. He used to talk about you. And you talked about him."

"Zero relevance, Anji. I don't care what the lunatic says. Or ever said. There's no connection between then and now. Dagge has disappeared into the abyss, and cannot be saved. Therefore, he must be removed."

"Funny you haven't been able to do it yet."

Hellen ignored that jab. "At the moment, you are at a complete disadvantage, between me and my backup." She jerked a thumb behind her. Beau fired off a shot, smacking the ground beside them and drawing Anji's attention. "Since you're here, though, I will be taking you prisoner."

She dug a hank of rope out of her pocket and waved in her hand in a circle for Anji to turn around.

Instead, Anji took a few steps toward her, holding up her hands in a rather noncommittal surrender pose—making it easy for her to reach a weapon on her back if she chose to. Hellen brought her rifle up to her face and sighted.

Anji stopped walking. "Look, I absolutely get it. I do. There's no reason you should trust me. Except I never killed you. I could have, but I didn't."

"Dagge wouldn't have wanted you to. He thought I'd marry him. He would have killed you if you'd killed me."

"Well, he might not have *killed* me. We have history."

Hellen looked around her scope. "So did we, and he killed me, and you're not doing too well convincing me you're not his puppet."

"Please, the man's a narcissist."

The rifle dropped to Hellen's chest. "Irrelevant. You're the one who's choosing to be there."

"Come on, you know what he's like. Sexy, and…sexy."

Hellen did indeed know. "You mean to tell me your entire value structure is built on your gonads?"

"Not my entire value structure." Anji let her hands drop back to her sides, looked down, shook her head, and brought her hands up to her hips. "I probably shouldn't tell you this, but there's no way you're going to trust me if I don't. I work for Shindao. Empress Dalang has assigned me to Tomius Dagge since some trouble we had on the

356

northern border. I met him then, and in some ways, we hit it off immediately, as I'm sure you understand."

Hellen sighted again. Anji put her hands up again.

Then she said a sentence in Shindaoan, and it sounded real.

"Speaking Shindaoan isn't proof."

Anji laughed. "Don't you want to know what I said?"

"Not particularly."

"It's about you."

"I don't care."

"Pow. Well, I'd say let's call the Empress, but I don't think you have a visaphone handy."

"You're right, I don't. And you're about to run out of time. That way," Hellen said, gesturing her barrel toward the monastery.

She didn't want to kid herself, Anji could be all the stuff she said, and still kill her. Or take her to Dagge, which was more likely. But Hellen felt in her heart the kindness Anji had shown her every day in Valdia—covering her work shifts, those terrible experimental dinners, the surprise birthday cake even when it wasn't her birthday.

Fake and manipulative, maybe, but she'd hate to be the death of someone if they didn't deserve it.

Chapter M.3

"Can we just stop a minute?" Anji said in that slightly panicked voice Hellen remembered.

"Stop for what?" They'd gone through the pines at a snail's pace. Every few steps Anji was stopping to pick pine needles out of her shoe. Now that they were in the clear, close to the monastery, it was dirt or rocks. Hellen was ready to start jabbing Anji in the shoulder with her gun barrel.

"Just stop!" Anji whirled around. Hellen shined the light in her face.

"Don't you wonder *why* I never killed you?"

"Not at the moment."

"It wasn't because of Dagge."

Hellen raised her gun. "Why were you sneaking up on us?"

"I wasn't sneaking! You know I wasn't sneaking. What kind of idiot would I be to yell for you if I didn't want you to know I was out here?"

"And yet you've just admitted you work for Dagge—"

"I work for Shindao—"

"And why should I trust anything you say?"

Looking at Anji, it felt terribly wrong to be holding her at gunpoint. Her movie buddy, eating buckets of popcorn, getting drunk. They'd done karaoke, for pity's sake. Was there any chance at all she was telling the truth about Shindao?

"What do you believe happened to Empress Ming?" Hellen asked.

"I know Mapo told the truth, that Ming was possessed by an evil being."

"Did you think that at the time?"

"Nobody thought that at the time. Those of us loyal to them didn't know what to think. Mapo wasn't crazy, something had to happen while they were here. It wasn't until we saw the developments in Pulari that we believed other-dimensional forces were at work, as he'd said."

"And in Valdia, you knew I was after those other-dimensional forces, yet you didn't see fit to help me."

"I was still undercover with Dagge. And I knew you'd get them."

Hellen scoffed. "Why would you turn me in at all to him if you knew I was trying to kill those things? Why would you report on me, and let him know where I was?"

"Better me than someone else, Hellen. I didn't tell him everything I knew."

Hellen was swayed, she had to admit. Anji was a liar by the nature of her job. She had to be good at it. But that didn't delete the possibility that she had good qualities, too. If only Hellen could contact Empress Dalang and ask if she had a spy on Dagge.

Maybe she could use the Treslo's visaphone. Just as soon as she got Anji in Beau's care.

"Keep walking," Hellen said, leveling her rifle at Anji's chest. Anji turned and headed into the cove.

At the kitchen, Hellen pushed Anji through the blanket that now served as the back door. Gun still raised and sighted, she followed her into the room. "Papa Bear!"

"Yeah!" His voice came from the great room, and seconds later he entered the kitchen. He had switched his long-range, nightscope rifle for an enormous handgun, which he trained on the intruder.

"The dog is not going to like our visitor," she said.

"Can't say I blame him, what with them sneaking up before dawn."

"I wasn't sneaking!"

"You got this Papa Bear?" Beau nodded once and Hellen lowered her rifle.

Anji had backed into the space between the fireplace and the first table, which could have made for a good escape had Beau not come in behind her. Now her hands were up and she'd turned her back to the fireplace so she could watch both of them.

Hellen pictured her backing up to the radiator in her apartment. She did that all winter. Wicker shelves had been wedged in beside the radiator, and it didn't matter how many times Hellen hinted about wicker and radiator being a bad combination. Anji would agree and promise to do something about it, but. Ah well, not Hellen's apartment. Every time she came home from somewhere, she wondered if the building would be charred rubble.

"Anji here claims to be a double agent. She's pretending to work for Dagge, but really works for Shindao. Does that sound likely to you? Because I am not convinced."

"Well, Hellen, I'd say it's a tossup.

Hellen had put her back to the dumbwaiter, so the curtain was in easy view when it moved. She glanced at Beau, who had seen her look at the curtain, and was dividing his attention between it and Anji. He moved closer to the wall for a better angle.

Nothing happened for a few more seconds, and then the growl started. The curtain lifted at the corner, and Wolf's snarling face eased through. He moved slow, and looked terrifying, eyes never moving from Anji.

Hellen didn't really want to step in front of Wolf, but she did. He looked up at her, still growling. Yikes. "Putting her back to Anji, she bent a little, showed her palm, and whispered, "Stay."

Beau covered for her, moving more to the front again and talking. "I'd say the fact that the dog doesn't like her is enough for me, Hellen."

"Good point."

"It's not a good point," Anji said. "Of course the dog doesn't like me. He—" She brought her hands down. "Do you mind?" She nodded singularly at them, rubbing her hands and loosening her shoulders.

Hellen bent to catch Wolf's eye, then she said, "Kill."

"Wait a minute!"

Hellen straightened, dangling three fingers in front of Wolf's face like that was all Anji had between herself and gory death.

"I saved that dog for you. I did. I snatched it up when its mother got shot, before the soldiers snapped up all the others. It bit me, too. I had to wrap it in a blanket, and I left it there again just before you got there. Yes, I was keeping an eye on you. And Dagge thought I was working for him then, too."

"He bit her even then," Beau said, raising his gun and sighting.

"I can prove what I'm saying." Her eyes were a little wild. "I have a tattoo that all Imperial Forces get. It's on my back, I can show you."

"Let's see it," Hellen said, bringing her rifle back up.

Anji turned slowly, hands moving down to the hem of her shirt, and slowly peeling it up. Then she turned back around, a small gun in her hand.

"You can't be serious," Hellen said, as Beau closed in from the side. Wolf lowered his head and barked a growl.

"Look closer." Anji raised her other arm, flipped the pistol in her hand, and held it out to Hellen. Beau maintained a steady aim on her head.

Hellen took the gun and examined it. It was a small revolver, old. Engraved on the handle was *Thanks, RP & HP*.

"Those were your parents. Rollo and Heloise Parker. They gave this to my father for saving their lives."

"This could be anybody. If it was true, why didn't you lead with that, instead of the b.s. about the tattoo?"

"I do have a tattoo. You were going to see the gun anyway, so I turned it over first. Let me show you."

"You know, I'm not going to go through a whole bunch of "proof" you could get at any tattoo shop. We can't trust you, so you will have to be our prisoner until we find out what Beast wants to do with you. Papa Bear, will you do the honors?"

Hellen raised her rifle, and Beau put down his gun. Pulling a wrist wrap out of his bulging pocket, he turned Anji firmly, and strapped her wrists behind her back. Anji cut her eyes and took it like a pro, Hellen had to admit, even leaning into Beau's body frisk and smirking at him when he finished. Sure wasn't the Anji she knew in Valdia.

"Where shall we keep her?" Beau asked.

"Stable. You can attach her to the trough. Take the dog—we can set him to watch her, he'll enjoy that."

"Yes, ma'am." Beau took Anji by the arm, grabbed his gun, and led her past Hellen toward the back doorway.

Anji trained her eyes on Hellen as she walked. Slightly past, she jerked against Beau and leaned back toward her. "I know more about you than you want me to." A smile lurked in her eyes and around her mouth. So slight as to be almost invisible.

Was that a threat?

Chapter M.4

Adia stood probably halfway back in the formation. David wanted the low singers up front, for power, he said. They all had to audition, to see if they could hold the note; it felt like an open call for a college musical. Now they all sat in their spots while David and Cary arranged people two at a time.

They'd started out with a small clock. There was a lot of closeness involved—too much, because David had to move them back a couple of times. He wanted them to stay near the rock, though, and eventually they used as many people as possible and got cozy. If you didn't count the time someone farted.

She loved listening to the people talk to each other. There were low voices, among small groups, and louder voices calling across the tunnel. Most of them were joking around, talking about memories, and saying what they were going to do when all this was over. When things were back to normal.

Adia wondered how normal things could ever be. So much had changed. The people had changed. They'd lost friends, children, parents, and lovers. You don't bounce back from that.

There'd be a new normal, one of these days. A restoration of many things, and the building of the new. Lives would resume their patterns: school, work, weddings, funerals. Children would be born. Commerce would come and go. And every person here would take great care of all that for the rest of their lives, because they would know how deeply valuable an ordinary, contented life was.

David's voice spoke loudly, just in front of her. "Edren! Will you hit the F for us?"

From the eleven, Edren's lovely baritone filled the space for about five seconds. As it played, other voices tested their pitch around the room. He picked up again, letting it stretch this time until everyone tried. When he stopped, they kept going, and it sounded like a perfect F to her.

"Thank you, Edren! Does everyone feel like they have a grip on it?"

"As long as Edren keeps singing," someone said.

They laughed. Some others probably felt the same.

"I'll keep singing," Edren said. "Is this going to take long?"

John answered. "I know when I put that balloon on that thing in the plaza, it took longer than I wanted, but not impossibly long."

"Then we have to be prepared to invest in this as long as it takes," David said loudly. "It'll work, right Dad?"

"It'll work."

"Okay. Does everyone have water?"

Some *ohs*. A few people passed her going to their packs. Then they passed back. Vartile had given Adia one, and she had to be careful not to drink too much so she wouldn't have to pee.

"Faces forward, let's go."

Edren started it. Others chimed in quickly, and soon the very air in the tunnel vibrated with sound. Adia felt a little buzzy from it, and couldn't help smiling—every voice was part of a tremendous whole. Sound echoed and reverberated on all sides, and the longer it went on the more she could feel it.

After a while she started getting blinks of light on the periphery. Tiny sparkles that popped on and glowed softly. What was that? She watched as the effect expanded inward and became a soft, more uniform light. As the singing went on, the light intensified, and the energy began to coalesce beside her, and in front of her in clumps, until she realized it was happening at every person. Every person was a glowing light. And as the music went on, the lights then beamed lines from point to point, connecting with each other in a complicated pattern.

"David!" she shouted, and the whole thing went dark. She turned to face the back.

"What is it?" he said from the back.

"I could see it…the formation. I can see the formation!" A murmur hopped around and she laughed. "We're making lines, glowing lines, and they make a shape. But I need to get up high to really see it." Holding out her hands, she let the people pass her toward the back.

"We need a volunteer to take the Queen's place," David said to the people behind him.

"I'll do it," Cary said, coming forward. She held her palm up, and he pressed it as he went by.

"Get on my shoulders," David said, tapping Adia's arm and offering his hand. "Just like we did in the forest, but up a little higher."

Adia stepped on his thigh, felt her destination with her hand, and swung up. She was careful to stay low, sitting up slowly so she wouldn't hit her head on the ceiling. Turned out she had plenty to spare.

"You set?" David asked.

"Ready." Adia held David's head as he settled them into place.

"Okay, Edren," he called.

The singing started. The lights didn't happen…and didn't happen…and then they did. She was so relieved. They twinkled, spread, and coalesced into lines.

"The formation is a little off. There are smashed places." She tapped him on the shoulder so he would look up at her. "About seven feet in that direction," she said, pointing toward the ten, "the third group is too close to the center. That's made the second and fourth off too."

"Dessara, I put you in the wrong place! Move your group one step to the left."

"Do we keep singing?" someone called.

"Yes, please!" David called back.

They kept singing, and as they moved groups around, the pattern crisped up and glowed brighter. For a few minutes she could see the reflection of the pattern on the walls. The lines on the right had to move out a bit to make it symmetrical.

When everything got straight, the walls began to glow. They were polka-dotted with carapaz at first, but as the glow increased, the spots disappeared. Walls and ceiling and floor became almost white.

The lines of energy thickened, and in a last expansion, beams of energy pushed toward the boulder. Within seconds, a rumble began, followed by the crackle of falling pebbles and dirt.

It rejuvenated the singers, and they got some real gusto. The intersection points glowed brighter, and with colors, which was interesting.

Between the rumble, and the falling rocks, and the singing, Adia couldn't hear what David said when he spoke upward to her. Bending down to him she could see him glowing, too. Down inside him, he was a sparkling blue star. It took her breath away.

"David, I can see you. I can see your energy."

Sound and awareness stopped for her as she looked around at everyone. They were stars, with their own colors, and every one different. Some were one color, some were many. Or a few. Some had halos, and others had rays, and one had flares, which was interesting. They were all burning brightly, and she wondered why people don't glow all the time. Or maybe they do, and we just can't see it.

With a final scrape, the boulder must have flown out, because a cheer went up and warm air hit her face. The cheer meant the singing stopped, the lights went out, and the boulder crashed down right outside the tunnel.

"Darn."

She didn't know who said it, but the dam burst, and everyone was talking at once.

"Were we supposed to keep singing?"

"No one told us that!"

"Can we get out?" Adia yelled, climbing down off David's shoulders.

"Yes!" Byron Taymer's voice answered. "It's farther away than it looks."

With David at her back, Adia made her way to the front, grasping hands briefly as she passed through the crowd hurrying to their packs. She couldn't see the people anymore, couldn't see the light outside. Just darkness, like before.

A few questions veered toward her, to which she responded, "Later," with a nod.

Apparently, something magical had happened with her sight. Or something scientific that had to do with the singing and the carapaz. Either way, the effect didn't last. Her vision wasn't going to suddenly manifest in this weird, amazing way.

Screw disappointment. No time for that right now. At least she saw it, right? And it was worth it, because now she knew what people looked like on the inside, and it was beautiful.

David's energy filled the space beside her as she crossed the little bit of open space before the warm, breezy hole. "Is it clear, Byron?" he called.

"Clear as day," the voice came dimly. "In fact, it is day; the sun is coming up."

Sigh.

"What?" David asked her, cupping her arm lightly.

"What what?"

"Your head was shaking. You didn't look at the people you passed. Can you not see again?"

She shook her head no, not trusting herself to speak about it.

"Then we'll figure out how to get it back. After we get rid of Dagge."

"Okay," her voice answered hoarsely, and she cleared her throat and swallowed.

David stepped out through the opening. Wolf's nose brushed her hand, and she bent her attention to him. "Hi, sweetie," she said, idly rubbing his ears. But instead of sitting and leaning into it, he turned away toward the opening, barked again, and went out. She followed him, stepping through the gap, feeling her way around the rock. Wolf barked again, from a few strides away.

"David, what is he doing?" she asked the air.

"He's heading back the way we came." David came from the left and tapped her arm.

"Toward the monastery," she said under her breath. "Something must have happened. I have to go."

"Adia," David said quietly, "you can't risk it."

"Don't tell me what I can do, David. All those times I couldn't help Hellen because she was too far away, well now she's not. Don't worry, I'll take someone with me."

Cary's walked out of the tunnel. "I'll go."

"Thank you, Cary. How about you, Byron? Will you go back with me to help Hellen and Beau?"

"Yes, ma'am, I will."

"Great, we'll take the tunnel." Adia squeezed David's hand and let go, then moved back around the rock and through the gap. "Who has a walkntalk?" she hollered.

"I've got one!" Vartile's voice said from the back.

"I have one," Byron said.

"Perfect, let's go. Vartile!" she called as she moved up the tunnel. "I'm putting you and Byron in charge of communications. Let us know when all the important stuff happens, okay? Luhe, Merv, you're in charge of setting up camp and figuring out some way we can mount that crystal, respectively." As she walked away, she shouted, "Somebody find the rock giants, we'll need access to that tear!"

Chapter M.5

Dagge sat at his desk and panned his harkener across the palace. It had been a long time since he'd had any fun with it. Since he'd had any fun, period. For the most part, there'd been a significant decrease in death over the last year. He'd have to change that when he caught the rebels.

Maybe his chemical weapons would be ready soon, and he could try those out. Biological weapons, too—he could release them in different places and see how they spread. That might be fun. Although, come to think of it, he couldn't risk catching anything, so it would have to be someplace far away. Easy peasy, now that he owned several countries.

Bored, he shoved the harkener back in the drawer and unsnapped his knife for a little target practice. He gave the King his full attention. Half the face hung in tatters, but the other half looked back at him. Still that smug expression, that bare, bare smile.

The temptation to sever that smile from Ol' Kingy's face was too strong to resist. With a swing of his arm and a flick of his hand, the knife flew, hitting the portrait…and bouncing off.

Kingy's face laughed. The mouth came open, and a glint flickered off the eyes just for a second. The head moved a tiny bit.

Dagge jumped back, his hands making claws in front of him. He rubbed his eyes, just like all the dumbasses in movies, and wiped back his hair. The picture was normal—same shreds, same holes. But he knew what he saw; it wasn't going to fool him.

His knife lay on the floor and he kicked it like it had betrayed him. It went spinning under the couch. Part of him wanted to get it, but he felt like the couch was hiding it, possessing it. The old man's couch. Why had he kept it? The man was in it. It should burn.

The Eye watched him, the mouth smirked.

Giving the couch a wide berth, Dagge headed for the shower. He had to wash this shit off.

Out the door, across the hall, into the bedroom, Dagge couldn't get to the bathroom fast enough. Once inside, he slammed the door behind him and backed away. Turning, he faced the mirror. He put his hands on his hips and struck his favorite pose. His breathing was strangely fast. He watched his chest heaving, his mouth open. There was no purple in his eyes.

He began to take off his shirt—unbuttoning, opening the collar. The grey had spread down his neck onto his chest on the left side, and up to his hairline on the right. He shook the shirt off his shoulders—it had spread over to his back. Turning slowly, he saw the grey covered more than half the distance to his trousers. He wiped and swiped at it even though he knew it wouldn't come off.

Something was taking him over. It used to be slow, but it was fast now.

A virus, probably.

He turned to check his other side. Different shape, same problem.

Turning back to front, he assessed the situation.

He didn't have to look at it, so who cared.

Satisfied, Dagge turned to the shower and started the spray. He wanted it hot, he didn't care if it was summer. Waiting for it to heat, he shed his pants and noticed a smear on the end wall tile. It looked like blood.

How was that possible?

He stepped in and examined it, warm water dribbling over his shoulders. It was dry, so it had been there a while. A blotch and a smear, like maybe a bleeding hand. Or shoulder. Maybe a head if someone had been killed in here. They could've fallen a little to the side, and forward.

Who was killed?

Nobody he could think of. He looked down at his hands—no cuts. His shoulders were okay, his head was okay. He put his hand up and touched his hair. Yep, okay.

Another fucking mystery.

He backed into the spray and let the water run over his head and face. The hot water penetrated the fog trapped in his hair and washed it away. He could feel the confusion slide off of him. The bad feelings. The fear. As he soaped, he gazed at the blood, chipping away from the water. He soaped his snake and sack, taking them in both hands and coaxing a stiffie. Eyes fixed on the blood, he stroked himself, and played, and pounded, and shot his jizz all the way to the wall. Catching the cream before it dropped, he pushed it up to the smear, rubbing the blood, adding water until it dissolved and dripped away to the swirling bubbles at his feet.

He felt better. Fuck this grey on his face. Fuck the grey on his back. Fuck Hellen and all those traitors and fuck Anji, who hadn't come back.

He knew what to do about them.

Chapter M.6

Hellen stepped out the kitchen door, checked the handgun she'd grabbed, and stuck it in her belt while she walked to the pyramid. The sun streamed golden over the tops of the trees, flowing onto the rock and scrubby bushes. A breeze tufted down from the mountain, cool and gentle. It almost made the day pleasant.

She should've made this trip earlier, but she'd had to lean on the table and take a minute to think. How many things were bad luck, or good luck, or not luck at all? Doubt opened a vast ocean of possible betrayals. Every conversation, every turn of events. How long would it take to reconstruct a semblance of truth? Even if she was working for Shindao.

Because Anji might be right about Wolf's reaction to her. He might associate her with his dead mother, which would render his reaction inadmissible. Do dogs suffer childhood trauma? Cats do. They'd had one at the orphanage that was obsessed with doors. It had grown up in a tiny cage, never let out until it was rescued, and ever after he had to go in and out of doors constantly just to be sure he could.

So yeah, Wolf could be traumatized.

At any rate, they didn't have to kill Anji right away. She could be their prisoner now, and Adia could help sort it out later. But…Anji would be a tough prisoner…better to contact Dalang asap. Maybe they could take Anji to the Treslo's with them. Put her on camera for verification.

Wolf met her at the pyramid door. His ears were up but his head was low. He looked back for several moments, then turned and faded into the darkness. Hellen pulled the gun back out.

Anji was standing halfway back into the room, and Wolf stood facing her, several feet away. "I'll make a deal with you," Anji said.

"Not likely." Hellen passed through the doorway into the cool stillness. It took her eyes a few moments to adjust, making her regret enjoying the sunlight. She stepped to the left, out of the doorway, and her foot bumped a soft, solid object that had to be Beau. She glanced down—he lay in the straw, body still, face dark. Hellen stepped over him and knelt, keeping her aim on Anji. His nose was slippery with blood, but warm air drifted out his nostrils, and she moved her hand to his chest and found his heart beating strong. Hellen stood and sighted, both hands on her pistol. "So, you're not alone."

Anji chuckled. "You must not think much of me if you don't think I can get out of a wrist wrap."

"It's not the wrist wrap."

"You think I couldn't beat him?" She tilted her pitying face. "Oh, I'm sure he's good, he's just…old school. You know, if you wanted, you could come study with me and I could show you a few things. Bring your game up more than you can imagine."

"You're actually right, Anji. I don't think much of you." Hellen said, almost meaning it. "You're a liar."

Anji raised Beau's big handgun. "And you're not?"

Hellen didn't have any comeback for that.

"Except for the knife in my shoe, I was unarmed, like I said. It's a short blade. I got him on the side of the face…and up under the jaw a bit. He'll live."

That wouldn't be enough to knock Beau out, of course, and Hellen was dying to know, but she didn't want to play Anji's game. "Why didn't you just kill him? Wolf, too? You could have escaped, why are you standing here?"

"I'm waiting for you."

"Why? I'll just kill you."

A pause, and Anji shrugged. "I don't want to fight with you, Hellen." Nothing more than that, just a little shake of her head.

Hellen glanced at Wolf: head down, ears up, focused on Anji. Not growling. "What do you want to do, Anji?"

"Let's put our guns down and talk."

Hellen didn't want to do that. "We can talk just fine like this."

"Aw, come on now, you're insanely outgunned. Let's just lower them. I'll go first." Beau's gun disappeared into the shadows by Anji's leg. Somehow that wasn't comforting at all.

Anji turned toward Hellen so half of her was washed in light and the other in shadow. Her black hair swung forward, striping her face with darkness. Beau's gun caught the light in teases as she moved.

A far cry from the person she'd been in Valdia. Or the person she'd seemed to be. Back then she'd acted flighty and a little stupid. Anji liked comedies and romance movies, and would talk loudly to the screen like they could hear her. Hellen missed that person—she lowered her gun halfway.

"Why won't you believe I'm working for Shindao?"

"Because you could say anything. Just because you say it doesn't make it true."

"All the evidence points to it being true."

"Horseshit. None of that's proof. If you're working for Dalang, why didn't you just kill Dagge? So many people have died because of him, and more will die. Proof of who you are is in your hand and lying here at my feet. Wolf."

Wolf came to her and she gestured for him to block the door. There, he assumed an attack posture and only growled when Anji turned toward him. Great dog.

"That's right, he's lying at your feet alive. Not dead. That's proof I don't want to hurt you."

"Yet you still haven't said why you didn't kill Dagge."

"So some other asshole would take over? Someone worse, maybe?"

"Now you're reaching."

"I didn't know the Princess was still alive."

"So when he told you, you didn't immediately think 'I can kill him now.'"

"Hellen, I…this isn't the conversation I want to have."

"I bet."

"Remember the time we tried to fry that chicken? We did the egg and the flour—"

"Twice."

"Right. Hot oil, turning it until it was nice and brown. It looked so good. We had everything on the table—the mashed potatoes, green beans, pickles—"

"You wanted the pickles."

"I did. And everything was beautiful."

"Smelled fabulous."

"So yummy, and we took one bite—"

"And it was raw. We had to spit it out."

"I was so disappointed!" Anji laughed. "I never was much for cooking. I don't think I've cooked anything since."

"Hand over the gun, Anji, don't make me kill you."

"Don't make me kill you, Hellen. You're the only friend I've had for a very long time."

"You know we can't be friends if you work for Dagge."

Anji was quiet, inscrutable behind the curtain of her hair. "I thought maybe we could go back to Valdia. We could get jobs and be normal people. Get a new apartment, learn to cook." She chuckled, then became earnest. "Aren't you tired of this? All the killing. The hunting, the manipulation. I have money saved. We could travel. You said you always wanted to go someplace tropical, let's do it. We don't ever have to come back."

What an offer. Hellen knew she'd be lying if she said it wasn't a tiny bit tempting. She *was* tired of the killing, and they had been friends. They'd taken care of each other, and filled those permanent holes people have, for a while. Anji might really be tired of the spy life, and mean this genuinely. She might also be completely snake oil. Hellen would never know, because quitting her job—her family—would never be an option.

"The difference with my work, Anji, is that I'm fighting for people I care about. We're all fighting for our lives. And everyone's lives. We're fighting to stop a tyrant who plans to unleash death on the whole world. Do you even care about that? Because you don't act like it. I'd invite you to join us, I'd like to do that, but you can't be trusted."

Anji reached her left hand up to pull her hair back from her face. Wolf growled and lowered his head. Light glinted off Beau's gun just enough to warn Hellen of what was coming.

She fired at the same time Anji did, but Anji's aim was down. Hellen tracked the path: fresh blood was spreading on Beau's side, below the vest. By the time she looked back, Anji was gone, Wolf running after her.

Chapter M.7

The kitchen was quiet when Adia slid the dumbwaiter door open a crack to listen. Silence. She felt behind her, found an arm, and whispered, "Look," then stepped aside to make room.

Cary bent over, then stood. "It's empty."

Adia pushed the door farther up and climbed out. Cary climbed out behind her, and Byron was climbing out when two shots went off in the direction of the stable.

"Ma'am…" Byron said.

"Go. Cary knows this place, Byron, he'll get you around." Warm air and radiance pushed in when they opened the curtain. "Watch your backs!" she said, but they were already gone.

Cool air enveloped her from behind. Was there anything she could do to help? Realistically, she should probably hide so whoever they were shooting at couldn't use her as a hostage. Adia turned to go back to the dumbwaiter and ran smack into a hard, leather-strapped chest.

Two hands cupped her head, one on her mouth and one behind. Panic ignited. She hit, kicked, and stomped, and she tried to find an eye. Whoever it was spun her around. He pressed her back to him. The hand on the back of her head let go, and a fist smashed into her temple. After that, she knew nothing.

Chapter M.8

Hellen had just jumped over Beau to follow Anji when she saw Cary and Byron running from the kitchen. She paused, pointing toward the stone steps. "Guys! Take the stairs, see if you can cut her off!"

Wolf had run up the stairs after Anji. He could be holding a grudge—maybe Anji was the one who killed his mother. That would make her evil as well as a murderer, so chewing her up would be a twofer.

She took the stairs two at a time. Wolf was at the top. He brushed by her and ran down the stairs without even looking at her. Anji stood by the open door, which framed Byron and his rifle. She stood to the side, half-lighted on the right this time. Beau's gun hung in her right hand, finger on the trigger.

"How is he?"

Hellen didn't say anything, just eased into the room.

"You realize I let the dog go, right? I didn't kill him."

"Is that your sole claim to a conscience?"

"I hope not."

Cary appeared at the top of the staircase to the third floor. They both watched him step down, and down, and down until he sat and they could see all of him. He watched Anji, his body loose and relaxed. Must be nice.

"Give Byron the gun."

"You're kidding, right?"

"I'm not kidding, Anji." Hellen raised her pistol.

The tip of Byron's rifle snaked in the doorway, looking around the corner. His shoulder came to the door frame opposite, his front hand reaching for Anji's gun.

Instead, Anji yanked the barrel of his rifle forward and down. Surprised, he bent forward. She grabbed his head, crushed his rifle to his chest with her knees, and rolled him into the room. Byron ended up on his back, with Anji on top of him, holding her gun to his neck. "Hellen, I will kill all of you if you make me."

Hellen tackled her off Byron, intending to pin her, but Anji rolled Hellen over and straddled her stomach. Cary's face appeared behind Anji's head. His arms got her in a choke hold, lifting her off Hellen. Anji swung Beau's gun behind her in an uppercut to Cary's crotch. Cary went down.

Hellen sat up and shot Anji in her right shoulder. Anji twisted, looking at Hellen, betrayal all over her face.

Byron had regained his feet. Anji raised the gun and shot at him, but her arm wasn't working right and she missed. Byron lunged toward her. She ducked and ran for the stairs to the ground floor, shooting in their general direction. Cary ran like a spider, crashed into her, and pushed her past the stairs. She landed on her ass, Cary on top of her, trying to wrestle the gun out of her hand. Byron walked up and loomed over her, rifle pointed at her head.

Anji let Cary take the gun.

Hellen walked over and took Beau's gun from Cary, then she gestured him aside, and took the task of sitting on their prisoner's chest.

Knees on Anji's upper arms, she said, "You have some good moves, I gotta give you that. Can you please now just give this up?"

"And then what, Hellen? Dungeon and trial? Do I strike you as the dungeon and trial type?" Anji's slight accent had disappeared. No more pretense about Shindao, then.

"It really is too bad you kept lying. You know I can't let you go. The only other option is death."

Hellen had made the mistake of letting Beau's gun rest on her knee. Anji bent at the elbow, grabbed it with her thumb on the trigger, and aimed Beau's big gun at her own head.

Brain and skull went everywhere. A spray pattern of blood coated the ground. Hellen's leg dripped with gore. The whole top of

Anji's head had been disintegrated, down to the left eye, which lay open, still looking at her. Horrified, Hellen jumped back off Anji, landing on her feet. Her hand clapped over her mouth, and she felt in danger of hyperventilating. Byron came to block Hellen's sight of the body and urge her downstairs. Cary followed them down.

Diit was there, bent over Beau. Hellen ran to them and knelt. Beau's eyes were closed.

"Is he all right?"

"His injuries are not irreparable," Diit said with a reassuring smile.

"We should call the monks. We need Beau, and they can save him."

"Yes, Miss. I imagine they are already on their way."

For a second, Hellen came dangerously close to breaking. How could kindness shatter your heart when rage couldn't? How could a small compassion melt you into your own cracks? She didn't know, but she wasn't sure she could pick herself up this time. Not after this ruin of a morning.

"Perhaps it would be better if you wait in the garden, Miss."

Unable to speak, Hellen nodded and led Cary and Byron out into the garden. Her hand was over her mouth again, and she was breathing suspiciously, but the sun beamed into her and pretty soon she could take her hand down and her breathing steadied.

"I didn't expect that. I thought she would take a trial!" She had to pace for a few seconds.

"It's possible," Byron said, "that she had more to hide than you realize." He paused, trying to be gentle, Hellen knew. "People do stuff. Sometimes it's bad."

She nodded. Shook her head. Opened and closed her mouth. Paced. Refused the images of Anji that came unbidden into her mind. No time for that now. With great effort she packed all the horror, all the worry, every damn thing that weighed on her for the last three years and shoved it down like a brick in her throat.

When she could speak, she said, "I'm glad you guys showed up; I don't think I'd be alive if you hadn't."

"You can thank Adia, really," Cary said. "She was right on it when Wolf started coming back this way. I should get her. She's in the kitchen."

"In the kitchen? Why didn't you say something?" Hellen jogged over to the blanket, lifted it, and stepped into the relative dark. "Adia?" She peered around, eyes adjusting. No one in there. Where was she? The dumbwaiter door was pushed up…nothing in there. Pipe ends, all quiet. "Adia?" she said into the pipe that went to Adia's room. Nothing.

Worry pushed that brick right back up. Hellen ran to the great room, pulling her gun back out of her belt. Nobody. She called…nothing. In the foyer she called again, opened the front door…nothing. She climbed the front stairs, jogged the length of the hall, and into the mountain. No one in the rooms. By that time the men were running around shouting, too.

Nothing.

Hellen called them into the garden again. "Tell me everything that happened." They relayed the story. "And the last place you saw her?"

"The kitchen," they both said.

"Right when the gunshots went off," Byron added. "She sent us to help you."

Hellen ran the events through her mind: she and Anji shooting; seeing Cary and Byron; running up the stairs; Wolf running down.

Wolf running down. That was when it happened, he was going to Adia. Where was Wolf now?

"Wolf!" she called, turning a full three-sixty. "WOLF!"

Cary whistled, Byron called.

Nothing.

Hellen focused on the forest. Not much else in the way of exit strategies. She hustled around the front of the building. Fresh hoof prints had left little crescents in the soft dirt. They disappeared onto the pine needles in the direction of the palace.

"Who's got a walkntalk?"

"I do," Byron said, and handed it to her. "Vartile will be at the other end."

"Vartile!" Hellen said into the speaker.

"Miss Hellen!" Diit called.

Hellen whirled around and saw him standing at the pyramid door. Her heart twisted; what if Beau had died? She'd started to run that way, but Diit held his hands up and stepped into the sun. "Mister Beau is all right, Miss. I was just wondering if I could speak with you for a moment."

Hellen blanketed her fire and said, "Yeah, Diit, of course, but Adia's been taken, and I have to—"

"Hellen!" Vartile's voice crackled out of the cheap speaker. "Hellen!"

"Hang on a sec, Vartile." Hellen released the talk button. "I need to go, can it wait?"

"Mister Beau isn't yet healed, Miss. You will need him to go to the palace, if you want to live and your mission to succeed."

"I want to stop them before they get to the palace. Adia would be Dagge's prisoner, Diit. He's crazy, he could kill her!"

"I trust her, Miss Hellen. We can all trust her." With a tiny smile he nodded once and turned to go back into the pyramid. "Wolf knows. It will be better to make a plan."

Chapter M.9

"No one said it would be easy, you know."

Her father's voice was louder than the birds, even though they were squawking enthusiastically. She looked down from the atrium treetops and into the King's eyes, which were teasing.

"I'm pretty sure you said it would be hard. Ad nauseum. Plus a few impossibles, and the occasional excruciating. Never easy."

"I'm glad you were paying attention." He chuckled, crossing his legs in his wicker chair. "I want to tell you something, my daughter. As many frustrations and challenges as I had in all my years of being King, none of it was as difficult as the things you've been through. I am inspired by you. I admire you more than you can know."

Adia's heart surged with all the love and sadness in the world. She missed her father deeply, and felt the loss of him every day.

"Well, thank you, Dad. But I wouldn't say it's been a smooth transition."

"That's all right. The hardest things are the biggest opportunities." He started to fade.

"Thanks for coming to see me, Dad."

"I'm always around, Birdie Girl. Stay strong, it isn't over."

As he said it, his face, and the trees, and the whole atrium disintegrated.

When Adia woke, the first thing she heard was someone talking, but she couldn't understand it. The voice sounded squeezed, like it was coming through an old timey radio.

Her head was killing her. She lay on her back, and the sound came from beyond her feet, giving her the strange sensation of being suspended over a metallic hole. She had to reorient…while not sitting up, or raising her head.

Where was she? Had to be the palace, right? What was under her? She moved her hand ever so slightly to see if she could tell. Smooth fabric…tight on the padding. Moving a little more…no cushions.

Her father's couch. In the sitting room.

That would make sense, of course, given everything. The tinny voices must be coming from the harkener, and Dagge was at the desk, because he'd never allow anyone else to play with his toy.

Adia steadied her breathing so she could take some time to think.

Hellen would be here soon. She and Beau and David would show up, probably Cary and Byron, too. Given they were all alive. Which they were, she was sure of it. The only question was when.

"What are you doing?" His voice startled her coming down from above. It had a smile in it, and she suddenly felt terribly vulnerable. How much had he looked at her while she was out on display?

"Fuck you, Dagge."

"Ooooh. I didn't expect such filth out of a Princess's mouth."

Of course he was joyful. He sat on the sofa table and loomed over her.

"I'm not a Princess, remember?" She sat up, careful to stay away from his face, and moved to the desk end of the couch.

"That's right! I didn't expect you to really embrace that, you know. In spite of its being true." He switched from the sofa table to the sofa. Adia could feel him put his arm along the back, just close enough to touch her if he wanted. "So how do you like what I've done with the place?"

Surely he could tell she was blind. "I'll let you know before I leave."

He huffed a short laugh and sounded like he crossed his leg. "Oh, you won't be leaving, I have plans for you. You are the perfect mascot. Plus, all your little friends will try to save you, and I can pick them off one by one."

"They're smarter than that, Dagge. You'll never even see them."

Adia leaned in, her hand went to her chest, and that was how she found out her shirt was undone. An overwhelming horror gripped her, mixed with rage at the theft of her most sensitive secret by this vile, twisted imitation of a man.

Even so, she calmly buttoned her shirt and said, "Why don't we do something even more depraved, and have a banquet? You can show me off to all your friends, and they'll admire you for having captured me."

"That's not a half bad idea. Except all those people are dead now, and I do take credit for that."

"Emperor Mapo isn't dead. He knows exactly who you are, and what you did, and that's why Shindao is forever out of your reach."

A pause, then Dagge's voice came closer. "Let's talk about you."

He shook the sofa getting up, and faded away toward the wall ahead as he spoke. Adia wondered what he'd put on the shelves there. A weapon, perhaps? A torture device?

"It must be hard for a pretty little princess to become a frighteningly ugly witch. What would you say is the worst part?"

"The worst part is knowing you killed my father. Knowing you're a murderer, and a traitor, and you're sitting in my father's chair so you can pretend to be him."

"You're so wrong," he whispered in her left ear. She jumped, hating that she couldn't help herself. By the rustling and pulling on the arm of the couch, Adia guessed he got down on a knee beside the armrest. "I've always wondered about scars. I have a few myself, and some of them are numb, and some are sensitive. I was wondering about your scars." A tiny prick pierced her cheek, and her hand flew up to it as a gasp escaped her.

"If you move, this might hurt more."

Adia's mind ran through everything she could remember of that one self-defense class she took three years ago. Very little turned up. Nothing usable.

"You could always just ask," she said. "But you have your answer anyway, so no need to go further."

"Oh, well, I'd disagree about the need to go further." His hand encircled the front half of her neck and forced her head back to rest on the sofa. "I think we need to test every square inch of it. Or more!"

Adia started to twist away, wrenching her hips to the other side, trying to break his grip. He squeezed tighter and she got woozy, and suddenly Dagge was on the sofa, pushing her over to lie down on the seat. His hand still clutched her neck, and he forced her to her back.

One knee forced its way up between her thighs. It went all the way up, capping with a little slam at the top. His other hand mauled her chest, undoing the buttons, pulling the fabric aside and tugging at her stretch bra.

Horrified, she thrashed, clawing at his face and neck, trying to ram her own knee up between his legs.

"Oooo!" he said, laughing. Capturing her flailing arm, he pinned it with his knee. It infuriated her even more. She pounded his head with her free hand, and he took his hand off her body to try and pin that arm. She kicked, managing to get one knee up between them. He kept laughing. She roared at him, and shoved, and worked to get her other knee up.

Dagge's core appeared, from nothing to unmistakable in a matter of seconds. Hot magenta with a lime green center. The magenta stabbed up at the top in fat spikes, smearing into his chest, and down...to his crotch, she realized.

Then his hand was all over her scars, rubbing them and massaging them. All thought exploded. She started screaming and pounding on him, kicking with all her might, bucking him, trying to knock him off the couch. She bit anything she could get close to her mouth, fought with everything she had, until a third hand clamped a cloth over her face and Adia ended up unconscious again.

Chapter M.10

Hellen moved as quickly as she could down the forest tunnel. Beau walked beside her, and he'd lost a lot of blood, so she was trying not to push it. Cary and Byron brought up the rear. Hellen was tired, and discouraged, and wanted to just go and get Adia by herself. But she hadn't managed to kill Dagge either time she'd gone to the palace before, so maybe alone wasn't better.

A plan meant more people. And weaponry. They could sneak in through the theatre, maybe. Liberate the Queen from the sitting room and escape through the vault. Simple dimple.

Liberating would be the trick, of course, but she was not without resources. She could hide in the hidey hole like all those mistresses and misters back in the day. She could appear when his back was turned and kill him. Or at the very least, distract him with hand to hand, and Beau and David could come from the vault and kill him.

Wharton would be another matter. Diit said he had one of those things in him now, so Beau would have to get him in the heart. Did he know that? "You know you have to get Wharton in the heart, right?"

"Yeah, that's permanently etched in my brain." He walked with his head turned toward her, watching. "Don't worry, Hellen, we're going to get this done."

She nodded at him, but couldn't speak.

The end of the tunnel became visible and Hellen broke into a jog. Uphill, it became a slow jog then fast walking. Her team kept up.

The boulder hadn't gone far. But the gap at the right had been large enough to get all the people and their stuff through. She could see tents nearby.

Hellen scooched herself through the gap, and the guys came after.

Outside, the sun was shining golden patches all over the ground. Beautiful and way hotter than she wanted it to be, but she really needed to stop thinking negatively.

"Where's David?" she asked Luhe, who was helping Donas set up a tent.

"He's helping Merv about sixty strides that way. They're hanging that crystal."

"Thanks," Hellen said, walking on.

She'd need as many fighters as she could find. Good shots, skilled with weapons. There'd have to be a general meeting.

"This is Hellen!" she said, turning a circle to call to everyone. "I need us to have a general meeting. By the boulder in five minutes! Guys…" she said, turning to them. "Would you take the perimeter? Just in case."

"You bet," Beau said. "I'll go this way. You guys take the ten and twelve."

They all ran off.

David had appeared by the time she turned back to her original path. He stood with his hands on his hips, turned to speak to someone behind him, and started toward her.

"Get everyone! I'm calling a meeting!" she called, got a wave, and turned back toward the boulder. All around her, people moved in, threading through the trees and bushes, walking in small groups. A few talked, but not many—who could blame them, calling a surprise meeting was never good.

Seeing Vartile made her feel better. Vartile walked up, and Hellen stopped. In a low voice Hellen said, "Dagge got Adia."

Vartile's hands covered her mouth, her eyes wide above them. Hellen's heart pushed up into her throat, and the rising panic must have shown because Vartile put her arms around Hellen, and said, "She'll be all right."

Hellen held on.

"She'll be all right." Vartile squeezed firmly while she talked. "He won't damage her, she's too valuable to him. And she's strong.

With everything she's been through, no way will he get the best of her. We will get her back. Every single one of us will do whatever it takes."

It poured over Hellen's heart like warm wax, cloaking and protecting it. "I know," she said, pulling back to look Vartile in the eyes. "Thank you." They resumed walking. "I'm about to call for volunteers to go to the palace. How many good fighters do you think we have?"

"All of us are good fighters. That's why we're here."

"Yeah, I just mean people who can…fight. Or shoot. Preferably both."

"We have…fewer than ten I'd say, not counting you and Beau. But don't forget trickery is a powerful tool, and we have a lot of people with brilliant ideas."

"Well, good point." Hellen nodded and rethought what she was going to say.

Vartile stopped at the inner edge of the gathering and let Hellen go forward alone. A lot of people were already waiting in front of the boulder when she stepped to its moldy surface and turned to face them.

"Can everyone hear me?"

A sampling of *yeses* came from all around the group.

"Good." She paused, suddenly realizing the news was going to upset all of them. How had she not thought of that? No help for it. "The Queen has been kidnapped."

Shock and quiet outrage ran like lightning through the crowd. Faces jumped in Os, and a collective gasp swept through the people, catching them on fire.

"We're going to need volunteers," Hellen said. David moved closer, as did John and Roberta, Vartile and Luhe. "I'm certain she's at the palace." Merv came walking up, Dessara, Donas—more coming than she had time to count. "We need to get in and help her."

Byron, at the twelve, raised his hand so he could be seen. "I can take a group with me to town. We have a stash of explosives near NHQ. We can bomb the wall. Draw a bunch of soldiers off the palace."

"Great idea, Byron. People, it's high risk. Anyone suited to it, form up back there. With the Queen there, guard will be at least doubled, so the palace will be high-risk, too. Some of us might be able to trickle in, like we did for the banquet. Be there for backup."

"We can do things too," Vartile said. "Like pepper bombs."

"Like blocking a hallway with a hundred chairs." Donas shrugged. "Stuff that would slow them down."

"Might make all the difference." Dessara nodded, looking around.

Beau raised his hand and let it down as he spoke. "Dagge will probably concentrate his soldiers on the forest side, since that's where you've gotten in and out before. Some can trickle in through the kitchen, but is there another way in?"

"I'm thinking we'll use the front door. Four of us in uniform, escorting a group of prisoners in from town. We'll need some volunteers to be prisoners. Firio, will you be one?" He raised his hand and nodded once. "Great. I'll need you, Beau. Where are our sharpshooters?"

Edren and Rack raised their hands. "Here."

"I'll need you guys, too." They nodded. "David and Cary, you choose. Your skills are probably better suited for town, but your call. Everybody, pick the team you have the best chance of helping. And don't feel bad for staying if that's what you need to do.

"It's going to be a long trip into town, but it'll be easier and safer to go by tunnel. If you've got easy food, bring it."

"I've got bars," Beau said, "and more at HQ."

"Thanks, Beau." Hellen held up her hand. "Any questions?" No one answered. "Palace people over here!"

The crowd moved quickly, separating into groups. David and Cary both showed up in front of Hellen, but the real surprise was Roberta.

"I'm going into the palace," she said. "Robert's still in there, and I want to get him out, too."

"Mom, you can't save Robert."

Roberta looked at David like she pitied him with a side of anger. "Robert is as much my son as you are, and I wouldn't leave you in there."

Hellen reached her hand out and grasped Roberta's. "We'll do whatever we can to help you, but you understand Dagge comes first, right?"

"Absolutely. Regarding that, I can guide people around the palace, if at any point it would help to split up. Other servants know me, and most of them support the Resistance. I also know who doesn't."

"Roberta, you are a bad ass."

"Thanks."

Chapter M.11

Awareness crept back to her on elephant feet—head-pounding, sound-distorting thumps. What happened? *Oh, yeah.* A tiny move of her hand told her she was still on the sofa. The urge to check her clothes was almost impossible to resist. Had he raped her? Could he have without waking her? How did she feel *down there*?

A mental inventory of sensation told her that her pants were on and her shirt was open. Her body felt normal between her legs—thank One. Surprising considering where Dagge had been.

He clearly had a thing for scars…a big, burning thing. Was that a little freaky, or was it just her?

The feel of his hands still lingered, like filth. He'd violated her in the deepest way, in the tenderest part of her psyche. And now here she was, laid bare, and there was no telling how long he had looked at her.

She'd seen his core. The true Tomius Dagge was magenta around a lime green middle. Magenta was the color of the 2D monsters in that dream she had before the murder banquet. Could that be a coincidence? Considering his behavior, Adia didn't think so. But he was committing atrocities way before those things came out of the tear, so what did that say?

Dagge's voice hummed off-key over at the desk. It was the song Roberta turned into their anthem that year. The one he interrogated John and Robert over—how strange that he would be humming it. Or maybe not, given that owning was his favorite thing. He sang the words in a soft whisper, and it was possible he didn't know she was awake yet.

A moment to think. His core had been…visible? Whatever sense it was, it happened without singing, or people, or carapaz. Heightened emotion, maybe, though she hadn't noticed her own light. Something else, then. Her Special Ability, perhaps, activated by the tunnel, targeted for him. If she could still perceive him when he was calm, that might indeed be useful.

She hadn't anticipated his morbid lust for her scars. Given the danger of attack, she wasn't sure she could wait however long it took for Hellen and the others to get there. Her best strategy might be to get to one of the secret passages. Escaping through the vault would be perfect, since it was close and let outside. The trick would be doing it when he couldn't see her, because it wasn't likely he'd let her out of his sight.

If she couldn't get away in the sitting room, maybe somewhere else in the palace. The royal bathrooms had escape routes to the Grand Ballroom hallway, and Dagge wasn't likely to think of that immediately. She was sure she could get help in the kitchen, and Cookie wasn't likely to tolerate soldiers hanging around in there.

The risky part would be navigating to the kitchen. But as many times as she'd been around the palace, as many years as she'd spent exploring and using every possible room as the set for an adventure, she knew a lot about the palace Dagge didn't. She wouldn't let the fact that she couldn't see slow her down.

All she had to do was need to pee.

With a sharp intake of air, she faked waking and sat up. Her hands went immediately to her chest, but her focus searched for the magenta and lime green smear. Nothing. Adia pushed back her disappointment. Clutching her shirt together, she hugged herself in a show of distress. And she listened.

He wasn't singing anymore. There was no telling where he was, except probably somewhere between the desk and the sofa. It amazed her how silently he moved—do people learn that or does it come naturally?

His hand lay on her shoulder from behind, making her flinch. "I'm afraid I've been a terrible host, and I hope you will forgive me."

What new crazy talk was this?

"I've arranged for dinner to be sent here for two. Like room service."

His hand disappeared, and his voice came slowly around the end of the sofa. Adia lowered her arms and began buttoning her shirt.

"I figure we deserve a celebration! Don't you? You're back in the palace, where you should be. I'm here, where I should be. Look how well things have worked out."

Adia wasn't sure what he was saying. That they both should be here? What did he mean, exactly?

"I told the cook I have a guest, but I didn't say who it is. I don't want to cause a panic." He laughed lightly, stopping in front of her on the other side of the sofa table. "If you like, I can take you to your old room. It's still exactly the way you left it. You know, I never intended for you to be forced out of your home."

It was everything she could do not to react. He'd intended for her to be dead.

A rush of fury engulfed her, battling with the compulsion for survival. She wanted to kill him so badly. For everything. Stabbing her father to death, abusing the country, being the absolute worst person she'd ever known…and putting his hands on her scars.

She hadn't known she could hate him more than she already did. However.

This Host Dagge was preferable to most of his other personalities, and if she could keep him in host mode, she'd have a much better chance of not getting killed. Or worse.

"I'd like to freshen up," she said. "But I don't want to be in my room. It has bad memories for me."

A dirty glow started in him, mixed of magenta and lime green. *(Warning, warning!)*

"Well, that's the place with all your clothes, so that's where you're going."

She stood, letting her hand brush the edge of the coffee table as she moved around it, hoping the path to the door was clear. "Fine," she said, walking toward the door alone in a wild shot at freedom.

394

Dagge said nothing, but his hand grasped hers and drew it under his meaty arm. He pulled her with him toward the door. Adia held her free hand out in front of her a little. One thing to run herself into something, another for Dagge to do it. Sure enough, at the doorway her hand stopped her just short of a collision with the jamb.

"Oh, I'm sorry!" Dagge said, his dirty glow subsiding. "I'm not used to this, of course. Please forgive me, I promise it won't happen again."

Uh huh. "I'm fine," she said, stretching her mouth into a fake but brilliant smile.

Down the long hall, she reached her hand out to trail the side tables that adorned the walls between the rooms. Dagge pulled her away from them, chattering away, and oops she'd better listen.

"…and I'd like to modernize the town some."

What?

"Great Hand is far behind other countries in some ways. The buildings are old…oh, they're quaint, don't get me wrong, but they don't allow for growth."

His voice rambled on, but she couldn't listen after all.

Maybe the Greeting Room door from her room's secret passage hadn't been discovered. Not a good chance of that, of course, it was obvious with the torch right there on the wall. Still, she'd check. Maybe she'd get lucky.

He stopped, facing her. "You know, we don't have to eat in the sitting room tonight; let's eat in the dining room, it'll be so much nicer." He resumed walking. "We can talk about fixing the place up, I'd really like to hear your ideas."

Conversations about decorating the house over dinner. The situation had gotten so much more bizarre in just the last minute.

"We can paint, if you like. Take down the old, dull tapestries. Replace the chandeliers with something modern. We could really liven this place up."

The man had no grasp of a world outside himself.

He stopped them in front of her door and turned the key in the lock. "Everything is just the way you left it. Dustier, maybe." His hand moved her through the door. "I'm going to lock you in, so don't get any wild ideas…" He paused, and Adia got the feeling he was giving her a little smile. "You freshen up and change, and I'll go tell the cook we'll be eating formally tonight. How does that sound? I believe I have party clothes somewhere." His voice leaned in to her, and got whispery. "Let's celebrate our beginning."

Every cell in her body wanted to rip his head off and shove it down the stump of his neck.

"I'm sure I can find something to wear," she said.

Like a knife, she continued in her head as he closed the door in front of her. The key turned in the lock.

There used to be several big knives in the museum. All old, from historic battles. Rusty, she hoped. Sure, she'd be the one to end up dead in a fight, but that would be far preferable to whatever Dagge was offering. Maybe she could give him tetanus before she went.

But of course she couldn't really throw her life away. She was the last Beldenet. Great Hand was counting on her, and all whiny Princess aside, she wasn't going to let them down. Dagge was the one who'd have to go.

He'd been so…anxious to please since she came to, aside from the snag re her bedroom. Probably that was just the scar-euphoria and would fade soon. But if it wasn't the scar, if all that agreeableness was pleasure from assaulting her, she was in serious trouble.

If she didn't manage to get away, she could at least be certain Hellen would come. And David, and Beau. Would she be glad to see them.

Before Adia could do anything else in her room, the shower beckoned. She felt fairly certain there were no cameras—she'd been dead, and no one came in here, so what would've been the point? Not to mention he'd seen her nearly naked anyway.

Standing in a shower as hot as she could manage, she soaped and soaped. Shampooed. Huddled under the water for a while. The old familiar smells comforted her, and also seemed like they were from another world. A world she no longer fit.

After her shower, she paused at the bathroom door wrapped in a towel. Something didn't feel right in her room. Tilting her head, she pretended to fiddle with her towel as she walked to the wardrobe, but all her attention was focused on her left ear. Nothing.

But as she passed the double doors to her room, she could feel him. His energy burned acidic. Her hand went instinctively to her bare arm, brushing it up and down. Canting her attention that direction, she picked up a faint magenta and lime smudge, smearing down to crotch level again. Looking for a peep show, no doubt.

Adia opened the wardrobe door and stood behind it. How was she going to handle this?

Still in her towel, she stepped around the open door, walked to the side of her bed and stood in front of Dagge, putting one hand on her hip and staring her blind eyes right at his face, she hoped. His light surged. Neither one of them said anything for a long time, and finally Adia heard the door open, his smudge disappeared, and the lock turned.

She had to sit on the bed for a minute. Reaching back and to her left, her hand located her mother's book pillow, still front and center in the place of honor on the bed. She grabbed it to her chest and hugged it, wishing it was her mother. Except then her mother would have to be here in this nightmare. So, nope.

After a bit, she put the pillow aside, returned to her wardrobe, and felt for an evening dress she could wear. One that would hide soft pants and a tank. If she could get away, or they rescued her from the dinner table, she didn't want to have to run anywhere in heels and a gown.

Her hands landed on the empire-waisted metallic gold silk she remembered from her last formal dinner with her father. It had tiny puff sleeves and a fairly full, lined skirt, so it would hide pants great. And a tank, too, if she got a string-strap.

In the drawers on the left-hand side of the wardrobe, she came up with all the hideable clothes she needed, and slipped them on.

Running her hands across the shoe rack at the bottom, she took a moment to truly appreciate the ladies who used to clean her room so long ago. The many pairs of shoes were always in the same order, grouped by season and occasion. That made it easy for her to pick a pair of black slippers she could wear with her dress, and she wouldn't have to hide shoes in her underwear.

Before the dress, did she have time to check the secret passage? If Dagge hadn't found the exit in the Greeting Room, she might be able to go through there and…where? Out the front door? Or maybe the East door. Deciding it was worth a look, she made for the other side of the bed.

The slender stone panel was chained open. They probably couldn't figure out how the sconce worked, and that felt good, but the open door also meant he had another way of getting in to watch her. He'd use it, so she'd have watch her back and front.

At least she could see him if he was excited. He didn't know, so that was her advantage. If she was clever, she could convince him she had powers, scare him a little, maybe. However, it was a fine line to walk, and she may not have long before it stopped working.

To think she once worried about him listening to her sleep.

On a whim, she cut across to the play room to check the doors there. The hall door was locked, and a lock had been added to the nursery doors as well. All access for him, no exit for her. She could wrap a belt around the nursery door handles to stop Dagge from coming in that way, but she had nothing to fix the hall door with, so what would be the point? Adia went back to the secret passage and started down the steps.

Maybe Dagge's new flavor meant he didn't see a reason to harm her or treat her badly. Maybe he wanted to try being decent for a while. Voyeurism not included.

Or maybe it meant he liked the scars so much he wanted to keep her as a sex pet. In that case it wouldn't be long before he'd forget all this niceness and rape her.

In the meantime, he might listen to her sleep, and watch her sleep, if she didn't manage to get out.

Which she would, whatever it took. It was only a matter of time.

Chapter M.12

The Greeting Room exit was blocked. The torch lever would barely pull, and no amount of pushing on the stone slab did any good. Diit had told her the outer wall exit was disabled as well, but she checked it anyway, and he was still right. She paced up and down the length of the passage a few times before she leaned on the short wall that made the end of the East Entrance coat closet.

It moved. She pushed it again. It moved, ever so slightly. She pressed it, felt around and found an edge of cut wood. Definitely a door. A skinny door. The coat closet had been added around a century ago, so maybe her Dad and Hilman hadn't known about this. Wouldn't that be amazing?

She ran her fingers around the edges feeling for the release. She found it in a recess of the stone wall, pulled the rod and the door came open.

A faint exhale of stale air met her nostrils. Various smells reminded her of the leather, the wool, the weatherproofs waiting silently for their owners. She wondered if this closet had even been opened in three years.

There was a choice to make. She could try to get out now, and either risk guards outside the east entrance, or risk trying to make it to the kitchen. Someone in the kitchen would hide her or help her get out. They'd get word to Hellen and the others, and she'd be rescued. They could figure out how to get Dagge again later.

But…what did her Dad say? *The hardest things are the biggest opportunities.*

What opportunity might she be missing? One: if she stayed, her friends would come, and she had no doubt that together they could defeat Dagge once and for all. Two: seeing their Queen in the fight would galvanize her people and give them courage. Three: the time was now.

Adia headed back to the stairs. She was going to earn her right to be Queen.

Chapter M.13

Hellen led the Resistance through the tunnels, past the well, and to the ladder lying underneath HQ. Cary helped Beau jam the ladder up into the hole, pushing the wheelbarrow bucket up and aside once Cary climbed to the top. Dirt fell in on them, but not too much. Joey hadn't been there to take anybody to his house, so they'd just done the best they could as they exited.

Beau was tired. His energy was down, and he'd kept to himself most of the way. Hellen was worried about him. She knew what it was like to have the hole fixed, but the body still traumatized. He needed rest. She'd call for a break once they got into the warren—they could all use one.

After Cary broke through, and people started climbing, she walked down the queue and looked for Vartile. Some of them smiled at her and grasped hands. Others were somber, and if they met her eyes, Hellen nodded.

"What's the plan?" Vartile said when Hellen pulled her to the side.

"Let's all rest a bit, get some water, whatever, then I think your team should go straight to the kitchen."

"Agreed."

"Great. It'll take a little time for the rescue group to get everything ready. We have to wait for Byron's explosions to start, anyway. Your group would benefit from going early. You have a plan to get through the checkpoint?"

"I've got soap, baby. We'll throw some in baskets, act like it's a summons. The checkpoint guards know me, I deliver. If it doesn't work, we'll come back."

"All right, but be careful, as always. Don't push if it starts going sour."

"Yes, ma'am," Vartile said with a smile.

"I don't mean to be bossy."

"You go right ahead and be bossy, that's your job."

Cary walked up with Edren and Rack.

"Cary, I'd like you to lead a team to clear soldiers from the front doors."

"Yes, ma'am. I'd like to have Edren and Rack on my team."

"I need one of you for the rescue group afterward. Volunteer?"

"I'll come with you," Rack said.

"All right. We'll wait until after the explosions draw the soldiers out." Hellen said.

"You guys coming up?" Beau's voice echoed down into the tunnel.

Hellen looked up at him, on one knee, silhouetted by the light, leaning his forearms on the low top of the hole. She knew he was looking at her, even though technically she couldn't see his eyes.

"We're on our way," she said, and moved toward the bottom of the ladder, grateful she didn't have to do this by herself.

Chapter M.14

The time in HQ stretched longer than Hellen wanted. Beau passed around food and water. A few got army uniforms and bullet-resistant vests. Trips were made to the bathroom upstairs. Scoped, concentrated pulse rifles appeared for Rack and Edren, who went over them with Beau off to the side. For the most part, though, people sat around the edges of the room, leaning their heads against the wall or talking in whispers.

Cary had gotten a rifle with a laser sight from Beau, which was brilliant. With the rifle leaning against the wall beside him, Cary kept checking and rechecking his stuff: knife, wound tape, straps, walkntalk, keys (?). No telling what else. His shoes got tied and retied. He patted his pockets and mumbled to himself. Hellen would worry if she hadn't seen it before.

David sat far from Cary, beside Roberta. David had gotten a uniform, and would be in the rescue squad. Roberta was dressed in black, courtesy of Vartile. The two Treslos looked somber, and were silent.

The plan was to wait until dark. Hellen hated waiting at all, but that was the deal. Byron had taken his team—two rabbit trainees and five fellow cops—to gather explosives from all the hidey holes. Dark was their deadline.

Vartile had already taken a group to gather candles and try to get through the palace checkpoint. Hopefully, word hadn't reached the guards that Adia had been captured. So far, no alarms. Vartile was supposed to radio when they made it to the back of the palace.

Hellen kept pacing.

Beau finished with Rack and Edren, and walked over to talk to her.

"How're you doing?"

"Okay, for this being the worst time in my life."

"Yeah. Can you sit with me for a minute?"

"Sure." She followed him to a bare spot along the wall and they sat. Cary was across from them with his head back and his eyes closed. Hellen was suddenly bone tired. How long had it been since she slept? Not all that long, she didn't think. Felt like it, though.

"How are you feeling, Beau? You look a lot better than you did."

Beau laughed. "I don't doubt it. I'm fine, Hellen, I promise. You don't have to worry about me. There is no way I will let you down."

In one brutal cleaving of her heart, all the pain, and hardship, and worry she'd collected broke open inside her, threatening her battered little boat. Of all the people in this battle, this man was the one she couldn't do without. She'd never find a better rock. And she didn't want to.

"I'm glad," she said. It was all she could manage. What was wrong with her? She'd never been this emotional in her life.

"Can I put my arm around you?"

She nodded, and leaned against his side, under his wing. The weight of his arm felt good around her, and the way he squeezed her to him. Eyes on her lap, she let out all the stale air in her lungs and took a deep, fresh breath. "Do you think she's okay?"

"I absolutely do. What do you think? You've been around him way more than I have."

"I don't think he'll hurt her. Not at first. He likes to pretend to be the perfect…whatever. He likes to be charming and use his looks. It's a part he plays. Or used to play. I don't know how crazy he's actually gotten, so I can't be sure of anything."

Static crackled down the wall. Hellen and Beau both looked. David was holding Roberta's little bug receiver; he'd fiddled with it and turned it on. Much to their surprise, a blotchy voice squawked out of it, covered in static.

David jumped up and ran to the bottom of the stairs. Hellen and Beau were fast on his heels, running up the stairs and into the smithy office. David held the receiver up and walked around the office, searching for the signal. Near the door, the static cleared. Dagge's voice shouted out of the dome.

"It's in a cage, Wharton! How dangerous can it be?"

Hellen met Beau's eyes. That didn't sound good.

Another voice mumbled, sounding farther away. Dagge answered like he'd reached the end of his patience.

"There's a big freight elevator in the back of the theater. Use that."

Mumbling.

"It's the entire front half of the west side, you moron! What did you think was there, a whorehouse?"

An attempt at mumbling was cut off by Dagge. "Get the fuck out of my sight!"

Several moments later Dagge was mumbling to himself. "It's gonna be great. It's gonna be great." A silent hurricane of a pause. "It's going to be beautiful."

With one loud slam it was quiet.

Roberta had joined them. She said, "He closed the drawer. It's in the drawer."

Hellen nodded blankly, her mind caterwauling over *what the hells is Dagge's plan?*

"We've got to go," David said. "We've got to get her out of there."

Cary came in. "Aren't we doing that?"

Hellen had to pace, hands on her hips. Turning back to the group, she faced David. "We have to wait for Byron to get the soldiers away. Otherwise we'll be overpowered. We just can't take on the whole army."

"Can't we sneak in?"

"We might be able to take the mountain path to the stable—John said he put a climb over in around there—but then what? Dagge will have all kind of soldiers surrounding the palace, and it's daytime. Look, David. Beau and I were talking about this very thing. I don't think he'll hurt her. More like…having big plans for her. But he'll put on his act, and be all nice at first. So we have time. Let's stick with the plan, okay? Trust me, I want Adia to be safe, too. You know I do."

David grimaced and had to pace himself for a few seconds. Grudgingly, he tucked the receiver in his shirt. "I know you do."

Roberta jumped in. "I can't believe the bug is working. David, this is great. We can keep listening and we may find out something useful."

A shadow moved across Roberta's face then—the ghost of John and Robert's interrogation over that song, Hellen imagined. She had watched Roberta cry when she talked about it. Dagge had danced, she said. Robert had been terrified. John almost died. It was the worst twenty minutes of her life.

There went Hellen's heart, searing again.

Please One, let us not hear anything bad.

Chapter M.15

A light glowed around a corner, leaving two reflections on the dark wall in front of her. The reflections were clear and round with small points at top and bottom: the top reflection was a warm golden white; the bottom was a perfect duplicate in a dark and intense blue.

Adia stepped to the wall. The bright reflection spanned from above her head to the bottom of her chest. She reached for it, pulled it into 3D out of the wall and held it. It was like a star in her hands, beaming and burning and bright.

Across from the star, her chest began to glow purple, and increasingly warm. The light grew until her chest and the star burned to each other and became connected. Suddenly she was standing in her college apartment kitchen, placing the star into the window over the sink. As she lowered her arms, she could see trees in it, and the light was so bright it shot rays all through the room.

The window merged with the star and became a mirror. She could see herself standing in front of the trees. Light beamed out of her chest, and the two beams met in the mirror. Together they created a barrier of light, covering her reflection. A voice erupted behind her, blaring one long note. She turned and it was David. He stood in the kitchen doorway, looking at her, blaring that note on and on, harsh and loud. It started to freak her out.

Adia woke with one of those snoring gasps. Her head jerked up from where it was lolled back on the wood trim of the settee. Her mouth snapped shut, dry, and she smacked it and tried to swallow. It had clearly been open that way for a while. No telling what time it was. One willing, Dagge hadn't already come to get her.

But since she was as dressed as she was going to get, she didn't stress over it. She did, however, listen. No breathing or rustling of clothes, and no sense of being watched. No smudge. If it was late, he'd be here.

He'd come when he came. In the meantime, she ran over the dream, fixing it in her memory: the bright reflection and the shadow; holding the bright one and making the connection; the dark wall becoming her old kitchen; the light becoming the window and the mirror. And David making that sound, not stopping. Not stopping.

The dream didn't make sense yet, but her brain needed time to percolate.

Adia sent her right hand wandering to the little table beside the settee, feeling for the old bird nest, some of it crumbling away as she picked it up. She remembered when she found it, fallen to the ground under a tree, and she'd given it a place of honor on this table, near her current books. It had a story to tell, too.

The sheer number of stories in this room could sink a continent.

Before she'd fallen asleep, she'd been waiting long enough to have touched every single thing in her room. She'd lingered over the council members in the chest, beyond glad they were still there. But the dolls and old art projects? Acorns and scraps of paper? A wasp nest? Why had she kept so much stuff? All of it sweet and useless, except for the council and the palace model. Other than those, she might need to have a lawn sale.

It amazed her to realize how changed was her sense of importance. All those treasures from visiting dignitaries, mementos from forgotten tributes. The last three years had stripped away so much, even the desire for useless things had disappeared.

Not entirely bad.

Adia gazed across the border from present to past with a curious eye. Had she really been so immature only three years ago? Did she think saving this stuff would give her substance? Or was she just afraid of losing things, like she lost her mother? Strange how the loss of literally almost everything else in her life did the opposite.

When Dagge knocked on the door (simultaneously unlocking it), she was still sitting on the settee, handling books from the basket on the floor. Smelling them.

"Come in."

The door opened, and Adia could hear the jingle of something as he entered. She stood, laying her book on the table.

"You look magnificent. The gold suits you. And if I may say, I'm glad you left your hair down. It's lovely." He had walked over to her, and his hand brushed her hair back behind her shoulder, revealing whatever could be seen of her scar. In a low and conspiratorial voice, he said, "You can't tell, but I'm also magnificent, wearing my dress uniform instead of a tux. It has gold on it, so we match." His tone was light, but she could hear the pleasure in it.

This was looking like a long night.

An awkward pause made her wonder if he expected small talk. She didn't know if she could drum up the stomach for niceties. What would he do if she spoke her mind? Considering what was in there, he'd probably kill her out of self-preservation. Or chain her in the dungeon, or something worse. Why hadn't she asked David how to escape the dungeon? That was stupid.

But her brain digressed. Time to haul those comportment classes into the light.

"Thank you for inviting me to dinner." She reached out a hand so she could be led. Should she run into some things, just to set the mood? "I confess I'm quite hungry (*she laughed lightly*), so I hope I don't embarrass myself." She bumped the table in front of the settee with her leg. "Oops," she said, extending her hand in front of her like it would help.

"Oh, you needn't worry about me," Dagge said enthusiastically. "I enjoy a good meal myself. You can't see me, but I've put on a few pounds."

She laughed with him—*oh hahaha, isn't that funny?*—picturing him in her father's chair, eating Cookie's good food several times a day. Mmm, mm.

Especially since she and Hellen barely had enough to survive that first year. Once her body got past the burn trauma, the pain eased and she was hungry all the time. They owed so much to Diit, who snuck a lot of things from the palace, but those things covered a wide range of necessary items and weren't always a lot of food.

The second year wasn't that great, either, even with the addition of John, and then Roberta sneaking stuff to them. They always had to ration, because the monastery was far, and the forest floor was treacherous, and Dagge had soldiers around the palace and in the town all the time. The third year got better, with Beau and Vartile and Luhe helping, but the monastery never could be called the lap of luxury.

Much of the time, they'd had to depend on Hellen's hunting skills, and thank One they improved. It got to where they had some kind of game most nights she was home. It was so delicious roasted over the fire. Adia's stomach growled again, and Dagge chuckled.

They passed through the door, and unfortunately, the jamb was too far away for her to run into it; he must have both doors open, which was admittedly thoughtful.

Out in the hall, he turned them left, so they were going the back way to the dining room. She wondered why. Were they stopping by the sitting room for something? She took the opportunity to step it off again, just to be sure.

"You're not much of a talker, are you?"

Adia laughed sociably. Understatement of the year. "I suppose I've gotten out of the habit," she said. "A lot of alone time will ruin your people skills."

"Then you must be glad to have company. I'll try to make your stay as pleasant as possible."

Well, there it was. Proof she had indeed slipped into the evil mirror version of her life. As if the last three years didn't already prove it, but this was just the touch of surreality that completed the picture.

"How very kind of you," she said.

Silence descended again, and they still had a long way to go down this hall. Her brain went right to what lay waiting in the sitting room. There was what, one pet freak left? Or was it two?

She wondered if she was going to be introduced. Would Dagge want one of those things in her? Physical skills-wise, she wouldn't be much use—unless he was looking for a giant air-breathing piranha, she could manage that. All she had to do was think of his face.

Goodness gracious, she had gotten violent.

Her smile was a lot more genuine when she turned up to him and said, "I'm looking forward to getting to know you a little better. We never had a chance before Camberton ruined everything."

What a lovely little pile of lies that was.

"Yes, you're right." Dagge was so pleased at her interpretation that he squeezed her hand to his body with his arm. Like a hug. A hand hug. Oh goody. "I found you very intriguing, even then," he said. "And of course, beautiful. But if I may say, you are more beautiful now. No, really! I know the scars on your face...and your body...must be very difficult to bear, but let me tell you, those are the marks of living your life. You have simply lived a lot more life than most people."

Well, krikey. She could suddenly see why Hellen liked him. Used to like him. Past tense.

What ruined it for Adia, aside from all the death and horror of the last three years, was the way he had of always bringing up either the scars, or the blindness. Over and over, even in the short time they'd spent together. What did that say about him?

She'd have to think about it later since he was talking. "I can't tell you what my plans for this evening are, because it's a surprise. I think you'll be excited."

Was she required to say something? Because she couldn't think of a single thing. Her training should be her salvation, except years in the woods had aloned that training right out of her.

She wished she had Wolf here.

The trick would be encouraging him to relax his guard without getting the idea she was ready to jump into bed with him. Keep it royal.

"That's very thoughtful." *Umm, what else?* "Will I be visible to the staff? I think many of them don't know I'm alive, and it would be good if I could address them and derail the speculation before it starts. It makes for a better work environment."

Dagge's long silence struck her as pregnant with a hundred little snakes. Well, maybe she pushed too hard in the wrong-ass direction. "You could monitor me, of course. I won't say anything...problematic."

"And you expect me to trust you."

"You knew my father. Was he ever untruthful with you?"

"No."

"I'm the same way. Besides, I know you'd kill me. Or imprison me, with possible torture."

He laughed, upwards, head back. A real laugh, which was good. Humor always did ease the tension. Even half-jokes about death and torture.

Maybe she could seem more funny and less smart. Get his guard down some that way. Did she know how to be funny? No, not really. It was generally a matter of luck with her. How she wished she was more like David.

"We're almost to the stairs. Would you like to stop by the sitting room for a moment? Your father's portrait is in there, and I thought you might like to put your hands on it."

Wow, that was...kind? Honestly, she wasn't sure how she felt about it. She'd rather it was hanging in the museum, safe, forgotten through this anomaly of time.

"Come on, you'd like it, you know you would." He removed her hand from his elbow and put that arm across her upper back, propelling her into the room. "It's in front of us, between the desk and the sofa." He pushed her faster than she wished, but she counted the steps and added to her mental map until they stopped.

"You're about two feet in front of it."

Torn, Adia didn't move.

When he couldn't wait anymore, Dagge picked up her hand and placed it on the frame. "It's right here," he said.

413

She ran her thumb over the front of it and felt the outer curve of the frame's design. Stepping closer, she ran her hand up the frame gently, respectfully.

It wasn't the same frame.

Her father's portrait frame had a very squared-off design. The lines were straight, the corners had nesting squares. This frame was not at all like that—it had bunting and curlicues and flowers. This painting was probably the one of the fat cherubs in the spa. She'd stared at it many times, and always thought it was funny some smart aleck put fat cherubs in a spa.

He was tricking her.

Adia paused and let her chin fall ever so slightly before she moved her hand to the painting. Very lightly, she ran her fingertips over the paint, stopped, and pulled her hand back. "I hate to touch it without gloves," she said, turning her hands to her chest.

"Certainly. I can understand that." A pause. He took her hand and put it on the painting. "I've heard that when you're blind, you can feel things without quite touching them, is that true?"

Adia lifted her hand from the painting and held it there, turning her face to him. "It depends on what it is." She didn't want to talk about being blind with Dagge. Too personal and...consumptive. Like he wanted to suck up all her soft middle and swallow it. She made an effort to smile as she lowered her arm. "I'm afraid I'm not myself at the moment. I feel a little lightheaded. Could you help me to the sofa?"

"Of course! Here, let me... You must be famished, and here I am trying to show off all the effort I've made for you. How about we just go straight to the dining room? Can you make it that far?"

"If there's food at the end, I can make it," she said, and he laughed. Two points for her.

****

David clutched the receiver so hard his fingertips were white. His mother put her hand on his arm, probably to soothe him, or encourage him or something. It wasn't going to work.

"She sounds fine," she said.

They were sitting back in their spot, downstairs, against the wall. Hellen and Beau were close, Cary sat across the room, staring at him. The whole room was staring at him.

"Was that the Queen?"

"What did she say?"

"Is she all right?"

"She's all right," David said. "They're just going down to dinner."

"If I know Dagge," Hellen said, "they'll be in the main dining room. He'll want to show off his mastery of the palace. When we get in, the rescue team will head there. The rest of you do your jobs as planned."

Chapter M.16

Adia's mental map showed the number of steps for each section: the hall, the sitting room, the stairs, the back hall. On and on. She kept repeating them to herself in the hope she could pull them out in the right fraught moment.

The Official Dining room seemed to be set up the way Hellen had described it after the banquet. Judging by the veer Dagge made toward the right, the table was still in a big U, with the bottom toward the far wall and the painting John Treslo tore a hole through.

Not really John, of course.

Dagge took her up the side and turned left presumably at the back table, stopping at what she guessed would be the center. Or, if he meant her to sit there, it would be just off center.

"Here we are," he gushed. "I've put you right next to me. We've got flowers, the fanciest dishes, and…four glasses each. I'm not sure what to do with them all." He laughed delightedly. "I had this room decorated for you. I wish you could see it."

Unbelievable. Where was that Face-Eating-Piranha superpower when you needed it?

"It has bunting—gold, in fact—and sprays of flowers mixed with green stuff. A sign that says, "Welcome Home, Adia.""

A chair was moved out on the other side of her, which meant there was another person in the room. Was it a servant? Could there be more than one? How could she find out?

Dagge took her hand in his and moved her to the front of the chair with his hand on the small of her back this time. Hopefully he wouldn't feel the pants.

As she stepped to the front of the chair, she called over her other shoulder. "Could someone please get the shawl from my bedroom? I'm a little chilled."

"You just need some fire in you," Dagge said, moving his body, clothes rustling. Seconds later, his coat landed on her shoulders, heavy and smelling of his cologne.

"I'm not sure I can eat in this." She laughed politely until she realized he wasn't laughing with her. "It's very thoughtful of you, but I wouldn't want to spill wine or get food on it."

A pause. And then, "You don't have to worry about that. You can't see it, but I'm smiling." He put his hand on her shoulder pushed her into the chair.

"Please don't push me," she said before she could think. The silence that followed was precarious, filled with her chair being pushed in by the mysterious person. Afterward, she redirected.

"Thank you for bringing me down here. It feels like a special occasion. What's for dinner? I'm excited to eat some of Cookie's food."

He began grudgingly. "She always makes my favorite meal for special occasions." But the tone of his voice relaxed some and began to regain some animation. "Pork chops. Perfection every time—plenty of salt, just the right amount of sear. I can cut yours up for you."

Wow.

"I might just pick it up with my bare hands." She smiled winningly, she hoped. "Cookie always was the best. Did you know I gave her that name when I was little?"

"Did you? It's very cute. I'm sure you were adorable. Let's toast."

He sprang it on her before she'd felt the layout of the table. Her hand reached to where she thought her wineglass would be, per tradition, but the water glass was there. So, she reached with her other hand to the other side, and it wasn't there either.

"Are we drinking…water?"

"Of course not! We're having the best wine; you just have to find it."

For a moment she was dumbfounded. Dagge's friendly demeanor had fooled her into thinking he really would be friendly tonight. But the entire evening was to be tests. Casual cruelty for his entertainment. What would be the best way to handle this? Given that she was unarmed.

"All right then," she said, scooting her chair up like she relished the idea of performing. Setting her back straight, she turned her face toward him, *because let him feel like I'm looking at him.* With a smile, she floated her hand up to the tabletop, and with the backs of her fingers, traced the edges of the stacked plates and the shallow bowl. Then she lightly caressed the silver and swept one finger along the glasses. When she found the wineglass in the center, she picked it up, faced him, and sipped.

Without throwing the rest of it on him. She felt pretty proud of herself for that, and set the glass within easy reach.

"There's also a candelabra behind the glasses. And flowers. Here, feel." He grasped her left hand and pulled it toward the back of the table. She had to stand up suddenly, in a half crouch because the chair was too far in.

Her hand landed on the candelabra her family had used in the small dining room every Winter Festival she could remember. It was tall, held three candles, and was sleek and heavy. She added it to her mental map.

Her hand was dragged over to the flowers and made to pat them.

"They're lilies," Dagge said, "a most beautiful flower, don't you think?" He paused a moment, then said, "I'm sorry, I forget you can't see."

Somehow she doubted that.

The subkitchen door opened and got Dagge's attention. Her arm got thrown back at her, his magenta-lime smudge blinked on, and he stood so fast his chair landed on the floor behind him. Unknown Person picked it up.

"What are you doing? Get out!"

"Overlord, sir, forgive me. I was told the soup was ready to be served," said a young male voice not far into the room.

"Where's Wharton?"

"I don't know, sir."

"Oh, please don't send it back," Adia said. "I'm so ready to eat something."

Her hand reached to Dagge's arm and rested on it. A tense silence descended, and his voice came down to her from where he stood.

"You know this person, don't you?"

Oh, that was a bad turn. His anger was palpable, the smudge had turned magenta.

"Not that I'm aware of. His voice is unfamiliar, but I can't remember everyone." Then she trotted it out. "Perhaps if I could see him. But I can't." She didn't know whether to feel smug or disappointed in herself.

"Shall I go, sir?"

"Please," Adia said again.

"Roger! Fetch the soup," Dagge said. Then he sat, taking his own sweet time, watching the exchange of the tray from one servant to another. Shortly, Roger placed the tureen on the table and Dagge's soup bowl was filled, then her bowl was filled, and no one said anything the entire time until he was done.

"I'm sure you believe your friends will rescue you, but I promise that will not be the case. We found all the secret passages. I found most of them myself, in fact. All of them, really. John always said it was a matter of unused space. He was right. Too bad Hellen killed him."

So many things Adia wanted to say, and she did. "Too bad she had to. But then, you'd already done it, really."

"I suppose I had."

There he was. That Dagge they all loathed. The killer. Would he still sound so proud of himself if she:

"I'm not sure I believe the secret passages were all found. Those monks were pretty good at hiding things." She sat forward and laid her napkin on her lap.

"That's why it took me so long!"

"I'd love a tour."

"I'll tell you what, you can ask me. Pick as many as you like, and I'll tell you if I found them."

"I'm flattered you think I'm that smart."

Adia picked up her soup spoon and dipped into the bowl. Some kind of chunk bumped against it. "It smells delicious, is it cream of potato with bacon?"

"Yes, it is. Another favorite."

Adia's stomach growled again, which made Dagge laugh, and his smudge flickered down and eventually went out. For a good minute the only sound was some light slurping, and it wasn't coming from Adia. Of course, if she'd had her way, she'd pick the bowl up and scrape the soup straight into her gullet, but that wasn't company manners either.

Yet there could come a time.

As they ate, Adia took a moment to make note of the ambient sound. The space felt cavernous after the modest dimensions of the monastery and the warren. Yet it didn't feel empty. There'd been so many people here, so many lives…the rock held them.

Were her ancestors watching? Would they be there if she needed them? She'd never given it a lot of thought, but found herself hoping.

She lay her spoon in her bowl and ratcheted up more company talk.

"I know I'm not supposed to ask about our plans tonight…" She shrugged Dagge's coat off and hung it on the back of her chair. "But will I need to wear something different? I should change if we're going to the dungeon, for example."

That irritated edge back in his voice, Dagge said, "We're not going to the dungeon." All the perfect host had gone right out of him. "You look fine. But if you're not going to wear my coat, I'll take it back." She felt the heavy fabric lifted from her chair, and he rustled as he put it back on.

She should have spilled wine on it.

"Are we going into the forest?"

Silence again. But not too terribly long.

"Why do you ask?"

"Well, if we go into the forest, I'll need to put on some good shoes."

"We're not going into the forest. We have no need to go there." He took a deep breath and exhaled slowly. "I'm glad you're excited. But I need you to trust me. I'll tell you everything you need to know when it's time."

Was he like this with Hellen? Because it was hard to imagine her putting up with it.

"I see."

"How funny that you use that word," Dagge said. "I would think a blind person would stop saying it."

"I have thought the same thing." She nodded back in Dagge's direction. "However, I find it useful, being the thing most people say." Her hand traveled to the wineglass flawlessly. So satisfying.

However, it might be time to shake things up a little.

Wine still in her mouth, Adia moved to set her glass down and caught the base of it on her bowl. Her glass slipped out of her hand and broke when it hit the opposite edge, no doubt spilling her wine all over the fancy setting. Shards of glass would be a bonus.

Dagge snapped his fingers and clapped his hands, barking orders for the staff to bring new table dressing. Many hands began taking the flowers, and dishes, and finally the tablecloth, and replacing them in opposite order. Adia sat back in her chair and willed the staff to understand her situation. Some of them might not know who she was, but some would. They had to.

After the sub-kitchen doors closed and quiet had been restored, Dagge sat for a few moments in silence, then rebounded with a running stream of chitchat.

"Here, let me get you some more soup." He got up, went around the back of her chair and took her bowl from the other side. "I wanted to surprise the staff later that you were here, but it's all right that this happened. Better to have the broken glass removed than for you to cut yourself. Or me." He chuckled like that was a joke. "Our server is not the best waiter, either, you're lucky you didn't have wine in your lap instead of just the table."

He laughed cordially. So did she, imagining the table in her lap. Weird that he would blame the server for her accident, though. Her bowl rejoined her stack, and she picked up her new spoon and ate.

Chapter M.17

After the soup Roger brought the pork chops. Adia was glad—she was so used to wolfing her food when she was hungry, she didn't want to waste time with teasers. Who needed them?

True to her word, she picked up her pork chop with her fingers before Dagge could grab her plate or do anything else deeply offensive. At least not to her food. Because he was certainly a steady stream of offensive in other ways.

"I honestly had great respect for your father. He wasn't the only king I'd worked for, you know." Something went into his mouth, blocking the words and turning them into a happy little grunt. Took all the fun right out of this experience.

But it was Cookie's food, so Adia compartmentalized and turned to the pork chop in her hand. Maybe if she tuned Dagge out he'd disappear.

That first bite was always the best—the taste of salt on the tongue, juice, and firm flesh. Ohhh, she wanted to grunt so badly. It didn't take too many chews before her forearms were resting on the edge of the table, and she was biting while she still had food in her mouth.

A chuckle erupted next to her, followed by a deep breath and a guffaw. Dagge's pork chop bone hit his plate, and the guffaw turned her way, blowing hot air on her she didn't need.

"Don't forget your mashed potatoes!"

Unfazed, she took another bite and talked around her food. "I warned you. I'm not the person I used to be. A lot can change in three years."

Dagge's utensils scraped his plate, clinked down, and the bone got gnawed as he talked. "Yes it can. Fighting for survival can make you an animal. You do things. Like ordering assassinations of myself and foreign leaders." He sounded a bit admiring, funnily enough. "I'm not sure Ol' Kingy would have done that. By the way, how does that look on the Beldenet resume?"

"Better than a dinner party where nine-tenths of the guests die."

He laughed again and dropped what sounded like an empty bone back onto the plate. "Are you sure about that? I got kingdoms, resources, exciting new weapons. What did you get?"

Adia put her bone down gently, wiped her hands on her napkin, and turned to him. "I got the satisfaction of knowing that with every one of those people you killed, you were one step closer to ruination."

Protracted pause. "Now you must think you're very close."

Adia turned toward him, hands folded in her lap. "Yes," she said. "I think we're close."

"You're not close." His napkin slapped the table, his chair slid on the carpet, and he came at her. One hand wrapped around her forearm and he pulled her up, smudge flaming. "You should know this: you belong to me now. Your little friends will never be able to get in here and get you away from me. You're mine." His other hand snaked around her back and pressed her to him, hard. She could feel the big knife tucked into his belt. "You will marry me. You'll wear what I like, you'll do what I like, and you'll give me sons." His breath spread over her face, smelling like pork and wine. "When we go other places, you'll walk by my side, and you'll laugh at my jokes, and you'll be happy. Am I perfectly clear?"

Adia's heart skittered in her chest. Her mouth had gone dry, and she put all her effort into controlling the fight-or-flight that could easily turn this for the worse.

"I hear you met my dog," she said.

"I killed your dog."

"Twice, I heard."

Dagge was silent.

"He's a good dog," she said.

"He's a freak."

"Maybe." Adia helped her arm fall out of Dagge's slackened grip. "The point is, you won't win," she said. "We'll just keep coming back, and coming back, and eventually you won't be around anymore."

"Oh honey, you'll go long before I will."

"But I barely matter. Don't you see that? It's the people who are this kingdom. Not me, not my father. The people are the reason Great Hand was a paradise. They're the ones who built community, and prosperity, and they made things beautiful because they care.

"The thing is, they will never stop caring. They will never stop fighting to reclaim this kingdom. They'll do whatever it takes, and one fine day, Tomius Dagge, a reckoning will come to you."

Chapter M.18

Why couldn't she just keep her fat mouth shut? Apparently, Tomius Dagge wasn't one to appreciate a good dress-down. After a tense moment, he'd grabbed her upper arms and shoved her back down into her chair. His smudge ramped up and flashed back and forth in hot magenta blinks. Shorted out, maybe. Or mechanized fire.

Barking, he'd ordered Adia's place cleared, except for her wine and water. All her senses trained onto Roger as he stood beside her, stacking her plates, laying the silverware on top. His energy felt like a skipping stone. She focused on where his core should be, and was elated when a spear of magenta stuttered into view a few times. Fantastic to see more than Dagge, sobering that it was another monster. Who did Roger used to be? Adia wondered if she knew him.

When the dishes had been cleared, Dagge activated the evening's entertainment. No more chummy conversation, too bad, but at least she'd have a chance to work at seeing. If she could teach herself how to expand this ability, to open it up, it could change everything.

Adia concentrated on the rustles that started to pass by in front of the table, doing her best to follow their movement. As she focused, she began to catch the barest colors of the people moving into the space. Soldiers, she guessed, by the heavy tread and rough clothes. Their core lights were small and hard to see, like they had invisibility icing partly scraped off.

The soldiers were walking to predesignated places and stopping. Clearly, they had worked on this during the time Dagge had left her alone. Chances were he was going to make her get through them—as an obstacle course, or a maze perhaps. And chances were he'd make it even more special somehow as a way to make her pay for her little speech.

But it had felt great to say that stuff right to his face. Let him stew over the idea of a reckoning.

Turning her left ear to the front hid her face from Dagge and allowed her to examine the right side of the room. As she practiced, the people-colors became more distinct—warm spectrum, mostly: dirty reds, bright reds, burgundy. Occasional orange and lime. Some browns, and even black. From one side of the room to the other, the colors stopped level with the table. All the soldiers were in front, and some stood where the other tables should be, so screw her assumptions.

The ballroom doors were unguarded.

The subkitchen door was also unguarded, but the main door had two guards in front.

Finally, all the lights were still, and loosely filled the space between the table and the doors. Any minute now Dagge was going to have her out there. She'd have to act like she couldn't see, stubbing her toes and tripping. She'd have to hold her hands out in front of her. Or would he tie her hands behind her back? Maybe she could trip and hit her head and wake up somewhere else.

Who was she kidding? One dose of humiliation would never be enough for him.

Pretending to sip her wine, she considered the viability of getting through the subkitchen door versus the ballroom door, while ignoring Dagge's monologue as best she could. Until something he said caught her attention.

"I kept her alive, I want you to know that. I didn't see why she should pay for your treason."

What was he saying?

His silence sounded gleeful in a teeth-sucking way. He expected her to react with some outrage or smart remark, she was sure. And she probably would if she knew what the hells he was talking about. She could hear him pick food off his dessert plate, which he had asked for when he sat down to presumably watch the show. None for her, though. Apple pie, he said. How wholesome. He didn't use his fork at all.

To be fair, she'd done it plenty herself. But who wanted to be fair?

"That's a strange thing for you to say to me, Dagge."

"What, that I saved your horse?"

Thank One. Her heart squeezed, but she pushed it aside.

"That I committed treason."

"Isn't that what it is when a person incites rebellion?"

"Against a legitimate ruler. We both know who committed treason, and it wasn't me."

"I wasn't a citizen of this country."

He had her there. It probably wasn't treason, then. Krikey, what was it? "You're still an illegitimate ruler, and I didn't commit treason either."

Wow, arguing like a married couple already. She had to get out of here.

"How long does it take for a ruler to become legitimate? What would satisfy your requirement for my right to sit on that throne? Oh wait, I don't care. This isn't my only throne; in case you've forgotten, I have several. Great Hand is only important because of the carapaz, and the tech it serves. When that's played out, Great Hand can become a slum for all I care. I'll just build the wall higher."

Adia's brain caught fire. Brief, wild ideas flew through her head: stabbing Dagge with his table knife; lunging and tackling him to the floor; smashing her glassware against his skull. None of those movies ended well for her, though.

Better to be smart.

"Tell you what, I'll take the throne and you can have the carapaz."

Dagge laughed. "Why would I give you the throne?"

"To stop having to worry about a rebellion. You can move your troops to Pulari and Valdia, and we can sign a contract for the carapaz. Everyone's happy."

"Except I'm not happy. Because I like the throne. The whole palace, in fact—it's much better than Pulari's."

The chink of a glass brushing a plate floated over to her. What were the chances it was more alcohol? Hard to say. Special occasion vs. liking to be in control. Hm, given his extra weight, special occasion just might win.

"I can see your wheels turning, but you're not going to escape." Dagge's glass thudded lightly on the table. "It's so cute that you think you could."

That would have done it, if it hadn't already been done. Her switch was so thoroughly flipped, though, she was to all purposes upside down. It was an interesting education for her mind and heart. Her fury wanted venting, and vengeance, and blood. Her training argued for strategy, wisdom, and justice. Honestly, she wasn't sure which would win.

"Cute was always my thing," she mumbled.

"What was that?"

"Nothing."

"It looks like everything's ready." His hand lay on her forearm. "Shall we?"

Her head turned to him of its own accord, but she was silent, drilling him with her sightless eyes.

The voice that came back was high and incredulous, the smudge alight: "You understand what's going on, don't you? You're a smart girl."

"That's so adorable that you would say that."

He was silent again, like someone who knows they've been insulted, but they aren't sure exactly how.

In two moves he stood over her. His hand grabbed hers and twisted it up between them, pulling her to standing again. With his other hand he cupped her jaw, fingers copping a feel on her scars.

"It doesn't have to be bad for you, you know. If you were to cooperate, we could have a nice time. You could have all the luxuries you used to have."

"What do you want me to say, Dagge? That I'll marry you? No. Fucking. Way."

Fury rolled off of him, smudge burning, his arm whipped around her back and pressed her to his stomach. His knife dug into her. His breath flooded her face—sour with a hint of cinnamon.

"You'll do whatever I say you will. Now let's play."

Chapter M.19

"We're standing about two-thirds of the way into the room if you're coming through the door. You can't see it, but I've had my men construct an obstacle course in front of us. Some of it is furniture from this very room."

Adia faced the main door, forcing calm in between the red flags and sirens going off in her head. Well, hells. The spaces between the people weren't empty. More stubbed toes than she anticipated.

"Others will have unexpected shapes and sizes. All you have to do is get out the door uninjured and I will let you go."

What were the chances he was lying about letting her go? A hundred percent?

"Any door?"

Dagge cracked his neck. His smudge had leveled out, but surged a little at her question. "Not the subkitchen or secret passage doors."

"Then the hallway and the ballroom are fair game."

"In the interest of sportsmanship, yes."

His voice had tilted ever so slightly into resentment and irritation, but he never would have allowed it if he didn't think he'd win anyway. That meant he had both doors covered with things that could injure her easily. What the hells could they be? She couldn't think of a single thing in the palace that could be that dangerous.

Except the polyphus. Fifty axe blades on long shanks embedded horizontally around a stone cylinder—all the long, curved edges facing out. As deadly a sentinel as you could have. Perfect for a large doorway, being taller than a man and thrice as wide.

The sheer death of it used to fascinate her. All her life it had sat in the museum, caged like a wild animal that might attack if she looked at it wrong. Both her parents told her she must never go over the low

431

wall built in front of it. She never did, but she came close. When she was eleven, she leaned way over trying to touch the cage and Hilman caught her just before she lost her balance. He'd said, "It just feels like metal, Miss. Nothing special about it. I believe Cookie has some fresh strawberries she wants your approval of. I'm here to escort you to the kitchen."

"Yes, of course, Hilman," she'd said, and they left. Only later did she realize her hand could have gone through the metal bars, and no telling how much of herself she might have lost. Her father never said anything to her about it, though, so she guessed Hilman didn't tell him. And she didn't get so close again.

No, she satisfied herself with reading the museum card after that. It said the polyphus was once mounted on a pegstone that helped it spin. Both the axe-wheel and the pegstone each had a large cut-carapaz crystal embedded in the top, and they worked on each other like same-pole magnets, both repelling and spinning.

It was made because several centuries ago, some criminal had found a way through the Apex Mountains. He and a small band terrorized the countryside: robbing, raping, leaving people dead. For months they avoided capture, until, as bad luck would have it, they tried to rob the Captain of the Kingsguard. Vicco Taymer outsmarted and outfought them until the crime spree ended with five men dead, three in chains, and the Captain holding all their weapons.

Adia soaked that in for a moment. What a hero he was. And she had people like that around her all the time.

The King in those days had the polyphus erected in the gap that made the raids possible. Legends said it had magical powers that drew living things to it, and the nefarious to their deaths. Reportedly, no one was ever found dead while it was there, though that might have been due to mountain lions. Several mountain goats did lose their horns and a fair amount of hair.

A few moons later, there were avalanches in that part of the range. Great sheets of mountain collapsed downward, taking spikes and razor-sharp edges with them into the passage. Up the mountainside, new spikes and sharper edges thrust toward the sky, freshly exposed and even more hazardous.

After the avalanches, the polyphus was no longer necessary, and the King had it removed. Dismantling the axe-wheel from the pegstone killed three people. One man reached to drape a chain around the axe-wheel, fell into it, and several blades sliced him wide open.

Two were rolled upon when the axe-wheel was lowered from the pegstone to the ground. It tilted over onto its side, and one man had both legs cut off, while the other got sliced in half lengthwise when he lost his footing and went under.

At that point, the metal cage was built for it, along with a special low cart. Once it was trussed, they moved it in through the palace theatre, and up to the second floor via a specially-built lift. Two doorways were enlarged, and it was settled into the palace museum, sectioned off in a corner by a little stone wall. The cart stayed with it, and the cage stayed on so no one would inadvertently die.

In an interesting side note, the pegstone got moved as well, but disappeared soon after. Most likely the monks had a hand in that, even though they were already gone by then ("gone" being a fluid concept). Yep, the far more dangerous part was left on a cart in an open room.

Until tonight. Because Dagge had put the polyphus in the doorway. Adia could tell now, because her crazy new vision kept improving, and she could see light radiating near the top of what would be the doorway. A faint glow had appeared there—the same color as the walls in the tunnel. Carapaz.

Knowing Dagge, the cage was off, too, just for grins. Which might mean the cage was also in the room, because why waste such a big obstacle? Likely it would be near the polyphus, and open so that it could be as big and confusing as possible. Yeah, no, she wouldn't be going out that way. But she could fake it.

Adia rubbed her fingers across her forehead before she realized it. Oops, can't show distress. She pulled her hand down.

The ballroom doors were her only real option, but what could he have between here and there? The only other dangerous things she could think of in the palace were antique hand-held weapons, and if Dagge wanted some soldier to kill her, a rifle would be far easier. Albeit less poetic. What would he choose?

Whatever was the most fun. Antique weapons it was.

"Sound off!" Dagge yelled to the room.

In front of her, behind her, all around the room soldiers counted off. Seventy-one soldiers, with around ten lining the walls behind. For those in the obstacle course, Adia mentally inserted unspecified antique weapons into hands.

"I know you've been listening," he said, "but as a gesture of friendship, I wanted you to know we're not alone. Well, you're alone, but you can pretend you're surrounded by friends. Eventually we'll get there. For now, they simply have orders not to strike you down."

"What if I don't do it, Dagge? What if I just sit down right here and say no?" She descended gracefully into her chair like she owned it.

His magenta and lime shifted into stakes. The magenta glowed, dominating the green until it looked thin as straw. When he spoke, his voice had a smugness to it that alarmed her.

"Do you really want to test me?"

Fear prickled her skin. "No, I don't suppose I do." Her hand lifted to her forehead and she pulled it away. If she went out there, she'd stand a far better chance of getting to a door, anyway. What she had to do to get there was inconsequential, because humiliation was only what you let it be. The way she looked at it, Dagge was far more pathetic than she was.

"Are they allowed to use weapons against me?"

"Only in self-defense."

His voice sounded giddy. His smudge morphed back to normal.

Even if he was lying about letting her go, he might be willing to let her get out as part of the game. Maybe she could make the family dining room, which had an exit that went outside.

Except she didn't want to go outside. She wanted to finish this. And for that she needed her friends, who were probably already here.

Realizing that gave her strength.

434

What were the chances she could get out uninjured? Some of the antique weapons would be sharp, so leading with her hands would be risky. She should find a way that didn't involve outstretched fingers.

And if she could keep him in Perfect Host mode, she'd be less likely to die prematurely.

She reached for her wineglass again, and tinked her fingernails into it. Oops. Grasping the glass, she said, "I propose a toast." Allowing a short pause for Dagge to join her, she continued, "From the morning sailors to the evening tailors, may we all have excellent luck."

"Hear, hear," Dagge said, and they drank.

"All right then," she said, putting her wineglass down and turning to him. "Are we ready?"

"Oh, I'm going to watch from over here." His voice faded away toward the subkitchen wall again. "It wouldn't be fair for me to do it, since I can see. But don't worry, I won't be far."

Adia wished she could see his face. His voice sounded so sincere she couldn't be sure he wasn't just insane. If she could see his eyes, she'd know. But what was she thinking? Of course he's insane.

She bent to the task at hand.

Fingers lightly trailing the tablecloth, Adia made her way to the right, down the long table to the end. There she stopped and faced the room, trying to get a sense of the presence of things between the people. It didn't work.

With a deep breath she stepped forward.

Chapter M.20

Extending her left hand, she felt for the next table, the leg of the "U." It was a ruse, of course, she could see the soldiers' lights where the table would be. The placement of the soldiers was too random to tell, but most likely those tables had been used as obstacles somewhere. Along with maybe sixty chairs. Krikey.

Adia made a tight left and walked down the front of the VIP table. Maybe Dagge would think she was coming for him, like she wanted him to rub her scars for luck. He'd like that.

Instead, she stopped at their place settings and felt for the candelabra. When she found it, she removed the candles, extinguished the flames, and laid them by the flowers.

"Wait a minute," he said. "No one said you could use the candelabra."

"No one said I couldn't," she replied, "and the deal is made."

"Oho, aren't you a clever one? All right, fine, you can use the candelabra, but nothing else."

"The deal is done, Dagge. I expect a sporting man like you understands that the rules can't be changed after the game has begun."

He said nothing for several seconds, then chuckled. "Fair point," he said.

She turned and faced the room. The nearest soldiers stood eight feet away at 2-3 o'clock, twenty feet at twelve o'clock, and five feet at 9:30-10:00. Plenty of space between. How to find out where things were?

Lowering the candelabra to hip level, she swept it in long back-and-forths in front of her. Greater reach would be better. She turned back and grabbed her water glass. Taking a mouthful, she squirted a steady stream to her right front, past the soldier. Nothing but carpet, so she was clear for maybe two strides.

At this rate, she'd run out of water way too soon. Still.

Two strides and she took a second mouthful. Nothing but carpet, so she took two more steps, still sweeping with the candelabra.

"What are you going to do when you run out of water?"

Should she answer?

Hells no.

Except she did want him to be Polite Host.

"I don't know yet," she said amiably. "Hopefully something clever."

She got no answer.

The first thing she hit with the candelabra turned out to be a chair. The extra reach saved her from stubbing her toe, and she wondered if a stubbed toe would qualify as getting "hurt." Compared to the polyphus it didn't amount to much, but technically it would be pain.

She'd just have to increase her protection.

Setting the candelabra on the seat and her glass on the floor, she turned the chair away from her and grabbed the back with both hands. The chair slid across the rug easily (being made for snottier people who couldn't suffer having to struggle with their chair), but it made a damn good shield, and instead of taking her time, she decided to rush it.

She'd barely gotten started when she plowed into a table.

"Oh, well done!" Dagge clapped delightedly. "You made that chair pay off!"

How she wished she could fly over and rip his head from his body.

Instead, she debated with herself over leaving the chair to go under the table, or pushing it the long way around. A lot of lights crowded the narrow space between her and the ballroom door on this side, but there were fewer on the other side, so she might do better going under. But what if she didn't come across another chair? Considering the number of chairs always in this room, finding another seemed likely. She grabbed the candelabra and ducked under the table.

For a moment, Adia felt quietly safe between the tablecloth walls—the exotic desert tents of her childhood. This time there was no treasure and no horses, though. Just her and a replay of the last eighteen months of dark.

She lifted the cloth and climbed out the other side.

The next soldier was in front of her, about seven feet away. She swung the candelabra, walking side first to protect her toes and shins. Trying not to slow down, she whacked him in the side, her arm making contact with the metal weapon he was holding farther out than she anticipated.

"Is she bleeding?" Dagge called from the side, level with her where he'd been keeping up.

"No, sir," the soldier answered.

"That's very fortunate for you, Princess. I'm glad we didn't sharpen anything. I'd hate for this to be over so soon."

Adia pulled the candelabra back a bit until it hit metal, then she ran it up and down and sideways to get a sense of how big the weapon was, and its shape. From what she could tell, it was one of the spiked battle axes, and she really was lucky not to be bleeding.

Behind it, the visible part of the soldier's core was half orange and half burgundy, divided down the middle. When she spoke softly to him, the orange flared briefly.

"I'm sorry if I hurt you."

There was a pause in which he shifted.

"You didn't hurt me," he said. He sounded young.

"Good." She nodded and smiled.

Dagge called over. "Please keep talking to him if you want to get him tortured and killed."

The soldier's whole core became visible—burgundy spiraling into the orange, churning the mix into a muddy mess.

Adia turned to Dagge. "I only apologized for hitting him with the candelabra."

Dagge said nothing.

Blocking the axe with the candelabra, Adia moved past the soldier, putting him between her and Dagge, squeezing his arm on the side Dagge couldn't see. His colors settled and brightened.

With that soldier behind her, she took stock of those ahead. Her perception had intensified and she could see them more clearly. One stood about seven feet away at the ten o'clock, another less than twenty feet at the eleven, maybe fourteen at the one, and the closest was five feet at the 2:30. Beyond the middle two, the path to the hall door was crowded with them. In fact, the whole front of the room was crowded.

"Roger, fetch the coffee!" Dagge called. "If you're just going to stand there, Princess, we'll be here all night."

The urge to throw the candelabra at him nearly overwhelmed her. But she couldn't waste her best tool. Instead, she took her time.

The likelihood was that the other long table was also placed to block the door. That would make the most inconvenience for her. How disappointed he must have been that she went under the first one. Worth having to give up her chair.

Since the middle area between the tables appeared the least crowded, the most efficient move would be to make for the second table and move along it to the right, aiming toward the ballroom. Judging by the distance to the line of people along the front wall, she had passed the ballroom doors slightly, enough to make Dagge think she was headed for the hall.

Behind her, a rattle of dishes let her know that the coffee tray had arrived, and she used the opportunity to turn as though she was listening.

"I SAID SILENCE!" Dagge shouted, his colors all spiky stakes again, squeezing the green nearly to extinction.

Adia chanced a glance behind. Roger's colors had appeared— emerald green flamed upward, into and around a block of magenta. The magenta dissolved everywhere it was touched, like ash, but it fought back, stabbing outward. The green surged, over and over, but slowly. Roger was fighting a battle inside.

Adia couldn't risk continuing to watch, and turned her head back to the front.

But it gave her an idea.

With careful sweeps of the candelabra, she moved forward. Pretending to listen, she turned her head searching for clear colors in people's cores. Several had blood red, which didn't seem like a good thing. A few had orange—two of them were between her and the door. The soldier at eleven had a big emerald green patch in his brown, and beyond him was a pale grey with a crown of yellow.

She turned sideways again to protect her toes and shins, giving her a good long look at the soldier nearest to her. He had a dark grey and maroon core—the grey dripping over the maroon like wet paint. She passed him by.

Judging by the space where no soldiers were standing, the table was probably in front of the guy at eleven. Behind the guy at one. That left four strides give or take until she was there. Hopefully room for chairs.

She waved the candelabra at hip level, sidling forward with her left foot and following with her right. In two steps, her foot hit something before her candelabra did. With her right hand, she felt for it and found the seat of a chair.

"Oh goody, another chair!" Dagge said, clinking his coffee cup onto its saucer.

Adia turned her head toward him, to see his core drifting a bit toward her. It had relaxed into its usual hot magenta spike-topped lime green egg. He refrained from getting too close, though, and she guessed he didn't want to enter the maze. All the better.

Laying the candelabra in the chair, she walked around to the back of it, narrowly missing ramming her toes into another chair. The side of her foot scraped the leg, her knee brushed the seat, and her hand hit the armrest. Surprised, she bent over, clutched the armrest, and drew her foot back protectively.

Dagge laughed. "Not what you expected?"

She didn't answer.

440

"I confess it wasn't what I expected, either. I expected you to trip, or maybe break a toe. Or both! But really, it's better this way, because now we get to keep playing. Would you like a drink of water? A sip of wine, perhaps? I'd offer coffee, but that would take too long, I'm afraid."

What she wanted, deeply, was to get out of here. To stop performing for his amusement. To sit in this chair, rest her chin in her hand and dare him to kill her. It sounded doable; she could be a martyr.

But what else she wanted was to see Dagge taken down in fine, sweet agony. All the twisted sickness of everything he'd done for the past three years ablaze in a glorious firestorm of justice. Once upon a time that meant trial and imprisonment, but not anymore.

And for that to happen, she had to get out of this room. She had to help her friends kill Dagge, eliminate the last 2Ders, and close the tear. Because what else she wanted was to save her kingdom from this ever happening again.

"I'm fine," she said, turning the chair with the candelabra in it toward the hall door. It knocked into other chairs all around it, and Adia wondered how deep the blockade went. She was just going to have to ram through to find out.

Dagge kept up a running monologue.

"I admire people with disabilities."

Uh huh.

"The ways you learn to compensate can be quite remarkable."

Sigh.

"I knew a man once who lost his arms…"

She tuned him out.

The heavy chairs didn't push so easy all packed together like they were. Still, she was making progress when she noticed people were moving. More soldiers were coming from the sides and behind her, their cores sparking. Dagge must have gestured them in, cheater that he was. They crowded silently to the front.

"You're not listening to me, are you?" he said.

"I'm a little busy." Adia wrestled her chair around toward the ballroom doors, slightly back from her position. No one was there. Of course, he wouldn't expect her to know that.

Sitting in the chair, she stopped "to rest," and the soldiers also stopped.

It'd be so fun if she could turn around and catch Dagge waving at them.

Oh, what the hells.

Adia stood, facing Dagge dead on with a tiny smile. His core stopped moving. Everything was silent except the pop classics streaming over the intercom. She turned away, jerked her chair around and pulled it back as if frustrated.

"It's creepy how you almost look like you can see sometimes."

"Thank you," she said.

Nothing happened for a few seconds, then the soldiers moved again, many of them making a solid line in front of the table. More and more crowded the area between the table and the main door.

Adia stopped again. They all went still. With a huff, she pulled her chair backwards out of the tangle of chairs and steered it to the right as though she was trying to find the way around. The soldiers blocking the way to the ballroom doors had moved more toward the front, and Adia faked her attempts to steer that way according to when she'd run into a soldier.

Soldier after soldier got a chair seat to the knee. Not too hard, but enough to look like she didn't know they were there. She apologized to everyone she hit, watching the effect it had on their cores. To a person, it was like adding a drop of light onto their colors. Seeing it helped her be sincere, and the more sincere she was, the more light it gave them. Fascinating.

Some of them blocked her with their weapons, though—a crack to the front of the chair, or pushback in the seat. Once, she heard the fabric of the chair back rip, only fingertips from her belly. The soldier's core behind it strobed two shades of red. Menace exuded. She backed away with a little smile and moved on.

Her progress was a little forward and mostly to the side. The chair, however, was repeatedly turned toward the front so it would look like that was the direction she intended. Dagge kept talking.

"Stop wasting all this time apologizing," he said. "You sound pathetic."

"I'm so sorry," she replied cattily. "I was raised to be polite."

"I don't recall your father being like that. But then, he died before I really knew him."

"You killed him, you mean."

"He died before I killed him?"

Fury inflamed her, bringing her to a full stop. The man was an ass. She wanted to turn on him and shout him down, but once he saw he could get a rise out of her over her father, he'd do it all the time. She dialed back.

Leaning on folded forearms, Adia turned her ear to the front and took a moment to gauge the position of the ballroom doors. Judging by the few soldiers remaining along the walls, the doors were about twenty feet away, closer for her than for any of the obstacle soldiers.

If the doors were locked, this would be the shortest escape attempt in history.

Chapter M.21

"SonofaBITCH!"

Dagge's voice filled the room, followed by a roar and a crashing of something against the wall. Adia whipped around, moving the chair between her and his explosion. Across the room, his magenta core burned twice its usual size, flashing harsh vertical flames, the lime completely gone.

She backed toward the door slowly.

The other person was the confusing one. Roger had become an entire person of magenta—only the magenta was stuttery, verging on dim, and the emerald green was now a big, bright core. The edges of the magenta dissolved where the core continually burned a hole in it.

Mesmerized, she watched Dagge's flames go after Roger. She could hear his fist landing on Roger as he shouted.

"You stupid fuck-up! (Punch) That was FUCKING HOT, you MORON!" (Punch. Thud of something.) "This is a goddam burn on my hand, you fucking (punch) Treslo (Punch) fucking traitor!"

Treslo? Adia's brain clicked into place. Dear One, it was Robert. Dagge had put one of his monsters in Robert! Fists hit flesh, and Robert's light got lower and lower, bending horizontal, then downward until it huddled on the floor.

Adia stood there in shock as the beating played out, until a burgundy and bright orange light crept toward her and a young man's voice whispered, "Run. When we get to the door, hit me in the head with the candelabra, and I'll block the door as long as I can."

The chair began to nudge her backward. "Is there anything behind me?" she asked, heart pounding.

"No," he said. "Twenty feet or so to the door."

She started pulling the chair, hauling it backwards.

"Somebody bring me a bowl of water!" Dagge shouted, leaving Robert prostrate, and walking fast back toward the table, complaining unintelligibly.

Adia kept an eye on him while she moved the chair backward as quickly and unobtrusively as she could. After a double handful of steps, the soldier snapped the chair back toward himself and said, "Stop! Now hit me in the head."

The chair had wrenched out of Adia's hands and she bumped the door behind her. The noise got attention from one of the nearest soldiers, who turned to look.

Her right hand was already over the back of the chair feeling for the candelabra while her left waved behind her for the door handle. Handle in her hand, she swung the candelabra to the side of the soldier's head, getting mostly shoulder and probably some face. "Sorry!" she breathed, and opened the door.

"Oi!" the other soldier said, moving toward her. Several turned then and started lunging in her direction.

Dagge apparently saw her at that point. A belly roar came out of his mouth, and she guessed the table went crashing over, because dishes broke and the coffee tray clanged on the floor. Voice all deep, he shouted, "STOP HER!" all long and drawn out.

The magenta of his core surged and filled his whole body with mechanized fire. Dagge had a monster, but it was different from Robert's. It had rounded parts and a neck, and when it turned it wasn't flat. But it did have purple eyes, and Adia knew what it was. It was all the death at the banquet, and death in the surrounding world ever since.

Adia left the chair behind, pulled the door just wide enough and slipped through. The young man's body fell onto the door, pushing it closed, and Adia could hear the chair tumble over, somehow tangled up with him.

She marveled at the kindness of some people. *Dear One, please help him not to be hurt for that*, she prayed as she jammed the candelabra down around the door handles on the other side. Hopefully that would slow them enough, after they got past his pretend unconscious body.

But there were other ways to get to her here, so she wouldn't have much time. On this side of the ballroom, the servants' door under the stairs let into the main hall, and from the main hall she could cut through the servants' hall over to the theatre. There she could hide backstage, or in the dressing rooms, or costumes and prop storage. Plenty of places to stay low until things settled down some.

The big dining room doors started shaking, and shouts could be heard from the servants' hall between the dining room and the throne room. One hand on the wainscoting, one in front of her just in case, Adia ran around the wall and under the stairs. With practiced assurance, she flipped the latch, pulled the hidden door open, and pulled it closed behind her.

Chapter M.22

Hellen led the rebels through the flipping fence and up the side fence bordering Luhe and Vartile's backyard. The explosions hadn't started yet, but they would soon and she wanted them to be ready.

Each person was outfitted and armed according to their job. Some had guns, a few fireballs, and miscellaneous personal weapons. Hellen's was the only bullet rifle—for monsters—and she had her carapaz knife, of course. Beau had a scope rifle, his handgun, and no telling what else in all those pockets.

Firio had a knife and hemp straps. Roberta was going to take him around the palace to all the double doors that needed their handles tied. It had been her excellent idea to block those avenues of pursuit.

Cary and his team would line the balcony in the foyer and shoot any soldiers who tried to come back.

Hellen and Beau and David were going in to get Adia.

Even after countless moonlight trips through the forest, it seemed like a dark night. Byron's team had taken out the few remaining streetlights. The crescent moon appeared and disappeared behind heavy clouds, and the air was still and humid. Hellen wiped the dripping sweat off her face.

Hunkering down, she gestured for the rest of the team to wait, and she made a beeline for the outbuildings she had escaped through just days ago. Beau halted the others and waved them sideways until they settled against the fence. Hellen stepped to the corner of the shed and peeked around.

No one in sight, even ahead, in the bottleneck, where Dagge had solar floodlights mounted on poles. The harsh ground was empty, bluish light searing the front of the palace in a fluorescent nightmare. The beautiful palace. Hellen grieved again.

"Not for long," she whispered.

On the upside, once the explosions started, they would have a lurid view of soldiers charging away from the castle. Out to get Byron and his team. *Dear One, please protect them.* Hellen turned to go back. *And bless their troublemaking.*

She checked her own team as she jogged back to the fence. They all looked alert and ready: Beau and David watched her; Cary, checking his pockets, held on to Beau's red dot rifle like it was a life preserver; Patsie, in uniform, looked a fraction of how lethal she was with her gun; Firio, Roberta, Dessara, Donas, Grovet, and Luhe, all in black, were the prisoners for the "patrol"; Edren and Rack talked together quietly, in uniform, rifles hanging on their backs. Soon, they'd clear the path to the door. Then Edren would join Cary's team in the palace, but Rack was coming with her.

Adia was probably in the dining room. Dagge would want to make a big production out of dinner to try and woo her. No way Adia would fall for anything, but Hellen felt bad for her anyway. Sometimes a woman's hardest job was navigating a man with an agenda. Especially a dangerous one.

Dagge would know the explosions were a ruse, but he'd also want to protect his wall. The soldiers inside would come out the front—however many he let go. Any soldiers he sent from the back were likely to use the gate at the road. There was a light there, too, but dimmer than those in the bottleneck. Hellen could barely see two soldiers leaning on the wall down there.

Hellen moved the Resistance to the wall so the east/west angle of it could hide their numbers. She took the front position and waved the others into the shadows behind her.

They hadn't been waiting long when the first explosion blew on the east side of town. Shortly after, a second went off to the north. A pause, then a whistle started blowing loud, rapid bursts downtown. A man's voice yelled from somewhere around the plaza.

"Fireball in the barracks!"

448

Shouts echoed off the buildings downtown, drifting in pieces through the dense night air. Soldiers poured onto the cobblestones around the buildings, some from the fire escape and some from the front. The ones from the front were wiping their faces on their sleeves and bending over coughing. Soon they were all looking toward the east, and an officer was shouting them into action.

The whistler came running from town up into the bottleneck, shrilling a pattern of two long, two short. Soldiers started hurrying from the palace—a few at first, probably from the door guard, then bigger groups. The whistler held his arm out, pointing them to the east side. A minute later, more soldiers were running through the gate beyond. When the flow trickled down, it would be their time.

Watching across the open space, something else caught Hellen's eye. In the shadows by the gate, a white dog was weaving through the soldiers, heading toward the palace.

"Is that Wolf?"

Beau checked his scope. "It is. Smart dog to wait for chaos."

"Wolf's crazy smart," Hellen said. They had no idea.

"We can't let anything happen to him," David said, crowding close. Cary craned forward behind him.

"No," Hellen agreed. "We can't."

"I'll go get him." David moved away from the wall. "Meet you by the doors."

"David, don't let anything happen to you. Adia and Roberta would kill me."

He turned and walked backward. "I'll be fine. I've got the perfect cover." His hands went to his chest. "I'm a canine unit." David grinned and opened his arms, then headed across the dirt and weeds toward Wolf.

Hellen grimaced, watching him.

"I'll keep an eye on him," Beau said, raising his rifle.

"Thanks, Beau."

Hellen moved around Beau, out of his way, and ran into Roberta, who was watching David jog away with a stricken look on her face. "He'll be fine," she said, her voice whispery with fear.

"He will, Roberta. Really. Beau's got him." If he had to shoot, that would change everything, but they'd deal with it. The night wasn't going to end pretty, anyway. Hellen put her arm around Roberta's waist and pulled her close while they watched David run through the shadows by the wall.

In the bottleneck, soldiers were rushing away from the palace in clumps. The whistler was talking to a man who looked like an officer. The officer stepped away toward a man who stormed against the flow of soldiers, striding toward the palace. He shoved the officer aside.

Hellen stepped forward and tapped Beau. "Is that who I think it is?"

Beau checked his sight. "Yeah."

It was Wharton, holding a walkntalk to his face. Hellen couldn't see a rifle on him, but that didn't mean he didn't have a gun. And a knife, and One knew what else. David had entered the bottleneck, and was going to cross his path right in front of him.

Beside her, Roberta clapped her hands over her face, head shaking no. A high voice slipped through the cracks between her fingers. "Not David. Not David." Her hands came down, made fists in front of her mouth, and motionless, she watched.

He stopped. About a stride shy of crossing in front of Wharton, David snapped to attention and saluted. None of the other soldiers were saluting. Hellen's alarm bells went off.

Cary leaned around her to watch, and the others crowded forward to do the same.

"What's he doing?" Cary asked.

"He's saluting," Firio said.

"Why is he doing that?" Patsie asked.

"Wharton's a general," Luhe said.

They all watched as Wharton slowed down, head turned to look at David with a thunderous scowl on his face. He stopped just past him, jaw flapping. Looked like he was chewing David out. Strangely, he shoved the walkntalk into David's chest and kept going.

David turned to face them, clipping the walkntalk on his belt, then held his hand up.

"He's waving us in," Beau said.

David looked toward the palace, gave a sharp whistle and Wolf came running. Together, they jogged nearer the far wall and up into the bottleneck.

The flow of soldiers had trickled and stopped.

Roberta took a shaky breath and blew it out.

Hellen faced her people. "Rack, Edren, it's time. Is half a minute long enough?"

"With both me and Edren shooting, that's slow."

"All right, we'll be right behind you. Clear that door."

"Will do," Rack said.

Edren nodded once, and they ran off toward the castle.

"Let's go!" she said, waving her arm at the people behind her.

Hellen set a fast pace, talking to Cary. "Half a minute after they start shooting, you guys go. Stick to the wall, out of their way. Fire if you have to, whatever it takes to get inside."

"Want me to wait downstairs in case Wharton makes it into the palace?"

"No. We'll take care of him. You get in and get to the balcony."

"Yes, ma'am."

Hellen gestured Cary's team around the curve of the wall. Wolf started barking, firing began, and she and Beau split off and ran into the bottleneck.

The scene was like something out of her nightmares. Wharton had a 2Der, and its burning magenta head stretched into the air probably five feet. It loomed, angular and flat, bent over Wolf, who barked and jumped from side to side in front of it. Wharton's arms raised into the air and swiped at the dog in big swings. Wolf jumped away.

The monster head swung over to the steady volley of laser fire from Rack's and Edren's guns. Hellen stopped, pulled up her rifle and sighted. In jerky steps the monster moved toward them, its grimacing mouth appearing in the tall head. She fired just as Wharton's arm reared back, going straight for Rack. She fired twice, missed him both times, and ran closer.

But Edren was already closer. He stopped shooting and ran at Wharton, laser rifle dropping to the ground, big knife emerging. He hurled himself at the body, grabbing at Wharton's arms and trying to stab him in the heart while the horrid mouth screeched down at him.

Rack jumped up and ran across the dirt in front of her with his crossbow, aiming for a good shot at Wharton that didn't involve Edren. "Edren! Move back! Move back!"

Then Wolf lunged at Wharton from behind, knocking him into a stagger which shoved Edren back. Wharton regained his balance and the tall slash of a head swung over Wolf and roared. By then Hellen was in better shooting range, took a knee and found Wharton in her scope.

Arrows started filling Wharton's back, shoulders, and chest. The purple eyes located Rack not far to Hellen's ten o'clock, and the monster went for him. Hellen fired and hit Wharton's face—a red splatter opened the cheek. Not what she meant to do.

She set herself again and sighted. Wolf attacked again, lunging at Wharton, knocking him back out of her shot. She tried to follow, but Wharton came for Wolf, and the dog jumped on him, paws on Wharton's shoulders, snapping at Wharton's bloody face. Wharton was trying to push Wolf away, and in those few seconds, the long, flat head of the monster sucked back into Wharton's body, and a hot magenta surge blew Wolf backward from his hands.

Edren rushed in again, pushing the arrows to the side, trying to get his knife into Wharton's chest. Did he know his knife could only kill the body? He didn't want to hang around after that. And she had to be there to finish it.

Hellen jumped into a run. If she could get Edren's attention, he could get out of the way, and she could kill it. She passed David who had run over to where Wolf lay on the dirt. He was lifting Wolf's head, talking to him. Explosions went off in the distance.

"He alive?" she said, not stopping.

"Yeah," David answered. "We'll meet you."

Hellen nodded and turned her attention ahead. Edren, built like a brick wall, was dodging Wharton's arms, darting in and out like a much lighter man. The arrows were mostly broken off now, and Edren had a clear path to Wharton's heart. She flung her gun back over her shoulder and released her knife.

But she wasn't close enough. Two spikes of furious energy thrust out of Wharton's hands and impaled Edren Taymer. They lifted him into the air, skewered from both sides up the middle. The magenta burned and crackled, and the monster's head pushed up out of Wharton's. It stretched slowly over to Edren's face and roared inches away. Edren's whole body shook violently. His head bobbled back and forth like it was held on with toothpicks. The spikes retracted, Edren fell, and Wharton moved away toward the palace doors.

Rack screamed at Wharton, firing his laser pistol all around him, taking chunks out of the portico balcony, the columns, and the front wall of the palace.

"Watch out for Cary's team!" she yelled.

Hellen scrambled for her rifle, fired at Wharton, misjudged his movement, fired again and hit him in the shoulder, then he got behind the big portico columns and she couldn't get a good shot.

Just ahead, Rack ran up to Edren's body and checked him, collapsing to both knees, chin dropping when he saw without a doubt that he was dead. Hellen's heart sank for him.

When she got to him, she put her hand on his shoulder. "You don't have to be here. Go help Byron."

"Are you kidding? I want to kill that motherfucker."

She paused. "All right then. I'll loan you my gun."

Wolf and David joined them from the left, Beau from the right. David scooped Edren's legs into each arm and helped Rack carry him to the portico, where they hid him behind a column.

They headed for the big main doors. Beside her, Wolf's hackles were up and a continual growl revved from his throat.

453

She was glad she wasn't Dagge.

Chapter M.23

Toward the kitchen, Adia could hear the clang of metal as soldiers worked on the problem of the polyphus. There was a lot of shouting and rattling of the cage. A high scream echoed in the hall, followed by a body tumbling to the floor just out the door. She looked back—his red light stuttered and dissolved.

Adia fled, skimming the wall, telling herself to assume the lights were on, and there was no new furniture. (Not likely Dagge would waste his attention on hall décor, unless it was something really special, like shrunken heads).

As she ran, the shouts and clattering coming from the dining room doorway increased. An enormous crash and several screams echoed up the hall. The polyphus must have fallen. Laser fire started, but it didn't sound like it was coming her way. For some weird reason there was the sound of firepoppers, and shouts turning into violent coughing.

Weaponized firepoppers. Her friends were definitely here.

Passing the closed doors of the Grand Ballroom, she could hear more shouting, heaving of furniture, and running echoing through the vastness. Dagge's voice boomed inside, screaming things like "You're DEAD! JUST LIKE YOUR FATHER, SO FUCKING DEAD!"

So much for matrimony.

Laser fire echoed. A scream faded down from one of the balconies and ended in a thud on the floor. "WharTON!" She'd gone twenty or so paces past the ballroom doors when they opened behind her. The door would screen her for a few seconds, so Adia tightened against the right-hand wall and sped up as much as she could.

Unseen, she rounded the corner into the front hall, praying no one would be there. No one was, except at the very end a single light flashing blue and orange, which disappeared, presumably through the conference room door.

Halfway to the end, the ballroom doors shook violently, and were pounded with something hard. It wasn't long before the laser fire started, and it apparently ricocheted off the metal plates around the doorhandles, because there was a lot more shouting and the shooting stopped.

She turned the other way and went left, toward the hidden door to the servants' hall. Her new plan was to double back, because the kitchen seemed like a better idea than the theatre now.

If her people were here, it was time for war.

Adia was in front of the foyer doors when they were hauled open. A hot magenta monster stood there, pulsing like a wound around a burnt orange core. It was enormous, filling the doorway with giant pointed arms as it lumbered through. Rays beamed from the purple eyes, the ragged mouth hung open, and inhuman shrieks tore the air.

Adia tried to make it to the servants' hall door, but she missed it, and couldn't find it. The monster saw her and came for her. Its arms shrank, and a human hand grabbed her by the neck, lifting her off her feet. She kicked, clawed at the hand, grabbed the thumb and wrenched it backward. The monster roared and slammed her against the wall, the face stretching over her head in a blade of hot fury. Purple eyes glared down at her, and the mouth hung open in a shaking black gash.

In fear and panic, she thrashed at where she thought the flesh body would be: the face, the groin, everything she could reach to make it let her go. But instead of letting go, the other hand attached to her neck, and it pulled her away from the wall, letting her dangle in midair. She fought harder, unable to breathe, pulling at the fingers and trying to get her feet up to the human head.

The burnt orange surged. It burst through the magenta in blooms of fire, in ones and twos and many. The monster howled and staggered. One hand let go, and that arm flew wide. The face started shrinking, looking down at its chest where the blooms began to meld together. Adia hung in the air, clinging to the other hand, watching.

The 2D arms receded, the head receded, and the monster shrank down until it was small and tight around the core light. Once it did that, the magenta burned so hot it incinerated the orange. Bit by bit the orange disappeared, and Wharton's voice—it was Wharton—moaned and gasped as the monster ate him until he was gone.

The magenta grew again, and the monster brought the other hand back to Adia's neck. It squeezed, and the hideous face bulged toward her. Hot nubs dug into her neck. She grabbed at Wharton's thumbs again, but it only squeezed tighter, and she kicked and clawed until the edges of her vision collapsed inward and blood roared in her head.

Then Wolf leapt, snarling, teeth first onto Wharton's arm, pulling his hand off Adia, knocking him backward. The creature's purple eyes widened as it staggered…the jagged mouth appeared, blaring a horrible metallic screech. Eyes narrowing to slits, it threw Adia to the wall and thrust its arms forward, stretching them into spikes.

Wolf snarled and snapped like something possessed—she'd never heard him sound so terrifying. His turquoise light was on fire. The monster stabbed at him, but Wolf dodged and lunged under the arms to get to the body. Fabric ripped, liquid hit the floor, mouth roared.

One glowing arm swung and hit. Wolf backed away, growling, and lunged again. The other arm stabbed, making Wolf grunt and shift to the side. It stabbed again, deeper, and pierced Wolf's light.

Adia screamed. Wolf yiped and yiped, falling away, the monster's spike still in him. She could hear his struggles to get away, see the light in him jerk around, but he went down. The spike pulled out and the monster looked up and froze.

A roiling green and gold was coming through the door, and it must be Hellen because she had carapaz in her hand. Someone else was already firing a bullet—it made a path into where the burnt orange had been. Another followed into the head.

Wharton's monster shrieked, head growing tall and much wider, but also dimmer.

457

Beau shouted, and she saw his gold light passing in front of her. "Incoming!" he yelled, and fired laser pulses down the hall. A blue-green light followed him, doing the same. Shouts and fire were coming back.

Adia had hit the wall hard, landing on the floor. Hellen crossed away from her, behind Wolf, advancing on Wharton to draw his attention. Adia scrambled toward Wolf to drag him from underfoot.

A bright blue with a spinning yellow galaxy slipped in, lifted the big dog, and started pulling him away. "Door's to your nine, come on!" David said to her.

She pushed to her feet, but her dress was long and she got hung up stepping on it. Next to her, too close, the monster screeched. Adia glanced up. It had become distorted, stretched into a sideways U. Wharton's body must have fallen, pulling the monster to the side. Hellen moved in on it. Abruptly, it shrank, sucked back into its core. Her feet now free, Adia slowed to watch, mesmerized.

"We really should go," David's disappearing voice said.

But she couldn't drag herself from it.

After a second, the lurid magenta shot back out toward Hellen. Ducking, Hellen swung her knife arm up and swiped at an eye. It left a blue mark, and the head jerked back, the eye drooping. The gold in Hellen made little explosions.

"Let's go-o," David said, pulling her by the arm. He didn't have Wolf anymore, so Wolf must be safe. Watching Hellen as long as she could, Adia let herself be pulled away through the foyer door.

Chapter M.24

The monster's head was so wide, Hellen didn't know how she was going to cut it off. Sticking it in the eye wasn't going to be enough, like it was with the woman in the magnetrain tunnel. It's brain, or whatever, was too spread out. This 2Der had learned some new tricks, too. No telling what there might be besides arm spikes.

The head sucked back into Wharton's body. It would be jabbing out again any second, looking for a new host. Past it, Beau stood against the far wall, firing. Return fire shot up the hall. "Papa Bear! Eagle! Get to the foyer—secure the Beast!" she shouted. "Watch out for the monster!"

Beau backed along the wall, still firing. The creature lunged for him, but he dodged and moved past, and the monster retracted again. "Ogre's in the hall," he said. "I couldn't hit him. Eagle's sighting."

"Eagle! Get out! GET OUT NOW!"

Laser pulses streaked up the hall, scorching the paneling and taking chunks out of the corner that blocked her. Beau fired back, still moving toward the foyer doors. Rack came running, laser pulses pounding into his body armor. He was almost to her when one shot exploded the back of his head. Mid-step, he stumbled, pitched forward, and fell. He lay with his face turned toward her, both eyes open, forehead a charred mess of brains and hair.

Horrified, Hellen forced herself to turn back to Wharton's monster.

It was staying in longer this time, which might mean it was building up energy to go farther, and if she didn't back away, she'd become the latest in a long line of whatever-Tomius-Dagge-wants.

But she had another idea. Instead of backing away, she rushed forward. When the monster shot out of Wharton's head, she sliced the top off at the outset, right through the eyes. The top of the head fell backwards and dissolved, and the rest stuttered and went out.

Only Dagge and one pet left. Her rifle was trapped under Rack, though, and she needed it. Hellen crouched and ran to Rack's body. Laser pulses zipped through the air. Making herself as small as possible, she worked to disentangle the strap from the crossbow and pull the rifle out from under him.

Dagge yelled something, and the firing stopped.

Beau's strong hands heaved Rack up by the vest. "Let's do this in the foyer," he said, and hauled Rack's body with him as he backed through the door.

But Hellen stood where Rack had fallen. She could see Dagge walking toward her, maybe fifteen soldiers behind him, rifle cradled on his chest. When he saw her looking at him, he began to run.

She flipped him off hard—spread-fingered with both hands—and fled.

Chapter M.25

When David finally got Adia out into the foyer, she'd hurried to Wolf in a straight, quick line, exactly like she could see him. Wolf stood to greet her, which was great, since he hadn't looked so good a minute ago. No blood, though, just like Edren. Just like Dad when that thing took him in the dungeon. Different kind of damage.

David checked the empty foyer as he followed the Queen under the stairs, and kept an eye out while she held and loved her dog.

"Wolf, you are so brave. Thank you." She put her arms around him and tears edged her voice. "I'm deeply grateful you're okay." Wolf licked her face, and Adia stood and led him to David.

"I'm glad you're okay, too," he said. Should he put his arm around her? "You are okay, right?"

"Mostly."

"Can you see?" he whispered.

"I can see people's lights agai—"

Laser pulses flew through the door, and Beau came running in the middle of a firestorm, ducking and dodging to the side, toward them. "David! Get a strap ready!" he said, pulling a bundle of wide hemp straps out of a pocket and tossing them. "Your Majesty, are you all right?"

"Yes, Beau, I'm fine."

He nodded. "Good. Rack's been hit. David, as soon as we come back through, you need to strap those doors. We'll have pursuit."

"Yes, sir."

Beau ran back in. Strap in hand, David followed him to the double door and started closing the nearest one.

Beau backed through the open door, dragging Rack by the vest. He laid him respectfully under the stairs next to the bathroom wall.

When Hellen came running through the door, David closed it and strapped the handles.

Based on what was coming, they all really should get moving.

Chapter M.26

Tomius Dagge stopped at the body of his ex-general, ex-supersoldier, ex-living thing, Somebody Wharton. What was his first name? Did he even have one?

No sign of the 2Der. It would still be here if it had taken someone. Another one gone. Damn, the last one was Roger, and it wasn't worth a flat fuck.

All of it thanks to the female. Hellen? The dangerous one. The one he killed. How could it be her? How could she show up again when he put a hole in her heart?

Revenge, so sweet. Like the insides of her thighs. He could almost remember. Where did she go?

Soldiers swarmed around him like flies. Rattling the doors, buzzing down the hall and rattling more doors. Big flies.

His head swam—a buzz growing, not louder but more potent. He felt there and not there, floating in muted sound. Tracers followed everyone as they moved. Shouts became slow-motion. His rifle clattered to the floor with a slow sound like bells.

He lifted off the ground, feet dangling as he floated. His back arched, his head lolled back, and his mouth dropped open. The hall and the wall and the men became a desolate wasteland before him. Bodies littered the dirt. Filthy, starving people cried. In a single moment he could see the vulnerability of humankind. How they wouldn't survive. They'd live their sad, pointless lives craving meaning. Not getting it. Ever so earnest…and ever the sweeping wind destroys them. His sweeping wind. Ravaging the land. Raising him to Godhood.

Useless, the striving, the efforts to save the world. There would be no saving it.

His head swiveled. Things hovered in the ceiling. Faces looking down at him, judging. Interfering. Fuck them.

A soldier appeared next to him and said, "Overlord…" Only it sounded like it came down a long tunnel, and he was wondering over that when—

"Overlord!"

Sound came back in a snap, and time resumed.

"All the doors appear to be tied, sir. I've sent soldiers to the back of the castle via the east corridor."

What was he saying?

"They'll go from there up the main east hall. I can leave some people here to break through this door…do you want to wait?"

It hit him just right. "NO I DON'T WANT TO WAIT, YOU GODDAM MORON!" Dagge pushed the man back, pounding his chest until he fell on his ass.

Aiming a kick at his leg, Dagge walked to the wall in the general area of the servants' door and began to feel around for the hidden latch.

Chapter M.27

"Wait."

Surprised, David stopped trying to urge the Queen away to the east hall (in order to avoid regicide by whatever came through that door), and he and his anxiety joined her stubborn streak under the stairs instead.

After retrieving her gun from Rack's body, Hellen and Beau rushed over.

The Queen continued. "He's going to come through that servants' door in just a minute, and you two could get him right here, if you were so inclined."

"Can you see?" Hellen asked.

"I can see people's lights. Here." She tapped her solar plexus. "And all of the monsters. Dagge has one of those things in him, Hellen. It's taken him over. But it looks different from the others. It's three-dimensional, so he may be harder to kill.

"We can do it," Beau said to Hellen. "Please. I've wanted a shot at him for three fucking years, and I want it even more now."

"Then I need you to go ahead," she said to the Queen. "Take David and Wolf. I can't be worrying about you with a bunch of soldiers and Dagge coming through the door."

"One more thing. David…" She turned toward him. "Robert has a monster in him, too. He's fighting it. I think he poured coffee on Dagge to help me escape. Dagge was crazy furious, beat him, and had him taken to the dungeon."

Wow…a surprising rush of sympathy for Robert ached David's heart. "Mom might be down there by now. Do the servants know Robert has one?"

"Almost certainly," Hellen said.

"What are the chances your Mom would get close to him?" the Queen asked.

"Very high," David said. "Why?"

"Because Robert's light is burning it, and that monster might think your Mom looks like a good alternative." She turned to Hellen. "David and I will go on to the dungeon. Do you and Beau want to come with us, or fight whatever comes through that door?"

"You guys go, we'll take the do—"

The servants' door burst open, slamming the wall beside it, vomiting soldiers.

"David! Greeting Room door!" the Queen hissed, offering her hand. David grasped it as Hellen and Beau opened fire, running to the corner of the bathroom wall.

Hand in hand, David and the Queen ran full speed the other direction, keeping the stairs between them and the battle. Gunfire echoed around them. Wolf slipped on the slick floor. It took forever to reach the corner of the greeting room. When they did, David placed the Queen's hand on the wall and brought up his gun.

"There's nothing but clear wall between here and the door. I've got your six."

He backed along behind her, checking over his shoulder every so often to see how close they were. The door passed by him on the right. Did she miss it? Because across the foyer, behind the stairs, Hellen's back came into view. Damn.

Shouts rang dimly down the east hall.

"Did we just pass the door?" he asked over his shoulder.

"We're not going into the greeting room."

"You want to go outside?"

"Trust me," she said, and pulled the closet door open.

"You want to hide in the closet?"

"David…" She disappeared into the dark. "Come on, Wolf," she called.

David guessed that meant him, too.

Tuesday

Chapter T.1

Soldiers dropped without Hellen having to fire a shot. Beau piled them one after the other outside the door until they tumbled into the walkway. It was like having her own dragon; nothing got past him. She wanted to kick herself for not letting him be there all along.

The soldiers stopped coming, and the strapped doors rattled. There was a pause, then the strapped doors down the front wall rattled. Dagge's only option was the servants' hall door, and when he finally came through, he had a soldier in front of him, one hand on the collar and one on the belt. They moved fast, the soldier looking terrified, Dagge's eyes blazing purple.

Beau pulled out his handgun and fired round after round into the soldier's chest and neck. Blood splattered all over Dagge, and with a strangled cry the soldier went limp, his legs dragging. Dagge wrapped his left arm around the chest and held him up. With his right arm, he pulled up the soldier's rifle and began firing, trying to circle around and trap Hellen and Beau under the stairs.

They started backing out into the foyer raining hellsfire on him. Beau fired with both hands: pistol shooting bullets at Dagge's rifle to knock his aim off Hellen, and the other shooting laser fire, blowing pieces of Dagge's shield away.

Hellen went for Dagge's unprotected head. Several bullets dug trenches in his skull. They erupted with blood, and made Dagge's head rock backward. One eye was blasted into goo, his jaw was pulverized, but he didn't stop. Bright rays of magenta beamed out of him, blinding her aim. She blasted away at the shield in front of his heart to try and kill the monster, but she couldn't see his chest well enough to hit the right spot.

One of Beau's bullets hit Dagge's rifle hand and the rifle clattered to the floor. Hefting what remained of his shield with both hands, he ran at Hellen, both eyes flashing purple as he closed the gap between them.

Hellen shifted her gun behind her shoulder and released her knife. From a few feet away, Dagge shoved the dead soldier's body at her face and knocked her down. Beau dropped his rifle, holstered his pistol, and tackled Dagge. Rolling over him, Beau landed on the ground above Dagge's head, rammed his feet onto Dagge's shoulders and pulled Dagge's wrists high and tight.

Dagge lifted his legs over his head and flipped onto Beau, trapping Beau's head underneath him. Beau leveraged one leg and tried to flip Dagge over on his back, but Dagge pressed his chest onto Beau's face and worked to jerk his hands free. Leveraging his other leg, Beau rolled Dagge to the side, but Dagge had gotten his right hand free and went for his knife.

Hellen grabbed his arm, yanked it up, and held her knife to his throat. Dagge's big knife was in his hand, but he was afraid of the carapaz, and got still. Hellen straddled Dagge, forcing him onto his back. "Drop the knife, Dagge."

The purple in his eyes faded, the magenta beams stopped coming out of his head. He loosed his grip on his knife to two fingers, lowered it, and slid it across the marble a few feet.

Beau came around and pinned Dagge's right arm with his knee, then pulled his handgun back out of its holster and aimed it at Dagge's crotch with a smile.

Chapter T.2

Explosions concussed the windows of Adia's room when she and David and Wolf reached the top of the secret passage stairs. The glass rattled, and it felt and sounded like very heavy things were being thrown at the castle. Wolf's breathing beside her leg reassured her. Taking David's hand, she led both of them through the open panel into her room.

Gunfire echoed in the foyer—first laser, then bullets. Dagge must have come through the servants' door. Adia stopped by the bed, listening breathlessly for the shooting to end. She wanted to think this could be over, but thinking stuff like that had a way of biting idiots in the ass.

She didn't want to be that idiot.

"We should keep moving," David whispered. "The sooner we can get to the dungeon and out, the better."

"I want to check on Hellen and Beau. Real quick." Adia nodded, apparently agreeing with herself. Or maybe trying to convince both of them.

She navigated around the toy chest and to the door. Battle raged in the cavernous space beyond—bullets and lasers shooting madly, echoing off the marble. Adia reached for Wolf and found his head. "Stay back from the banister, okay?"

Adia felt her way forward, and looked down into the foyer from the side of the hall doorway. Hellen's green and gold was backing away, and Dagge's magenta appeared, advancing on her. Heart pounding, Adia ducked and ran to the pillar at the corner of the balcony. Squatting and peering between the posts, she watched Hellen's bullets make little trails in the monster's head...but they disappeared immediately. The monster didn't dodge, or jerk, or act like it felt the bullets at all, it just kept coming for Hellen.

It charged, the carapaz knife appeared, and Hellen stumbled backward and fell. Adia's fists flew to her mouth, thumbs pressing her lips. Bright gold flames raced out from under the stairs and flew at the monster, taking it to the floor. Beau and Dagge rolled and thudded, grunts echoed through the room. Beside her, a low growl took root in Wolf's chest.

Then a stream of lights poured onto the balcony from the hall on the other side of the ballroom. Lots of different colors, no red theme, so they had to be her people. One of them was that flashing blue and orange she'd seen going through the conference room door. Half a dozen lights positioned themselves along the railing facing the front doors.

Adia stood away from the pillar so she could be seen, and felt for Wolf, just in case. A teal and burgundy light started toward her along the front balcony. Wolf had stopped growling, so it must be okay.

Cary's voice whispered, "Roger, Cap. Ready for the onslaught." He clipped the walkntalk back on his belt. "What are you doing here? You're supposed to be going to the dungeon."

"We're on our way," David said behind her.

"What did you stop for? I thought Beast's safety was your job."

"Back off, Cary." Adia had had enough. "What I do is up to me."

Pounding started on the front doors below them, followed by laser fire hitting the wood.

"Yes, ma'am," Cary said, "but soldiers are coming back to the palace, and you need to get out of here now."

"We're going," Adia said, and reached for David, who took her hand.

"Which way?" David asked.

"Straight to the back." She gestured to the hall past the ballroom. "We can use the stairs in the servants' quarters."

"See you in the forest," Cary said, moving back the way he came.

Adia turned to follow David, Wolf at her heels.

As they ran toward the hall, she glanced down into the foyer and saw that Hellen was on top of Dagge, carapaz knife at his head. But Dagge's magenta looked strange. It wasn't a full-size human shape anymore; it was shrinking, collapsing at its extremities, curling up like a leaking balloon.

Maybe it was dying? Adia slowed, pulling back on David's hand, and they stepped to the banister to watch.

The magenta was pulsing, the brightness increasing instead of diminishing. Like Wharton's monster, Dagge's was gathering itself— strengthening and preparing for a fight.

But Hellen and Beau couldn't see that. Adia's mouth dropped open to scream.

Chapter T.3

Hellen felt pretty good, holding her knife to Dagge's throat, seeing him overpowered and reduced. He'd loomed so large in her life, in all their lives, for forever it seemed, even though it was only a few years. So much had changed because of him.

Would Adia want her to kill him? Right here, right now? Or would she want to be here? Have her final say? Funny they had never talked about that.

"HELLEN! RUN!!"

The scream snapped her attention. It was Adia, above them on the balcony.

What did she say? Run?

Beau looked at her, confused. "Do it, Hellen! We need to get out of here."

Dagge watched her from the floor. The purple was gone, and he looked like he used to.

"Help me, Hellen. It's killing me."

What the...?

A picture of John Treslo flashed into her mind, leaning over her on the stone steps, eyes glowing purple. She'd told herself it wasn't John, and she'd killed him.

Guilt grabbed her, shook her, squeezed until she couldn't breathe. All this time she thought the tragedy of what had happened in Great Hand, and Valdia, and Pulari was Tomius Dagge's fault, but maybe it wasn't. What if he was a victim?

There'd been good in him, she had to believe that. Could that person be saved? Kill the thing in him without killing him? Because she didn't know how many more people she could kill.

It had taken a toll.

Beau eyed her closely. She looked over at him.

"He's not going to stop if you let him live. It's why he's here."

The monks told her that. Dagge wouldn't stop. She'd die, her friends would die, Adia would die. Bombs and chemical weapons would be used everywhere Dagge wanted something. All it would take to protect the planet would be this one life.

As she started to press her knife into its neck, its left arm swung up, a magenta spear thrusting out of the hand toward her head. Instinctively, she blocked it with her knife hand, cutting the magenta partway through, knocking the arm back. The cut closed up immediately, which wasn't good at all, and the arm hit her like a club, knocking her sideways into Beau. Beau caught her, firing into Dagge's legs as the two of them toppled to the floor.

Dagge's trapped arm got free, and he pushed them down as he stood, driving Hellen onto Beau's firing arm. Sheathing her knife, Hellen rolled off Beau, grabbed her rifle, and pulverized Dagge's chest with hot metal, blasting a saucer-sized hole where his heart should be. From on his back, Beau emptied his clip, shredding Dagge's fancy uniform, blowing his neck wide open, and turning half his face to hamburger. Still he advanced. Blood flew, flesh hung, and he kept coming.

Its mouth dropped open and a screech pierced the air, wailing higher and louder until all the humans in the foyer had to put their hands over their ears. As the monster shrieked, it grew. Magenta boiled through Dagge's skin—giant pustules bulging and receding all over his body, his mutilated flesh disappearing and reappearing in between.

The screeching stopped, echoes fading in the enormous room. The boiling shrank and slowed until all that remained were the purple eyes and smooth magenta filling in the gaping holes in Dagge's body.

Dagge smiled, the remains of his teeth awash in blood. His eyes—one mostly human and one completely purple—swiveled up to the balcony. Hellen followed his gaze to see what he was looking at, but she already knew. Adia was up there. Hellen dropped her rifle, released her knife again, and lunged at Dagge's head.

But Beau caught her from behind. "Hand-to-hand will only get us dead."

The monster laughed—a sound like sand on metal. It spoke with that same sound. "You can't kill me; you should know that by now. I'm a god. Your puny weapons are pointless."

It stretched its neck and loosened its shoulders the way she'd seen Tomius Dagge do a hundred times. That was when she understood there was no separation between the monster and the man. Dismissing her, it made for the grand staircase at a fast clip.

"Let's get the Queen out of here," Beau said, snatching their rifles off the floor as he pulled her away. She glanced up at the balcony as they ran, but no one was there.

Chapter T.4

Adia had met Dagge's eyes. After all the boiling and blistering and shrieking, after the jagged mouth smiled, the eyes had rolled up and found where she was standing. The purple glowed brightly, magenta filled the human form, and dread washed over her. She could be certain it would come.

"David!"

"I'm right here," his voice said above her right shoulder. "Ready to go?"

"Yes."

They were turning for the hall when the snapping blue and orange light jumped up from behind the banister and ran toward Cary on the front side of the balcony. Firio's voice was tight with urgency. "Soldiers are running down the east side. Many of them. I saw them through the big window."

"Damn, they're headed for the back," Cary said. "We need to get to the south end, but I don't know the palace."

"Come with us!" she called to him. "I know my way around."

Cary let his people go in front of him, just like Beau would've done. "Oh, shit, don't look now, but Ogre is headed our way." His teal and burgundy were sparking.

"We should get a move on," David said.

"Let's use the royal suites hall," she replied. "We'll access the servants' hall from there."

Wolf beside her, she reached for David's warm hand, and they ran.

Chapter T.5

Roberta's hands shook as she sprinkled the red pepper into tissue paper squares and tied them to firepoppers. Across the table, Vartile poured pickled pepper juice into tiny rubber balloons and tied them to more firepoppers. Up and down the long kitchen table, servants and Resistance fighters—all Resistance fighters, really—made firepopper bombs, strapped the remaining knives and forks to outdoor grill racks, and attached hoses to cans full of hot cooking oil. All to protect the palace.

Hellen had told her about the secret passage out of the kitchen. She said it was accessible from the laundry room, too, and the spa, and let outside. Just in case the people needed it. Roberta hadn't told anyone yet, because it didn't seem right to tell palace secrets unless she had to. Hopefully she wouldn't have to.

Robert was in the dungeon. He had one of those things in him, Cookie said, and he wasn't doing too well. The time would come when his mother could help him, but it wasn't yet. How she'd help him was still in question.

She set her pepper bomb aside and clenched and unclenched her hands.

Vartile watched her, compassion in her eyes. "The important variable is that he's away from Dagge."

"Yes."

"Dagge can't use him, or hurt him now."

"Yes." Roberta nodded. They'd told her Dagge had beat Robert, and that Robert had probably helped Adia escape. Hopefully that was true. She clenched and unclenched, then dabbed at her sweaty top lip with the back of her hand.

She and Firio had strapped the south doors, but it took a key to lock the exterior dungeon door, so the soldiers could get in there, once they thought of it. Whenever they did, two racks of knives and meat forks already blocked access to the kitchen, anchored with chains so they couldn't be moved from the hall.

Some of the servants had guns, and although three of them went with Cary earlier, a few remained. Two went with Luhe. Two of them planned to shoot from behind the dumbwaiters if they had to. One guarded the servants' stairs, along with firepopper throwers, and hot oil pourers, and they had blocked the staircase with a stack of beds.

Two of the apprentice cooks had invented and tested the firepoppers much earlier, and they worked, but it took a lot of them. Hence what she and Vartile and a bunch of the others were doing now.

The soldiers had tried to come in the kitchen door a few minutes ago, but Marly had poured oil on the stone outside the door, laid a string of firepoppers in it, and run the fuse under the door. When they got to the porch, they slipped in the oil, she set the firepoppers off, and a fire started. Cookie hunkered by the window, peering out, holding a fire extinguisher, but she wouldn't let anyone open the door. One soldier shot the window, but the laser pulse just bounced off the glass, and the soldiers decided to try something else.

Once the soldiers got in through the dungeon, they'd cut the strap on the south doors and flood the castle. She and Firio had strapped all the other double doors, too—most of them on both sides, so that would slow them down. For a little.

Several more knife and fork racks waited by the main kitchen door.

She sure hoped they'd gotten Adia away.

Roberta grabbed another tissue paper square, but dropped it when the crash came from the dungeon.

Chapter T.6

The balcony had emptied, but he knew the place she would go. She and that wolf. She and that wolf and those weak underlings. It desired to cast its power upon them.

His step felt light. Even with the body a damaged wretch. No matter. Could he change it for a new one? He was not like the others, the ones from the portal.

He was better. Stronger.

Unstoppable.

Joy consumed him. Lifted him. Made him sparkle.

He didn't need a new body. Let the world observe his magnificence and feel envy.

Chapter T.7

The servants' hall was filled with lights. Blue, pink, lava, smoky topaz—they were lavish. Sparking, flaming, pulsing, whirling. Thrilling to look at.

Adia turned to the nearest one, which was pink, and spoke while David, Wolf, Cary, and the others filed in behind her. "What's everyone doing?"

A young female voice whispered, "We're helping the Queen."

Adia's breath caught in her throat. "I'm the Queen," she said, extending her hand toward the girl. A little gasp squeaked out, and after a confused moment, the girl's fingers met her own.

"Your Majesty, I'm sorry, I—I—"

"It's okay, I've been gone a long time, I know."

"Yes, ma'am. We've all been so worried about you. Mister Luhe!" she whispered loudly down the hall. "Mr. Luhe!"

"Your Majesty!" That was Luhe's voice. His core was the smoky topaz, and as he moved, it lit with rainbow facets like a cut gem. Others moved toward her as well, until a crowd of lights surrounded her.

"Everybody back up a little, okay? We're running out of oxygen." As Luhe loosened the pack, Cary spoke to her ear.

"We don't have time for this, we need to get to the kitchen, and the dungeon, right now. Dagge's not going to take a break just because we disappeared. The soldiers aren't either!"

"You think I don't know that?" Adia worked to keep the irritation out of her voice. "These people matter, Cary. I will not treat them like they don't. At some point we may owe them our lives."

"In other words, shut up," David grumbled. Adia pressed him with her shoulder.

Once the group had settled some, she said to the crowd, "We need to get to the dungeon, and I want Dagge to follow us down there."

Mumbles of surprise and protest swept the people, but Luhe quieted them. "Sshh, listen!"

"Don't worry, I have a plan for Dagge," she said. "But we need you to stop the soldiers. We think they'll be coming from the back, and the strapped doors won't hold them for long. I need you to slow them down and do whatever you can to keep them off us until we get out. Stay hidden. You know the palace, most of the soldiers do not. Use the hidden halls and doorways, stay safe."

"Don't you worry about the soldiers," Luhe said. "We'll stop them long enough for you to get away."

Chills raced over her, and again Adia was grateful for the people she knew.

"If Dagge's going to be following us, I'd like to have a decoy of you. Just in case," Cary said.

"That's a great idea," David agreed, stepping forward. "That incredibly beautiful dress glows in the dark."

Adia had forgotten she had it on. After all that planning and worry, too. She should have left it in a puddle outside the dining room doors, melted like a wicked witch. That would have been satisfying.

"I'll just take it off. That's what I meant to do." She lifted the skirt, turned around because too many people, and began to pull the dress up. Patsie helped from the top.

"Your Majesty, I will decoy for you." Firio's voice came forward.

Of everyone she knew, he would be the perfect choice. She remembered him from her one self-defense class—not much bigger, medium brown skin, dark hair, and way more athletic.

Patsie lifted the dress off her head. Adia took it, tugging her shirt down as she turned back to the crowd. "No moustache these days, Firio?"

"No, Ma'am. Or sideburns. They outgrew me." The grin in his voice tickled her. "And I can take my shirt…"

481

He rustled and moved, and David chuckled beside her. "The neck of his shirt is around his head, and the rest is hanging down his back like hair."

Adia chuckled and handed him her dress. Judging by his movement, he put it on.

"It will be perfect, ma'am. That monster will only see my back, from a distance, and never know it's not you. If he has a gun or a knife, I can move out of the way better than anyone."

"What if he has crazy, bizarro spike arms?" David asked.

"Let's find out," he said.

"Thank you, Firio." She reached her hands toward him, and he grasped them and shook them once. "Cary, get Hellen on the walknta—"

Behind them, a scrape grated across the wall, loud and skin-crawling, capped by a shrieking roar.

They panicked and ran.

Chapter T.8

It stood at hall's end, willing itself to feel the direction of the vermin (it's pleased to have named them. his privilege as the god he is). The damaged body felt heavy now. The eyes and ears were near useless. Far below the all-range of frequencies. And the pants were too tight.

It fed attention outward, reaching down halls, around the balcony. Heat started in the belly and pushed out. He looked down. A hundred little tentacles stuck out of the arms, shoulders, body. They waved in the air like those things in the ocean that catch and sting others to eat.

And it could feel the vermin! Not far, just past that wall. Many, many of them. And her, too. The one who humiliated him.

Anger changed the feelers, sucking them into the heavy body, and pushing the arms into long, pointed blades. Excellent. It stepped to the wall and swiped, shaving off wood. Rock underneath hissed at the touching. The blade scrapes long and hard, and breaks, the tip flying and disappearing mid-air. Fucking stone! He screeches at it, strains his left hand to be a big…badass…motherfucking…hammer.

But no…

The vermin were running.

Chapter T.9

"Stop! Everybody stop!" Adia held her hands up and watched the lights ahead trail into stillness. "Let's not panic. Dagge will be expecting us to go to the dungeon, and the quickest way there is the way we're going. He'll know that, and will expect us to do this very thing. We can't afford to give him the time or place to ambush us. He's...no longer human. We saw what he is, but it's too hard to explain right now.

"Soldiers will be coming up the halls. My team will draw Dagge away from you, and them, and run him on our terms. This is our best chance to defeat him. With all of us. Anyone who's here to help by holding the soldiers back, thank you." Shouts and pops could be heard in the back of the palace. A scream, followed by gunfire. "Now is the time for courage."

Adia held her hands up, palms together, and opened them outward over her people. As they ran back down the way they came, she could hear Luhe behind her.

"We need groups at all three doors. I'll be with the group at the first door, and will signal when soldiers are spotted. Group One will deploy pepper bombs to slow them down, Group Two will man the wires to thin them out, and Group Three has the rifles to stop them."

His voice faded as Adia's group reached the last door on the right and slipped out into the hall.

Chapter T.10

Hellen was leading Beau through the last royal bedroom door when Adia opened the servants' door opposite.

"Hellen!" Adia rushed over to hug her, bumping Hellen's nose with her hand because of course she couldn't see Hellen bending. It reminded her of when Adia was little, running into door jambs, smacking furniture, all elbows and knees. Back when her life wasn't on the line. When all their lives weren't.

Hellen's heart ached. Nothing to be done about it.

"How did you guys get away?" Adia asked.

"Conference room. Thank One for all the secret passages."

"Hells yes. I'm glad you're safe. Luhe's got a contingent in the servants' hall. They'll keep the soldiers back while we get Dagge to follow us to the dungeon. Firio will decoy me in the middle of the pack, and I'll be in front with you, if you're in."

Firio's dress glimmered in the dim light of the hall. "We're taking Dagge to the forest? Where our people are?"

"We're taking him to the tear."

Of course they were. Send him back to the hellshole where he belonged, because there'd be no getting rid of him otherwise. "I'm in," she said.

"Beau?"

"Always. I'll take rear guard."

Hellen took a good look at the people who had come through the door. David, Wolf, and Cary made a shield around Adia's backside. Patsie and a few others with guns stood behind them. Hellen nodded their direction, grateful.

"Would my arm be helpful?"

Shouts echoed faintly down the hall. Soldiers were coming up the stairs.

Adia nodded. "How about your hand? It'll make it faster."

Hellen took Adia's proffered hand in hers. "Let's go get him," she said, and they headed for the foyer.

Chapter T.11

Hellen peeked around the edge of the open foyer doors and found herself face to face with the last place Tomius Dagge had his tongue in her mouth. Her eyes closed, her head shook the tiniest bit, and she never wanted to think about that again.

"Are you okay?" Adia asked behind her. "Your light went…flat for a second."

"I'm okay." Hellen answered, opening her eyes. "Just remembering." She shook it off, and led the group into the cavernous foyer toward the back side of the balcony.

When she spotted Dagge, he had his back to them, far down the dark hallway, just standing there. Magenta glowed around him, so he must be looking at himself, or maybe he was practicing that neat bubbling trick. *(Watch this, Mom!)*

Hellen gestured everyone to crowd into the corner by the hidden door. "I'm going to get his attention. We need three of you to surround Firio and Wolf, and several more behind. When you run across the hall, Dagge will be looking. But he doesn't have a gun, and any freaky hand spears shouldn't be able to reach you."

"I'll go with Firio," Cary said. The rest of Cary's team also volunteered.

Beau was the last to say. "I should go with the Queen. Soldiers will be coming up the kitchen side, too."

"We can take the servants' hall downstairs instead of the main hall," Adia said, "the soldiers aren't likely to know it."

Firepoppers started going off upstairs, the noise drifting around the corner through the open doors behind them.

"Let's get you across the hall," Hellen said to Adia.

She looked at Firio.

"I will know when to run," Firio said. "Trust me."

Helen clapped his shoulder, and moved Adia into position.

"Where's Wolf?" Adia asked suddenly.

David stepped aside so she could see. "He's beside Firio. I think he knows what we're doing."

Hellen looked back. Wolf was standing by the gold dress, mouth closed, watching them intently.

Adia blew him a kiss and he snapped on the air like he caught it.

Damn, things were getting crazy.

Adia held out her hand to David. "Let's go."

After checking to make sure Dagge's back was still turned, Hellen waved them across the hall. He didn't respond at all when they ran, and they made it halfway past the ballroom before Hellen stepped out to yell down the hall.

"Tomius Dagge, why won't you DIE?!" With that she opened fire, sauntering into the hallway, round after round hitting the wall and punching holes in the back of his jacket.

He turned toward her and she could see what he'd been looking at—enormous, glowing magenta hands, flashing and sparking with power. He held them up, as if to show her, and they lighted up what was left of his face.

It was horrible. His cheek and jaw hung in tatters, his remaining eyeball dangled and swung. In all the holes, glowing magenta, except for the purple eyes and black swamp mouth.

He couldn't repair. That was good. With a little effort, they might be able to shoot Dagge's entire body away.

In the meantime, the magenta fill looked dim compared to the hands, and the barest purple glowed in the eyes. The monster looked tired, which struck her as strange. Out of all the 2Ders she'd tracked and killed for the last eighteen months, not one of them had ever looked tired. Welcome to 3D, asshole.

If the hands, or spears, or whatever he used, took energy from the rest of it, well, time to wear that freak out.

Firio and the others crossed to the ballroom corner at a full run. Hellen pretended to try and block them from Dagge's view, firing as they crossed.

The glow in the hands stuttered and the purple eyes flashed. He stumbled forward, legs apparently weak, hands sinking. Stopping, it opened its mouth and roared.

The hands came up again. Dagge stared at them, jaw hanging. They spread wide apart and he looked down at his legs. After a few seconds, the hands began to flicker and shrink, and new magenta legs began to grow. Thick, and long, they raised him up, his own legs dangling to the knees in front of them.

"Run!" she yelled over her shoulder. "It's got legs!" she cried, firing down the hall, not caring whether she hit him because at this point it didn't matter.

It was coming.

Chapter T.12

Firepoppers were going off behind them and in front of them. It sounded like gunfire coming up the hall from the kitchen. Or maybe it was gunfire, Adia couldn't be sure.

"Down the stairs," she said to Hellen, who had taken her left hand. David had her right hand, Beau's equipment rattled behind, and an army of feet thundered the carpet, then the marble as they fled.

The monster started shrieking, closer than it should be, gaining on them fast.

"We're almost to the bottom," David said. "Three more steps." He jumped, anchoring her until she made it. "You're there."

"Around the bathroom," she told Hellen, who led her to the left. David and Beau stayed tight on their heels, rounding the corner with them, into the narrow passage between the ladies' room and the theatre.

Firio, Cary, Wolf, and the others ran in. The smell of blood was strong, reminding Adia of the firefight earlier. How could she have forgotten? The door to the servants' hall was probably surrounded by bodies. It sounded open—she could hear shouts and screams and laser fire.

She turned to David. "Can you see him yet?"

He stepped away, and leaned out into the foyer. Laser fire from the other side of the foyer pocked the theatre wall. David jerked back and retreated. "He's out on the balcony, looking down. There are also soldiers coming out from the east hall."

Cary spoke. "My team can hold the soldiers back while you draw Dagge." His people parted, going to either side of the bathrooms and opening fire.

"Dagge doesn't know where we went," Hellen said. He may not come down."

"He's got to see Firio." Adia twisted her hair up and made a knot, hoping it would stay for at least a few minutes.

Laser pulses streaked through the hall door and went past them so close that Adia felt the air move. Hellen pulled her to the side, saying, "Time to go."

David's hand encircled her arm, and pulled her toward the front of the castle. She looked over her shoulder into the foyer as she ran, hoping not to be shot.

Dagge's monster had jumped from the balcony. It dropped from way overhead and landed on the marble floor, cracking it with the force of its massive legs. The soldiers, who had hidden behind corners and pillars and furniture, loaded it with laser fire and horror. The monster reveled in the pulses that hit it, and its dim magenta brightened until it shot beams through all the holes in Dagge's body. It held its hands up, roared, and turned to them.

Shouting and screaming, the terrified soldiers fell over themselves and each other to run back the way they had come.

Chapter T.13

David only glanced back once when the scary, fucked-up monster landed with a crackling thud on the marble. He'd taken the initiative and grabbed the Queen's hand and Firio's hand, and run with them to the theatre door. No point in waiting around when the laser fire was coming from two directions.

David released Firio's hand and opened the door. Behind them, Hellen started shooting, and the crashing footsteps got closer. David held the door until Beau took his place, nudging him on. But David couldn't stop staring. Magenta dripped from the monster's thighs like lava. It hunched forward, walking like those giant birds in prehistory, little human legs swinging across the front of it.

Yikes.

Hellen backed in past him, and Beau closed the door. Just to piss it off, probably, since a little door wasn't going to stop it.

"I think there's a light switch on the wall," Hellen said in the immediate blackness.

But David couldn't help her out because the Queen was pulling him along, his toes stubbing on the seat mounts. "Let's not turn on the overheads," she said. "Firio, link up, stay as close as you can. Hellen, Beau, you too. These are simply rows of seats; run your hand along the top. We're headed for the main aisle."

David marveled at her. Fearless and brilliant. Confident, adaptive.

Along with the dark, and the monster chasing them, and the threat of death around every corner, she scared him a little.

Chapter T.14

Hellen held Firio's hand, and Beau's, as they threaded through the seats. They reached the main aisle and Adia ran them to the stage. Hellen kept glancing back toward the faint rim of light around the door, and when Dagge crashed into it she spun around and walked backward with her gun up. Beau did the same. Not that it would stop the monster from coming, but they might slow it down.

The door splintered and shook. At the next hit, cracks of light appeared, and the next one sent shards and splinters flying. By then they were at the stage, and the others were climbing up onto it instead of trying to make the stairs on the sides. Hellen was just about to make the climb when the door flew open.

All she could see were the enormous legs. The head bent down, peering below the top of the door and roaring. Then the head disappeared upward and the legs began to flicker.

"I've got your six," Beau said, holding steady aim with his pistol.

Hellen hoisted herself onto the stage and shouldered her rifle. "I've got you," she said to Beau, and he followed her up. Onstage, they backed away, Hellen looking for Adia over her shoulder.

Outside the door, the legs were shrinking. Dagge's body came into view, then his head. He stepped through the door and stopped, looking for them. The glow in the gaping wounds beamed, magenta lighting up the seats and wall around it.

Adia was talking to David just behind the proscenium. They'd turned on a tiny light at a lectern and were examining the wall. "Look for five switches that say 'work lights.'" She reached her hand out and pulled Hellen, then Beau, backstage. "Now flip the top two."

The stage flooded with light. "Are they on?" Adia asked.

"Holy cow, it's blinding," David said.

"We're going to follow the back wall to the lift—it's center left from here. Hellen, Firio, we need you to run where you're just visible. Beau, contact Vartile and let everybody know we're coming. And what to expect."

Adia's gesture to the seats turned all their heads. Dagge was standing in the seats, magenta spears thrusting forward from his hands. They all watched in horrified fascination as he stabbed into the spaces between the seats, lifted his body into the air, and vaulted over them to the stage.

"Let's go let's go!" David hissed, urging Adia into the darkness.

Hellen took Firio's hand and they ran along the edge of the curtain legs, catching Dagge's eye as he landed on the boards. The monster loosened its neck *(did it even need to do that?)* and raised its spears to the sides, narrowing and shortening them into long blades— not a smooth or fast transition, but faster than before. Which didn't look good for any of them.

Hellen and Firio rounded the back curtain. Adia and David had reached the lift; Adia waved at her while backing farther down the wall. She waved at Beau, too, who was behind, whispering into his walkntalk.

"Don't know yet. Tell Cary to have both halls manned, keep soldiers clear. Ogre will be right behind us." Vartile's voice said something unintelligible and Beau clipped his walkntalk on his belt.

With a screech, the monster began slicing through the back curtain. Darkness parted in huge swathes. They all ducked, and Adia nodded at David, who pressed the button. At a run, she led them to the next door and they disappeared into Props and Costumes.

"He knows we're going to the dungeon," Adia said in a low voice, navigating around the sewing machine tables to the right of the door with her hands out. "But maybe he'll think we've taken the lift to get away. We need to slow him down, he's too close. These are small spaces back here, it'll be hard for him to get around and use his...weapons."

Hellen and Beau changed their clips while she talked. The magenta glow outside the door was increasing.

"I'll take David and Firio to the servants' hall. Beau, if you'll stay—"

"I'll stay," Hellen said. "Beau needs to go with you."

Adia paused. "All right. When the lift stops, make a loud noise and run. Please run."

"I will, I promise."

Just one thing first.

"David, the do—" Adia was pointing to the back corner when Hellen realized she could see her clearly.

The thing that had stepped into the doorway was unlike anything they'd seen before. Glowing magenta tentacles stuck out all over Dagge's body. They were probably a foot-length and waved in the air, alive. Hellen could see the eyeball hanging on his face by the light of the tentacle coming out of his jaw. And the one at his temple. The purple eyes were dim in comparison. She backed between two costume racks.

"Run!" she said, and the others took off for the back door, weaving through shelves and around tables, David in the lead. Beau lagged, wanting to wait for her. "I'm right behind you," she said, and he went, too.

The monster took several steps into the room, feelers reaching out, searching. Hellen sank a bullet in one purple eye. The monster screeched and a clump of tentacles pointed her direction.

Hellen stepped out from between the costumes, rifle raised, and walked slowly toward Dagge. The glowing, waving, total freak parts were making aim difficult, but after one lucky shot, Dagge's dangling eye exploded in a little fountain of blood. The creature shrieked and shoved Dagge's hands forward. The tentacles shrank, moving the glow through the body, down the arms, and out the hands, which grew in bursts until they were the size of wagon wheels.

Dagge made fists, held them in front of him, and advanced.

Chapter T.15

"That way," Adia said. The small hall they were in had a way to go upstairs, a way to go outside, and a way into the servants' hall. Adia pointed to the door that opened to the servants' hall and they hurried toward it. "See if it's clear." She looked back—Beau was waiting for Hellen, who ran through so fast she lost her balance, crashed into the door jamb, and Beau had to pull her into the hall by her arm. Staring into the costume room, he closed the door in a hurry.

"We'll see if he can work a doorknob with those hands," Beau said, rattling up beside Hellen.

"It's got giant hands now," she said. "I shot his better-than-nothing eye, too…he might be pissed."

The door splintered behind them. Beau turned to face it, gun raised.

At the servants' hall door, Adia could hear fighting at the kitchen end—laser pulses, bullets, firepoppers, shouts and screams. A lot of it sounded farther away, down the south hall.

The people she loved were fighting, risking their lives. Anxiety clutched her ever harder.

"The hallway's got overhead lights on," David told her. "I don't see anyone at the kitchen end."

"At the foyer end?"

"No."

Adia moved to pass him.

"Me first," Hellen said, passing her and David both. They all followed, the door to the costume shop breaking up as they slipped into the servants' hall. Beau closed the hall door and their little team got moving quickly in the narrow passage.

Like the servants' hall upstairs, and the one in the back by the dungeon door, an entire wall had been covered in storage space—all the cabinets, drawers, and stand-by shelves a person could want. In this one, the whole center section consisted of floor-to-ceiling cupboards for the massive curtains used in the ballroom, dining room, and throne room. Three doors opened for each cupboard: one at floor level, a mid-door, and one up high. Ladders could be pulled down from the ceiling and rolled along a track embedded in the wood. Adia had climbed the ladders many times, but only once all the way to the top. Being so high had made her heart pound, much like it was doing now.

More gunfire and laser fire erupted in the echo of the kitchen. Glass shattered, things crashed, there was shouting. It sounded like Cookie's heavy tables were moved, and something was pushed over. Her outraged tirade rose over all of it in unintelligible fury.

Laser pulses went off in the hub at the end of the hall: Hellen stopped running; David stopped; and so did Firio and Wolf.

Beau closed in behind her, putting his hand on her shoulder, talking into his radio. "Roger that. I'll tell Beast."

"Tallulah!" Adia called, and the others returned. They huddled in the dim light, halfway down the hall, listening to Beau as Dagge's monster pounded on the door they just came through.

"Soldiers have taken the kitchen, demanding to know where Dagge is. They think we have him. Cookie and a couple of servants are trapped in there. The soldiers have set up a guard in the hall and Resistance fighters on the south side have been overpowered."

Another pound on the backstage door, and splintered shards hit the floor.

Adia seethed. "They want to see him? We can show them who he is."

The door shattered. Adia watched in horror as two monstrous, glowing fists punched through the broken wood. Pieces thumped to the floor in the hall.

A cabinet door squeaked open and Hellen urged everybody over behind it. Adia found herself with her back to the open cabinet and

Hellen's hand on her arm. "We've got to lead him the shortest way, but we can't risk taking you into the kitchen. I'll radio Cary and Luhe and round up everyone I can. Firio, you'll be with me. Adia, I'm asking you to get in the cabinet just for a minute. Follow us when the shooting stops."

"I'll go with Firio," David said, and moved close. "You stay with the Queen—"

"David…" Adia said.

"She's best able to protect you."

Wolf started growling and Adia peeked around the door; the giant fists had become giant legs, coming down the hall toward them.

"We better do something quick," David said, and his hand squeezed her arm. "See you soon," he whispered, then stepped away, Firio with him.

"Take Wolf and Beau," Hellen said, "it's got to look real."

"It should be you if you want it to look real," Beau said. His gear rattled and his warm hand lifted Adia's. "I'd be honored to be your escort, Your Majesty."

"Accepted," she said.

His hand squeezed hers. "I'll radio Swamp Witch and we'll get you to the tear in time, I promise."

"Come on, Wolf." Hellen cupped her cheek, and Adia felt a surge of that old worry, that old fear. Wolf's nose nuzzled her hand and they were gone. Despite everything she had to lose, she didn't say anything as the waving green and gold and the bright turquoise ran off down the hall.

Adia stepped up into the cabinet and let Beau close the door.

Chapter T.16

Through the cabinet wall, Adia could hear Beau talking into his radio but she couldn't hear what he was saying. Out in the hall, Hellen's bullet rifle went off at intervals, setting off a pop and a tinkle of glass that got dimmer with each one. She was shooting the lights, which was smart. Not only to make them harder to see, but to keep the monster's attention.

The heavy footsteps pounded closer and closer, vibrating the stone, shaking the wooden doors. Beau stopped talking.

Outside her door the running stopped. Aside from the fading pops, all was quiet. Adia backed farther into the velvet Winter Festival curtain and held her breath. The air seemed to hum and crackle, and the door of her cabinet began to squeak.

Chapter T.17

When Beau shouted, Adia shot out of the cabinet and ran as fast as she dared—one hand brushing the cabinet doors and the other out in front of her because she didn't know where a ladder might be. Behind her, Beau was firing his gun over and over, but they all knew bullets weren't going to kill it.

The monster screeched and wailed, and Adia almost felt sorry for it, until she heard a crash and a thud and Beau grunting. He shouted "Go Go Go!" running up behind her. "Ladder in three steps," he said, passing her. "Climb on."

She did, swinging up on one foot, Beau pulling the ladder down the hall as fast as it would go. Garbled noises followed them, angry and stumbling. She looked back (aren't you not supposed to do that?). The monster stayed close, running on normal legs this time, magenta burning low, every thud of its feet stuttering its power. Its ragged mouth hung open. Another grating screech filled the narrow space.

The ladder stopped, jerking her back, caught by Beau who pulled her around the side and into a space that could only be in front of the door. Adia frantically felt the wall for the hidden latch, but Beau bumped into her, pushing her against it. She swiveled and faced the monster.

It was at the ladder, magenta arms waving. The cabinets were deep, but not more than arm's length, and the ladder only allowed a few extra fingertips. A glowing hand thrust at Adia's face, grasping and clawing, stretching to reach her. Beau rammed the ladder onto the other one, trapping the monster's right side between the ladder and the cabinet. The monster roared and struggled, flailing its good arm at Beau, the magenta hot in its head but getting dimmer everywhere else.

Adia ducked and searched for the latch again. She frantically ran her hand along the moulding, glancing over her shoulder every few seconds. Panic surged when she caught it glaring at her.

It knew who she was.

By then it had gotten its trapped arm around Beau's head or neck, and judging by the banging of the ladder, Beau was having a hard time keeping it trapped. The monster's free arm reached for her again; she slammed herself into the corner, pressing her back to it, trying to get herself out of its reach.

The glow in the head traveled down the neck, through the arm, to the hand. As the glow increased, the hand extended.

"Get down!" Beau said, and grabbed at the arm while Adia sank into a squat. But when he grabbed, the ladder moved, and the monster shifted. The shift freed the trapped arm a little, but it also freed Beau, who shoved the ladder back into place, folded that arm around the ladder and held it with his body.

But the free hand stretched, pulling the glow from the rest of the monster. Still a hand, it pawed at her arm, clothes, and hair. She knocked it away, fought with it, but it came back and grabbed her, trapping her wrist. The glow increased, the heat on her skin felt scalding and she panicked, thrashing and crying out, prying at the fingers.

Beau lashed at the arm with his knife. The cuts went through it, and the thing bellowed, but the gashes mended themselves and the glow kept increasing.

The door opened behind her.

Chapter T.18

Two hot, purple eyes met Roberta's when she opened the door, and she froze. She hadn't seen one of these before—magenta glowing through the bloody holes in Dagge's face and body. The thing was terrifying: all piercing screeches and gore. What was left of the mangled flesh hardly looked like Tomius Dagge.

Behind her, Vartile yelped and nudged her aside, looking for the Queen. She found her squatting in the corner to the right of the door. Vartile grabbed the glowing hand and wrenched the thumb out, releasing Adia's arm. Then she shielded Adia with her body, ignoring the hand grabbing her clothes and hair, gathering the Queen to them. Roberta took the shaking girl and pulled her to safety. Vartile tried to follow, but the monster had her by the hair. She turned back and shoved her walkntalk antenna into its eye.

It shrieked and roared and punched the empty space where Vartile used to be. The hand faded, and the glow began to burn in Dagge's face.

Outside the door, Vartile tried to gather Beau, who wrestled the monster for the ladder. It held its face away and fought Beau with its free arm. Beau sliced at any part of it he could, putting all his weight and strength into keeping the right arm trapped.

"Beau, come on!"

"Get away first! It's going to come after us!"

The monster shrieked louder and began to push its head through Dagge's hair and flesh. Magenta came out in pops, forehead bulging between the rungs, overlarge and tumorous-looking. The eyes followed it, rolling independently of each other.

Moving upward, the glow concentrated in the bulging forehead. Dim now, the body began to come through: a leg, then one side of the torso pushed out of the flesh and between and through the rungs, and the free arm dropped Dagge's arm, which swung down and back. Roberta shoved Adia behind her and backed away.

The jaw passed through the rung. The mouth opened, screeching, and Roberta could see the rung inside. Beau tried to fight the monster back, but his knife passed through it, going into the head and arm and body with no damage. In a moment, the entire left side of the monster was through the ladder.

And the freer it got of Dagge's corpse, the brighter it glowed. The monster's eyes were locked onto Roberta's, the open mouth stretched into a smile like Tomius Dagge's, and a high-pitched laugh sliced the air. The arm reached for her.

Beau shoved the ladder, catching the half of the body that hadn't separated and throwing it off balance. "Go!" he shouted.

But none of them made a move to run; it was like watching inevitable death.

The separated half was glowing bright now, and the waving arm bumped against the ladder, unable to move through. Surprised, the monster tried to step forward, then backward, then just to free itself from the rungs, but it was stuck.

Furious, it squinted its eyes and the end of its free arm began to glow fiercely.

David appeared on one side of the ladder and Hellen appeared on the other. David yanked Dagge's attached arm behind him, and started to haul the ladder away from the door. Wolf snarled, and growled, and helped David, pulling on the corpse with a mouthful of tattered coat. Dagge's dead body lost its feet, and the weight pulled the monster backward, stretching the magenta hooked around the rungs, and the monster roared while the entire mess was dragged down the hall, loose body parts flopping.

"Hellen, he knows I'm me," the Queen said, leaning forward. "I could tell by the way he looked at me."

Hellen nodded. "I'll tell Firio. Want me to save your dress?" she asked with a smile.

"Nah. Just your own hide."

"We're going to put that horror where he belongs, Adia. Go to the forest with Vartile and the rest. Beau and I will take him through the tunnel. Yes, Beau?"

"Yes, Hellen."

"I'll meet you in the dungeon. See you in the forest, Adia," she said, and followed after David.

"Can you see?"

Roberta's true blue was very much like David's, minus the yellow galaxy. Adia found that reassuring for some reason. She wanted to laugh at Roberta's shock, but she hadn't quite gotten over it herself. "I can see essence, not bodies. There's a light inside us. People, animals. And monsters, as it turns out, only they're full body."

"So it's like the tunnel," Vartile said, green and brown leaves waving.

"That's what started it. I'll fill you in all about it later. Right now, we need to get to the laundry." Gesturing toward the door across the hall, she said, "What's our status?" Roberta's true blue took the lead.

Vartile gave her the rundown. "The kitchen's been taken. Soldiers attacked the patio. We sent our folks with guns up to the roof to chase them off, and other soldiers in the dungeon hall laid a plank and walked over the knife racks. People got hurt. A few tried to fight and got killed. Most got out through the family dining room. Hellen had told us about the secret passage when we left the warren. I just wanted you to know."

"All good. She and I talked about it, and lives are the important thing."

"It saved a bunch of lives, that's for sure." Vartile's hand patted her shoulder. "Three hostages were taken, including Cookie. She wasn't going to leave. A lot of the soldiers know her, and she says she knows how to handle them."

Adia hoped so.

They passed through the door under the ballroom stairs. "We moved base up to laundry, and the soldiers haven't gotten up there yet. The back stairwells are blocked. Luhe got the big one secured, and it's guarded now. Some of the others have defended the servants' stairs, and that's worked really well."

"I want to hear that story later."

"Me, too, ma'am." Vartile stepped through and Roberta latched the door behind her. "All the chairs and tables from the ballroom and dining room and waiting room are packed into the southeast corner, blocking access from the south door. That's the only one the soldiers will use, not even the greenhouse. I guess it scares them. Cary said some of them got an eyeful of Dagge, so you know the stories are flying."

"We need to introduce Dagge to the rest of them," Adia said.

"I'm all for that. So around the center block here, all the double doors are strapped at *least* on the inside, and the service doors are as yet undiscovered. The polyphus is still outside the dining room."

"I know, I could see the carapaz in the hall. Carapaz is on the short list."

"Nice," Vartile said.

They passed through the dining room doors, and Roberta bent over to pick something up.

"Is it a candelabra?" Adia asked, holding her hand out.

"Yes," Roberta said, and gave it to her.

"I hooked it over the door handles."

"That's brilliant. I can't wait to hear your story," Vartile said.

"Same here," Roberta agreed.

"It's a doozy. I want to hear yours too. Someday soon." Adia held her hand out and they grasped it. She felt like the three musketeers walking into the dining room.

"This room is empty, so no worries about running into anything," Vartile said. "We've been using the old secret passage stairs to get back and forth from the laundry to the subkitchen. The subkitchen is manned and waiting for the next move. For the time being, the center block here is safe."

"You guys are amazing," Adia said. "Thank you for all of it."

Roberta laid a cool hand on Adia's arm. "How do you feel about making a straight escape? I believe all of us would be glad if you headed for the forest."

"We would," Vartile chimed in.

It consternated Adia a bit. She'd proven herself today, she thought. She had no doubts left about her own worth.

"We just want you to be safe," Roberta said.

Of course that was it. Roberta was the perfect person to remind her. Adia felt bad about jumping to defensive conclusions and smiled. "Hellen wants me to go overland, too, so yeah. She and Beau are taking the tunnels to the tear, and nobody better for wrangling Dagge. Meanwhile, I happen to have an old friend in the stable, and I'm sure we can all find rides. Is there an escape plan?"

"Not really. It's fluid." Roberta patted her arm and pulled her hand away.

"Okay. Well, we're going to need Wolf—he can get us through the forest faster than anyone. Hey, has anyone seen Diit? I haven't heard from him since I've been here."

"No, now that you mention it," Vartile answered.

"Me neither," Roberta said.

"I hope he's all right." How could she have not thought of him before? Wouldn't he be here with her if he was okay?

Cookie would know, but Adia couldn't ask while she was held hostage in the kitchen. David and Wolf would be around there somewhere. And Cary, and Hellen and Beau. Should she help her friends, or run to the forest like they wanted her to?

"How far are we from the subkitchen?" she asked. "I can't leave while so many of us are still in trouble. And we need to get Wolf, and David, and Luhe, and Cary. We can't go without them. I can't."

"We just got you out," Roberta said. "Dagge is that way!"

"He was stuck on the la—" Adia said.

Screams and laser fire blew through the subkitchen as the swinging doors slammed open. Several flashing lights tumbled in, the monster's harsh metallic screech overtaking them.

"What the fuck is that?" one man said in a squeaky voice.

Adia, Roberta, and Vartile rushed to the open doors.

The big circle windows of the hall doors hung in space across the subkitchen. In one, a gold light stood next to a blue and yellow light, next to a blue and orange light, barely visible.

In the other window, Dagge's mutilated face hung silhouetted inside the monster's head as the thing stood at the kitchen doorway and shrieked.

Chapter T.20

They'd gotten the monster close to the end of the hall before it figured out how to transfer enough energy to get off the ladder. It still couldn't get out of Dagge's body, though, and it dragged the corpse around, left side hanging off its back, the head an alarming mismatch of mutilated flesh and bulging magenta.

The four of them had ducked around the corner and through the greenhouse door, hiding while they watched the monster stagger toward the kitchen light like a moth. The monster's glow had gotten dimmer again. It moved slow. Hellen wondered if it had reason or thought at all.

They wanted it to go into the kitchen to scare the soldiers away. Or kill them.

"I need to get Cookie and the others out while the soldiers are distracted. I'm going to cut through that way."

"Let me do it," Beau said.

"I'd rather have you behind it, making sure it doesn't turn back." Hellen nodded once and gave his arm a light squeeze, then went quietly through the family dining room door while Beau led her little group creeping back into the hub.

She was standing at the door to the kitchen when the screaming started.

Chapter T.21

It took Hellen a few seconds to locate Cookie, even with the screaming. She and her two staffers had huddled down in front of the cabinets by the side door, Cookie fumbling through her keyring with shaking hands, one girl wide-eyed, the other crying.

Eight soldiers were backing away from the monster, tripping over chairs, screaming and shouting. They could tell it was Dagge, and weren't sure what to do. Some wanted to shoot, others kept yelling it was the Overlord, two faced off over a rifle with another trying to break them up.

Hellen hunched over and ran to Cookie. "Let's go," she said, helping her off the floor and back to the family dining room, where she left them by the table. "Don't go back in the kitchen until we get Dagge through."

"Oh, we won't. You can believe that." She hugged her girls to her.

The shouting faded when the shooting started. Hellen stuck her head into the kitchen and watched Dagge's monster take laser fire.

"Don't shoot!!" she shouted. "STOP SHOOTING!" But they didn't listen.

All the laser pulses lit the monster up. It shrieked and thrust its arms into the air, stretching them into pulsing blades. The laser fire petered out, the soldiers pushed each other and rushed frantically for the door they came in. The first guy slipped on the plank and stumbled sideways onto the knives. He grabbed the next soldier by the sleeve and pulled him over, but that guy missed the knives. Two others pushed by them both.

Hot with energy, Dagge's monster rampaged, heaving the table over, knocking chairs and kitchen tools across the room. Bearing down, it swiped through the men still trying to get out. The blades slashed them open, blood flying, bodies falling. A few tried to run the other way, around and behind it, but the blades were long, and they went down in the mess around the table. The second guy got up and over the knives, hitting the first guy's hands away, and escaped down the hall. Screaming and crying, the first guy grabbed the edge of the door and tried to pull himself out, but the monster stabbed him and ripped him in half gut to head.

After that, it was quiet. Dagge had lost a lot of his glow and was moving slowly. His blades shrank back into his hands. Now would be the perfect time to get him to the dungeon. With a "wait" gesture to Cookie, Hellen cut back through family dining to the hall.

The first thing she saw was Wolf standing at the subkitchen side door, whining softly. Adia must be in there. What the hells? Hellen opened the door and let Wolf in, raising her rifle in case of trouble. But Adia was fine. She, Vartile, and Roberta stood at the main doors with two young servants holding guns, all of them staring through the round windows into the kitchen. Adia greeted her dog while Hellen gave them the same "wait" sign she gave Cookie, and backed into the hall.

Beau, David, and Firio were gathered to the right of the main door, also peering into the kitchen. Beau glanced back, saw her coming, and waved her in to join them watching the monster. It was across the room, sucking the head of some dead soldier, but it must not have gotten anything, because it threw the guy down and shambled over to pick up another. The flesh right hand held the neck, smashing the face onto the monster's mouth and pulling it away again, like it was trying to figure out how to eat it. Dagge's mouth blended with the monster's mouth on the right side, but his left side swung in and out: his nose appeared and disappeared inside the black mouth; the empty eye socket cut through the flat face then receded.

"That's messed up," David said.

"Yeah," she agreed. "And it's still stronger than I was hoping for, but we've got to get that thing into the dungeon."

"Those escape hatches are small, Hellen," David said.

"Could Dagge fit?"

"Well, yeah, but—"

"Then it'll work. We can use laser fire to tempt it."

"Aw, hells. Okay."

"Let me lead it," Firio said. "David should go with the Queen. He can tell me what to do for the escape. I have lots of experience with this kind of thing."

"You good with that, David?" Hellen asked.

"I am."

"Excellent. Thanks, Firio, we'll get you a gun."

"I have a laser pistol right here." He patted his belly.

The subkitchen side door opened and Adia and the others filed out into the hub. Seconds later, Cookie and her two helpers came out the family dining room door.

"Oh, Your Majesty." Cookie met Adia with outstretched hands. "I'm so happy to see you. We were terribly worried. That monster wouldn't let us know anything all day. Keeping you locked away like that."

"Cookie…" Adia said, "I'm glad you're all right." She grasped Cookie's hands. "I knew you were all there, supporting me. The footman was a bold move."

"He insisted! We told him he might be killed, but he was determined. He let us know you were at least sitting up and talking."

How are your people?"

Cookie's mouth tightened and tears shined her eyes. "We've lost some good souls to them soldiers." She swallowed. "Most were upstairs with Luhe, though, and his group did all right."

"Please introduce me to that footman later, will you?"

"Yes, ma'am, I will."

Adia nodded, released her hands, and looked toward the kitchen. "What's it doing?"

"Still trying to suck heads," David answered.

"Where's Cary?"

"He took a team to search the castle for soldiers," Beau said.

"Will you call him, Beau? And Luhe. It's time for us to leave."

"Yes, ma'am." Beau stepped away with his walkntalk.

"A lot of the soldiers already ran," Cookie said. "They were passing the windows even before that thing got to the kitchen. Some of them stole horses—they won't be coming back."

Adia's brows pulled together in a worried frown. Hellen hoped upon hope Starseed wasn't taken.

"Roberta," Hellen said, "are you still planning to go to the dungeon?"

"Yes. I'd like to go ahead of you."

"You know Robert has a monster in him. You could get down there and he'd take you over."

"I'm willing to risk it. It's what I've been planning, and there's no talking me out of it."

Were all mothers like that? Well, how many times had she put her life on the line to protect Adia? Plenty, and no talking her out of those, either.

"I have no idea how this'll play out, Roberta. It might take some work to get the monster into the dungeon, so you probably have a little time, but if you want to go ahead, you should go now."

****

David watched his Mom, standing at the edge of the group, a little behind Vartile and the Queen. She looked pale, like she did after Dad died. She didn't make eye contact. She kept her arms crossed in front of her. He stepped around Vartile and wrapped her in his arms. She squeezed him hard.

So much loss. Grieving interrupted by new, distant versions of Dad and soon Joey…they had separate lives now, as monks. Not the worst, but not the best, either. Is it okay to grieve when you've been given so much back?

And Robert to top it off. Still alive, as far as they knew, unless that thing had finally beaten him.

David doubted it, knowing Robert.

Chapter T.22

Roberta planned to cut through the servants' dining hall to get to the dungeon door. She'd have to go through the game room to get there, and if she had to move chairs or tables stacked in the hall, she would. The back hall by the dungeon was what scared her—soldiers coming from the south doors, through the dungeon pass, or Dagge seeing her from the kitchen. Her terrified heart pounded. There'd be no way she could outrun anyone, or fight. No help for it.

"Want me to come with you?" David asked.

"No, you stay with the Queen. Robert will respond better if it's just me." She let go of him, and didn't want to make a big deal of leaving, so she simply walked away.

"Take him to the monastery, Roberta," Adia said. "The monks may be able to help him."

Roberta held her hand up. "Thank you, Your Majesty. We'll see you there."

Firio was watching her as she walked around the group. The two of them had become friendly as she took him around the palace, strapping doorhandles. He knew about John and Joey, of course, and told her how sorry he was, and how much John had inspired him. She told him about the big hole in her life now, and how she couldn't let Robert die too. He understood, saying his wife and two sons had gone back to Tirlan before Dagge closed the border, but Firio believed Great Hand was worth saving, and had stayed to fight.

He was probably worried about her. Maybe it would be better to wait until they got Dagge out, but she was sure Robert had suffered enough, and she didn't want to wait too long. One willing, she hadn't waited too long already.

Roberta's hands clenched and unclenched against her chest. Her brows were down and she breathed through her mouth. For a moment, her eyes met Firio's, and he nodded at her ever so slightly, sending strength and courage. That was why he had no idea when the monster stepped through the doors and grabbed him from behind.

The other two men screamed, nearly running her down as they stumbled backward to get away, pulling their rifles up.

"Don't shoot it!" Hellen shouted, moving into the middle of the hall, motioning the young men to get behind her. "Adia, get out now!" she yelled over her shoulder, bringing her rifle up. David had taken rear point, like Beau, making sure everyone was safe as he followed Adia, Wolf, and the others into the family dining room. Roberta was so proud of him in that moment.

The monster screeched. Firio's eyes bulged with terror. The monster had trapped his arms with its arms, and it squeezed him and lifted him off the ground until his head was level with its mouth. Firio's legs and body thrashed.

The black mouth opened. Glowing magenta worked its way over the top of Firio's head. He started screaming then, in long, gasping breaths.

Roberta's knuckles flew to her mouth, panic plucking at the thin threads in her mind. She didn't know how to help him. *How could she help him?*

Firio's eyes rolled back, whites gleaming in their sockets. His head appeared to stretch, lengthening into the monster's mouth as it pulled, sucking and slurping. Firio's screams broke and mixed with sobs.

Hellen put a bullet in his chest. He went limp, head falling forward out of the monster's mouth.

Furious, the monster roared and shook him. It threw Firio's body at Hellen and stormed at her. Hellen dodged and opened fire on the monster's head. The bullets went through the magenta and blasted bits of bone and flesh off what was left of Dagge's skull.

It was horrifying. Roberta shrank against the wall, looking away, staring at Firio's body, wondering if there was any way at all he could still be alive.

John's voice came from the left. "Roberta, it's time to go."

Looking left, she saw not John, but the doorway of the subkitchen. Roberta turned, pushed the door open, and escaped.

"Run, honey," John's voice said, and she did.

She ran as fast as she could and wished like hells it was faster.

Chapter T.23

Hellen straddled Firio's body to protect it from the raging monster in front of her. Bullet after bullet pierced the head, which bulged lopsidedly in its fury. The attached side stayed small and dark, but the entire side that was free of Dagge boiled, like before. Not a good look.

The bullets just pissed it off.

"You!" she called over her shoulder to the two young guys behind. "Get around behind it and fire just above its head. Hit it only if you have to get its attention. We're going to take it through the kitchen." She could hear them hit the family dining door as they ran through.

Where was Beau? He'd disappeared, and all she had was her rifle and her carapaz knife.

Swinging her rifle onto her back, Hellen reached down and grabbed Firio's wrists, and pulled him toward the subkitchen door. By then the guys were in the kitchen, and laser pulses started hitting the wall high above her head. She crashed through the double doors and left Firio's body next to the worktable.

The monster had been distracted. It's back was to her, and it was roaring into the kitchen from the doorway. Hellen cracked one door and pulled the other one open. Leaving her rifle behind her, she released her carapaz knife and walked into the hall, closing the gap between them.

Tomius Dagge's body hung half out of the magenta imitation man. His flesh sagged, the arm flopped, and the leg dragged like a piece of toilet paper on a shoe. Hellen had thought herself in love with him once. Horror and grief intermingled. On so many levels.

Where was Beau?

Hellen veered to the left, following the monster into the kitchen. "You know where to go, right?" Laser pulses flew over their heads.

"Yes, ma'am," both said. She didn't know whether to be annoyed or gratified.

They made progress through the kitchen: tables, racks, and chairs were moved; bodies were dragged out of the path. Hellen kept to the left, since the carapaz worked better on the magenta than the flesh. She had to stay close, too, because a knife was, after all, a contact weapon.

Despite her proximity, though, the guys were taking the real risk right now. That monster wanted them.

Chapter T.24

They found Starseed in the very last stall. Most of the other horses were gone—the few left were saddle shy, but got saddled anyway for the people who couldn't manage the walk. Starseed was glad to see her, and whinnied and nickered when Adia approached.

Her light was lavender and baby blue. It wasn't built like people's and Wolf's, though—more like a cloud. And the other horses' were even more that way…big, nebulous lights with varying degrees of color. Lots of pale grey.

David put the saddle on while Adia petted and talked to her horse. She wished she had treats, but that was going to have to wait. Instead, she petted her all her favorite ways.

Starseed settled, Adia stepped into the walkway and took a knee to talk to Wolf. He was so smart, she had no doubt he understood her. "We need you to take us through the forest to the tear. It's going to be a lot of people, and we'll need the easiest, quickest way. Will you do this for us?" He licked her face. She took that as a yes.

Cary's voice called out from the direction of the stable doorway. "Majesty?"

David growled, yanking Starseed's strap.

"It's okay, David."

"It's not okay. The more he gets away with things—like hollering for you from a distance—the more he'll push that envelope."

She couldn't argue.

"Come back here, Cary," David called, with a fat edge of irritation.

In a few moments, Adia saw Cary's teal and burgundy at the end of the row. He jogged toward them. "We're heading into the forest. Luhe left a few minutes ago. Do you guys have a radio?"

"Cookie has one, so I thought we'd go with her," Adia said.

"Great." Pause. "What's your problem, big guy?" he asked, sounding genuinely clueless.

David took a silent moment while his galaxy spun wildly. "You don't holler for a Queen, man. You walk into the building and look."

Some tense air happened. A silent standoff. Adia could imagine the looks between them, and dug deep for the tact the situation required.

"Thank you, David. Cary, I know this is an unusual circumstance, so no damage done. David is right, however, for…normal…times." Change the subject. "Are the other riders ready? Did you notice?"

"No, ma'am."

"No, they're not ready, or no, you didn't notice?"

"I didn't notice. Ma'am."

David cupped her hand. "We're ready," he said, and guided her hand to the stirrup. Adia moved to mount, and as she raised herself, he asked, "Want the reins?"

"I think we'll be safer if you have them," she said, settling herself in the saddle and patting Starseed on the neck. "Wolf!" A high bark answered. "Let's go!" she said.

Cary stepped back and let her go ahead, which was an improvement over the past, she noted. He might get the hang of this someday.

David followed Wolf, leading Starseed toward the stable doors. A horse whinnied at them from the first stall. It had to be Dagge's— Sephone, as Adia recalled. Sephone's light was concentrated even more than Starseed's—a cotton fluff of Dagge's lime green spotted with royal blue. Like her own lavender in Starseed's light, Dagge had left his imprint on his horse. She was so completely Dagge's, no one had taken her. But Dagge would never use her again. Adia wondered if Hellen might.

That reminded her. "Cary? Any word from Beau or Hellen?"

"We haven't heard from them, ma'am."

Chapter T.25

Roberta found Robert in the last row of cells. He lay on his back on a stone block, one knee up and the opposite arm draped over his face.

"Robert."

His arm came down and head tilted up. One eye was swollen shut, and dried blood smeared the bottom half of his face. He looked at her for a bit, and when he spoke, she could tell his lip was split.

"What are you doing here?"

Always the sweet kid.

"I'm getting you out." She'd found the ring of keys on the table at the bottom of the stairs. There were no guards around at all—not much point in staying if your boss only wants to eat your soul.

The keys jingled as she looked through them, trying the ones that looked the most likely.

"Are you sure you're not here to say 'I told you so'?" Robert sat up slowly, clearly hurting, though he would never say it.

"I'm not interested in doing that."

"But it's such a prime opportunity. You all tried to tell me, didn't you?"

She looked at him. "Robert, you're my son, and I love you. What I feel is sorry that you had to go through this. That it turned out the way it did."

He fell silent after that. "To be fair, I couldn't have known he'd go mad."

Roberta didn't say a word, just kept trying keys.

"You couldn't have known, either. Not for sure."

"The crazy part was pretty clear, honey. But he also has a monster in him—like the 2Ders, only 3D. None of us knew that."

Another key, while she watched him for a few seconds. "They say you have one in you."

He didn't answer.

"They say you're fighting it."

Still nothing. She noted the tension in his shoulders and the arm he held across his gut. Her heart panged, all the old hurts vanishing. "You must know I will never abandon you."

"I do know that," he said, and looked up at her. "You were always a good mother."

It ripped her heart. Of all of them, she was probably the worst mother for this one. How much of this struggle was about her own redemption? How much was about saving him…and was that even possible?

He folded his other arm across his chest. "It feeds on me," he said, staring at the floor in front of him, his voice a near whisper. "I'm not sure how much of me is left."

It nearly killed her.

The lock turned and the door opened. Robert stood, but Roberta pushed into the cell instead of letting him out, and she wrapped her arms around him. It didn't matter how much he hated hugs.

But to her surprise, his arm went around her, his hand lay flat on her back, and his head lay on top of hers. She held him as long as he let her.

"Aren't we leaving?"

"Not that way. We need to get down into the tunnel, and we need to hurry. I'm taking you to the monks, they can help you."

"Do you know how to get into the tunnel?"

"I do. I've actually done this before." Roberta made a move to reach for the hinge, but Robert's arm stopped her.

He stepped over to the cage door and bent down. "You know, you and Dad always thought David was the smart one. The golden boy, the perfect one." When he turned to face her again, his eyes twinkled ever so slightly, and he held a hinge pin in his fingers. "But he was never any smarter than I am."

Chapter T.26

Beau showed up just as they were trying to get the monster to go through the dungeon door. It didn't want to, it wanted to go down the hall, and Hellen had had to circle around through the servants' stairwell and stand in the way, shooting Dagge's body, making more and more of it drag the floor. The guys fired laser pulses from the dungeon stairs, but the monster didn't care, it only had eyes for her.

Talk about screwed up. They'd had to feed it more laser fire than she'd wanted, and now it had plenty of energy, all ready to launch out on its own. It grimaced at her, Dagge's nose thrusting out of its mouth, shredded skin hanging in the cheek area. At least it had shrunk back to human-sized—pushing parts out did seem to drain it faster.

Beau came up behind her carrying an enormous jewel of carapaz in his hands. A mesmerizing depth of colors and shapes flashed in the overhead light. The only other turkey-sized chunk she'd seen was Merv's, but it wasn't nearly so fancy.

"What's that for?"

"I don't know," he said, bouncing the carapaz and making a quick assessment of the status quo. "I got it from the polyphus. That thing's afraid of carapaz, so I figured the more the better."

The monster roared when Beau looked at it. It was growing. Head and hands expanded, half-caught by the dead flesh, bulging around it. As it bulged it became something else, more blob than human. The glow dimmed quickly. Two laser shots fired into the ceiling hit the monster's head and waves of bright magenta swept its body.

"Stop firing!" she yelled at the doorway.

It shrieked with new energy, popping more of its head out of Dagge's skull.

Aiming the jewel's point toward the monster, Beau edged to the right wall and squared off. It bellowed at him, raised its fists, and opened its enormous hands high in the air. Dagge's trapped arm had ripped in the armpit.

In Beau's hands the carapaz began to spark, and blue-white energy snakes formed along the slope of it, writhing and snapping.

Beau lunged and impaled the monster's chest, deep into the solid energy of the left side. Snakes bled into the magenta, and the monster howled and jerked and flickered. Beau pulled the jewel back and struck again, swinging into the monster's head. With a choked-off grunt, the monster staggered backward through the door and onto the landing of the dungeon steps. But the hanging, flopping half of the companion corpse got in the way and the monster tripped over it, pitching headfirst down the stairs.

They rushed to the door. Dagge's body flipped the monster over and over down the steps. Halfway down it fell off the steps entirely and the body hit the floor below with a thump.

Hellen led the way down the first few steps. In the center of the room lay a tangle of compound fractures and stuttering light. Ryin and Balisba had run down the steps, but not all the way to the floor, and they kept their distance about a quarter of the way up.

"Nicely done," Hellen said to Beau, giving him a big smile as they headed down. "We can drag it now."

Chapter T.27

It was harder to get Robert into the tunnel than she expected. His collar bone seemed to be broken, and every movement cost him. Getting him to lie down and scooch into the secret passage took forever, and Roberta could hear the shooting in the hall before she even got him all the way in.

Then he wouldn't slide. His clothes and skin were sticky with blood, and Roberta had to get him to roll to his side so she could squeeze around him. It wasn't an easy squeeze. They hadn't been that close since birth.

But once she made it, she sat between his feet, tucked her skirt up in her waistband, and pulled him by his legs, her own feet pedaling them forward. A little way down she had to tie a knot in her skirt so the tail end would quit coming out of her waistband. Bare skin wasn't cutting it. After that the occasional yank on the wedgie did the trick, and they finally made it all the way down.

She pulled Robert out until his feet touched the floor, knees bent, and he could sit up.

"Did you leave the key in the keyhole?"

"Really? That's what you say after I bust my ass getting you down here?"

He frowned and looked like several retorts came to mind, but what he said was, "Thank you for getting me down here."

It would have to do. "You're welcome. And yes, I left the hinge pin in the keyhole. The door tried to close too soon if I took it out, and I didn't think to rush to put it back while I was wedging myself between you and the wall."

"Let's hope Hellen finds it then, and not Dagge."

"Dagge is out of commission. Permanently."

"What does that mean?"

"That means the last time I saw him, he was hanging halfway out of a glowing magenta…biped. Dead."

"But the biped is not dead?"

"Not when I saw it."

"Then we should probably hurry."

"Now you're talking."

Roberta helped him up and they hobbled off toward the monastery.

Chapter T.28

They did have to drag the body. The magenta bounced along, its free half stretched out on top of Dagge's body parts. Some of those parts were barely hanging onto each other.

Hellen removed all the iron bars and pickaxes the soldiers had used to try and find the tunnel. She tossed them beside the upended chair which was no doubt Dagge's supervisory throne. Evidence of his tantrum at not being able to get through.

Around the corner, she was glad to see that Roberta had left the cell door open. And the secret passage door—she'd have to remember to thank her for that. Hellen squatted at the end of the block and peered down into the darkness. Looked like a slide, but there was a curve and she couldn't see where it went.

Did it matter?

Beau and one of the guys dragged the monster in and laid it on the floor.

"I'll get down in there to pull," she said.

"Why not me?" Beau asked.

"If there's anything that'll help, it'll be my knife."

"Then let these guys go first. I'll take rear."

"What are your names, anyway?" Hellen asked.

"I'm Ryin."

"Balisba."

They squeezed past, stepping over the edge of the corpse.

"Got your bulb torch?" Beau asked her.

"I do," she answered, patting her hip as she moved aside. But neither of the others had one, so she gave up hers, and Beau gave her his. His was nice. She smiled.

She also handed Ryin her rifle to take down. Balisba went first, then Ryin, rifles in their hands, giving long whoops like kids at a playground.

Hellen laughed.

Looking at the nasty mess on the floor, even as tight as the quarters were going to be—and she'd have to have her hands on it—dead weight was better than fighting it all the way down. (Not *dead* since it still had light. They could probably revive it when they got to the tunnel. Laser fire. Enough for it to walk) And if they had to drag it the whole way, they could do that, too. Because it had to be taken to the tear, so they could get rid of it forever.

Hellen backed into the tunnel opening on all fours.

Chapter T.29

Dagge's body was halfway into the opening when the thing woke up. The carapaz had started to glow, reacting to the magenta, and the magenta reacted, probably protecting itself. The monster's head lifted, right in front of Hellen, and she stabbed it in the eye.

Maybe she shouldn't have done that. It shrieked in her face, all of its energy rushing to its head, which started growing toward her. She backed away, letting go of Dagge's body, which had hung up on the side of the stone block. As she retreated, the head stretched for her, and the rest of the monster came with it, leaving Dagge's body behind.

Fuck. Fuck. Fuck.

"It's free!" she screamed, letting herself slide, but not too far. She wanted to remain its best option, instead of it turning on Beau. The body was so dim it was transparent, and Hellen could see Beau behind it, pulling Dagge's body out of the opening.

Hand over hand, the monster dragged itself forward. The head began to flicker, feeding the arms with faint pulses of energy. It got faster. Hellen got faster. And it watched her, no doubt wanting to suck her head.

When she reached the bottom, Ryin had her rifle up and aimed at the monster.

"Want me to shoot it?"

"Not yet. You got it, though?"

"I got it," he answered, squaring off with the slide opening.

Hellen backed a step or two to the right. The magenta glow came first, then the bulging forehead and purple eyes. Below that, it stretched away and got smaller until there was no chin, only a skinny neck. Past that, it lay flat. Like it had lost the ability to be three-dimensional.

Too bad she couldn't take a picture, Adia would be fascinated. Hells, everybody would be. She could win a prize.

Ah, well.

She continued backing. Ryin didn't waver. Balisba shined the flashlight onto the opening from the other direction.

The head came out and went upward, the body slithered over the edge, touched the floor, and backed over itself until it was standing. The head shrank, draining energy into the body, giving it some volume. It was still thin, and dim, but not harmless. It might get stronger away from Dagge and the solid carapaz slide.

"Where do you want me?" Ryin called.

"On the other side," Hellen answered. "But don't shoot me!"

Ryin backed toward Balisba, and Beau came sliding in with the jewel. The monster screeched at him weakly, and backed toward the opposite wall.

Hellen clicked Beau's torch on. It made a wide circle of light to walk in, and she settled in for the long haul, hoping Roberta and Robert were well on their way.

Chapter T.30

They didn't get very far before Robert collapsed. She'd had to feel their way around the outer edge of the space, which was large and dotted with random slide openings. Roberta hadn't thought to grab a light, and keeping one hand on the wall while holding Robert up with the other arm had been slow going. They were both exhausted, and the dark had been absolute, which they both hated.

She had just gone to her knees beside him when light appeared back the way they came. Sounds had been echoing behind them for a few minutes, and Roberta had hoped to be out of the way by the time Hellen and the others got there. No such luck. Warm white flashed around the walls, ceiling, and floor, silhouetting a wide stone column in the middle of a round room.

They hadn't even made it to the tunnel.

She should have let Hellen's group go first, but she didn't think about that. Now they were going to have to let them pass, and who knew what would happen.

Roberta hooked her hands up under Robert's arms and pulled him across the floor toward the column. Despite how thin he looked, he was still heavy enough she had to pull him in spurts, using her back to get him moving.

His feet got lighted up just as she was reaching the back of the column. Roberta fell to her bottom, Robert on top of her. She scooted out from under him and pulled his knees until he was in a fetal position around her, facing the wall. She plastered herself against the wall and tried to control her breathing.

In two seconds, Hellen was walking backward past her. The bulb torch swung at Hellen's waist, washing her and Robert with the edge of the light every step. About three feet past the edge of the column, Hellen saw them. Her eyes met Roberta's then looked away quickly. Her face showed no reaction, and she kept her slow backward progress.

The monster appeared, holding itself upright, no longer hampered by Dagge's body. It stopped maybe two steps past the column and turned slightly toward her. Hellen unclipped her bulb torch and shined it in the monster's eyes. It screeched weakly.

But it didn't move forward. A patch of bumps started growing on its side. All the glow went into them and they became feelers, waving in the air and finding her and Robert. The monster turned more to them and screeched louder.

"Balisba! Ryin! Go around the other way! Beau, we need you!" Hellen clipped her bulb torch on the back of her belt facing up. It lit up the space and made her look like a superhero. Knife in hand, she spread her arms and prepared to fight.

Beau came running, holding a huge jewel in front of him that the monster screeched at the sight of. It turned to face Beau—hands up, feelers disappearing and dimmer than before—and backed away toward Hellen.

But it knew they were there. The purple eyes shifted between Beau and Robert. Roberta didn't like the way it had focused on Robert, and she climbed over him to block him with her body.

Hellen had backed around between them and the tunnel opening. The two boys came running around the other side of the column, meeting her.

"We'll need to you draw it down the tunnel. Ryin, give me my rifle." She waved her left hand, eyes not moving from the monster.

"When do you want us to start firing?"

"Do it now," Hellen said, slinging the rifle over her shoulder.

The two boys backed toward the tunnel, firing into the ceiling. Panic lit Roberta up for a few seconds, but the laser pulses didn't bounce. They crackled on the rock and left glow spots that faded.

Distracted by the laser fire, the monster turned back around and shuffled toward the shooters. Hellen edged closer to Roberta and watched the monster pass, knife at the ready. When it got farther on, she closed in behind it. Beau held the carapaz ready in the rear.

Maybe they'd get it to the forest after all.

Roberta had just moved to Robert's head to check on him when the glowing tentacle snapped out of the darkness and pierced Robert's back. Roberta screamed, grabbed onto it, and tried to pull it out. It wouldn't budge, and she shifted closer to get a better angle. A flickering dim magenta appeared on Robert—in him and extending from him. A sharp angle thrust out of his head, flat, stretching purple eyes through the border of Robert's skin. It looked at her.

Roberta's mouth fell open. Behind her she could hear the sounds of fighting, and voices, but she couldn't understand them. She didn't know what was happening, all she knew was the tentacle wouldn't budge and she needed to save Robert's life.

Chapter T.31

It had tricked them. When it got close to the tunnel, the glow ramped up and two tentacles shot out the ends of its arms. One got Balisba's gun and the other went straight back to Robert. Hellen attacked that tentacle, slicing it with her knife, but unable to cut all the way through. The monster closed in on her fast, tentacle reabsorbed into its body as it came.

Beau swung the jewel at its head, sparking and crackling the magenta when it made contact. The monster shrieked and surprised them all by reversing through itself so it was facing Beau, and it knocked him aside with the rifle, splitting his temple open. Beau went down.

Hellen sliced at the tentacle and the back, trying to cut chunks out. Balisba circled around, grabbed the rifle, and tried to get it away from the monster while Ryin fired laser pulses frantically into the ceiling from the mouth of the tunnel.

Balisba got his rifle rammed up through his jaw, freezing him, eyes wide and mouth open. The monster yanked it out, blood pouring down, followed by Balisba's limp body.

Hellen attacked with all the hot fury in her. She jumped onto the monster's back, left arm around its neck, and used her carapaz knife to scramble its brain, if it had one.

It ignored her, trying to figure out how to shoot the gun. But it couldn't, and a hand started to form. As it did, the face came through it again, and it was looking at her, inches from her own face.

Then, by One, it laughed.

Chapter T.32

Roberta watched the fight with rising panic. Beau might be dead, the boy was certainly dead, and Hellen wasn't stopping the monster. In fact, she fell off of it, and it kicked her to the side. Then it came toward Robert. Roberta didn't know what to do.

The thing inside Robert had stretched out more and more. Its light was dim and stuttery, but it watched everything, even her. Robert was still breathing, so she had hope.

Behind the monster, Hellen got to her feet, took the rifle from the second boy, and shot the monster. It looked back at her, but aimed its rifle at Robert and fired.

The pulse zipped by Roberta. Robert's body jerked and the thing in him flashed brighter. Roberta tried to stretch out to block Robert from being shot, but the tentacle was in the way, so she lay across him, on top of the thing inside, willing it to take her instead.

It passed right through her. No matter how she grabbed, or pushed, or made herself available, the thing was unaffected and uninterested. She could barely feel a hum where it intersected with her flesh. Below her, the tentacle lit up, and parts of the thing stretched out of Robert's body, through hers, and latched onto it, merging energies.

The monster shot Robert again.

Roberta lost it. She wasn't going to let that thing just kill him. Not while she was there. Not while she could do something.

She pushed herself up, ran at the monster, grabbed the rifle, and wrenched it upward as hard as she could. Hellen yelled at her, but Roberta couldn't understand what she said. More laser fire hit it, and it arched backward, but it wouldn't let the rifle go.

Roberta yanked and wrestled for the gun while the thing in Robert got brighter. The head came completely out, and harsh screams blared through its open mouth. The big monster walked toward it, jerking her along.

Hellen grabbed her arm, but Roberta shook her off. She was saying something; Roberta had no idea what. They were close to Robert now, and Roberta's only focus was keeping the monster from killing him.

With all her strength, Roberta yanked the rifle downward, breaking the monster's grip. The rifle clattered to the floor. She scooped it up and pointed it at the monster's gut, then she pulled the trigger and pumped pulse after pulse into it.

Its mouth opened and eyes went wide with surprise. Magenta flashed with every shot. A scream came from somewhere to her right and someone tackled her. Once she was on the floor, she realized it was Hellen.

But Hellen was too late. Robert's monster climbed up the tentacle and joined with Dagge's monster. Two heads—one flat and angular, the other round—protruded from the shoulders, both of them glowing and pulsing and happy. The tentacle shrank into the body, the 3D head looked down the tunnel, and the body turned to go that way.

Hellen leapt to her feet and snatched up the rifle between them. "Ryin, it's coming your way! Roberta, we've got to go."

"I know," Roberta answered, and crawled over to Robert.

"Beau!" Hellen shook his shoulder. "BEAU!" Getting no response, she picked up the jewel and ran down the tunnel. Bullet fire crescendoed, monsters roared, and the last time Hellen shouted, it trailed off, and she was heard no more.

Robert's pulse was faint, but still there. There probably wasn't a whole lot of time.

He was a monk, though, right? He'd be around.

Beau stirred, then sat up quickly. "Where's Hellen?"

"She's taking it down the tunnel. Things went bad. The monster has two heads now," Roberta said. "That boy didn't survive, as you can see."

Beau glanced over at Balisba, then got up, touched his head, looked at the blood, and looked around for the jewel.

"Hellen took it."

"You okay here?" Beau asked. "Because if you are, I'm going."

"We're fine. You go."

Beau nodded and ran off.

Robert's voice was faint when he spoke. "You realize I'm not fine, right?"

"Robert..." She turned him over so she could see his face. "You'll get better. We're in a tunnel. I'll call Dad, I'm sure he can help get you to the monastery. Or bring somebody here. Monks can heal people, you'll be fine."

He was quiet for a long few moments, not looking at her. "Do you think I've been a bad person?"

Ugh. Her brain stopped. She knew why he was asking, of course. People think about a lot of big things when they're dying.

"I think your life has been a mixture of light and dark, just like all of us. It's true you made choices I didn't understand, but I am particularly proud of your actions in the last 24 hours. You have behaved with courage, and you've been willing to admit you were wrong. That's a big deal for everyone. So, nicely done, son. On *all* of that."

"Thank you." He took a shaky breath. "I want you to know my family has been the only upside to this life." He looked for all the world like he was going to cry.

"That, and saving the kingdom," she said. Robert looked at her. "The Queen told me she may never have made it out of that room if it hadn't been for you."

Tears did actually leak across his temple and into his hair. "I'm glad she made it out," he said.

Roberta put her hand on his cheek and smoothed his hair. Not too much, though, just in case.

"I'm about to go," he said. "But you'll see me again."

"Yeah." She nodded, glad and heartbroken. Half wishing she could go with him.

"You're not done yet, you know. Mom. We all have our parts to play." His voice faded out, and Robert was gone.

Mom.

Roberta wept. For herself, for Robert, for all of them. What a crazy, awful time to live through. Absorbed in grief, it took her several minutes to notice that she could see. Her head jerked up and she looked around. John was sitting against the wall off to the side, softly glowing.

"What are you doing?" she asked.

"I'm waiting. It seemed like you might need some room."

Roberta crawled over to him and sat against the wall. "I'm tired, John."

"I know. You have every reason to be."

"I've still got to get to the monastery."

"Or you could go home."

"I could, couldn't I?"

"The others will be fighting Dagge in the forest later."

"Yes." They'd be fighting for their lives. And they would all understand why she wasn't there.

But Roberta realized she wanted to be there. She wanted to do whatever she could to take that…that scourge of the world down. If she could blow its damned head off, that'd be great.

Age and stiffness had settled into her while she sat, but she ignored them and pushed herself to standing. She knew what she needed to do. Brushing off her hands, she said, "Will you come with me so it's not so dark?"

"I was hoping you'd ask," John said, getting himself up. "No more questions, though." He put his arm around her. "Let's talk about the old days instead."

"I'd like that."

Roberta couldn't feel John's arm or body in the usual way, but she could feel his energy. And that would be enough to get her where she needed to go.

Chapter T.33

The sun was well over the trees, shining right in David's eyes with every clearing. He walked in front of Starseed, the Queen on the horse's back talking sideways to Vartile and Cookie. Cookie had ridden up to say they'd heard from Byron—he and his people had just exited the forest tunnel.

The Queen took the radio. "Byron, this is your Queen."

It tickled David and he turned to look at her. She winked, grinning.

"Yes, Your Majesty!" Byron was very enthusiastic.

"Would you tell Merv we're at…where are we?"

Vartile said, "I have no idea."

At the same time Cookie said, "Lost in the woods, most like."

And David looked back over Starseed's head. "I know we're not there yet."

"Did you hear that, Byron?"

"Uh, yes ma'am."

"Great. Tell Merv to get the other rock giants to move away. We'll be there as soon as we can. Anyone who hears from Hellen talk to me immediately."

"Yes, ma'am," he said.

The Queen handed the radio back to Cookie. "Thank you, Cookie. If anyone sees a landmark, let me know."

"Yes, ma'am," Cookie said, and turned her mare back to the servants' group, radio at her mouth.

"David." His Dad's voice sounded right beside him. David looked around, but no one was there.

"Dad?" David said, a little too loud because the Queen heard him.

"David?" she asked.

"Yes, that would be me," the voice said. "The Dad who changed your didies."

Yeah, it was Dad, alright. "Please don't ever say that again."

"David? Care to share with the class?"

"Son, I need you to *not* tell everyone you can hear me."

David turned around to face the Queen and walked backward a few steps. "Just talking to myself…making plans…you know." Facing forward again, he whispered, "Why? We all know about you."

"I need this to not be a big deal. If you tell everyone, it becomes a big energy generator and I'm not supposed to be helping. Know what I mean? Listen…how much did you get out of that book?"

"Pff, I don't know. Didn't seem like much."

"Don't get any closer than thirty feet." A moment of silence, then "Gotta go!"

Really? David shook his head and sighed. He hated not knowing what he was doing.

"That was a heavy sigh."

"It's nothing." David dropped back so he could walk beside her. "I'm talking to myself, but I promise you I am not crazy."

"I believe you."

"So do I," Vartile said, "and maybe you'll tell us what you discussed someday, but for right now I'm going to catch up with Luhe and get some sweetness of my own." She smiled, clucked her horse into a faster pace, and went ahead.

The Queen lowered her voice to a whisper and bent toward him. "That was your Dad, wasn't it?"

"You could see him?"

"Very faintly. Bright green with sparkles."

"He was trying to hide—he didn't want to cause a big fuss. He told me not to let everyone know, but you already know, so…" He shrugged, then realized she couldn't see it. This seeing/not-seeing thing was confusing. "I'm clear."

"Yes, you are. What did he say?"

"To stay thirty feet away."

"That was it?"

"He had to go. I think they're keeping him on a tight leash."

He and Starseed walked in silence for a bit, and the Queen said, "What do you think we'll need to do?"

"I think we'll need to use a formation, but I don't know how that relates to the crystal."

"I had a dream about the crystal."

"Yeah? What was it?"

"I held a really bright light. It became a window in a wall, then turned into a mirror."

"And you can figure that out?"

She laughed. "You'd have to be there. And, in fact, you were."

"Really?"

"Yes, you came up behind me and started this awful blaring. It kept going and going. Freaked me out a little, if I'm honest."

"Absolutely be honest. I'm not the best singer, I know that."

She chuckled. "I think it means we need to use sound, but I don't know if it's a different note, or quality of sound, or what."

"Okay!" he said. "We don't know what we're doing, but we have half an idea! That's fifty percent more than nothing. I have one hundred percent faith in the two of us, and in all these people. We'll figure out whatever needs to be done."

"I completely agree."

They rode and walked in silence, passing through a shallow gully. David stepped over the trickling water, but Starseed stomped right in it.

The Queen's hand found his head and squeezed her fingers through his hair. It was surprisingly arousing. He leaned into it, untucking his shirt.

"David, I want to thank you for coming with me. For taking care of me—amazing care, really, almost as good as Hellen."

"I take that as high praise, Your Majesty."

She leaned down toward his ear. "Just between you and me, could you call me Adia when we're alone together?"

He turned his face up to her. "What about Starseed?"

"She told me I should ask you. She says it's tiresome, 'Your Majesty this' and 'yes, ma'am that.'"

"Well, I wouldn't want to irritate her."

"Oh, she is a prima donna."

"So, if I wanted to call *her* Your Majesty, she'd probably be okay with that."

"Yeah, I imagine she would," Adia said. They went along in silence again, both of them smiling. "It's hard to believe we've only known each other a few days."

"No kidding. And what a few days it's been."

"I know! And the last three years...I swear, I feel a hundred years older."

"I think we all are. I think this kind of trauma ages you in very real ways. We're not much like the people we used to be."

"What did you imagine your life would be?"

"I thought I'd go to school, get a degree in architecture, maybe? I mean, Dad had a great life. Periods of intense, creative work, then a week off, or two or three weeks. Raise the kids, be a Dad. Seemed pretty perfect."

"So you want kids?"

"Yeah! Don't you?"

"I worry about how much time it takes to be a Queen. I loved my Dad, but it was all about the kingdom for him. I wouldn't want my kids to have to go through that. To miss their mother."

His heart ached for her. He never thought about what it would be like to grow up an only child, no Mom, and a Dad who always had important work. "I'm sorry you didn't have your Mom, Adia. I can't imagine life without mine."

"Yeah. Thanks. I did have Hellen, and she was great. Love her like a Mom. And I'm glad we both have your Mom. She's been kind to me, and incredibly giving." She smiled down at him. "So, how many kids do you want?"

"At least two. Possibly three. Siblings are important. They shape us like our parents do."

"I'd like to have three kids," Adia said. "And I want to make sure the crown doesn't have to pass to the oldest, or the male, or whatever other bullshit monarchies think of. I want the crown to go to the child most suited."

David understood that. In his family, the crown would have gone to Robert, and David couldn't imagine any good coming of that.

Would David want the crown?

No way. He'd have had to talk Joey into it.

"Okay, let's say you're an architect. Do you want work in Great Hand, or do you want to go to a different country?"

"I'd like to stay here if there's work. Get married here, have kids here, the whole thing. Especially now."

"Why now?"

Oh, crap. Like she said, they'd only known each other for a few days. How was he supposed to tell the Queen of an entire country he wanted to stay for her? He wanted to marry her, and have a family. Was he crazy? Wasn't it way too soon to know he wanted to spend his life with her?

And did he really want to be Prince, or King Consort, or whatever they'd call him? It would almost be like being a king, and he knew he didn't want that job.

But she'd need him. She'd need him to make her laugh and have her back. And he wanted to be whatever she needed.

David looked up at her. Her face was turned toward him, and a little smile tilted the corners of her mouth.

Yeah, there'd be no hiding it from her. His light was going to give him away every time.

"Well, you're going to need help with those three kids."

544

Chapter T.34

Exhaustion and stress had worn Hellen thin by the time they reached the tunnel hub at the monastery. They'd been on high alert the whole way, she and Ryin largely going backward, keeping an eye on the monster, shooting laser pulses. Its legs stretched to twice their usual length, trying to eat up the distance despite getting weaker even without the dead body.

A few times it tried to turn around and go back. Thank One Beau was all right (despite the blood running down his face) and had followed them. He stayed behind the monster and fought the thing back when it turned on him. The giant crystal crackled and flashed as Beau jabbed it into the monster's belly and swung it at the flat head looming out over him.

Hellen tried to get the flat head to loom over her—she'd cut that asshole right off—but it wouldn't do it.

It did release a tentacle once, trying for Ryin's gun. The monster had to slow down, and the legs shrank so it could make one. But the tentacle was thin, and Hellen cut it off as it passed her—the severed end dropped to the ground in a smoldering black line. The monster roared at her, pulled the stub back and cradled it. So it did feel pain, or loss, or something. It was pissed after that, and they had to run again.

Now, at the hub, all she wanted to do was take a minute. Could they trap it somewhere? Like in the thumb tunnel? They could take turns guarding it with the carapaz.

The monster screeched as it walked into the hub from the pinky tunnel. Hellen's bulb torch lit up the space enough to see the entire 10-stride by 15-stride room. The monster's legs had shrunk, and the magenta flickered, but Hellen had learned her lesson about believing it was weak. She backed away, knife up, Ryin behind her and to her left.

545

"You guys mind if we take a breather? Maybe we can pen this pain in my ass and take turns on guard."

"If you have a plan, I'm all for it," Ryin said.

"I'm in," Beau agreed.

"Ryin, there's a tunnel opening about eight strides to your six. It's a dead end; let's get the monster in there. You all right with first watch?"

"I'm just fine. You guys have been taking the bulk of this, so you rest."

Carapaz knife out in front of her, Hellen backed around the curved wall of tunnel openings, leaving a wide space for the monster to go by.

The monster shuffled sideways, the flat head looking at Hellen and the round one at Beau. It kept going, shuffling along the back wall, flat purple eyes drilling a hole in her. "Beau, if you'll get it to come at you, I can get behind it and cut off that skinny head."

The round head turned and looked at her. The monster stopped. *Did it understand what she said?*

Ryin fired a shot into the ceiling over the heads, trying to get its attention. It ignored him. Then it turned and stepped into the dumbwaiter.

Feelers on its back were reaching up toward the fresh air. They shrank quickly, and two long tentacles shot upward from its hands. Hellen heard a splintering, and a faint light washed the stone shaft. The monster hooked onto what must have been the dumbwaiter door opening and tried to haul itself up into the shaft. It hung crooked, by one arm, apparently, because the other one thrust back through the shaft opening right at her. It was the one she cut, and the end was black, and it wrapped around her neck and squeezed.

The tentacle was thicker than it was before, and Hellen couldn't slice all the way through it. She hacked at it, but it healed itself like it always did, leaving only smoky scars now.

Beau placed the muzzle of his pistol on the middle of the tentacle and rapid-fire released it from its body. The free end dropped, and Hellen yanked the thing from her neck and threw it aside.

But the live end didn't turn black. It grew back, and Hellen barely had time to dodge, grabbing the tip with one hand and stabbing repeatedly with the knife.

Beau had picked up the carapaz and was rushing the dumbwaiter shaft. Before he reached the opening, the tentacle yanked back into the shaft, and the monster shrieked at them. Beau dropped the crystal, squeezed into the tiny space, and wrapped his arms around the monster. The two tentacles pulled it upward, and the monster slipped through Beau's grasp like an eel.

Hellen sprinted, getting there just in time to grab the monster's leg. She pulled down and sideways out the door. Beau had shifted his hands to the other leg, but the space was tight, and he couldn't get a good grip.

It slid through their fingers, rising up the wall to the broken door. Hellen said, "We've got to stop it! Ryin!" she called, pushing past Beau and grabbing the dumbwaiter's pull chains.

"I'm here!" Ryin said from the opening.

"You guys take the steps. Don't use the laser!"

Beau grabbed the carapaz and they disappeared into the stairwell. Pulling the chain, Hellen hauled the cart upward, gaining on the monster. It was moving slow—the carapaz in the rock weakened it. Hellen could see tiny white energy snakes crackling where the magenta rubbed the wall.

Above her, Beau's head stuck out from the stairwell into the shaft. He tried to reach across to the tentacles hooked over the bottom of the door, but it was too far.

"Let it get to me before you do anything," he said. "I'll hit it in the heads."

"Want me to shoot it?" Ryin stuck his head into the shaft.

"Not with me behind it! Give it bullets if it gets level with the door."

The monster shrieked furiously around its arm at her. The flat head stretched down its back, scowling and screeching at her, but staying out of her reach. It examined the chains, and her hands, and the head shrank back into the shoulder. Then the whole monster dropped on her, crushing her to the floor of the dumbwaiter. Both tentacles whipped over to Ryin and pulled him down on top of them.

He landed neck first. His face was crammed into the monster's lap just above her, and he looked very dead.

Chapter T.35

Rage leapt up in her, and a grief so sharp she knew it wasn't just for Ryin. It was for all of them. And she'd had enough.

The flat head leered at her, its eyes slitted and mouth in a grimace that may have been a smile. She struggled, trapped under the monster's weight, and the head came closer, around Ryin, mouth sucking toward her head.

But her knife arm wasn't trapped, and she swung it up, slicing the head right across the eyes, relishing the surprise as the top folded down and dissolved, and the rest of it flickered and went out.

Sometimes a small win is all you need to keep going.

Beau had grabbed the chains and was frantically pulling her upward. The remaining head watched for a few moments, and the monster's tentacles retracted. It turned its gaze downward to meet Hellen's eyes.

It knew her. She was certain of it. All those months of lust and passion had left a mark, and what would it do now?

The arms, just arms again, reached past Ryin and cupped her head gently. The round head lowered toward her, purple eyes gazing solemnly into hers. Its mouth puckered, and it began to suck.

Hellen felt the pull like a giant vacuum, sucking her brain, and her eyeballs, and sinuses. Her tongue stuck to the roof of her mouth, blocking her breathing. She forced it down, gasping, her knife arm slashing at every part of the monster she could reach.

Ryin's face filled her vision. Beau's voice shouted in the background…muffled, but close, she thought.

The pull had deepened into her chest, terrifying and overpowering. Her arm no longer worked, and lay limp against the dumbwaiter floor. Black holes appeared in her vision, took over, and her vision dimmed and went out.

Movement jostled her. Some kind of scuffle overhead. The pull had stopped, and Hellen's eyes began to work again. Above her, Beau straddled the shaft, beating the monster with the carapaz. Sound began to penetrate the haze, and the monster's shrieks filled the narrow space. Its hands left her head and its arms went up, grabbed the bottom of the opening to the kitchen, and the monster slithered past the broken door into freedom.

Chapter T.36

When they got to the tear, David felt like he was looking at a movie set. People were running around, clearing brush, moving stuff. The rock giants had made a wall behind the tear, and David couldn't tell whether their…personalities were in them or not. The rock giant containing the tear sat in the middle of the all the activity, complaining.

"When are they going to get here? This thing is burning a hole in me and I'm tired of my ass being wet. Has anyone heard from *anyone*?"

"We're here now," the Queen called, climbing off her horse. "Wolf!" She knelt as the big dog ran over to her, a sandwich hanging out of his mouth.

"Looks like Vartile has already rewarded him with one of her famous egg sandwiches." David said. "I am *so* jealous."

"You and me both! But you totally deserve it, you Best Dog Ever. Thank you for getting us here." The Queen rubbed his ears, and Wolf chucked her chin gently with his nose before he bent over to eat his sandwich. She gave him a quick squeeze and left him to it. "David, would you please get me to the rock giant?"

"Yes, ma'am." He tossed the reins to someone leading another horse, tucked the Queen's hand in his arm while they walked, and when they got there, she cranked up the charm. "We're grateful you're sticking this out with us. It would be nearly impossible without one of you guys stepping up. We do need you to stay a bit longer while Hellen gets here with Dagge's monster. Can you manage that for me?"

"Well, sure," he said, all traces of irritation gone. "Now that you're here, Your Majesty, that's progress. Where is Hellen?"

"She and her team are coming through the tunnels. It shouldn't be too much longer."

"I can hang on. I'm tougher than I look."

David chuckled. What a flirt. How could you look tougher than an enormous boulder?

The Queen laughed. "I'm sure you are. Where's Merv?" she called to the group at large.

"I'm here, Your Majesty!" He stooped to pick up a plain pyramid of carapaz and brought it with him. As he got near, David could see that there was actually some cut work around the base, making it jewel-esque. The body of it was clear as pink water.

"We thought—" He remembered the customary greeting for the Queen and stopped to close his eyes and bow his head.

She held her hands in the air. "Everyone! All head bowing and eye closing is suspended until this is over! Got me?"

"Yes, ma'ams" came from all corners, and she turned to Merv again.

"All right, Merv, what did you think?"

"We thought we'd strap it in the branches, but that wrecked maneuverability, and given the nature of what we're trying to do, we decided maneuverability was probably more important. The stone isn't that heavy. Well, it's a little heavy, but I think someone like Beau, or even David could hold it without any problem. I believe a distance of thirty feet would be optimal."

"Will I be able to hold it? Because I'm pretty sure it has to be me."

"Oh," Merv said, for a moment speechless. "Well—"

"I can do it," David said. "Let me do it. We don't know what will happen once the energy builds. Sound can move a boulder! Something like this might be dangerous to the person holding it."

"I don't disagree," she said. "But I've dreamed about this, and it's not negotiable."

David had no words for five seconds, and that was unusual for him. "Your Majesty, you are far too important to take that risk."

"Oh, baloney," she said. "I appoint you my successor should something happen to me."

"Don't even joke."

"I'm not joking. Who are my witnesses?" she called at large.

"I'm a witness," Vartile said.

"Me too," Luhe chimed in.

"I as well," said Dessara.

"Likewise me," Donas said.

An unintelligible noise escaped his mouth and his head snapped back around to the Queen.

"There, then. I'm holding the crystal." The Queen tilted her head and smiled at him, golden eyes twinkling, and he couldn't help but laugh. Sheer horror, maybe.

A shout came from the north. Cary's voice cried, "The monster's out!" He came striding toward them through the trees. "It got out at the monastery, and Hellen and Beau need help!"

Chapter T.37

Hellen supposed she shouldn't have been surprised to see the sun, but the last three hours had turned out to be ten, so she was discombobulated. Not to mention sad, angry, and wiped. To cap that off, the monster gained wind once it got out of the tunnel, and nothing she and Beau did slowed it down at all.

It had gone immediately out the back door, feelers waving, Beau said. By the time he'd gotten her out from under Ryin and boosted her up to the door, the thing was gone.

They'd run out immediately, and of course it was hiding beside the door. But Beau had insisted on going first, and he shoved the monster back to the wall with the jewel, and held it there while Hellen got a running start. When he caught up, he was running like hells, arms pumping, vest slung over one shoulder cradling the jewel.

That was when she radioed. The monster was in full pursuit, and feeling much better now that it was out of the tunnels.

"Cary! Cary!"

"I'm here!"

"It got away from us at the monastery! We're in the forest, heading straight for you, but we're going to need help."

"We'll be there before you know it. Out."

Hellen clipped Beau's radio onto her belt, and suddenly thankful for all the lean, hard times she'd had, settled in for another long haul.

Chapter T.38

"We need anyone who has a carapaz weapon!" Cary's burgundy and teal vibrated hard as he hurried through the trees and people, shouting.

Adia wondered where Hellen's lightning weapon was. Nowhere handy…not that it would help, anyway.

Cary rushed up, all rapid breathing and agitation. "Your Majesty, request permission to lead a group toward the monastery to assist Hellen and Beau."

"Permission granted," she said.

"Where's Firio? Did he go with Hellen?"

Adia's heart jolted. She assumed someone had told him.

David took the burden. "Firio didn't make it, man. The monster got him." Cary's light slowed, and he was silent.

Many other lights joined them, and she asked, "Who have we got here?"

Byron Tamer said, "I'm here, Your Majesty." His light was half chocolate and half royal blue. "Rack made me a carapaz knife."

"This is Donas, Your Majesty. I have carapaz arrowheads."

"Donas!" He had an orange and aqua stripe. How interesting. Adia held her hand out and Donas put his in hers. She squeezed and let it go.

"Your Majesty—"

"Okay, let's dispense with the 'your majestys' for the moment and speed this up." Adia pointed at a snapping red and orange light.

"I'm Kata, I have carapaz arrows." A young woman's voice.

"I'm Cadiz, and also have arrows." A man, true blue and turquoise.

"Good. From what I saw, Hellen's knife hurt the monster but didn't kill it—cuts healed up as soon as the blade was out. Arrows will go deeper, the deeper the better. As long as they're in there, they're doing damage. You'll need to weaken and distract it strategically, keeping in mind it does need to get here.

"Take horses." She called to the clearing at large, "Will someone please get the horses ready to go again?" A couple of "yes, ma'ams" floated through the trees. She spoke again to the group. "Hellen and her team will need rides. Bunk up if—"

"Hellen can have my horse. I'll lead the monster." Cary's burgundy and teal glowed very hot. Adia wasn't sure if that was a good or bad thing.

David said, "Cary, don't interrupt the Queen."

Cary's light sparked and twisted like he might erupt. Thank One for those diplomacy classes. She said, "Thank you, David, I'll handle it from here. Maybe you could talk to the others and get them ready for the formation."

"Yes, of course, ma'am." David walked away, galaxy whirling.

Adia turned back to Cary. His light had slowed a little. "I know you know what you're doing. I appreciate you taking this on."

"I'm used to running, ma'am. And I want to lead that fucking monster to its death. I owe Firio." His light swept with a series of bright waves. "And I won't let you down."

"I know you won't," she said. "Byron…" She reached her hand to him and he laid his fingertips on hers. "Tell the archers what to expect. I'll send Wolf to get you there. Wolf!" she called, and his nose bumped her other hand from behind. She bent her head toward him. "I'll need you to lead them, okay?" Stroking his head with her thumb, she continued with the people. "Dagge's monster has to go back through that tear. Lure it, shoot it, chase it, fight it, whatever you have to do. Just please stay alive."

"Yes, ma'ams" were said, and Donas added, "I'm too young to die." The others laughed because he was the oldest by far. A couple of "me, toos" chimed in.

A voice called from her 4 o'clock, "Horses are ready, ma'am!"

"Go," she told them, and the small group of fighters hurried away.

"Wolf…" She leaned down to him and cupped his face. "Find Hellen." He licked her nose and trotted away with Cary toward the horses.

Adia faced the clusters of people working among the trees. "Hellen and Beau are coming through the forest with Dagge's monster." she called. "If you haven't seen it, be prepared. It's horrifying and dangerous, and we have to force it into the tear. Soon will be the time for courage. For all of us. We cannot falter. And we cannot fail!"

Voices bounced from group to group: *We won't fail!* and *"Courage, everyone!"* and *"We're feckin bad ASS!"* They all laughed, and a cheer went up, and Adia's heart felt a wee bit better. The lights surrounding her were every color and countless styles, weaving a tapestry of magic, and Adia was again overwhelmed by the beauty of people.

Chapter T.39

The monster had grown.

It was three times human height now, not full strength, but better and better. Too tall under the canopy in some places, though, so it made giant fists to break through the branches. One arm was stunted—the one she cut off in the tunnel—and its fingers were black, but that didn't slow it down much. Leaves and sticks went flying. Its fat head would appear in the gap between the broken limbs, grimacing.

Not far into the trees, it had put feelers out on its chest, pointing forward, and Hellen wondered if it could sense the people ahead. Or the tear itself. Maybe that was why this little perp walk was going well. It wanted to get to the tear because it had friends there.

That would be a nightmare.

Beau worked hard at keeping the monster focused on them: firing laser pulses; occasionally grazing the magenta to whet its appetite. Twice the monster caught the laser pulses with its hand, lighting it up, face grinning open-mouthed just like Dagge used to do. Beau was more careful after that, and a few times, when the monster got tired of that game, Hellen had had to get in close and remind it how much it liked sucking her head.

It was chasing her when the first arrow embedded in its side. Hellen heard it crackle as it hit, and saw the shaft had gone deep when she turned to look. The monster stopped, its hands held away from the arrow, a surprised roar filling the air. Hellen scanned the trees and found several people ready to shoot—two on her side, one on Beau's side.

All of them waited to see how the first arrow worked. Hellen slid around some rock to hide while she watched. Wolf, growling, appeared to her left, then Cary to her right.

The monster's eyes narrowed. Its mouth hung open, and it sneered at them, then it put both hands on the arrow and pulled. Chunks of crackling magenta oozed out the entry point, white snakes more and more visible as the tip neared the surface.

"FIRE!" Hellen shouted. Three more arrows pierced the monster, two in the body, one in the head. It screamed, furious, threw the first arrow aside, grabbed the arrow in its head with one hand and ripped it out. The tip brought more chunks of magenta, crackling with energy, oozing down the monster's face. As the white energy faded, the magenta reabsorbed. The monster threw the arrow aside and turned toward the forest, searching.

"Hide!" she yelled, backing away. "We need to keep going," she added, looking to her left for Beau. He stood at the front curve of a tall jut of rock, rifle up, keeping one eye on the monster and the other on her. She signaled him to back away.

"I brought a couple of horses for you and your team," Cary said. "Is it just you and Beau left?"

"Yeah." Horses sounded great at this point, if the monster would follow them.

Cary nodded. "They're back in the trees, one on each side. You should go ahead, let me take this."

They'd backed about ten strides and the monster wasn't following—it scoured the forest for archers instead. "I don't think it'll follow you, Cary. It's got no reason to."

"We'll see about that," he said, and crossed in front of her, sticking his finger and thumb in his mouth. He blew, and Dagge's special whistle for his horse pierced the air—not a perfect imitation, like Firio's, but good enough. The monster's head slowly came around. Cary did it again. It stared at him, mouth hanging open, eyes slitted. He did it again. A change transformed the monster's face…it got a nose, and cheekbones, and eyebrows. It became a giant magenta Dagge face with glowing purple eyes.

The head swooped forward, body stretching long so its face went right up to Cary. Surprised, Cary stumbled backward and fell.

"YOU."

The thing spoke.

Wolf barked and crouched. Hellen rushed forward, brandishing her knife. Byron appeared on her right, breathing hard, a carapaz blade twice the length of hers sticking out from his fist. For a brief second, she felt knife envy.

"FIRE!" she shouted, but the Dagge thing jerked upward and only one arrow nicked him. Hellen put herself in front of Cary. "Get back, asshole," she said.

"What are you going to do, Hellen? Poke my eye out?" The Dagge thing laughed, and it sounded just like him.

Cary jumped up, Beau had pulled out the jewel, and they flanked her on her left. Hellen saw them in her peripheral vision, but she couldn't stop the horrified fascination gluing her eyes to Dagge's face. It looked at her, too.

"Happy to see me? Bet you didn't know I was in there, did you? DID YOU!" It thrust and roared in her face, pulling back just in time to avoid the sweep of Byron's knife. "Oho! Big man!"

The face weaved through the air above them, back and forth on a long body like a snake. "It's been me all along, Hellen," it said. "All the sex. All the pillow talk. How does that make you feel?"

Horrified, to be honest, but this really wasn't a conversation she wanted to have.

"Let's talk about what happens to evil assholes when they die, instead."

It regarded her in silence for a moment. "You can't kill me, no matter how hard you try. I'm beyond that now. I'm something this world has never seen before; my human brain just didn't know it. The third dimension isn't all it's cracked up to be. You people are stupid."

That did it. Hellen had enough of listening to this monumental shit pile.

"Fuck you, Dagge. You couldn't catch us while you were alive, and you can't catch us now."

Cary whistled Sephone's whistle again, and they all turned and ran. Behind them, Dagge's angry shout turned into the monster's roar, and it came thundering after.

Chapter T.40

Adia watched David arrange the people in formation. Some of the lights he moved around were bound to be people she knew, but she didn't know their lights yet, so it was impossible to pick them out. A few she recognized: Merv's bar graph of plum, peach, and celery was in the front of the formation, and Cookie's gold and toast cluster was behind Vartile, who was near front center where Adia would be. The pink girl was there, and Luhe was walking around—on guard, she imagined.

But she didn't know Dessara, who was out there somewhere, and Patsie...workers from the palace, too. She wished she knew who they all were, because it meant something very significant that they were here.

She wondered about Roberta. There wasn't much chance she could save Robert, but there was a good chance she didn't die. *Please stay away.*

Pulling her head back into the moment, she watched David. Something was wrong—it suddenly all seemed like wasted time.

"David!" she called to him across the clearing.

"Yes, ma'am!" he called back, and his light moved around the edge of the formation toward her.

"Something's off," she said when he got near. "This isn't the way it's supposed to be."

"It's the only formation I know."

"I know, it's not that, I don't think."

He made a frustrated sound, the blue of his light sparking. "I don't know what else to do. I have a hundred people and not a lot of time."

"I know." Adia glanced around, hoping an answer would come to her. Something obvious.

"What was in your dream?"

"I had the crystal…" She raised her spread hands to head height. "I put it in the window…and I could see myself in the trees on the other side." With both hands, she indicated a path. "The beam from me met the beam from the other me, like a mirror."

"Then we need two formations. A mirror, why didn't I think of that?"

"But we only have one crystal."

"Maybe the sound will mimic the beam…I don't know. I'm winging this. Do you have a better idea?"

"No, I think you're right about the mirror. Let's do that. We'll figure the rest out as we go."

David stepped toward the rock giant, who was chatting with the people at the front of the formation. "Cliff, are you squared with the tear? Not turned at all?"

"I haven't moved since you made me check. Only my head and arms. Tell me you aren't going to start all over."

"We're not going to start all over," David assured him, moving away from her. "Only a little over. I need half the people on the other side! If you're in the last two layers, come with me. And all you free people, come too."

She'd been counting on all the people being behind her, connecting their energy with hers so she could put it through the crystal and fry that thing. Would half of them be enough if it didn't work that way with the mirror side?

Adia's chest tightened another notch.

Chapter T.41

Hellen found herself running alongside two of the archers when she veered to get the horse. "Who can shoot from horseback?"

"I can," the young woman answered. Hellen didn't know her, but she didn't know everyone.

"Great, what's your name?"

"Kata."

"Let's go, Kata." Donas, pick up the other archer and meet us at the tear." Donas dashed off old man style to his horse.

Their horse was Starseed, as luck would have it. She whinnied when she saw Hellen, and was only a little skittish considering the shrieking magenta monster mere strides away.

As they went, Hellen kept them around ten strides to the left, level with Cary. Wolf ran between them and the monster, Beau and Byron kept pace on the other side. Cadiz, the archer on that side, was one of Rack's apprentices. Donas picked him up and they kept pace with the monster behind.

Whenever the monster started coming their way, her archer fired. When it veered the other way, Cadiz fired. The thing had nine or ten shafts sticking out of it before long. Some of them broke in the trees, two it pulled out, a handful of unbroken ones bobbed on its back. If the monster stopped or slowed, Beau would shoot it with his laser rifle. Then Cary would get its attention again.

Cary knew just how to piss the monster off. He teased it, slowing down and speeding up, whistling insulting variations on the horse whistle. Laughing at it. The monster had gone back to its thrice-human size and had its fists again. Occasionally it would swing one at Cary and he'd dodge and laugh.

The terrain was tricky, but smoother than a lot of the forest. Hellen kept Starseed in the open space between the trees, away from roots and rocks as much as she could. Kata had wedged herself in the saddle behind Hellen, which was snug, but made it easier for Starseed.

Cary, on the other hand, took the monster through every rough spot he could find. He flipped over fallen trunks and swung on vines and branches over gullies. Doing somersaults and shit. The monster would have to slow down and Cary would perch on the other side of whatever obstacle it was, mocking it. It got dimmer, slower, and shrank some as they went, until it was only twice human size.

And seriously pissed off.

It shrieked at Cary when he climbed a high jut of rock and smiled down at it. The monster took a swipe and broke a chunk out, but Cary jumped down the back and came around to the side, just feet away. It lunged at him and he skipped away, laughing.

That infuriated it. The face writhed into Dagge's again. He sneered, and the upper half of his body spun around and grabbed Donas in one hand, Cadiz in the other. He spun them back around to face Hellen. Dagge looked at her, lowered his mouth onto their heads and sucked.

Hellen freaked. She jumped down, unslung her rifle, and dropped it on the ground at a full run. Reaching the nearest leg, she dug long slices up and down with her knife, trying to hurt it. The magenta sparked with white as the carapaz passed through. Byron ran over and started using his knife, slicing its arm everywhere he could reach. Beau swiped the jewel across the monster's feet and pounded its ankles.

But it wouldn't stop sucking.

Donas and Cadiz began to jerk and shake. Hellen sheathed her knife and pulled on the two men's legs. Their eyes were blank and mouths open, absorbed by the consuming of their lives. Byron pulled at the arm holding Donas. Kata pulled at the one holding Cadiz. Beau climbed the tree next to the monster and smashed Dagge's awful face, over and over.

It wouldn't let the two men go. Hellen tried to climb up an arm, but it flapped her off. Beau dropped onto it, and the carapaz hit the monster's head, but he bounced off, jewel sparking. By then it was too late. Their friends' eyes had hollowed, they gasped for air, and their skin hung slack and gray.

A gunshot came from behind her. Then another. Cary had the bullet rifle, and both men hung dead in Dagge's arms. The monster raised Dagge's face and looked at Cary.

Hellen ran to him. "Good shots, Cary. Where are the horses?"

"Behind the rocks."

Beau came running. "Let's go let's GO!"

Dagge dropped Donas and Cadiz and came for them, shrieking.

Hellen and Kata ran for Starseed, Beau and Byron ran for their horses. Even Cary caught Donas's horse and rode.

They wove through the trees, leading it. It smashed through branches at a dead run behind them. Triple-size again, ripping out arrows.

And then it stopped. The ground stopped shaking, branches stopped breaking, and everything was quiet. Hellen swung Starseed around. Kata's arms clutched Hellen's waist and they teetered almost out of the saddle. Hellen stopped the mare facing Dagge, and walked her through the trees to get a better look.

It had feelers out, waving in the air, tasting. Little by little, all came to rest in one direction. Straight toward the tear.

It shrieked. And ran.

And so did they.

Chapter T.42

Adia rubbed her forehead with her fingertips, unsure what to make of the formations front and back of the rock giant. The other rock giants were hollering advice, David was strung out, and the people standing in the formations were restless. She couldn't blame them. This enterprise was a mess.

The new formation had gotten skewed to one side. It had been impossible for David to see through Cliff, of course, and lining the people up perfectly on the first try would have been miraculous. What they'd needed was a bird's eye view, and David asked Cliff if he could climb up and stand by his head.

"Sure, man, that's what I've got big shoulders for," Cliff had said, and now David was directing people from on high.

At the moment, David was moving everyone over two steps.

"No, look," he was saying, "line the center up with my arm."

"Who's the center?" someone called.

She was tired. They were all tired, and the cranky level was high. A lot of people on the original side were sitting in their spots, which was a great idea as long as they didn't get surprised. Hellen or Beau or Cary needed get on the walkntalk and update them—the fact that they hadn't worried her. But she didn't want to think about the possibility that they were dead.

All she let herself think was that her own team needed to hurry. If Hellen's team were to show up right now, they'd all be screwed.

"I want to thank all of you for being so patient." She said it loud enough for everyone to hear, though she was speaking primarily to the first group. "Hellen and the others could be showing up any minute, and it would be smart for us to have a practice run using the crystal." Adia's place would be at the front, and she made her way that direction.

"We're going to sing, like before, but this time I want you also to physically connect. Hands, hand to shoulder, arm, whatever. The people nearest to me will connect with me, and together we'll power the crystal."

As she rounded the front corner of the formation, Merv met her with the carapaz, and she carried it to the center of the front row.

"Are you going to point that thing at me?" Cliff was closer than Adia expected. She couldn't see his light, or the tear, so déjà vu all over again, right? Just like old times. Must be the rock. Or maybe the whatever-dimension energy he was.

"Not if you move," she answered.

"Ohh," he said in a high voice, "she's funny!"

Adia chuckled and settled herself in her spot. The people in adequate earshot also laughed, which was good, because the tension was taut. "David, are you close to ready?" she called.

"Yes, ma'am," he yelled down over his shoulder. "You guys on the end, a little more...a little more...perfect!" He jumped down bit by bit to the ground. "We should be good for a test run," he said, walking toward her. "So, after this, want to go get some coffee or something?"

She laughed, chin dropped to her chest, crystal on her hip like a toddler.

"Sure, I'd love that," she said, her face rising to meet his.

Chapter T.43

David wanted to touch her so badly, to smooth the worry away between her brows, or wrap her in his arms. But not the time or place for that, obviously.

"Is that heavy?" he asked.

"Yeah, but I can manage."

He nodded and smiled, as pointless as that was. "I know."

David, turn to the side a sec.

David jerked his head around, looking for whatever was going to clobber him over the head. Nothing there.

Be subtle! Are you twelve?

He turned more slowly. Just looking around… "I thought—"

Don't think! I don't mean that. Just listen…you have to mirror.

"*I* have to mirror? I thought I was supposed to be behind her." Only he thought it to his Dad instead of saying it.

Did you hear me?

So much for two way telepathy. "I need to be the mirror?"

Hear me, okay? You'll know when the time comes.

His voice faded out and he was gone.

What was with all the cryptic bullshit?

"Was that your Dad?"

"Yeah, could you see him?"

"Not this time. He's really hiding, getting you to turn around like that. What did he say?"

"I have to be the mirror."

"That makes sense. We probably could have figured that out."

"I thou—"

She held her hand up, quieting him.

Shrieking. Still in the distance, but not for long.

569

It's time!" she shouted.

The sitting people stood, and David checked the formation behind the Queen to make sure it was still tight. After waving a few people over, he stopped beside her and put his hand over hers on the crystal. "This side is ready to test."

"We should look at the other side, make sure both are lined up, and start singing." She put her other hand on top of his and gave it a squeeze, then patted it and turned to business.

"Cliff, it's time to go," she told the small mountain of rock in the middle.

"Yes, ma'am."

Cliff pushed himself up off his haunches, the power moving his rocks making an audible hum. Standing, he realigned his invisible joints, reminding David of a boxer, and David had to wonder how good these guys would be in a fight. They might be about to find out. On mismatched feet, Cliff slid his heavy body toward the rock giant wall.

David hadn't seen the tear before. It hung in the air, about six feet off the ground, two feet tall, give or take, and a little more than a foot wide. Pink and blue light danced in it. The edges burned.

How the hells were they going to get that huge-ass monster into that tiny hole?

Chapter T.44

Gunfire popped in the forest, not close, but too close for comfort. All niceties disappeared, and Adia pushed David toward the formation opposite.

"They're warning us. Everyone connect!" she said. All around, the people adjusted their positions and placed hands on shoulders and backs. "The monster will be scary. Don't let go! Don't move! No matter what happens. Send your energy to me, and I'll do everything I can to keep the monster from us." She called to the other side of the tear. "You on that side, send energy to David. He'll connect with me."

How in blazes were they supposed to do that? She had no idea. Maybe David could throw his heart out of his chest like old Mahab.

"Okay, everybody! Here's your note!" A strong F rose out of David's belly, through his throat, and into the air.

In a few seconds, both sides of the formation had picked it up. As they settled into it, she glanced around her, but she was too short to see.

"What is it?" he called over the loudness.

"I can't see well enough," she yelled.

"Stand on my shoulders," David shouted, and hurried over. As he rounded the tear, he could hear it crackle. That was new, but he didn't give it much thought.

Luhe jogged over from the side. "Stand on mine," he said. "David might need to hold the crystal." Adia handed David the crystal and climbed onto to Luhe's shoulders.

Holding Luhe's hands, Adia steered him in a slow circle. The connections were fainter than they were in the tunnel, and it seemed to take forever to make out the formation. When she pointed, David rushed to the problem spot and fixed it according to her hand motions. There were three of those, not bad, plus some minor edge trimming. But no connections across the gap.

Those old fraud feelings raised their ugly heads, but she refused to give in. She was in position and ready for the crystal back when the rock giants started shouting.

"It's coming! IT'S COMING!"

Chapter T.45

Half the voices shut off like a faucet. David didn't blame them, he trickled off with the rest, and would they even be able to get going again? Possibly not with Dagge's freak show bearing down on them.

David ran the pyramid to the Queen, worried about her using that thing. It was huge, and what if this process fried her? Or liquefied her, or something else equally horrible?

He pushed that out of his mind and ran back to his own spot. The people looked over their shoulders, or watched him, a few hands in the middle reaching toward him. They looked afraid. So was he. All their backs were to the monster, and that was the worst.

David hoped they hadn't gotten out of place, because they really needed this formation to work. No time to test the crystal now—at this point it was all about faith. In Merv, in the Queen, in the monks.

Maybe Dad meant David would know when, and hopefully how, to connect energy with the Queen. Magically. That seemed likely, right?

The roars were closer. Closer and closer. They could all hear branches breaking now, over a low thundering of feet and hooves.

He felt pale. Was that possible? Sweat ran down his face and neck. Every cell in his body wanted to run.

Chapter T.46

They paced the monster, weaving the horses through the trees, sometimes having to veer pretty far to stay on less treacherous ground. But they kept up, and that was how Hellen could see the feelers stretching, yearning you might say.

It had shrunk to fit under the trees so it could move faster. Mostly legs now, too—its body was the size of a child. The magenta was fading, which was good, though there was no telling what other new tricks it could be pulling out later. She wished her knife was a three-foot sword, she'd cut those legs off right now.

At least they'd have Merv's pyramid. Beau had made good use of his jewel, and they did move a boulder once with that formation. They didn't move it very far, but she wasn't going to think about that.

Kata hung on behind her, bow in hand. She'd landed a couple of arrows in the monster's leg, but it was a waste of carapaz. The thing acted like it couldn't even feel the arrowheads, despite the white snakes flashing around them.

Wolf still ran between their horse and the monster, his attention strictly ahead. On Adia, Hellen was sure. She would have to be in front of everyone, closest to the tear. And if the monster was feeling the tear, the tear might be feeling the monster.

But as long as Wolf didn't suddenly race forward, Adia was still okay.

They were nearing the tear. She waved to catch Beau's eye, and made her hand into a gun, pointing in the air. He pulled out his pistol and fired again.

Using her feet, Hellen urged Starseed into a faster run.

Chapter T.47

"Rock giants! Please, place yourselves so you block the monster's view of the people, and create a funnel to direct the monster to the side, between the formations. The less the monster sees beforehand the better. Position your rocks to look natural, and if you don't want to stay, please leave your rocks on the far side of the funnel. This isn't your fight, no one will blame you.

"People! Everyone who is not in the formation, get behind us. There's no telling what will happen. It could get bad. Be ready to fill in if needed."

Adia hated asking people to risk death. Good people who never trained to be soldiers. But what else could she do?

As the rock giants placed themselves, between them she glimpsed the magenta glow—unclear, broken up by the energy of the trees—maybe 90 strides away. And closing.

Gunfire popped again. Horse and riders galloped toward the tear, flashing across the gaps between the rocks. A few seconds later, Starseed came running into the clearing, Wolf at her side, Hellen and Kata on her back.

Chapter T.48

Hellen swung her leg over Starseed's neck and jumped down. "Stay with the horse," she told Kata. "We might be back on her if it doesn't take the bait."

Kata nodded, and Hellen started toward Adia. A waving arm in the middle of the formation caught her attention. It was Dessara, her forehead furrowed.

Hellen wished she could nod, or give a thumbs-up, or anything that would let Dessara know Donas was okay. That he'd come riding up in a minute and continue this fight with them. But that wasn't going to happen. Instead, Hellen had to shake her head and watch Dessara break, see her eyes roll back and her head fall forward...see her life crumble in a single blow. Someday Hellen would have to tell Dessara about her husband's courage, and what happened in his last moments. She'd tell her it didn't hurt, and she wouldn't be lying. But she would never tell Dessara about the sightless, sunken eyes and hanging skin. She didn't need to know about that.

"I've got the giants funneling the monster to the side," Adia said as she approached. "The tear's firing up, and the less that thing sees, the better."

Hellen looked at the tear. The rim burned hot, and the inside looked more magenta than blue. Good thing David had given it some space, because they couldn't catch a freaking break today.

"A funnel's perfect," Hellen said. "They can close in behind Dagge and trap it. Browbone!" she shouted.

"Here," he answered, at the front edge of the formation.

"We'll need three or four of you to close the monster in when it gets into the funnel. Don't worry, it doesn't like rock, it should stay away."

"Bellyboy! Ig! Get ready to hem it in!" Browbone moved to the edge of the funnel, Duncecap taking his place blocking the people.

"You called it 'Dagge'," Adia said.

"Wait 'til you see it." They stood side by side, listening to the scruff of tree limbs and ominous pounding.

"Where's Wolf? I saw he came back with you."

"I don't know." Hellen glanced around. "He was with us the whole time. He's okay, don't worry. He'll be back. In the meantime, you've got me. I'm staying right here." Hellen said.

"Yes," Adia said, relief and gratitude all in it. She shifted the pyramid left, and found Hellen's hand with her right. "Let's kill this sick horror show."

"Hells yeah," Hellen said, and they faced the front together. "I've never seen this many rock giants before. Eight are in front, blocking us except for a curve opening away to the right. It looks like six more left their rocks on the west side. They define the funnel and block us up to the trees."

"Okay, thanks. It's good to know what I'm working with." Adia squeezed Hellen's hand, let it go, and got her pyramid crystal positioned in front of her.

Bits of magenta flashed above and between the rocks. Beau and his horse flew past the last few, and he was out of the saddle at a full run, carrying the jewel to the Queen. David was off his post and running toward Beau before the Queen could say anything.

"Mirror!" he shouted to her, and she nodded at Beau, and Beau handed David the carapaz. David ran back to his spot and started to sing.

But the people were mumbling too loud, shifting nervously, and didn't hear him. Hellen picked up the note as loud as she could, and a few others did the same.

Cary and Byron ran their horses around the curve and into the clearing. All singing stopped as they dismounted and tossed their reins to a horse guy.

"Kata!" Byron called.

Kata handed off Starseed's reins to the horse guy and took her place at the welcoming end of the funnel.

But when the monster got to the funnel, it stopped. The bare front edge of it was just visible through the rocks. The legs shrank to normal human size, the body grew to normal size, and the feelers came out again.

The tear was hard to see from the side, but that didn't mean it was hard to feel. Hellen had no idea how sensitive those waving worms were.

Cary trotted back into the funnel and whistled. It just looked at him. Then its face morphed into Dagge again. The head grew bigger than the body—but thin, like a mask—and stretched out on a long neck. It tilted out over Cary's head.

"Fuck you," it said. "You think I'm here because you were whistling? You're a moron." It looked for Beau and found him between the funnel and the formation. "Thanks for all the laser fire, by the way."

Hellen couldn't see Cary's face, but he had to be fuming. Dagge's right fist shot out and landed a surprise punch on him. Cary hit the ground, slid into a rock, and the asshole kept talking.

"I know who's in there!" Dagge's face called.

Only he didn't know everyone in there. The incredible people fighting for their lives. He wouldn't care about them, they were filler. What an idiot. Not that she was complaining.

Of course he knew the Queen was in there, but that wasn't going to change anything.

It continued. "Princess, if you will come out, and stop fighting, I will consider forgiving you."

Next to her, the Queen laughed.

"Rock giants!" she called. "Open a sightline between Dagge and me, please!"

Chapter T.49

Slowly, the rock giants shifted until Adia could see the magenta Dagge thing they'd been blocking. The giant head was a good look for him. Accurate.

"What's that you have in your hands, Princess? Aren't you happy to see me? Oh, I'm sorry, there's that word again."

"You are an unbelievable dick. Do you know that? What am I saying, you have no idea. You're a classic narcissist. Anything that isn't you is for use by you. Which is why the vast majority of people will kick your ass until you're gone. And that's going to be very soon."

"Such big talk," it said, face weaving side to side, up and down. "For such a tiny person. Tiny, and blind, and mutilated. You used to be pretty, you know."

"You are so pathetic. If that's intended to hurt, you're hammering the wrong nail, buddy." Adia handed Hellen the pyramid as she passed. It wasn't far to the mouth of the funnel, and maybe her movement would get him moving.

"Am I though?" The magenta mockup of Tomius Dagge smirked. "Any pretty girl mourns that kind of loss."

"I've lost a lot of things, and the least of them is the way I look." She stopped at the edge of Dagge's vision, using the rocks to tease him out. Backing a little. Waiting.

He moved slowly toward her. "You don't have to lose everything, Princess. I'd still let you come back to the palace. You could stay in your room when you weren't in mine."

She had that sudden drop feeling and the resultant urge to vomit. She knew what it felt like to be underneath Tomius Dagge and no thank you ever again.

But it was an angle she hadn't considered. And loathing didn't mean she couldn't use it.

Adia stepped into full view at the end of the funnel.

With her right hand, she languidly wiped the left side of her shirt up over her skin and showed that monster her scars. She turned and got the sunlight on them, raising her chin, showing the bumps and shadows to their greatest advantage.

It screeched and snarled at every rock giant it passed on its way to her.

That's right, it couldn't resist the scars. Again, she didn't know whether to feel cheap or brilliant.

Chapter T.50

David had followed his Queen, flanking Hellen, who was at her four. Hellen carried the pyramid; David had the jewel. Beau had helped Cary to his feet, and they all stood with Byron, weapons out.

Beau made eye contact with David and pointed to the jewel. Then he mimed using it to ram something. Given that it was carapaz, it made perfect sense, but it sure wouldn't be his weapon of choice.

When the Queen moved into the opening and fired the monster up by showing it her scars, it kinda took the wind out of David, he had to admit. Then the sicko started coming for her, mouth open, making this panting, growling noise like it wanted to eat her. David copied Hellen, rushing past Browbone to the Queen's side, carapaz raised.

The monster was terrifying. The big face swooped forward and backward, eyes wild, feelers waving. Its right arm and hand stretched in Adia's direction. David watched Hellen for cues…how close were they going to let this thing get?

Behind the monster, the rock giants were trapping it in a shrinking space, forcing it forward. Browbone stood at the funnel mouth, his side to the clearing, fists twitching, weight shifting from foot to foot.

Dagge edged away from him, toward the other side of the funnel. Backed against the rock, he looked out at the people. He raised his big left hand toward Hellen, almost gently. Like he thought she might help him.

And while everyone was distracted, he slung a blade out the end of his right arm, arced it into the air, and cut Browbone's head off. The rock flipped into the air, tumbled onto the shelf of his shoulders and dropped into the funnel opening not three feet from David. The small rocks of Browbone's face pattered down the big chest and landed at his feet. The people in the clearing started screaming.

"Get back!" Hellen shouted, her hand pressing the Queen. David wrapped his arm around the Queen's shoulders and pulled her with him. Browbone's heavy body collapsed with a monumental crash, blocking much of the opening, his smaller rocks thudding around him.

Hellen filled the air with fury, bellowing and showing her teeth. In her hands, the pyramid was sparking, and she ran toward the monster. Its head thrust into the gap, eyes flashing, dreadful grin stretching its mouth. The big left hand waved Hellen forward, but when she got close, instead of ramming the monster, she swung the pyramid into an uppercut. Lightning sizzled, and the magenta mask broke, spreading its jaw into the air in sharp pieces that disintegrated into ash.

Wide-eyed with fury, Dagge caught Hellen in his short, fat fist. But the pyramid burned him, because he howled and hurled her into a tree. Next to David, the Queen gasped and jerked in that direction.

"I'm a GOD!" the broken mouth screamed. "How DARE you defy me!" Whirling, it sliced its blade along the tops of two rock giants behind him. Sparks flew where the edge dragged on the rock. The giants tried to dodge, they started to bring their arms up for defense, but they were too slow, and their heads rolled off their shoulders to the dirt.

It turned back toward the people, and the mask started shrinking, its twisted grimace changing in macabre fits.

That was enough for David, he had no need to see what was coming. "We've got to get to the tear." He found the Queen's hand and ran her to her place in front of the formation. He handed her the jewel and said, "I have to find Hellen and get the pyramid. You want that or this?"

"I'll take this," she said, "and get the people going."

"Okay," David said. "I'll be right back." He ran toward the funnel and saw Byron stabbing at Dagge's hand, Cary shooting its feet with bullets. Kata had an arrow in her hands, using it like a knife when the fist came for her.

The monster screeched in fury—its blade was too long to get to them, scraping and bumping the rock in the tight space. The magenta flickered, the blade shriveled into the body, and they ran.

Beau met David at the end of the formation, carrying the pyramid.

"She's alright," Beau said, and shoved the carapaz into David's hands. "It's time. We're counting on you." He ran off to join the others as Hellen limped up to the monster, carapaz knife slashing.

Luhe and several of the other free people had made a line between the monster and the formations. They held rocks, rifles, whatever they could get their hands on.

But Dagge wasn't paying any attention to them. Dagge's attention had moved to the tear.

And the magenta creature sticking out of it.

Chapter T.51

David gave the tear a wide berth on his way back to his spot, staying outside the ditch around it. He'd put the front line of the formations at thirty-three feet, but it looked like the people had backed up and smashed to the side. He couldn't blame their instinct, but he didn't see how they were going to fix it, either.

The 2Der coming out of the tear watched them intently. It stretched and shrank, stretched and shrank. The eyes were on both sides of its head, and it reached out from one side of the tear then the other. The Queen jabbed her jewel at it, and it avoided her. Seeing no other options, it withdrew into the tear and the flashing resumed.

Vartile stood at the Queen's eight, hand on her arm, face taut. Others had hands on her. All the people were nervous—glancing and agitated…crying, some of them—but the courage of the people facing the monster raised their own courage. Resolute faces everywhere, built over abject terror.

"Connect!" the Queen shouted. David felt many hands on his back and arms, and saw the same on the other side of the tear. Her jewel got a glow in it. He looked down—his pyramid had one too.

Screaming started when a magenta tentacle shot over their heads. Straight at the Queen.

Chapter T.52

Hellen felt ripped apart, trying to keep up. Her leg was weak, pain exploding every step, but when the tentacle shot for Adia, all she could think about was getting there.

Vartile grabbed it before it got the Queen. Both her hands wrapped around it, squeezing, her face a tight landscape of determination. The tentacle fought to get free, thrashing and glowing so bright it lit Vartile in magenta fire.

Adia shoved the jewel at it, snakes writhing and crackling. Hellen yelled, "Stay connected!" as she reached the formation. For the most part they did, shouting to each other to stay, and roaring on their own.

David started the singing again. It picked up in an irregular wave, and the power in the crystals increased. Adia moved the jewel to Vartile, touching her with the point of it, and energy exploded from Vartile's hands, shuddering the tentacle with crackling power.

Waves of magenta pulsed toward them, down the length of the tentacle, over Hellen's head. The tip stretched, whipped around Vartile's waist, and hoisted her into the air. Adia shoved the jewel at the tentacle, and Hellen cut and stabbed with her knife, but it would not stop. "Cut it!" Hellen yelled. "Byron! CUT IT!"

But Byron had been caught by Dagge's fist, which had grown enormous, and wrapped around him from knee to chest. It held him in the air, Byron's knife hacking and plunging into the fingers to no avail.

Cary shot at the feet and stabbed the leg with his rifle. Beau shot the face, and it snarled and snapped at him. Energy pulses passed across her knife, crackling. Hellen slashed and sawed at the tentacle, but couldn't beat the heal.

Vartile kicked wildly as the tentacle carried her toward the tear. The flat head lunged out of the opening, black mouth open. Vartile screamed, kicking, and clawing at the tentacle around her waist and near her head.

Luhe ran past Hellen, arms reaching up, hands grasping at the tentacle, but unable to hold it. He called Vartile's name in between strangled grunts, but he was too late. The flat mouth opened wide.

Vartile's body flattened as it was forced into the second dimension. Feet, then legs, and torso thinned and stretched as she was sucked into the jagged black hole. The monster's eyes glowed. Bust and shoulders went in as the tentacle let her go. Her face distorted into a nightmare, frozen wide-eyed and mouth open as it compressed into only an image of the woman they knew. Then she was gone.

Horrified and heartbroken, Hellen placed herself in front of Adia, ready to give her life if the tentacle came back to get her.

But it didn't.

Chapter T.53

Adia watched in grief-stricken fury as Vartile's light disintegrated. What should she have done? Vartile had saved her, and she didn't save Vartile. Like she didn't save her father.

Hellen moved in front of her. Luhe stood at the tear, and he must be pulling on the tentacle because it yanked and dipped. It had plunged into the tear when Vartile and the 2Der disappeared. The pulses were going the other way now. The monster was feeding off whatever energy it was getting from the tear. Maybe Vartile's. If it decided to pick them all off one by one and shove them in there, could they stop it?

Adia wasn't going to let anyone else die. "Get behind me!" she shouted. Hellen moved to her right side. "Luhe! LUHE!"

Luhe turned. Cracks in his faceted light were leaking. Violet bands reached out and faded. His rainbow colors had dulled, and the smoky topaz was dark.

"Fight with us," she said. "Let's be rid of this thing."

He nodded once and took Vartile's place beside her.

Chapter T.54

Hellen felt torn between staying with Adia and fighting Dagge up close and personal. Sure, she had faith in whatever these crystals were going to do, just not whether they'd do it in time. The people around her were all going to be dead if they didn't stop this thing.

Dear One, please make this go the way it needs to.

A small, bald man stepped out of the crowd, swinging a sling. The rock flew, and hit the monster in the eye, imbedding in the magenta. It screamed and threw Byron down. Its tentacle snapped back, shrinking into another hand, and the monster swiped at its face where the rock sparked inside it. The eye had tightened like a sphincter, and the rock was visible behind, making sparks in the monster's head.

It erupted in rage, put both giant hands under Browbone's rock, and flipped it into the air. The people screamed and cowered, ready to run, but the rock flew over their heads and into the trees on the other side.

Fists clenched, it came for them.

Chapter T.55

"Adia. It's time."

Adia heard David clearly across the gap. She tore her focus from the monster and looked at him. His pyramid was sending a tenuous beam across the space.

Beau and the others had gotten in its way, trying to slow it down. It glared at them with its one good eye, and swung at them with both hands. But its depth perception was off, and the big fists hit some and missed some. Kata stabbed at its foot with her arrow, and it kicked her. Byron grabbed its short fist and tried to climb onto its arm, but the monster flung him into something and he bounced off.

They were never going to beat it in a normal way, anyway.

"Forget the formation, gather close and connect!" she yelled.

Hands lay all over her back, arms, and even her head. Her stone started glowing and ramped up in seconds. Energy coursed through her—all the people's fear, courage, and determination. It filled her and made her strong.

A beam stuttered its way out the end of her jewel. Adia relaxed and concentrated on moving the energy through her—hands and chest in particular. The beam steadied and grew.

Having a head start, David's beam met hers on her side of the tear. They resisted meeting, like the same poles on magnets. Her beam was wider, and cupped his.

"Put yours in the tear!" Adia yelled.

David's spinning galaxy hitched, then sped up. "Are you sure?"

"Yes!" She wasn't, really. It just popped into her head.

He aimed his pyramid upward. People around her ducked as it shot into the air above their heads. As it moved, the beam cut through the frame of embers at the edge of the tear. The cut gapped open, and

David jerked in surprise, cutting it more, making the hole even bigger—maybe three feet wide and four feet tall. Glowing ash consumed the jagged edge, smoothing it in clusters of falling bits.

The blue and pink were 2Ders. Some of them had stopped to look, but when David got his beam into their dimension, they swarmed.

The beam shined straight through the tear, looking unchanged.

Luhe came close and said, "I'm getting down on all fours. Stand on my back—it'll put you about the right height."

Hellen tapped her arm. "I've got you," she said, and wrapped both hands around Adia's waist. Adia raised her left foot, had to go higher than she expected, and with Hellen's help, lifted herself into a wide stance on Luhe's back. She raised the jewel to neck height, thankful Hellen had her by the waistband of her pants.

Across the gap, David adjusted until his beam was cupped in hers again.

But now the end of David's beam carried a perfect replica of the tear.

What the hells?

That could be problematic. Or good. Because if the carapaz worked like magnets, given that same poles repel and opposites attract, what would happen if she flipped her stone? The fractal would be sucked into it. And maybe, in some mysterious, cosmic way, that would help.

Adia grasped the tip of the stone with her right hand and flipped it toward her, resettling the weight in her left hand.

"What are you doing?" David called, a touch of panic in his voice.

"We've got to see what this does," she said. "Be ready."

David's beam had felt like a presence on her skin, warm and pushing while she spun her stone. Always worried, he veered it off of her. But when she got the opposite pole facing out, the pull of Adia's stone bent David's beam and drew it in. The beam rushed into the flat top, and the churning, burning tear was projected in a thousand windows around them.

Chapter T.56

Oh, shit.

David's first thought was that they had really screwed themselves. Dimensional tears zoomed out along the gap in both directions, onto the ground, into the air…onto people.

Adia's mouth was hanging open in shock, which meant she could see them, and that was good. After a good look around, she frowned, and smiled, and David knew she knew. But maybe the Dagge thing didn't.

The monster froze in its attack, one fist raised, eye wide and mouth open. Lunging, it stormed over the fighters and toward the tear. Its fists stretched into tentacles again, but branching this time. It was clearly planning to juice up, and after that there might be all kinds of fun new things it could do.

They only had seconds.

"Give it all you've got!" Adia yelled. The glows grew brighter, the energy stronger, and the beams from the facets of Adia's jewel filled the clearing.

Tentacles reached out of the shadows, going for the tears. When the light hit, smoke swirled into the air, and the monster screamed. That didn't stop it. It knocked Elzibieta backward into Patsie and Mieko. She had a tear on her. On the other side, Merv had a tear and was sent staggering. He came back, tried to grab the tentacle, and the end wrapped his neck and started carrying him away. Several people ran up, held Merv down, and wrenched the thing off. The monster snarled, let go, and swept its tentacles across the people, knocking them down or pissing them off. Or both.

The people were on fire. They came together, a group on each side, yelling and shouting as they tried to resume their formations.

There was no way. David waved them back away from the tears. They moved back, still yelling.

Furious, the monster melded and hardened all those tentacles into two blades.

A flash of white way behind the Queen stole David's attention. It was Wolf, and behind Wolf was his Mom.

Chapter T.57

Roberta had been glad to see Wolf. The walk was awfully long, and even with John's company most of the way she was tired and out of sorts. Wolf meant she was close, and that gave her renewed vigor.

Seeing the light at the end of the tunnel struck her as funny until she heard the screaming and screeching and gunfire that came with it. The monster was there, the fight was in full swing, and she was frightened.

Roberta knew what she was supposed to do. John had confirmed her educated guesses in the most not-telling way possible—looks, and movements, and noises. She felt like she was trying to wring information out of Joey while he was playing a game. In the end, John had to go anyway because he'd said too much. Turned out being frustrated was better than being alone.

Roberta patted her pocket. It was still there.

Wolf led her around the boulder, into the trees, and broke into a run. Something lit up the forest in golden white light. Bits of magenta glow moved through the leaves. She knew what that was.

Hefting the lightning weapon in her hand, she went toward it.

Chapter T.58

Adia broke the connection with David and all the beams and images of the tear blinked out. "EVERYONE GET BEHIND ME!" she shouted. "COURAGE!" Adia watched a second while their sparking lights rushed around the end away from the monster. Tucking the jewel under her left arm, she patted Hellen's hand. "Let's get me down," she told her. "David! Get right behind me!"

On the ground, Wolf's cold nose bumped her hand. "Wolf! Honey! I'm so glad you're here." She stroked his head and turned to face the monster. "Stay right by me, okay?"

Luhe stood beside her. "I'll be at your eight if you need me." She squeezed his arm and he took his position.

The fighters had lined the front of the group and were slowing the monster as much as they could. Cary had climbed to the tops of the rock giants right next to it. He was throwing rocks at the head, dodging the blades, and turning the thing around. Byron stabbed the foot. A blade swung down, and he jumped away, but it kept going until a scream ripped through the air. Kata had been hit, and her red and orange light went out.

Luhe's big hand landed on her shoulder and she felt the strength and courage in him. It sustained her.

David came up behind. She said, "Point the tip of the pyramid at the monster." He held it over her head. "No, in front of me," she said. "As far as you can reach. They'll have to connect with you, and you'll need to press your body to my back to transfer as much of the energy as possible." She called behind her, "Tight connections, everyone! Get as close as you can!" Hands lay on her shoulders and upper arms. Wolf pressed her right leg. Hellen's hands grasped her right forearm, and two others, no three others, held her left.

David's arms went to either side and positioned the carapaz in front of her. His chest and stomach lined her back, arms encased her head (not ideal, but no help for it.) He leaned his head down to hers and whispered, "I think I know what you're doing."

"What we're doing," she said, positioning her carapaz flat side out, but holding it below David's. "You go first."

Adia could feel the hum of energy from all the people connected behind her. They felt like a single living thing: breathing, beating, rushing blood; fear and fury and courage. David's crystal began to glow, and built a beam in fits and starts toward the monster.

Above the blades, the monster's face became Dagge's and watched. "You're so cute to think you can beat me. Do you really still think that?"

She wouldn't dignify that with an answer.

"Your father was a loser, Princess. You should know that. I gave him every opportunity to have a backbone, and he skulked around and got himself killed."

Rage rose up and ate her every thought. She wanted to unleash a fury hurricane on that colossal shitbucket. Her carapaz sucked all that energy in, sparking and flashing.

David's beam had reached the monster, which deflected it with its blades, taunting and posing, wearing Dagge's insufferable arrogance.

"Now me," she said softly, raising the jewel behind the pyramid. The repel flung the jewel to the side. She wrestled it into alignment. Luhe's strong hand left her shoulder and helped hold the jewel in place. A beam exploded out the top, meeting the flat of David's stone and lighting it up. Light came out the apex of the pyramid in a hot stream straight to the monster's chest.

"Fire it up, everyone!" she yelled, and all the righteous anger of the last three years burned through her, sent by the people of Great Hand to the monster that was Tomius Dagge, odious source of all the suffering and tragedy and loss.

Surprised, the monster held its blades stacked in front of it as a shield. They glowed fiercely, taking most of Dagge's energy, and the beam couldn't penetrate.

But that wasn't Adia's intent, anyway.

Roberta trained the little white dot on the monster's leg. She was not a marksman, but was prepared to keep the light on for as long as it took. To her surprise, it didn't take long. Pretty much as soon as she aimed, the explosion went off, making a milky white burst in the leg.

The monster lurched to the side. It snapped its head in her direction, one eye closed, the other glaring a hot purple. Roberta wanted the thing to see her, wanted it to know who the pain came from, and stepped out of the trees into the clearing.

Would it know her face? Her maid's uniform? Would it feel her hatred through the beam? She hoped so.

Roberta covered the body with bursts, everywhere she could aim the white dot. Before long, she just held the button, moved the dot around, and exploded the thing's insides.

David and Adia's beam burned it. Acrid smoke rose into the afternoon sunbeams. Black scorch marks stained the magenta like scars. Screeches shook the air, reverberating off the rocks and rebuffed by the trees.

Singing rose to meet the screams. Branches began to shake, and leaves filled the clearing. The long vibration of the one note became deafening, and drowned the desperate shrieks in a sea of sound.

Dagge's monster began to collapse in sections, only partially rebuilding before the next collapse. The arms drew back into it, trying to save the energy and heal itself. Dagge's face appeared and melted. Appendages bulged and disappeared. It tried to turn and run for the opening in the rocks.

But David and the Queen did something with the crystals they were holding. Their beam wasn't firing at the monster anymore…it was sucking at it. The jagged black mouth was pulled into a long, screaming gash…the purple eye a wild smear. Part by part, the monster lengthened into thin streaks and shredded into the beam.

The stones took the thing, and it was gone.

Chapter T.60

As the monster collapsed from the explosions, it became soft. It sucked into the pyramid, and Adia's jewel drew it from there in a meaty feed that made her sick to her stomach. The flat top of the jewel was right at her chest, and made her wonder if Dagge could get out again.

They needed to hurry.

"Break off," Adia said. "Let me take it."

David lifted his pyramid away. Cool air rushed in, chilling her back and neck. She was sweating.

"Have you got it?" Luhe asked.

Adia spread and repositioned her hands. "Yeah," she said, nodding. Luhe removed his hand, and the jewel got heavier. Adia looked down and saw movement. A purple eye glowed in the thousand facets.

Heart surging, she strode to the flashing and sparkling tear in front of her, reached up, and stuffed the jewel into it. The consistency was like pushing a rock into gelatin, except the jewel went flat as it crossed the threshold. White snakes of energy erupted, a storm of lightning that grew and filled the tear.

Adia backed away, stepping between David on one side, and Hellen on the other. They held hands. The crowd spread around them, hands connecting to her back and shoulders. Luhe and Cookie were there. Merv and Dessara. Cary and Beau were beside Hellen. Byron farther on, standing beside someone Adia didn't know. Everyone who had fought, or had died fighting, was there. Adia could feel them.

They all watched in silence as crackling snakes melted the glowing edges of the tear into a blue and magenta shimmer. That shimmer became opaque, and shrank around the jewel. Dagge's face appeared in its flat top. It grimaced and morphed as the hole got smaller, mouth opening in silent shrieks. One eye was still a sphincter.

The 3D world took its space back and closed the tear. For Adia it disappeared. No remnants that she could see.

After a few seconds of cautious silence, a cheer exploded around her. People started laughing and whooping. Wolf barked, and Adia pounded him on the side. She put her arms around Hellen, who swayed and patted for two seconds then thrust their arms into the air, turning them both to see the people behind them.

Lights glowed and flashed and jumped and swarmed all over. Adia saw sparkles, rockets, flames, all kinds of moving parts, all alive with victory and joy. She wished she could have a snapshot of this moment, and took a few seconds to try and imprint it on her mind.

David took her hand. She could tell by the size and heft of it, and where the callouses were. "Mind if I hold one of these for you?" he asked.

"I do not mind."

"I was thinking maybe I could give you a hug."

Adia suppressed a smile. "Do you really think you need to ask?"

"Well, I don't want to make assumptions." He turned to face her.

She faced him, too. "I appreciate that."

"So-o, what do you think?"

Hellen's face shoved into their moment. "I think you guys need to tonsil-swab each other and get it over with. Adia, it's almost dinner time, and Cookie wants to raid the kitchen for everybody. Let's have a bonfire! In the east meadow, so we can gaze at the forest and tell stories of all we've done."

"I love that idea." Adia grinned up at her two favorite people. "You guys, I'm amazed at us. Look what badasses we are. Every single person here."

"Couldn't agree more," David said, that smile in his voice.

"Me too." Hellen squeezed her arms around Adia's shoulders, and David somewhere, so they were tight. "We've done each other

600

proud. Now you guys kiss, and let's get going. See you at camp teardown." Patting Adia on the shoulder blade, she walked away, Beau on her other side. "Cookie! Whatcha got in that kitchen?"

Smiling, Adia turned to David and said, "I guess we better do this so we can get going."

"The hug part, or the tonsil part?"

"Um, I'm thinking let's start with hugs. That back-stomach contact was, um…" Her head nodded while she searched for the word. "Powerful."

"I'm really glad you felt that way, because again, I couldn't agree more."

David's arms wrapped around her and she snuggled into his chest, arms around his waist. The electricity between them soothed and excited her at the same time. She gave a quick look down, and his yellow galaxy was spinning and throwing sparks.

"That's not really fair, you know," he said. "You can see all my secrets."

"You can see my face, so I don't feel bad about that."

David laughed and kissed her on the head. Around them, people were moving through the trees toward camp. The two of them looped arms around each other and went along. Adia completely trusted David to get her over the forest floor pain-free.

And that was saying something.

Over their heads, birds twittered and flew under the canopy. A high breeze soughed in the treetops, and washed in waves across her skin. Afternoon sunshine warmed her in spots as she moved through them. Ahead, voices hummed in conversation, laughed, or shouted across the space to each other.

They were going home. Really their home now, changed and damaged though it was. Almost all of it could be reclaimed…just not the people. The greatest loss. Memorials would be needed. Medals and honors. Burials. This evening they'd move the fallen to an interim place. Everyone would help, so it would go quickly.

So much to do yet. But tonight was for celebration.

Epilogue: Reign Dance

Chapter E.1

Hellen stood at her bathroom mirror putting the finishing touches on her makeup. One last dab of mascara…some lipstick…and she was done. Adjusting her form-fitting black dress, she pulled a strap back into place, and reminded herself she needed to get her necklace. The square neckline would make a perfect frame for it. She checked her hair twist one last time, and noted that the tan line around her neck was indeed gone, thank One. Not that anyone she knew would have been surprised to see it, but a tan face and white shoulders might have ruined the effect of the party frock. So, all the lazy sunbathing with Beau had been worth it. Wink wink.

The light went out as she left the bathroom. She was going to miss the palace, especially her room. Marly, who had assumed her duties while she was gone, said it hadn't felt right to use her room, so she hadn't. Hellen was touched by that, since she never had much of her own all her life. Adia had told her she could take whatever she wanted when she moved out, but she couldn't take the closet, and that would have been the main thing.

As much as she was tempted by Beau's offer to cohabitate, she wanted to live on her own for a while, so she was hunting a place in town. There was a lot of empty property. Adia had a team searching for the people who'd left all the houses and shops. If and when they were found, either purchase deals were made, or the people came back. Of the current owners-not-coming-back collection, a cute little house not far from Roberta was very appealing.

Hellen's shoes waited in front of the open closet doors, and as she slipped her feet into them, her eyes went to the lightning weapon lying on the shelf. The one weird artifact she'd inherited from her parents had made a big difference in the end.

Roberta said she'd gotten it back from Merv when the Resistance workers stopped going to the mine. So much was happening, she'd tucked it away and forgot. Brilliant of her to think of it for the monster—it worked like it was made for it.

Hellen picked the weapon up and turned it in her hand. What incredible strength Roberta had. Losing three quarters of her family and still kicking ass. Taking a deep breath, Hellen laid the weapon back on the shelf and closed the closet doors.

Joey had finally shown up, in record time, according to John. Roberta had been walking the tunnel from their basement in the mornings so she could visit with John, and one day Joey spoke to them. A month or so later he showed in glowing sheen form, and the month after that he was nearly normal-looking. Still the same Joey, Roberta had said, smiling.

Those trips down the tunnel thinned out once she got busy with the university, but they'd helped her a lot.

Hellen had seen John every time she went to check the tear. He'd walk with her, and start telling her about some new science thing he was learning. That would pass the time, with a lot of "I can't tell you" and "Um, let me just say…" included. He'd ask about Roberta, too, and Hellen would tell him she was getting better, which was true.

And the tear was still closed. But you could bank on Hellen scouring the air for new signs every time.

Strange to see the rock giants still lined up and lifeless. So far, she'd only seen Duncecap there, and only one time. His jokes had fallen flat when Hellen tried to thank him. He said they'd all left their rocks after Browbone and the other two got their heads cut off. Hellen told him that was only smart. He said he'd pass their thanks along, and his rocks settled without him.

Hellen wished it could have been Browbone.

And she'd never stop being haunted by what happened to Vartile. The image of her getting sucked into the tear was burned into Hellen's mind. It showed up mostly in the middle of the night, along with dread that she might still be alive in the second dimension somehow. But Adia said she'd seen her light disintegrate, like they do when people die, so Hellen could mostly let that go. What she did know was that Vartile wouldn't want to be remembered as a dying smear, and Hellen tried to replace that image with good ones. Every time.

The same with Firio, Edren, and Rack. And Anji (who she found out had worked for Shindao years ago, but was exiled around the time Dagge was there—no explanation of why). Anyway, all of them weighed heavy on her heart.

She tried to stay busy.

The last six months had been a whirlwind. The first thing Adia did was ask Empress Dalang if she had stonemasons who could tear down the wall. The Empress was happy to send her best people, and between them and an astounding number of volunteers in town, the wall was nearly gone. A section had been left in the east side park—plaques were mounted on it with the names of all those lost. The park had gotten a lot of traffic while the weather was warm.

Hand at the base of her throat, Hellen walked to the jewelry box on her desk. A smaller box lay nestled inside, brand new and mostly alone in there. Lifting it into her hand, she removed the lid and smiled at the gold heart on its delicate chain. It was a locket. Adia had given it to her, having put carefully-trimmed pictures in it of herself and Beau.

When Adia told her about the worst parts of her time with Dagge, Hellen had wanted to kill him all over again. The horror of his mauling was so vivid, Adia had cried and curled up with her arms over her scars. Hellen could only wrap her child in her arms and hold her, hoping and praying the monster suffered in his flat carapaz prison for a long, long time.

Hellen fastened the heart around her neck and patted it on her chest. Time to think about happier things.

In two weeks, she and Beau would be taking one of those fancy dirigibles to an island on the other side of the continent. After all the hardship, and grief, and terror, she was finally getting that vacation, and she was excited. A new bikini was even now hiding in the drawer, but she wasn't sure she could really wear it in public. A sensible one-piece was in there, too, just in case. All she could see in her mind's eye was lounging on a beach with some kind of frosty drink in her hand. That, and slathering lotion on Beau's muscles. Maybe that wouldn't be happening on the beach, though. She chuckled.

It had been a great six months with Beau. They'd worked on the wall, cleaned out his underground room, and walked the forest in between all that sunbathing. The sex was fantastic—what a difference real love made.

They'd explored the extension of the well tunnel, too. The end had a trapdoor in the ceiling, and no way to get to it, so they went back and got the ladder. Beau had to work to get the door open, and when he did, something heavy fell over and rolled a short way.

Up top they found a real cauldron over on its side with a spill of rocks out of its mouth. She and Beau had looked at each other with open-mouth smiles.

Beau said, "I guess she really was a witch."

"Suppose she was trying to keep the monks out?" Hellen rolled the cauldron a little and looked inside. Lots of rocks.

"I'd say yes. Think this was the last thing she did before the townspeople hauled her off?"

They nodded together.

"Glad it wasn't me," Hellen said.

"Me too."

The rest of the tiny stone building was plants and rubble. A lot like the west wing of the monastery, interestingly. Trees hung overhead, and it was fairly well hidden at the base of the hill. Not undiscoverable, though, so maybe there was a veil, too.

They'd gone back into the tunnel after that, with Beau pulling the righted cauldron back onto the door as best he could. Their walk back to the warren had been full of musings about witch life, with Hellen saying she wouldn't mind learning some of that herb stuff. Vartile had taught her a few things, but barely brushed the surface.

Beau said, "Let's do it. I can learn about plants."

He was so fine.

The smithy had been overrun after the victory, prompting Beau to hire a new guy from Rofland. Devy had a good head and ten years under his belt. Plus, he and Beau's first guy, Siler, got along great, so it was a win, win, win.

Beau was also helping Cary settle into his new job as Chief of Police. Byron had recommended him, even though he hadn't been on the force. He'd said the courage and leadership Cary had shown was the lion's share of what he'd need, and the rest could be learned. Then he recruited a bunch of police officers for the Queensguard, so Cary was having to learn a lot.

Hellen gave herself a final check in the full-length mirror beside the closet. Simple but elegant. Black had always been a good color for her, and all the work at the wall had given her muscle. The heels were for the birds, but they did look good, she had to admit.

She felt strong. And happy.

They'd talked about having kids. A little late on the draw, maybe, but who knew? That Protector bloodline shouldn't dry up, right? Not on her watch. At any rate, they weren't trying to stop it. Marriage wasn't off the table, either, whichever way it went.

Joy glowed her, as Adia would say.

Hellen crossed to her nightstand to get the tiny bag she was strapping to her wrist for the evening. Inside was a folded wad of tissues and three aspirin. Crap, she'd forgotten her lipstick. Bag in hand, she went back to the bathroom, where her heels clacked on the stone.

She was going to have to get used to that, she supposed. With her Queensguard forming, Adia had officially released Hellen from all her old jobs—including Protector, though Hellen wasn't sure she could be released from that. But they pretended, and Adia offered her a different job if she wanted it: Special Envoy to the Queen.

Hellen dropped the lipstick into the bag and hung it on her wrist as she left the bathroom.

The job would be to travel to different countries and meet with leaders when Adia couldn't go *(or didn't want to, let's be honest)*. No doubt it meant a lot of high heels, but still, a different kind of Protector,

Hellen told herself. And she did have some experience dealing with leaders of other countries. Killing them, sure, but they'd been monsters, and now everyone treated her like they wanted her to like them, which was great.

Hellen knew that because she and Adia had traveled a few places together soon after Dagge's defeat. Pulari and Valdia had celebrated Dagge's death, and Adia wanted to officially return their sovereignty to them and apologize. Her reputation was already legend by then. One rumor they heard in Pulari said the Queen could see a lie, and Adia had confirmed that was bonafide truth.

In Valdia, she had heaped her legend higher by offering to clear out the chemical and biological weapons plants Dagge had opened. Talking to the new President, she said they had a team of scientists working on ways to neutralize the components. He'd been skeptical, like he thought she wanted to keep that stuff for herself. But Adia was sincere, and told him of course it was for Great Hand's benefit. Ridding Valdia of such danger was for everyone's benefit, and she was sure the people of Valdia would agree if she asked them. At that point, with a large audience outside the Capitol watching, he couldn't say no even if he wanted to.

Good times.

Laughter and shouting erupted in the servants' hall on the other side of her room. Lots of activity over there for the last hour or so. All the servants would be guests tonight, in new party clothes and no work until noon tomorrow. What wasn't to be happy about?

It would be the best Winter Festival ball ever. All their friends in snappy outfits, dancing, music, and endless champagne. The foyer, ballroom, and dining room had been filled with lights, fresh garland, and velvet ribbon. Pine cones, and apples, and clove-studded oranges were piled on tables everywhere. The scents of cinnamon and glorious food wafted through the air.

And Beau would be down there. She could hardly wait.

Hellen left her room to go get the Queen.

Chapter E.2

Adia stood in front of her full-length mirror, looking at the phoenix in flight rising from her amethyst light. Wings raised, feathers spread. Born of fire.

In everyone else's eyes, the tattoo spanned the scar from her chest to her face. Adia had described the design she'd like to have, and the woman had run with it. David had the brilliant idea to put carapaz powder in the ink so she could see it. She couldn't see the colors, but Hellen said the palette was incredible. Starting at the tail, the feathers went from different shades of blue, to purples and violets, and the whole thing surrounded by blue fire. It was temporary, of course, but she'd see how she felt later about making it permanent.

For now, it was the perfect emblem for the Winter Festival ball. The whole of Great Hand—the people, the town, the prosperity—was rising from the ashes of what Tomius Dagge had wrought. She wore the phoenix for her people and for herself. Triumph belonged to all of them.

Also, it would match her dress, which she'd finally get to wear after three and half years. The first time she'd tried it on, it hung on her, and she was forced to eat as much of Cookie's superb food as she could, darn it. But she'd suffered through, and the dress fit nicely now.

She was pretty sure David would like it. That familiar rush swept through her body at the thought of him. The last couple of months had been electric. His scent and feel had become part of her. She licked her lips, and her mouth dropped open so she could pant a little. It made her laugh.

They'd have to keep their hands off each other, or at least only on the polite parts all night. Difficult and tantalizing at the same time.

Adia opened her underwear drawer and dug around for something that wouldn't give her panty lines. Locating a slick, loose panty short and a satin bustier, she took them to her bed to put them on. Dropping the damp towel she'd worn since her careful bath, she began the assemblage.

The entire country had been invited to the ball. They'd had to import tailors and seamstresses from surrounding nations to clothe everyone. Carapaz paid for it. Likewise, it paid for the food, servers, childcare, and transportation to and from the palace that night.

Turned out Dagge had left a huge pile of the stuff in a hidden room under a shack on Camberton's old property. Adia guessed she was going to have to learn some resource economics so she wouldn't have to open the mine again anytime ever. Or maybe she could hire someone for that job, someone she trusted. After she spent all the money she needed to.

Carapaz had paid for the rejuvenation of the town, as well. For the past six months, Shindoan builders had been supervising the dismantling of the wall, starting at the palace, and moving outward in both directions. John had done a good job, of course—the big wall took a long time to bring down, but much shorter than the time it took to put up. Some of the rock was used for repair, some to construct new buildings in the public parks, a science complex was in progress on the old Camberton property, and the remainder was laid at the base of the outcropping. Anyone who wanted some could come get it.

Rising from the ashes.

Trees had been planted in the Merchant District, too. They were small, of course, but well-loved. Someday they'd be grand, and she'd be able to walk in their shade. Whenever she saw Luhe, he'd say something like "Vartile would love" whatever plant he was getting ready to put in the ground. And he would be right. Adia's heart ached with it.

All the people who fought had been awarded for their service. The families of those who died were awarded additional. Not that money could ever make up for what they'd lost, but it could take away some uncertainty of the future, and that was meaningful.

The funerals had been hard. They all went to every one of them. Due honors were paid—flags raised, and singing. So many tears. People's lights were dark, and barely moving except to sag.

She'd had a ceremony for her father, too. The whole kingdom came, packing the royal cemetery, flowing out the gate and into the meadow. Empress Dalang was there, and Mapo, who cried.

Her father's body was long gone—burned in a pit, she heard—so she'd had his mutilated portrait buried in his place. The discovery of the portrait had been devastating. Hellen answered her questions about what parts had been pierced, and the one eye Dagge had clearly been saving. For a long time, she'd stood there with her hand on it, crying, and also strangely glad to have something to bury. Weird, maybe, but true.

Adia picked up her towel and carried it to the bathroom, hanging it on the rack to dry.

She'd been back to the monastery a few times. The first time, she'd told Hellen and David she wanted to get the stuff she'd left, and they wanted to come with her. David told Roberta, and she wanted to go. Hellen told Beau, and he wanted to go, and it ended up being a big excursion on horseback. Wolf went too, of course. He was still the best guide, and they opted to go overland to visit the forest and check on the tear. Starseed was the only one who didn't want to go—she kept trying to turn around and head back to the stable. Adia really needed to ride her more.

When they got there, the mural had beckoned her right away. Turned out much of it was carapaz—like the nebula, which dominated the upper left, and was swirled through with flecks of rock she couldn't see. The stars were carapaz, too, and the sheer number of them crowding the background wowed her. They framed the planets and comets and asteroids so she could see them as well. The large planet in the lower right had rings, but only three of them were carapaz, and she knew from all the times she'd touched them that there were twelve rings there.

That first trip was the time the monks showed up. Adia had wanted to tie Starseed in the shade out front, so they'd all done likewise and gone in the front door. The echo in the foyer was the same, but when they reached the great room, a bright light swept over them, and familiarity disappeared. Adia could suddenly see everything: the fireplace, strange glowy people, Hellen, Beau…and David.

"You can see me," he'd said, while she couldn't say anything.

And Diit had been there, too. Of course. Once Adia realized he wasn't a prisoner somewhere in the palace, or dead, the only explanation for his absence was that he was a monk. Once she realized that, so many things made sense.

Hilman was there, too. He got hugs from her and Hellen, and some big thank yous. It had been a little hard to recognize him and Diit without their wigs, but they had manifested faces, unlike the other monks, who sported smooth all over.

Diit had taken her down into the tunnels—just her by herself—explaining that day even though she didn't need explanation.

"It was terribly hard not to help." They stepped out of the dumbwaiter staircase, and he led her toward the thumb tunnel. "What you were facing was unprecedented, and that doesn't happen much anymore, I can tell you."

She had questions, of course, like "Who are the monks really?" and "Are you coming back?" But she wasn't sure she wanted the answers. Instead, she'd said, "It was you who hit the monster in the eye with the rock, wasn't it?"

He'd laughed and said, "Nobody told me I couldn't."

They had reached the end of the thumb tunnel and stopped. Pulling a golden key out of his pocket, he'd blown a single note on it, and the wall they'd all thought was a dead end dissolved. At first it was only darkness, but as they stood there, lights began to glow. Lamps and bulbs came to life, scattered about on tables and the floor, the growing light revealing a cave of wonders.

Star maps and land maps of other worlds hung on walls and projected into the air. Scrolls and books were stacked on floor-to-ceiling shelves. Gizmos and gadgets were clustered on tables, tools hung on walls, and unidentifiable machines crowded the floor.

In front of that sat careful piles of the artwork, musical instruments, and other valuables Dagge had stolen from the people of the kingdom. Portraits of bygone men in hats and ladies in very little clothing gazed steadily at her. Silver trays and candlesticks gleamed dully around small, ornate boxes. A harp stood half covered with a tapestry full of horses and dogs. Adia had walked in a few steps, and her mouth hung open.

"I moved all the treasures in here after he picked out the pieces he wanted," Diit said.

"I wondered what happened to all their things. I figured he sold them, or they were burned, or he bribed people. But here they are. You saved them, Diit." Her eyes roved over jewelry and abstract paintings and statues. "Can we give them back now?"

"Yes, ma'am, we certainly can. I'd like to take care of that, if I may."

"That would be brilliant, Diit, thank you." She turned and looked at him. "You know, come to think of it, that's probably not your real name, is it?"

He grinned. "It is, actually! The monks call me Servant, but you can call me anything you like."

Adia had taken his hands and said, "Then I shall call you Diit, because that's who you are to me." She hugged him. He felt surprisingly solid, and looked 3D when she pulled back again. "Besides, calling you Servant would sound really weird in the palace, and I'm hoping you'll come back."

"You don't feel like I betrayed you?"

"No! Why would I feel that?"

"Because I wasn't there when you needed me."

"But you were. You took care of me when I had nothing. You brought food. You made a couch. How many people can say that?" She smiled and he laughed lightly. "I know you had to stay away at the end because we needed to fight Dagge. We needed to win with our own steam. And even with all the losses—" Grief seized her throat of a sudden. Adia wondered if her heart would ever stop hurting. Probably

612

not. "Look what it's given us." She smiled under her runny nose. "Now we know what we're capable of."

"Yes, ma'am." Diit paused, his eyes shining. "I think you should know, if you haven't thought of it, that we can restore your eyesight, if you like, ma'am. But you'd have to give up your perception of souls."

Wow, what a choice. She hadn't thought of it, and for half a second, she was tempted. Her heart longed to see Hellen and David and Wolf for the rest of their lives. But did she really want to trade seeing the truth of people for seeing appearances again?

"No thanks. I'm liking myself just the way I am."

They'd gone back upstairs then, after Diit closed the room and put the key back in his pocket. She'd asked him why he showed her that secret.

"I believe you have earned it," Diit said in his soft way. "What you do with that knowledge is up to you. If you want the key, I will give it to you. But I would like to warn you that humankind isn't ready."

That seemed completely believable to her.

Adia located her dress hanging on the inside of her armoire door, carefully removed it from its hanger and went in from the top, out of consideration for her up-do, which had taken two women and a ridiculous amount of time earlier in the day. None of the servants were working tonight, though, so she'd practiced getting into her dress herself. Once upon a time, she was used to doing everything herself, but it had been easy to get re-spoiled, she had to admit. The buttons in the back were a different story, but a knock on the door announced Hellen, who was just in time.

"Come in!" Adia called, wrestling the heavy brocade onto her shoulders. Hellen's capable hands pulled and buttoned as she talked.

"People are arriving," she said, "music's playing, and the palace looks beautiful. It's a miracle all the repairs got done, especially the marble in the foyer."

"It was the cayenne that got me. Every time I walked down to Dad's sitting room, I'd stir some up and end up crying."

"You sure that was the cayenne?" Hellen asked.

"Okay, maybe not entirely. I am constantly reminded of my last day there, with Dagge. And the discovery of Dad's portrait still tears me up."

"We'll find someone to reproduce it, I promise."

"I know. It was just…like Dagge killed him, and killed him, and killed him."

"Dagge was a sick fucking monster, and you know what? We killed him."

"Yeah."

"I'm changing the subject now," Hellen said, finishing the last button and turning Adia to face her. "You look incredible. Your skin is glowing, your eyes sparkle, and your hair and dress and phoenix are worthy of the hero you are."

Adia chuckled right through her big smile. "Thanks. Your green and gold are magnificent, too. Glowing and alive."

"Thanks," Hellen said. "We should get downstairs. Cookie is already in the dining room examining the food. I saw her sneaking down the stairs when I walked by." She dug Adia's shoes out of the armoire and placed them on the floor in front of her. "It's a good thing you banned her from the kitchen, or she'd be in there, sweating through that beautiful dress."

Adia laughed, holding onto Hellen's shoulders as she worked her feet into her fancy shoes. Hellen adjusted the straps for her—Adia's dress was so form-fitting, bending was not the best option.

"Thanks," Adia said. "Am I ready?"

"No jewelry?"

"I've got the hair pick." She reached up and made sure it was staying tucked in. "But I need the gloves and bracelet." Hellen's light moved to the armoire. "I didn't want earrings or necklace to detract from the phoenix."

"Good choice." Hellen returned with the long white gloves, which Adia put on, and Hellen clinched the diamond bracelet around her wrist.

"Let's go then," she said, and walked over to open both bedroom doors wide. Music and the hum of conversation swept in, along with laughter and calls across the big foyer. She tucked Adia's arm into her elbow, and they made their way toward the grand staircase, their shoes tick-tacking on the hard floor between the carpets.

A hush fell as people saw her walking across the balcony. Whispers and murmurs floated up. At the top of the steps, Diit's white light floated outward in disappearing waves, the rainbow sheen catching the light. Wolf stood next, panting audibly, turquoise light sparkling. Next to him, David's galaxy spun as he stepped out to meet her.

David would be leaving soon to go to university for the spring semester. Double engineering major: mechanical and architectural. It wouldn't be an easy train trip if they wanted to see each other, but it was the best school on the continent. When admissions heard he was instrumental in the moving of the boulder and the capture of the monster in the tear, they fell all over themselves to accommodate him. Adia was proud, though she'd miss him terribly.

He'd almost promised that he'd be back unchanged, but she didn't want him to. He needed to get out there, have some fun, make some mistakes. If he was meant to be in Great Hand later, with her, he would be. That much she'd learned. Until then, they both had work to do, and if David ended up back home, they could take it up then.

She was hoping more than she let him know.

Maybe one day she'd get to mention what his official code name really needed to be.

"You look breathtaking," David said, wrapping her hand with his big warm one as Hellen passed her off. "Are you sure you don't want to do this yourself?"

"No way." She snorted. "These stairs would be a death trap for a blind woman in heels. Besides, I'd much rather have my two guys with me." Reaching down to rub Wolf's head, she smiled up at David with all the love and gratitude and joy she felt, and that was considerable.

Adia put her left hand in David's elbow and they started down. Wolf's nails clicked softly on the steps to her right. Water trickled and gurgled in the crescent garden on their left. Quiet conversation had started back up below. It sounded excited, and the energy was palpable. An image popped into her mind of floating on it, out over the crowd. She grinned to herself.

As they rounded the curve, the people standing at the bottom of the stairs came into view. Byron Taymer stood at the corner where the steps met the wall. He was a fixture at the palace now, dedicating his life to the protection of the sovereign, like so many Taymers before him. Next to him stood Cary, who'd been voted in as Chief of Police because of his courage and dedication. His light carried a new quality now— less fractious, more substantial. Adia was glad to have him protecting their people. Roberta was next. She'd been working tirelessly to open the university, searching for the professors who'd fled in the early days of Dagge's occupation, hunting new replacements when she had to. Her blue light burned steady. Beau stood beside her, his gold flames waving gently. He'd finally won the thing he most wanted in the world, Hellen Parker. Just ask him, he'd tell you.

Beyond these loved ones, a sea of lights glowed and waved and sparkled through the entire foyer. Some were raised on the entry steps, more were slipping in through the doors. An excited murmur swept around the room. From the back someone shouted, "Long live the Queen!" Then everyone had to shout it three times, they burst into applause, and the joy of it parted Adia's mouth in the biggest smile.

David whispered in her ear. "I'm going to leave you here. You're four steps up, but I'll come back and get you when you signal me." He lifted her hand out of his elbow and kissed it. "Feel the love, Your Majesty. Come on, Wolf." And she was on her own.

Adia couldn't quit smiling. She raised her chin and showed her phoenix, and a cheer went up, echoing in the enormous space. Hellen went around her and joined Beau in front, Wolf barking in excited little yips beside her.

But they weren't just cheering the Queen. All of them cheered and applauded themselves and each other. After the years of death and deprivation, after all the fighting and suffering and loss, they had earned it. The people of Great Hand clapped until their hands were surely sore and their throats worn out from so much shouting. They hugged and cried and laughed, and Adia watched them, feeling very aware that she had family.

When the fire subsided, she held her hand out to David, standing beside his mother, and he took her hand.

"Let's dance," she said.

And they did.

Chapter E.3

The forest rests in the quiet. From the sharp and ancient rocks, long sighs breathe down, brushing the treetops with snow. Pouring the night.

For a time the quiet will last, and life will remain. Until the next need, the next fight.

Tonight, peace sings under the invisible moon and the endless, enduring stars.

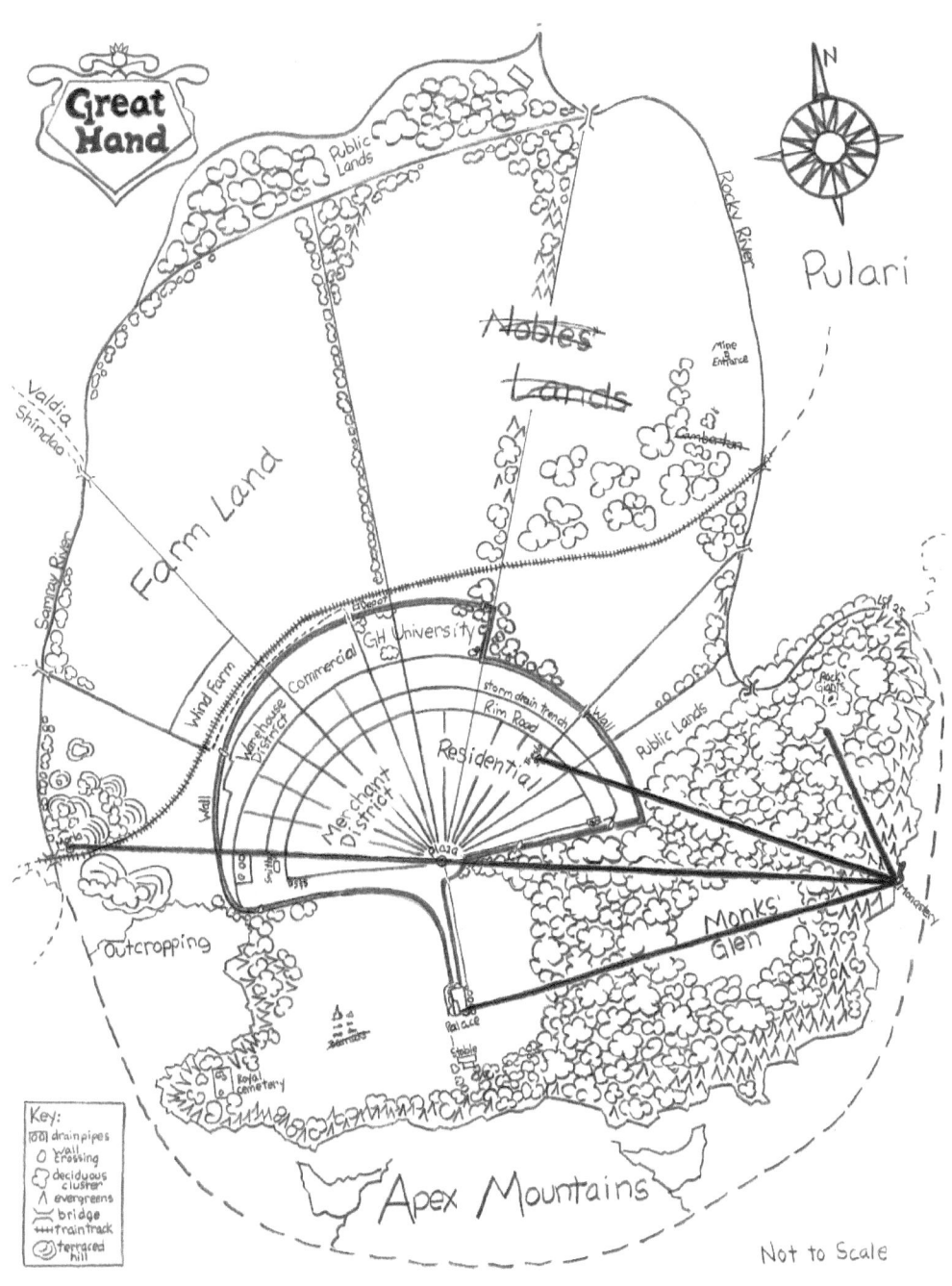

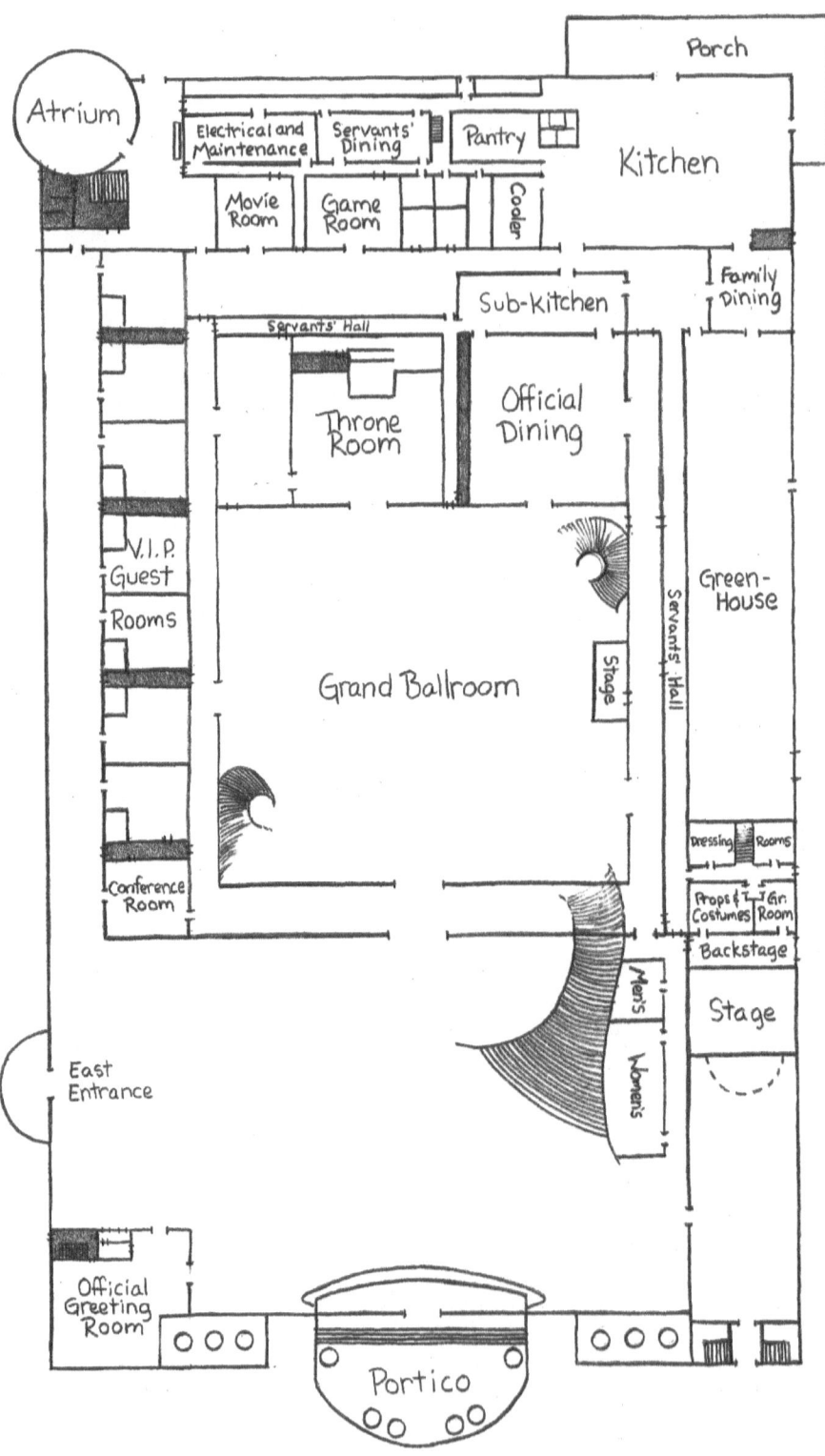

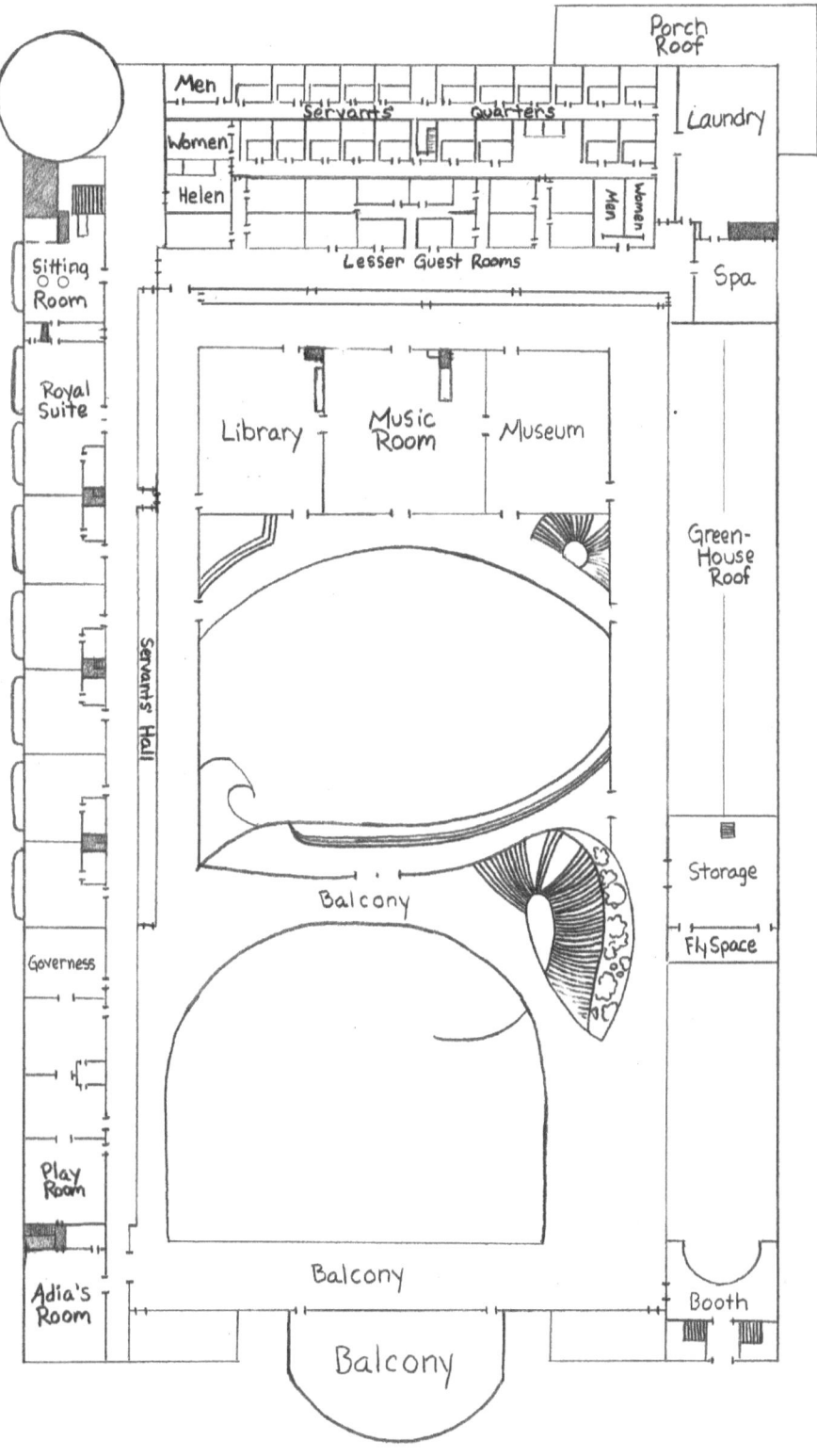

Porch
Roof

Men

Servants' Quarters

Laundry

Women

Helen

Men

Women

Spa

Lesser Guest Rooms

Sitting
Room

Royal
Suite

Library

Music
Room

Museum

Green-
House
Roof

Servants' Hall

Storage

Balcony

Fly Space

Governess

Play
Room

Adia's
Room

Balcony

Balcony

Booth

Balcony

Acknowledgements

A couple of years ago, our son Sam had three copies of Reign Fall printed as surprise Christmas gifts for the family. It was a touching and validating moment for me. Now, I have a much clearer understanding of how much effort he put into it. Thank you, Sam, for your thoughtfulness and good heart that shines like the sun. You are and have always been an inspiration.

And Rocko, without your savvy creative input, these book covers would have been much sadder affairs. Thanks for all the ideas, not to mention the lightning-fast executions (Honestly, he's a blur. I can't follow what he does at all. And yeah, I'm a dinosaur, but he's really fast, no joke).

Thanks also to my husband Kimball, who has been beside me both literally and figuratively—supporting, weighing in, and seeing things I don't. We make a great team, honey. I love you.

Lastly, this story began as a play in Sherman, Texas. My friend Deb Shaw and I put it together with the help of many people. They all added their own spices to the characters and settings that flavor these books. My love and gratitude to all of you.

In loving memory
Susy Parker as Tallulah as the Chef

About the Author

LP Rothrock has had a few nicknames in her life, but sadly, "Long Play" was never one of them. Her favorites were "Smiley" and "Sidekick" because they made her feel like she was somehow tethered to an old Western. While Smiley would never scoff at tradition, Sidekick thinks it's silly to write about herself in third person.

But that's neither here nor there.

We're all just glad these books are done. It's been a wild ride for fifteen years, and our dearest hope is that you find this story satisfying.

www.ingramcontent.com/pod-product-compliance
Lightning Source LLC
Chambersburg PA
CBHW021931110726
47901CB00003B/800